Half a Chance

A survival story from the seedy side of Sydney in the '70's

Danny B. Mortison

DEDICATION

In loving memory of Denise Shirley Mortison

(The Mouse)

18/4/1951 – 29/7/1

CONTENTS

ACKNOWLEDGMENTS

The author would like to thank Shirley Flett of Dunolly, Victoria for invaluable research assistance; Dr. Rosie Craig of Meerschaum Vale, NSW and Max Tomlinson of Townsville, Queensland for editing assistance on different drafts of this work. I would also like to thank the friends who read and commented on the manuscript plus family and friends, many of whom may see themselves somewhere in these pages.
Cover artwork original acrylic on canvas by Genevieve Mortison.

Chapter 1

He had the taste of dusty roads in his skin from the very start. The Gypsy spirit was ingrained in his ancestral lines. The doctor had no sooner spanked his backside to provoke the first yelp before he was out there, on the road. Just three months old, Terry Bruce Martin, cradled in the arms of his mother was on his first journey in the cabin of an old fruit truck on which his folks hitched a ride with from the Melbourne markets. They were headed for Cobbin Station where 22-year-old Stephen, had secured a job as a station hand.

The truck rattled along with Stephen and two older children, Suzanne, aged five and Delia, three, lounging on the canvas tarpaulin seat they had made on the back of the truck. Another tarp had been slung over a crude metal frame to protect them from the relentless sun which bore down on them. Now the truck was driving into it providing them with some shade. Stephen was playing 'Summertime' on the harmonica, the girls cuddling in close on either side under his arms. His young wife Shelly who was just 20 sat up front cuddling baby Terry.

Fred Jackson was cranking down a gear to negotiate the creek crossing and was asking Shelly what possessed them to bring the family out here. He was making conversation more than anything. He'd heard Stephen's tale a couple of days before when he was approached at the Flemington markets.

"Stephen has done a bit of shearing over the past few years, but I was with the kids in Melbourne while he was away. This looks like a good job though. There's a bit of everything. They have sheep and horses to care for and I'll make a bit of money myself, helping out with cooking and cleaning at the station."

"Why all the way out here? The nearest town is Hay, and that's bloody ten miles away from Cobbin."

Shelly's thoughts took her to the last town they lived in. Healesville was only five miles away and Stephen seemed to spend a lot of time away from home, spending their money on drink. She hated his attitude after he'd been drinking. He scared her, although to date he had kept his hands to himself.

The truck reeled over a bump as she continued, tightening her arm over the baby asleep in her lap: "We were on a stud farm near Healesville for a few years," she hesitated, looking out at the endless plains. "Stephen really liked it there. Delia was born while we were there." She continued to stare out the window. There were no trees here. "I really don't mind being out of the way of the towns. There are bad influences in towns, I reckon." She turned to Fred; "I'd like to see a few more trees around though."

"Better get used to not seein' too many trees and the like for a while. Not out here," he laughed. "She's the little one there?" Fred motioned with his head over his shoulder. "Delia, I mean, is she the little dark-haired one?"

Shelly turned to see the girls asleep on Stephen's lap again. He had pocketed the harmonica and was now quiet too.

"Yeah, she's the cheeky little one; the little brunette. Gee she's been a handful; since she could walk she's been into mischief. A real handful, I tell yer!"

"Looks like you've got a bit of a handful now, with another one there to boot. Mine are all growed up now. They're out there in the big world trying to make it on their own. Just like you two I s'pose."

Stephen was awakened from his doze as the truck shook while Fred slowed for the crossing. He looked down at the girls asleep on either side of him. He thought for a moment of the baby in the cabin with Shelly and smiled. The whir of the engine told Stephen they were getting back to a straight run. The road behind soon straightened out into a long strip of gravel stretching on forever.

The truck finally pulled off the road as Terry woke up and bellowed. The driver timed his run well, but could not have stood much more of that noise.

Stephen instinctively gathered branches from the few trees by the creek bed for a campfire. He paused at the trickling creek and listened to the quiet as he dipped the billy that Shelly would use to heat up a bottle for the baby all the while keeping an eye on Delia and Suzanne who were heading straight for the water.

"I reckon the station may be a good start for you lot. Good clean livin' out here." Fred was poking more sticks under the billy. "They reckon there's gonna be a lot more sheep here in a season or two."

"If this job works out we might look at buying our own place around here one day," Stephen was optimistic.

Fred sat up proudly filling out his shirt with his chest as he responded: "I've had me own place outta town there now for twenty-five years. It's only small. Too small to make a living from but big enough to run a house cow and a few head of cattle and sheep as killers. It's bloody hard work. I have to do these runs down to Melbourne just to keep it goin'. We'd be stuffed if I didn't have the truck and the work."

"I don't mind hard work, Fred. I just reckon I'd feel better if I was doin' it on me own spread." That was Stephen's dream on this warm February evening. "With half a bloody chance, I reckon we could make a good go of it out here."

"It's gonna be pretty tough you know," said Fred, giving Stephen a steely eye. "You know what Morgan's shearer's quarters are like?"

Stephen looked at Shelly shuffling in her makeshift seat made from the tarp. "Yeah Fred, we're aware of that. The missus will just have to put up with the conditions. I did the sheds around here for a few years. A mate, Wally Turner, wrote me to tell me this job was comin' up."

"Do you know the cocky, Harry Morgan? They reckon he's a tough bastard to work for."

"Yeah, I did his shed with a few other blokes in '49. It was hard yacka, but the pay is good if you can keep up in a shed like that. Harry's okay, I reckon. At least we all got paid."

Stephen was wondering how Morgan would take to the children. He hadn't told him about the three children. He'd only mentioned himself and Shelly.

"Shelly could help out with the cookin' over at your house," he'd said on the phone to Morgan, not thinking of the task ahead for his young wife of cooking and hand washing for three little ones.

They sipped the tea from tin mugs and watched the sun disappear into a shimmering haze of dried grass which seemed to stretch forever.

Fred decided they would camp overnight, "to allow the youngsters a decent rest". They rolled out the tarpaulin to make a ground sheet and pulled a flap over the top to make a huge swag where the five of them could snuggle in. Dinner this night was beans on toast.

The remainder of the journey next morning showed them the wide-open plains leading into Hay and then out to the station.

Shelly had expected an impressive farmhouse complete with out-buildings. She was forlorn as she looked at the ramshackle house they drove in to.

"Well good luck you lot," Fred meant it with all his heart as he dropped them off, but knew deep down that Stephen would not last out here. He was too cocky. One glance at Shelly's eyes when she looked across the dusty yard to the shearers' quarters, was enough of a memory for him. He had done the same thing to a young woman twenty-five years earlier.

The quarters were rough and hot, no more than a tin shed with a dirt floor. It had only ever been used as a bunkhouse for a handful of shearers. This was the first time Morgan had been confronted with a man, his wife and children. He looked at the shed then Shelly and found it hard to hide his embarrassment: "You didn't tell me you had kids Steve."

"Didn't I say that? Sorry Harry, but here we are." He turned and waved to Fred driving slowly down the track before turning back to Harry. "We can put up with the quarters."

"They're a bit sparse for family living though. Anyhow you better come along and clean up."

"They should be alright," Shelly lied, forcing a smile as she looked at the structure. There was a door and two windows on the front; the rest just roofing iron nailed to a rough sawn frame. For now it was home.

To Stephen the shack was comfortable, compared, that is, to some of the shearers' quarters he had stayed in. Shelly hated it but soon made it feel homely. It's amazing what a tablecloth will do for a laminex table. The dirt floor annoyed her more than anything and after a few weeks she took to running a straw broom across it. On one such occasion Stephen walked in on her: "Cripes woman, you can't sweep a dirt floor."

"I just want to get rid of the extra stuff. The dust," she pleaded.

"You're creatin' more bloody dust ev'ry time you sweep it though."

He suggested straw. She couldn't come at that, but did try wetting things down by sprinkling water about. This only splashed mud around the cabinets.

Stephen soon got used to Harry's lists which kept him occupied for most of the daylight hours. He didn't mind the hard work and loved the station life. Shelly was happy to see him content. The girls were happy and spent their days outside of the quarters following either Stephen or Harry about on their chores.

Harry came on a bit grumpy to them at first, but soon got used to having little Delia or Suzanne close by.

Stephen warned them of the dangers of wandering into a herd of sheep, or walking too close to horses, but they had no fear of the animals. This kept everyone around the place a little on edge, especially when the sheep were being moved about.

Harry Morgan was a hardened bushy, although he proved to be a fair man and anxious to help Stephen and Shelly along. He made a couple of spare beds from the house available and even helped Stephen carry them to the shack.

"Well it's best they be as comfortable as possible, ay Steve?"

Stephen responded with a smile. "Yeah, thanks Harry."

Harry believed in a hard day's work for a day's tucker. If you couldn't ride a horse, you were no good to him. He'd seen men come and go for all of his fifty years and tried most of them on in one way or another.

He was not a very trusting man and would check up on people coming to work for him, before they got there. Armed with what he knew he'd ask probing questions, in the most open of situations, just to get a reaction. Sometimes they'd be embarrassed by his where-with-all and apparent knowledge of where they'd been. He'd see how they responded. It was a position he assumed most of the time. It was a game to him. He'd have a lend of some people all the time and this provided a social screen to his more probing realizations about people. He liked to work the bush telegraph.

There was a lot of work to do and Stephen proved a willing hand. That first day he asked if Stephen could ride a horse, knowing full well that he had worked almost two years with one of the best breakers in the Gippsland district.

"Done a bit," was Stephen's reaction.

He was just 15 when he learned how to break a horse at his first station job. He had worked on many properties since, choosing brumbies from a pack and breaking them in as stock horses one by one. When a mob was run in for a day's work he would sometimes pick out one that he had broken, and ride it again to further its education.

At the stud farm his grooming and horsemanship skills were found to be less important than his attentions to the boss's daughter. That was the side of him Shelly knew of but was always afraid to ask. He didn't tell her the boss had caught him out in the stables.

"I wished you had got on better with Snowy Lawton," she probed one evening under a hurricane lamp. "The stud horses were more challenging for you than here, Stephen."

"He just didn't want me trying out any new things, Shelly. This'll be OK. You'll see. The beauty is that by living out here we don't spend any money. Who knows, if we can stick it out for two or three years we may be able to get enough for a deposit on some land of our own."

Shelly agreed with a sigh, and hoped, deep in her heart, that would be the case. She had mentioned the same to Harry's wife, Ethel, when cleaning the house that very morning.

"I'd love to bring the children up on a good block, although I reckon there are a few better towns closer to Melbourne where we could look."

Ethel had said the same thing; she'd like to be closer to a town or even live in town and just stay on the farm when there was work to be done.

Shelly drifted off to sleep dreaming of forest-clad mountains and green rolling hills, a far cry from the barren, flat dust bowl of Cobbin.

It did not take Stephen long to pick out a good riding horse for mustering time. He knew the big black stallion hadn't seen many riders before, only a few very experienced horsemen had dared go near him.

His sheer size, almost 17 hands, and his flighty nature kept most riders away. He was keen to take the bit between his teeth, but Stephen maintained a tight hold keeping his hands low. He was a good horseman alright. After a couple of weeks he had Jet, as Stephen named him, coming on a whistle, walking right up to him, as placid as a lamb. Then he'd nuzzle the grain from his hand.

Stephen was industrious with his time. When the work was finished for the day he'd be looking at fixing something else up. He liked to have something to do. When Harry complained of not being able to get anything from town, "without having to take the truck in," Stephen was quick to respond by building a sled to drag behind the tractor.

"Christ it's so flat around here I don't reckon we'll need wheels," he told Shelly. Sure enough, the next day he took an axe to a steep angle at the front of the skids and it went even better, by not digging in as much. When the kids sat in the back of it, it went even better.

After that he dragged the sled behind the old grey Fergie tractor to do the mail run once a week. The girls loved to jump on board the sled and take a ride, although Shelly thought little Delia was a bit young for such things. She usually got a small ride around the house before Shelly would swoop and take her off. Suzanne loved it and would run after Stephen to hitch a ride anywhere it was going. He would usually oblige.

The ride to town was a couple of miles down through the paddocks to the railway track which he would then follow for another eight miles into town. The journey was long and boring across vast flat plains of yellowed straw and dust colored by the blue of the sky. As they ambled along the sled tended to go off-track a little until the tractor jerked it back into line. On one such adjustment Suzanne slipped off.

It was a typically clear western day and Stephen had maintained a brisk pace for most of the journey mesmerized by the shimmering heat haze as he looked to the horizon. He was almost into town when he realized Suzanne was missing. He found her half way back home, sitting on the ground sobbing, where she had slipped off. As he got down off the tractor she let out a full bellow.

"I looked back and noticed the sled a few times, and you know, I wondered if she had come along this time," he told Shelly over dinner in the shack. "Then I thought I'd better backtrack and check. And there she was, about three miles back, sitting in the middle of the road. When I stopped she let out a huge 'waaaaah waaaaaah'." He held his hands up to his eyes mimicking what he had seen.

Suzanne was not impressed, the event had been an ordeal for her as she fell off and watched the tractor and sled disappear in the dust. The five-year-old didn't want her father to make fun of her now.

The wide open plains country appealed to Stephen. The peak summer months were incredibly hot and winters bitterly cold, but they were comfortable, and earning their keep. He experienced the Zen of hand milking the cow and tended the vegetable patch most mornings before breakfast at 6:30. Stephen's garden sprouted bountifully until the winter frosts came.

The shack proved to be easy to warm up with a second hand wood stove he picked up in town although he had to scour far and wide to bring in enough wood. Morgan occasionally took him out with the truck on firewood missions.

"I reckon we should be gettin' things ready over the next day or two. How are the horses?" he asked Stephen.

"Jet is a bit jumpy, but I think a ride will do him good. They'll be okay, I reckon."

He liked the crisp winter mornings riding out with Harry through the mist to bring a mob in. On this day Stephen walked his horse away and looked around at the vast paddock, the grass browned by the frost going on forever to the horizon. He had to get a mob in for crutching. The spread covered nearly 70,000 acres of flat plains country, and was this year running an estimated 15,000 head.

Stephen didn't give much thought to Harry's talk of a boom in the industry. All he knew was he had a job he liked and a roof over the family's head, and three square meals a day. His pay packets were adding up and by shearing time he would make extra money shearing around the sheds throughout the Riverina district.

Stephen did not realize the Koreans had shown a huge interest in the Australian product which was giving graziers their best chance to make some ground in an industry which could fluctuate dramatically due to seasonal factors or market demand. At the moment demand outstripped supply and the graziers were reaping one pound sterling for a pound of wool. The whole country was riding on the sheep's back.

Jet responded as the horse ahead, ridden by Harry, stepped up the pace and Stephen raised himself in the saddle slightly, allowing him to break into a natural slow canter falling into the rhythm of the day. This was the part he loved about the station life.

They rode for less than an hour before finding a mob, taking care not to spook them as they slowly circled around for the push in. Stephen liked the way the old dog, Spike, and the bitch, Lady, worked the mob. They went on with the job guided by the odd whistle and shout of, "get behind" or "go around". The yards took most of the mob of about 3000 they had worked up.

Trimming dags off sheep was not Stephen's cup of tea, but he did it with few complaints.

"Just like cutting a three-month-old nappy off a baby," Stephen remarked to Morgan who almost threw up at the thought.

The turnaround seemed to be a lot quicker. Morgan realized it was Stephen's efforts around the place that had made things seem easier, but he was not going to let him slacken off.

The first six months was hard work, and things were going well. Stephen had shown a fair bit of initiative with the chores, but there was always something else Harry could add to his list. The main house badly needed a coat of paint. Stephen was uncomplaining as he sanded the old paint off and applied an undercoat before the main coat. Many sections needed replacing which prompted Stephen to ask Harry for the money to get the materials. Harry always complained about the cost but Stephen copped it sweet and proved himself to be pretty loyal and trustworthy to his boss. He was pretty good with his skills too. He could put his hand to just about anything and he got the job done.

By the time he had finished painting the house, it was looking like new. Even the new fruit trees he planted in the yard were starting to get a go on, although Harry found another reason to complain about that use for the water. Stephen's answer was to use the cold dishwater and bath water to spread around his vegetables and the trees.

Stephen was as fit as he had ever been in his life. He had hardly had a drink except for two occasions when they were invited to the Morgan's for dinner.

It was a long way from the confines of the reform school where Stephen had spent half his teenage years. There he met up with a collection of Melbourne's bad boys, who were put into the home for a variety of misdemeanors. There were others there, like himself, who had done nothing wrong, who found themselves in the home simply because their families could not cope. His mother, Daisy, found it very hard trying to bring up four children by herself in the Melbourne suburb of Auburn. Her house-keeping work barely paid enough to feed the family.

Harry just shot out the question over dinner this night: "So, tell me Steve, how long were you in Boystown?"

Stephen stiffened up: "Never been in; just .. .. So, you've been checkin' up on me have you?"

Harry swung back on his chair and gripped his pipe: "It's my business to know some things, you know. I usually check up on all the shearers and workers who come through here. "As a young fella, you spent a bit o' time in the home, I hear. What did you do?"

"Nothin' really, except being a boy in Melbourne."

"That's no reason to put you in a home."

"I used to hang with the local publican's son. And, as boys will be boys, occasionally we would wag school and catch a train into the city to look around."

"So, what about your old man? Surely he would have kicked yer arse for you for wagging school."

"My mother had turfed my father out when I was young and she didn't really know how to handle me, I s'pose." He slowed and thought for a minute.

"She had four of us but could hardly afford to keep us. She asked for help from the welfare and they suggested I go to Boystown. She just let them take me."

"How old were you?" Harry took another puff on the pipe, "when that happened, I mean."

"About twelve."

Ethel gasped: "Oh that's terrible, putting you in a home, at that age."

She looked up to see Harry glaring at her. She knew well enough not to 'butt in' on Harry's conversations. Harry maintained the glare and turned back to Stephen: "What did the home do for you?"

"Made me go to school every day, that's for sure," they all laughed.

"They did teach me how to read and write better and how to add up enough to know when some store-keeper was touching me for a bob or two."

Stephen didn't tell of the night schooling with the inmates. They knew how to nick a car and drive it. It was these unruly youths who taught him to drive. There were some wild rides around St Kilda for them, and a few chases through suburban back streets to get away from the law.

He did tell of his liberation: "I was almost sixteen when I was allowed to leave there. And then it was only because I had met a bloke who worked in a travelling show. They allowed me to go on the premise of getting a job in the show with Tex Morgan. He showed me how to blow a harmonica."

He didn't tell them it was a tent boxing show or how he'd make a few bob having a stoush with a cowboy here or there. Although only small in frame, Stephen was quite stocky. He could easily have been a jockey with a bit of wasting but his travels had taken him on other trails. His days in the boys' home taught him how to fight and he had mixed it with plenty of blokes in the tents and come off without any visible or permanent scars.

"Tex Morgan used to sing and tell stories on these shows. He'd play guitar and sing and then start reciting his poetry. I would accompany him on the harmonica."

"Tex Morgan, aye? He did some pretty good stuff for a bush poet. Couldn't see how you'd make too much dough outta travelling around doin' those shows though."

"It was pretty tough for 'em all, I reckon."

Harry was amazed that Stephen could recite a number of Morgan's poems off by heart. He was able to quote a few lines of Lawson and C.J. Dennis too to Harry's amazement and he held a fine tune on the harmonica.

Shelly got the children comfortable with books in another room before helping Ethel with the dishes. She wanted desperately to comment on Harry's attitude to her but felt she would come and speak to her when she was ready. She tried to make small talk but Ethel was not in the mood to converse about anything. There was something amiss here.

Back at the quarters after the children were asleep Stephen was concerned about how much Harry had unearthed about him. He wasn't keen on too many people knowing about his tent show fights.

"Shit, he's been pokin' around, Shelly."

"Don't worry about it, Stephen. He said he checks up on everyone." Shelly was not concerned.

"It just shits me that he would check up on me, that's all."

"Look Stephen, he has every right to check up on anyone he has working for him. Anyone has. You know there are lots of undesirable types in this world. He's just being careful. Anyway, you seemed to handle things really well tonight when he asked you about it. You can't help where you came from or what your parents did, now can you?" Stephen cuddled her close and dozed off within minutes as the day's and night's activities caught up with him.

Stephen proved to be a terrific hand in the yards when shearing time came around and Harry was amazed at the numbers he brought in from all corners of the block. He was also pretty handy in the shearing shed, and although not making the ringer's tally, was primarily responsible for keeping the shed running quickly. The eight-stand shed had the whole flock done in less than three weeks. The shearer's count topped 19,000, certainly something to put a smile on Harry's face. It was his best year to date and he wondered if Stephen hadn't rustled some of the neighbour's sheep to make up the numbers, although he didn't ask about that one.

As part of their deal Stephen was able to sign up with the gang of shearers after Morgan's shed and spent the next two months shearing in other sheds around the district. He made some good money in a short time and spent a couple of weekends in town with the lads.

Shelly stayed on at the station and enjoyed the quiet and her leisure time with the children. Morgan even took them to the lakes for a swim on one hot day.

The children frolicked at the water's edge as Harry and Shelly watched: "Gee, they're having a great time aren't they, Shelly?"

"Sure are! Gosh, I never thought these shallow lakes could be so nice. They look so gloomy in the winter time."

"Yeah. Summertime is the best here. So, Shelly, how did you come to pair up with Steve?"

"I was working in a milk bar at Sandringham and one day he came in and asked me out to a dance."

"Crikey, you must have been young then."

"Sixteen. I was the eldest of twelve kids in our family. Being the eldest I seem to have always been helping Mum along. I think meeting Stephen gave me a chance to do something else other than look after kids, my brothers and sisters."

"I dunno about that, Shelly. What, you're just twenty and you have these three young ones hangin' off you already."

Shelly told him of her father's background doing theology in England before coming to Australia and his time in the ministry in Perth and Adelaide before they moved over to Melbourne.

"He was a fighter too, in his early days, while my mother was a concert pianist and violinist."

"So your Dad would win the fights and your mother would lull them with piano and fiddle." Harry was trying to be funny.

"Not really. Dad held the welter weight and middle weight titles of WA at the same time and it was suggested he turn pro. At his first pro fight some men had offered him money to take a dive and he knocked his opponent out half way through the first round.

"That's how he met mum. He went to a cafe after the fight where mum used to work reading palms and tea cups. He was having a cuppa and a bloke came in and shot him five times in the stomach."

"Wow, and he lived, obviously?"

"Yes, my mother went with him to the hospital. That's how they met, but his fighting days were over. He ended up reading Tarot cards for patrons in the cafe where he had been shot. They fell madly in love and somewhere between then and the time I was born, he found the Lord again, prompted by his remarkable recovery.

"My father's passion for the church meant we all had to follow his wishes. He was very strict. He became even more passionate about religion when we moved over to Adelaide."

Harry lay in the shallow water as Shelly continued her father's remarkable story. She told him how he only had enough money to put his wife and two young kids on the train and decided to walk across the Nullabor.

"He had a water bottle and rationed himself to drinks between water stops, which were pretty well marked. However with about a week to go he smashed the bottle and so had to try and make it from water hole to water hole.

"He made it to one water hole and threw himself in and drank his fill before he saw a sign that said it had been poisoned.

"My mother went to the train station every day expecting to see him and was really worried when he was about two weeks late when suddenly he showed up.

"His survival, not just from the walk, but also the poison water made him even more convinced he was here for a reason, to preach. Mum ended up having twelve kids, but lost a couple in birth. Dad became known as the fighting preacher and would spruik the Lord's word to anyone who would listen.

"He never really liked Stephen and wasn't prepared to give him any chances either.

"What about you Harry? How long have you and Ethel been married?"

"Nigh on thirty bloody years I reckon. Though I reckon it has been pretty rocky for the last twenty years or so. She only talks to me when she wants something now. Couple of times a year she comes into my bed, when she wants it."

"Do you mean you don't sleep together all the time?"

"Yeah, we have got the separate rooms and all now."

"That must be pretty hard on you Harry."

"Oh I don't know. Maybe she'll snap out of it one day. I really used to love her a lot. Now she seems distant and just comes to me when she feels like company."

Tears welled in his eyes as he continued: "You know what Shelly? I would like to be able to just talk to her normal like, just normal like. Trouble is, any time I talk to her now she wants to argue about something. And it usually has something to do with bloody money. We've had so many crook seasons now we have just been able to keep the place chuggin' along. We had one hell of a row when I told her I was employing a station hand."

"Don't worry too much Harry, things will work themselves out," Shelly's words were comforting and Harry knew the season had been good.

In fact, the wool season would exceed all expectations for Morgan; they only needed a few good rains to kick the grass on now to see even more money in the bank for more additions to the sheds, although these appeared less urgent now with Stephen on board.

Stephen could 'bush fix' almost anything. And he did a good job too. By their second clip together he had managed to "find" about 6,000 head of sheep more than Harry even knew he had. All of the fencing was up to date and he had been through two excellent clips, records for the station.

Stephen returned home from shearing just two weeks before Terry's second Christmas. This hot summer day he had completed most of Harry's list of chores. It had grown while he was away.

Shelly sat on a stump he had erected outside the door at just the right height to chop the wood for the fire, she pulled her summer frock up exposing her legs to the sun, lifting her hand through her long curly locks: "The kids are bored Stephen. How about we do something today? See if you can get a loan of the truck and we can go across to the lakes for a swim. I'll pack a nice lunch for us all."

The children were excited about the idea. They had a wonderful time by the water's edge on their previous rides to the lake. But they were all with Harry.

"Look darl, Harry piled me with jobs for today. Seems he's decided that gate needs fixing; you know, the one that ram bloody flew through, well he wants it fixed today for some bloody reason."

"Oh come on. He's not using the truck today, is he?"

"Well he said he was going into town this morning when I saw him. Do you think he's been in already?" Stephen was warming to the idea of the lakes himself.

"I don't know, can't hurt to ask him though. It'll be a good day out, you'll see!" Shelly was keen to get away to escape the heat. All they had was a small piece of shade at the edge of the shack which provided little solace for the unrelenting still heat of the day.

Stephen made a beeline for the homestead but soon found Harry had plans of his own for the truck which was still parked around the back of the house. "And anyway, it's just for cartin' goods," he told Stephen.

"Listen Harry, Shelly told me you had been taking them all for a swim while I was away. I just want to give them a day out too, away from here."

"What about the jobs I gave you to do? Have you done the gate on that catchin' pen yet?" He picked the one task Stephen had not done from his list. Harry knew there was at least a couple of hours in that one.

"Well no, I haven't done that yet Harry, but I'll do it as soon as we get back. It'll be done before dark."

"Sorry Steve but I have business to do in town and I'll need the truck meself. I have to see some people today."

The heat was suddenly unbearable. Stephen was on a short fuse; pissed off: "Can't your trip wait a day Harry?"

"No Stephen and that's bloody final. Now get that bloody gate fixed before I get back from town or you're out of here!"

"What do you mean out of here? Are you threatening me?"

Harry pulled the fly wire door closed as Stephen's tone became menacing. "Well go on then, get to it."

"Look Harry, we've had a bloody good year. You've made your money on the clip. I'm not going to wreck the bloody truck. You're just being a miserable old bastard."

"Bloody-well no! And don't you call me a bastard. There's plenty more where you came from, you know; you're not so indispensable."

"Listen Harry, just because I've worked for you for sweet bugger all for two fucking years, doesn't mean you can treat me like fuckin' shit. You know I made more money in two months shearing each year than I earned from you for the rest of the year."

"Don't you talk to me like that you fuckin' little bastard or I'll clip you round the ears."

Stephen pulled at the door handle only to find Harry had locked it on the other side.

"Oh yeah, you can have a fuckin' go if you think you're good enough Harry," Stephen was shaping up. It scared Harry who shut the main door on him. He yelled through the door: "You're bloody finished here Martin. Pack your bloody things and get out."

"What about my pay? And the bonus you promised, for getting the last shed through so quickly. I haven't seen any of that yet!"

Harry yelled through the door: "I'm going to town, I'll get your money for you. But you can forget about working anywhere around here again. I'll make sure everybody knows about you, you bad tempered little dag."

Stephen was on exploding point but realized Morgan may not pay him out properly if he took things any further. He had made him know he would not be intimidated, but he wasn't going to get anywhere by taking things any further. He knew that. Shelly knew by the sounds coming from the verandah that he'd done his block and they'd soon be on the move.

Harry waited until Stephen had left the verandah and stormed off in the truck. He returned late in the afternoon with Stephen's pay packet and walked solemnly over to the shack where he stood in the doorway watching Shelly fold clothes into a cardboard carton.

"Where's Steve?"

"He saddled a horse to ride over to the Arnold's place. He said Fred's truck was due in to cart off their bales to Melbourne. He was going to see if we could get a lift with him."

"I'm sorry Shelly, but he made me do my block." Harry held out two envelopes. "This one is Stephen's pay. There's extra in it too. I know you'll be doin' it hard for a while. The other one is for you. The kids are going to need proper schooling, you know. It's not much, but it might help you out a bit. You need to be near a town again anyway."

"Yes Harry, I suppose you're right. Look, don't mind Stephen. Sometimes he has a bad temper. It is probably because I told him how much we loved to go to the lakes with you."

"Shelly I will always remember those times we had too. You look after those little ones." Harry bent down to give them each a hug good-bye.

"I'll just stay out of the way when he comes back, I think."

Stephen was unsaddling the horse as Fred drove the truck up to the quarters. Within half an hour of Fred showing up, they were packed up and on the road again.

Chapter 2

Stephen soon found a job on a dairy farm near Lilydale, about 30 miles from Melbourne. The job would give him an opportunity to work with horses again and he was now close enough to the city, he thought, to hitch a ride to town when he had the time.

Shelly liked the hills, especially the Dandenongs. The accommodation was much better; a real farmhouse with three bedrooms, lounge room, kitchen and there was a bath, a real bath, inside the house. A small chip heater outside had to be lit before bath time each night, but Shelly didn't mind the routine. It soon coincided with Stephen's afternoon milking.

Each hour of the day would throw different light across the mountains whose hues would herald the coming of rain by turning a deep blue. That was handy to know when you had a line full of washing. There was something about the mood of the mountains; an energy that seemed to envelop them and make even the most mundane of tasks interesting.

Stephen was up at dawn through the summer months and would allow Shelly an extra hour's sleep before the children surfaced.

"Did you see that big black horse yesterday?" he enquired. "He followed the cows right up to the yards." Stephen had a gleam in his eye that Shelly could notice even in the meagher rays of first light.

"No Stephen, I didn't see the horse, I was busy getting the children clothed and fed.

"He was beautiful Shelly. If he comes up today I'll try and catch him."

"Yeah, yeah Stephen, see you later," she pulled a pillow over her head.

He pulled it off again and kissed her on the cheek. "You'll see," Stephen stood in the doorway, adjusting his hat, "I'll get him."

This farm work was totally different to what Stephen had been doing at Cobbin. Sure, the general maintenance and fencing were much the same but here, there were no sheep; that was a bonus to him. With the added attraction of the city close by, he was a willing worker on a herd of 80 cows.

His day started with bringing in the herd from the run of paddocks, milking them, and taking them back again. The turn-around was between two and two-and-a-half-hours.

The boss, Clarrie Burke, lived more than a mile away in the main homestead. He had the dairy breeders there, plus a few beef cattle and half a dozen horses in the paddock. Two of the horses, a bay mare and the black stallion had seen a few race tracks, according to Clarrie, but he had lost interest when they didn't do any good. "Might as well have the buggers chewin' grass in the paddock than pay any more entry fees," he told Stephen.

"The mare was a pretty handy galloper, but she just never had any fight in her. The bloody stallion could gallop though, but he'd play up in the barriers all the time; knock 'imself up before they even got started. When he did get goin' he'd be trippin' over 'imself until he got into a stride. He never really settled as a colt. He didn't like work at all, the lazy bludger of a thing."

"So why not geld him," Stephen asked.

"Naaah, not him, I don't reckon it would make much difference; he's not worth the time, I reckon. Anyhow, he has a nice line. We may be able to get him over a few mares one day."

Stephen knew his horses and added comment: "I saw him about a week ago running down that adjacent paddock. He's a bit full but he seems to be able to gallop alright."

"Naaah, that couldn't be 'im, he's confined in the next paddock to my place, unless he's takin' to jumpin' bloody fences now," Clarrie seemed annoyed.

"It was a big black horse, seventeen hands or thereabouts, came bolting in here near the cows; scared the shit out of 'em."

Clarrie tilted his hat back on his head: "Sounds like 'im alright, wonder how he got through. The gates have been closed and none of the fences are down anywhere. I'd better bloody well check on me way back.

"Listen Clarrie, what do you reckon I try and get him galloping for you. I like a challenge, especially one that big," Stephen was expectant. "Do you mind if I ride him a bit; looks like he might need some work. He must be bored if he's jumping fences all by himself."

Clarrie paused for a moment, scratched his chin. He had a worried look on his face. "Look I just don't want anyone gettin' hurt. He's a rogue that bastard. He bloody nearly killed the track rider one day. Dipped and pig-rooted and threw him fifteen bloody feet in the air."

Stephen jumped in: "I used to break horses, I know what he's capable of. I'll be real careful not to put any of the other animals at risk."

Clarrie saw the eagerness in Stephen. 'Maybe, just may be this bloke could handle the bludger,' he thought. "It may be a way to get him on the go again. If you can catch him, that is. He's been playin' round the paddock there for months. He may be a bit frisky for you!"

Stephen assured Clarrie again, reminded him of his horse-breaking days and his time at the stud farm. "I've had to handle some of the roughest, meanest bloody horses in the bush. That bloke's already broken, I reckon I can get him goin' for yer. Maybe I can use him to bring in those few new cows you want taken back over in the morning. Get him used to walking in amongst them."

"Shiiit no," Clarrie whined noticeably, "that's why he didn't do any good before. He gets spooked near other animals. Keep him away from the cows, he might kick one of 'em. Don't want a bloody good milker goin' off just 'cause of a bloody horse. Just keep 'im clear of the milkers." Clarrie was adamant about that.

"Look, I'll open the gate into that central paddock on my way over. He'll find you, but I reckon you'll have a real job catching him. He's not real fond of people, either you know. I can't get near the bludger without 'im racin' off into the paddock. If you can catch 'im, well; then if you can ride 'im, maybe then we'll have a think about what we may be able to do. He was over near me house paddock t'is mornin' I'd say he may take a while to find the gate's open. Then I reckon it'll take yer a week to catch the bastard."

"Thanks Clarrie ..."

"But I don't want any of this 'orse business interferin' with the work at hand here with the cows, yer hear?"

"Righto Clarrie, the cows come first. I'm aware of that."

The following morning Stephen scoffed down his tea and grabbed a handful of sugar lumps as he went out calling his new dog: "Ginger, come on boy." The dog responded and walked at his ankles to the yard where the old mare was waiting for her saddle. The clouds over the mountains shone pink, triggering the 'shepherds warning'.

"C'mon Betsy, come on girl," he held out his hand and the old mare leaned in his direction prompting her to walk towards him. She was a good old mare, but had seen better years. Some mornings Stephen had felt guilty about throwing a saddle on her. He really thought she was too old to do this work. All he really had to do was ride out and open the gates, so some mornings he took off his gumboots and ran the paddock.

This morning Betsy was looking alright and they ambled their way to the task. Stephen noticed the sky was a deeper blue than he had seen before. Like a first light dark, dark blue. The horizon tinged with red and yellow. A storm was brewing and lightning began to crack to the west. All the way out to the far paddock he kept looking across for the stallion but soon forgot about him for this day as he got stuck in to the work at hand.

The cows were heading in the right direction and Betsy had assumed her position behind them when he heard the hoof beats across in the other paddock. The stallion was storming towards the lead cow at such a rate the animal veered from its course along the fence line and started into a trot. The rest of the herd followed and Stephen realized he should get Betsy into the fray to straighten them back onto the right course.

"Get out of it you big bludger," he screamed at the stallion which turned and swished his tail high in the air as he accelerated into a fast gallop swinging away in his own paddock. "Bloody Dark Horizon; they named you well you big bludger," he felt he was talking to the breeze.

"Ginger get around boy, git around, Go on!"

Stephen managed to get Betsy into an even canter, which matched the speed of the cows and steered them into the yard with much haste. He finally jumped off and swung the gate closed as the last cow ambled begrudgingly in, followed by the dog.

'He'd need some work too,' he thought as the stallion galloped right to the fence three metres away and skidded to a halt. A roll of thunder broke his whinny and he bolted away again, the ground shuddering from a mixture of thunder and hoof beats.

"I'll be back for you today boy," Stephen's voice was loud enough for the animal to hear as it accelerated away. Stephen's heart was pacing and the milking went off without a hitch. He had left all the gates open to his third yard of grass and was confident they'd find their way.

His attention turned to the road and the Dodge ute piloted by Clarrie.

"Gedday Stephen, how did they go today?"

"Pretty good Clarrie; they're on the way back now."

"Well why aren't you following them out."

"I can catch 'em up soon enough. Anyway, I saw the horse this morning, the stallion. He looks like a fine animal. He was just out there before," he pointed toward the adjacent paddock and looked up to see the horse standing there. "Shit, there he is; right there."

Stephen approached him with a bit of meal from his pockets in his outstretched hand. The horse responded by walking quietly up and licking it clear, allowing Stephen to stroke him gently. Then he slipped him a few sugar cubes which disappeared through Darkie's soft nuzzling lips.

Clarrie was impressed, but didn't want to praise him up too much. Not just yet. "Righto son, just start slow on him. Can't say as I'd be takin' him anywhere near the cows though."

Stephen opened the paddock gate and ran the stallion into the yards. He took his time to show him a halter, offering another handful of the dairy meal as incentive. With this he wasted no time and, within minutes, he was brushing the shaggy coat. Great clumps of excess hair rubbed out with each stroke, but the animal enjoyed the attention. He rubbed his hand over the black horse's chest and watched the wither shake gently as he accepted a saddle blanket. He was a beauty alright; 17 plus hands. Stephen was talking all the time in gentle tones. When he had nothing to say to the horse he would sing a little tune, watching the tell-tale signs of the horse's ears as they enquired to the sound.

He was calculated with each change of action, but saw the horse starting to take it all in. As the saddle went on, he became twitchy, pulling against the halter, tied to the railing. Stephen was quick to respond unhitching the rope as he moved to his left.

This gave the horse something else to think about, and soon he was walking in circles on the halter behind him. Stephen would break out of a turn and head straight up the yard before turning again, first one way and then another. As soon as Darkie started to over-run him, Stephen would turn him around again. Just as the horse would predict a turn Stephen would stop. Within fifteen or twenty minutes he was able to tie him to the rail on a loose halter.

He waited maybe ten or fifteen minutes and was off again and every so often he would stop suddenly, bending down in front of the horse, pulling up a hoof, or offering a handful of grain. The animal received the bit with ease thinking there would be another palm-full of food.

Clarrie was returning from town and stopped to take in Stephen's training. He laughed out loud watching his antics: "Yer silly bastard, you could have jumped on his back from the top of the barn and he wouldn't move for yer. Not with that fat gut of his."

Stephen laughed it off, but knew in himself that he had done the right thing with this horse. The horse had his own little way and would seek Stephen's own response to things he did; Stephen acted like the horse and responded, only when he was ready.

By the time he was ready to mount him, Dark Horizon was ready for the ride himself. Stephen was in his element and enjoyed the ride as they got to know one another.

Before long Stephen started walking the cows out in the mornings from the dairy to the paddock using Darkie. He learned not to spook them and have the horse settled to a walk long before he reached the cows. When he did reach them he would often walk the horse straight through the herd, making him bullock his way gently through.

On the way back his track always took him around the perimeter fence, just slowly at first, but in a matter of weeks they had a reasonably clear understanding of each other. Dark Horizon, willingly approached the obstacles and stepped over with ease. Stephen would count the seconds in his head between landmark trees or stumps. He knew the horse was responding to his meal, but it was now time to see if Clarrie was prepared to dip his short arms into his deep pockets to buy some decent oats.

Clarrie was impressed when this day he watched Stephen working the horse; he hadn't paid too much attention to the workings for weeks, he had other things on his mind, but one look at Dark Horizon made him realize the horse was shaping up.

Stephen had not told him about his habit of ploughing through the mob of cows or the log jumping; he simply wouldn't understand, he thought.

"Look, if I shell out money for him I gotta be able to get something back. How are his legs?"

"He appeared a bit dicky at first, but he's getting a lot more sure-footed now. Overall he's pretty confident of his own ability I reckon." Stephen responded.

"There's a race at the locals in about eight weeks that carries five hundred pounds in prize money, the Country Cup. You reckon he can be ready for that?"

"Cripes Clarrie, you may have to give him a start before a race like that. Those horses will have been running in town."

"There is a meeting coming up at the locals at Healesville. I'll see if there's somethin' over a mile or thereabouts."

"Even further, I reckon. He settles down really well. He's almost asleep sometimes walking up behind the cows." Stephen was keen to tell of the antics of the horse, "but when we get going he settles real well, just finds his gait and sights it up really well. I have been taking him on a circuit of the big paddock and then goin' 'round again. He even jumps the logs down the lane there!"

"How does he go over them?" Clarrie's head lifted with interest.

"Does it easy, he's really relaxed and sights them up really well."

"Maybe we should be looking at a hurdle race, they're bloody long though. How far do you reckon he could go?"

'Bing,' thought Stephen, thinking for a moment before answering.

"With an easy run he could go two miles or better. The hurdles are easy for him. He just steps over them easy. In fact it gives him something to think about, I reckon. Remember he was jumping the paddock fences by himself there just a month or so ago."

"Look I'll get some feed, but I'll come over tomorrow after the mornin' milking and check him out."

The next day Clarrie watched the horse gallop and was impressed by the way Stephen had brought him on. The jumps were no real obstacle; rather they provided something to keep Darkie's mind occupied, as Stephen had said. He liked the way he handled the horse.

"He sailed over that log down the bottom there both times. For a minute there, I thought you were goin' round again," he was genuinely excited as he shouted to Stephen as Darkie wheeled to a halt.

Stephen was puffing more than the horse from hanging on, holding him back: "We've had days we've just poked along steady and gone four times around and he's still picked up the bit in the run home there."

"Gee, that paddock has to be a mile. How fit do you think he is?" Clarrie stood back and looked at the horse. "He still has a bit of a gut on him I see. Let's get him in that hurdle race then. Can you ride him?"

"Well I haven't had a real race ride before."

"Well, who do yer reckon we put on him then?"

"I dunno."

"You can ride him over the hills there the day before the race. Maybe give him a hit out on the course early. We'll have to see if we can get one of the local boys to ride him. Trouble is, not many of them could ride him before. Sure you couldn't make weight for a hurdle?"

"Well, maybe I could, but I'd 'ave to give him a trial first. Just see what he's like."

"Goodo, they've got some jump outs coming up the end of next week. It'll be worth giving him a look at the barriers. That's one of the problems we had with him last time. He just wouldn't get near the bloody barrier stalls."

"He should be OK, I've been getting him used to crowds with the cows. He can walk right through them now without even spooking one." Stephen opened the gate to show Clarrie a narrow race he had made from a couple of gates. "Watch this." Darkie responded by walking straight up to the narrow entrance and with a gentle prompt with his knees Stephen had him walk up into the centre of the gates.

"That is very impressive Stevie. I'm amazed at the way you have worked on him in such a short space of time. We'll just get him to the jump outs and see how he jumps out of the gates. Just don't let him go in the trials. Keep him under double wraps."

"You get the feed, I'll have him ready; look at him now, though!"

Clarrie brought the feed home and the mix brought Dark Horizon up another notch. His coat was now really shining. Whether it was the oats or the attention that sparked him up was not really clear. Stephen would spend hours grooming him. He even set up a sand roll by shoveling sand from a creek bed. He could appreciate the athlete in the animal.

The work was also bringing it out in Stephen himself. They were both getting to the peak of their physical fitness and the Cup Hurdle was on in just six weeks.

In the weeks to come Stephen seemed to be on automatic pilot to get the cows through quickly so he could spend more time with the horse, giving him a day off galloping work occasionally.

The day before the trial he danced into the yards. After one hard hit out from the stables Stephen allowed him to bowl along loosening the reins for the last mile of the second round and he found the horse knocked up. He blew for hours after. Stephen was glad Clarrie wasn't around.

He floated him to the track for his trial. The horse appeared to have recovered well enough for the gallop. They were in the third barrier trial and Dark Horizon spooked a little when heading towards the gate with another runner. Other jockeys yelling also spooked him. Stephen turned him around away from the other horses in the stalls to unhitch him. "I'll bring him up meself." He reeled him around in a huge arc and made another go of it, saying as he went: "gently through the cows", and he went in with ease.

The starter knew Darkie and was amazed at how Stephen was able to settle him and walk him straight up, once all the others were in.

He yelled: "All clear," and the gates were released. Darkie reared slightly at first, but Stephen had a tight hold on him and they were away last in the field of six. The six furlong gallop was against horses used to going quickly and he simply could not keep up. Rounding the turn Stephen scrubbed his ears a bit and realized Darkie was starting to pick up on the others. By the time they reached the post they had made up about four lengths and ran into fourth place. Darkie was just starting to warm to the task when Stephen was putting the brakes on. He pulled up so well that Stephen was beginning to believe even more in the horse's ability. He was galloping well and was frisky enough when they arrived home for Stephen to use him again to walk in the cows for milking that afternoon.

Stephen was so excited about the gallop he started looking up the form on other horses nominated in the hurdle race Clarrie had selected. He looked at the times they had done, and decided finally it would come down to the best horse on the day, and he and Dark Horizon would be giving their best. They would just have to let the race pan out.

He eased up on the work over the following week, giving Darkie just one full gallop of the paddock each week for the four weeks before the race, gradually building up in distance with each gallop. Two days before the event they went for three miles with Darkie responding well in what Stephen considered to be fairly even time and still showing some dash across the final paddock. As they pulled up he realized the horse was hardly blowing at all. Darkie was as fit and as ready as he'd ever be.

"Shelly, he might even win on Friday," he skited, excited by the prospect.

"You just be careful Stephen. We can't afford you to get hurt, so don't take any foolish chances."

"Well you be careful milking those cows while I'm gone."

The following day Stephen kissed Shelly and the children good-bye and drove the horse the ten miles to the course in Clarrie's float truck. He slept there overnight in the stables. At daylight he decided to give him a look at the course and slipped out in the early light for what he termed his "final conditioning". Just an easy work over to the six furlongs post where he allowed him to stride out just a little, keeping a tight hold on him down the straight.

Clarrie arrived on course about an hour before the race. Stephen had Darkie in the stall and was ready to weigh in. Clarrie borrowed a saddle and lead bags and handed the silks to Stephen.

"You'd better go and weigh in. I'll be over directly to pick up the saddle."

"Say, Clarrie, are you going to have something on him? He's forty to one in the ring."

"I might just wait a bit and have a look at them, I think."

"Well if you do, you reckon you can have a couple of pound each way for me?"

"Yeah, OK Stephen, I'll do that for you."

The favorite of the race didn't look like much of a race horse. He stood about 15 hands and looked as round as a barrel. The two that looked pretty good to Stephen were also well in the market.

There were just eleven of the original sixteen nominated left in the race. Dark Horizon was number eleven, having his first start over jumps and his first start at anything more than a mile. He had the bottom weight which gave him a stone and a half on the top weight and half a stone on the next in the field. Despite this Stephen had to pack half a stone of lead into the bags.

There was a late plunge in the betting which saw Dark Horizon firm up to 15/1, the price Clarrie told Stephen he had got, "at the death".

The barriers didn't bother him at all. He strolled in as though he had done it a hundred times before. Stephen let him get up to speed then gently rolled him away from the rail and settled him in about sixth place on the outside. This gave him room to move with his big loping gait. All he had to do now was maintain his momentum and not let the leaders dash too far away. He positioned himself well for most of the jumps and was sure footed on all but one of the landings. They were fifth coming up to the turn but had given the leader about ten lengths. Stephen rode him out and found another gear and was moving into fourth place at the furlong when the saddle suddenly slipped, slowly sideways at first, and then up along the horse's neck. Stephen displayed miraculous skills to stay aboard as the horse veered out near the line. The mishap, he believed, cost him the race and in the run to the line he finished third going down by just two lengths.

As he crossed the line Stephen held Darkie's mane with one hand while trying to stay on board. He finally got his other hand back between his legs to pull the horse up. He immediately dismounted and, with the help of a race goer, checked the girth strap. As he centred the saddle and pulled up the strap he noticed a neat slice between two of the buckle holes. The saddle had been tampered with.

He walked the horse back into the enclosure. He hardly said a word to Clarrie who was jabbering away at him: "You were lucky to stay aboard over the line there Stevie."

Stephen glared back at Clarrie as he gathered the saddle: "I was lucky to go any distance at all in that race Clarrie. Someone cut the bloody girth."

"What do you mean Steve?"

"You know what I mean Clarrie," Stephen turned away and walked in to weigh in.

Stephen changed from his silks and headed back out to Darkie's stall where Clarrie handed him his riders fee and winnings for running the place. Thirty pounds all up.

"Not a bad run, for first up."

"He could have bloody well won for us you know," Stephen looked straight back into Clarrie's eyes which shifted away immediately.

"Well, gotta go and see some of the congregation. We've got a whole crew from the church over in the Member's. See you then."

Tips from the jockeys' room saw Stephen lay the lot on two other gallopers on the day. They both got up. He also learned Dark Horizon had blown out to 66/1 before someone laid money all over the ring taking every bit of each way he could find. The eventual winner, at the same time had eased in the betting until someone plonked on him at 12/1. Clarrie and his mates must have had a really good day, Stephen thought, but he knew he wouldn't get the truth from him.

Two weeks went by before Clarrie came over.

"When are you going to give him another run Clarrie?" Stephen was anxious.

"You gotta give 'em time to forget this run. That's how you get 'em," Clarrie was firm.

Stephen didn't understand.

"Hey Clarrie, he could have won the other day if someone hadn't slit that notch in the girth."

"If he'd won, I wouldn't get any price on him next time. You can put him back out to the paddock in the mornin'; maybe bring the bay mare in."

Stephen was disappointed. Dark Horizon was looking better than ever, but Clarrie had his own reasons for holding him up.

"No. Turn him out. You are supposed to be looking after the dairy cows too, not just that bloody horse. Anyway, everyone knows he's running well. Those bookies'll never bet anything about him like that again."

"All that work for just one run," Stephen was pushing. "Clarrie, he can win some races for you. He'll win in town, you watch," he was almost pleading now.

"Yeah, maybe he will, but only when I want him to. He goes to the paddock tomorrow."

Two months later Stephen heard that Clarrie had told the locals the horse had gone shin sore and may never race again.

"The cunning old bastard," he told Shelly, who really appreciated the work Stephen had done with the horse.

"It's all about money Stephen. He wouldn't have the guts to tell you he took the big odds each way and had a sizeable saver on the winner that day. Can't you see by his actions that they don't really care about the horses, it's the money."

She had seen the big horse when he first came in and noticed the difference in his temperament as Stephen worked him nearly every day.

Now the mare was here and she could see the frustration in Stephen. He handled her just as well, but after a month he was looking for work elsewhere. He did not like the ethic here and he told Clarrie as much.

"You'd rip off your own grandmother Clarrie. You set me up in that race. I know. I heard the price they bet down there. And my mate saw you collect on the winner as well as Darkie. You could have killed me you bastard."

"Nothing personal Stevie, it's just the way you gotta do things. I'm sorry that you may have been in danger, but as it turned out, no harm was done and we will have something on Darkie in a couple of months' time in town. Just remember to be on him."

This was now a Dark Horizon for Stephen; time again, to move on.

Chapter 3

The northern suburbs of Melbourne were pushing their way out from the city. East Reservoir was the new housing commission development built outside the Olympic Village at East Preston, now also a suburb to provide low cost commission housing.

Stephen and Shelly were allotted 22 London Avenue, a three bedroom cottage, the same in size and design as another dozen within sight of the front gate. There was just one of the original properties left in the street, surrounded by its shade trees, just the surrounds of the house block within the original picket fence which had needed painting for a long time. Nonetheless the move from the country had its good side. The girls needed a school to go to and that was just two blocks away. There were so many new friends for the children to meet.

As they all found their way the children were unaware of the nickname given to the suburb they had moved into although 'Little Chicago' was to live up to its name for Stephen.

He had taken on several jobs in the first year but found it hard to stick with any. His resourcefulness gained from the country resulted in quite a few surprises in that first year, including the appearance one morning of Baaa, a month-old lamb.

"Cripes you shoulda seen him running after them sheep Shelly," Bert Baxter said. "I was just drivin' along and he says: 'Stop. Stop here.' When I pulls over, he is outta the bloody car creepin' along on all fours, going 'baaa, baaa'. Suddenly he was surrounded by 'em and grabs the little bludger out there."

"He'll be good tucker in a few months," Stephen chimed in.

When he was working, usually as a truck driver or storeman, Stephen would leave home before the children were up in the mornings and would not be home until after they had gone to bed again.

The children were rostered onto bottle feeding the lamb until it started eating the back lawn. They called him 'Baaa' and played with him daily until he grew big enough for them to try to ride him.

This Monday they arrived home from school and the sheep was gone. The next weekend they sat down for the traditional Sunday roast. This week it consisted of a leg of prime lamb. As they each stuck their forks into the meat on their plates Stephen couldn't help himself: "Baaaaa".

"Oh no! You're kidding," Delia protested.

"That's not Baaa, is it?" Suzanne opened her mouth to release the first bite.

"Stephen, cut it out," Shelly was firm. "Don't be silly, I got this from the butcher yesterday. Stop teasing them Stephen."

"It doesn't matter. They should know they are eating lamb when they are eating lamb chops or a leg of lamb or lambs fry..."

"Just cut it out."

"I'm not eating any of that," Delia insisted.

"Oh yes you are young lady," Shelly tried to calm them all.

The event got out of hand and all of the children left meat on the side of their plates that day. However the refrigerator appeared to be well stocked with other products from Baaa. Eventually they succumbed, unknowingly, to eat their friend.

As the first year in the new suburb met the next Shelly had settled into a routine as Stephen chased the next bout of work. She was used to him coming home with another story of 'doing his block'. It was a habit he attained more often now. Although it usually only happened when his bosses were concerned about the quality of his work.

Making the wrong deliveries on the Mornington Peninsula run didn't help either: "You gave Mrs Watson of Marine Parade the lounge suite which was purchased by Mrs Jackson, and you gave Mrs Jackson the refrigerator belonging to Mrs Green and you gave Mrs Watson's stereo to Mrs Green," The boss blurted out.

"I delivered them to what was on the dockets; have a bloody look at them," Stephen was, by now, waving the dockets in the air.

"I already have looked at the dockets Stephen, and you have stuffed up, so you had better spend the morning driving out there and getting things straightened out."

Stephen's ventures into the suburbs often resulted in a sidetrack with visits here and there. He knew people all over the place. By the time he'd get back this day he knew he'd have the sack again.

Bert Baxter lived along the Peninsula and Stephen could not resist calling in again, seeing he was in the district.

"Gedday Bert, I told you I would drop in whenever I was over this way."

Bert laughed: "Howdy Steve, but you were just here yesterday weren't you?" he scratched his head. "Yeah, I'm sure that was you who helped me finish that bottle of Black Label."

He told Bert about the mix up and he laughed heartily: "Shit man, you probably stuffed up after you left here."

"Didn't matter, they all signed for the fucken things. What was I to know?"

"Come in yer bastard and have a drink with me. Geeze, so what have you got to do now?"

"Go and get them back and deliver them to the right places. Then I reckon I have got the boot. I think one of the bitches smelled my breath and dobbed me in."

"It sounds like they all bloody-well dobbed you in mate. I don't reckon that's bloody fair. You shoulda told them that you were pissed. Ha ha ha!"

"Hey listen Bert, if he does give me the arse, I tell yer, I reckon we can easily knock the store over one night. He'd be fucken insured anyway. No loss to the bastard. I don't have a decent vehicle though. I'm on Shank's pony after tonight."

"I know where I can get hold of a truck."

"Nah, too big. It would be noticed there. Maybe a van might do."

"How the fuck am I going to get my new fridge, television, washing machine and vacuum cleaner all into a bloody van."

"Shit, I s'pose you're right. And where's my one of all of them gonna go?"

"You two bastards will end up in the can doing that stuff," Maureen Baxter was slurring a little. She and Bert had drank well into another bottle of Black Label and it was only 11am.

"Shut the fuck up or I'll clobber you," Bert retorted.

Maureen simply retreated to a safer vantage point and kept on nagging at him. "That's right you bastard. Threaten me again why don't ya," She paused and turned away into the lounge room: "Go on then, get yourself pinched again. What do I care? Things are more peaceful 'round 'ere when you're in the bloody nick."

"Piss orf yer bitch." She left the room as Bert attempted to stand up: "Fucken women Steve. Yer gotta put 'em in their place. And to think they gave them the vote. Worse fuckin' thing they coulda done, I reckon."

Shelly simply could not take to some of the people Stephen called on or brought home, especially Bert Baxter. She wondered how Stephen could possibly get tied up with anyone like that. She saw through Baxter the first night Stephen brought him home to party on after a Buck's night. She knew they'd be trouble together. It was just a matter of time. Then there was the sheep. The trouble now was, when she expressed her opinion, he shut her up. That was his way now, especially when he'd had a few.

She smelled the liquor on him when he arrived home and forgave him when he told her he got the sack. Then he blew it by talking about his day with Bert: "Bert reckons we could make a real killin' if we knocked over that Blaine & Blaine Store."

"He's all talk Stephen. Just don't get involved. So what if you've lost your job? There'll be another one for you soon. I don't want to hear about your plans if they involve anything illegal."

"Don't you fucken tell me what I can or cannot do. Just shut the fuck up or I'll belt you one," he raised his hand to Shelly. She was shocked that he'd threatened to hit her so quickly this night and cowered away. She had no defense for this. He was a different man to the one she knew in the bush. The city had just too many diversions for him. She knew he was a better man in the country but whenever she mentioned going back he would explode into a violent rage. It was his way of ending such conversations.

She could not understand why he was so violent in defense of his mates; too violent for her to argue. He would force her to wait on him, hand and foot and if anything was out of place or not to his instant liking, he'd belt her one.

The next morning Shelly did her best in getting the girls off to school. They were helpful and could now get their own breakfast, although Shelly's routine meant she would automatically put Terry's out for him.

"What happened to your face Mum," Suzanne was staring at the blue black of her mother's cheekbone. Shelly lifted her hand to her cheek to cover it up: "Nothing much dear. Mummy slipped last night and hit herself on the silly chair."

Delia knew that was a lie. "I heard Daddy when he came in last night." She looked straight at Shelly forcing her to turn away.

"Come on you girls. Eat your breakfast and get off to school. You'll be late."

Terry toddled about following Shelly around all morning until he discovered Stephen in bed. Shelly caught him by the arm just before he stuck his fingers into Stephen's eyes to wake him.

Stephen surfaced after midday, showered, dressed himself in his best suit and walked up the street. Terry spent the afternoon at the front gate waiting for Suzanne and Delia to get home.

Like many of the other families in the street, the Martins had a very tight budget. Every penny would count. The gas meter ran on shillings and sixpences. The washing was done in a copper, when there was enough money for gas to heat it up. Shelly was washing for five, and now, had another one on the way. Tears flowed down her cheeks as she looked down at her three-month swell.

Stephen came home shortly after five with the news. He had flowers and chocolates, which went around the children twice as dessert. "Shelly, I am going to buy me own truck. Stuff this workin' your arse off for other bludgers. I can sub-contract out. Do deliveries, like old Barry."

"But where did you get the money?"

"You told me not to tell you if me and Bert were doing anything. Let's keep it like that. We got enough from the job for the deposit but I'll have to start earnin' with it pretty fast to keep up the payments." He thought he had it all worked out.

A few contracts were enough to keep Stephen on the straight and narrow for a while. He managed to contract three local companies to do pick-ups, mainly from the wharves and deliver through the suburbs.

Things were looking all right although nowhere near what he had expected. Now and then he allowed Terry to ride with him for the day.

On one occasion they were heading down Glenferrie Road and Terry recognized a familiar turn off: "Nanna is down there Dad. Let's go visit Nanna."

He had a mouth full of cream bun Stephen had bought for him and was finishing the last of it as they turned into Station Street, Auburn. Stephen looked across at Terry holding his hand over his mouth.

"Hold it in. Hold it in."

He stopped the truck and quickly opened the door and ran around the front to open Terry's side. He let fly just as he did, wearing the first gush of regurgitated cream bun down one shoulder.

Stephen took his shirt off and washed it off under the tap of the front yard he had grown up in. He then wet a handkerchief and offered it to Terry after he'd emptied himself out.

"Are you okay mate?"

Terry wasn't really but he responded with a quiet: "Yep."

"Let's go see Nanna then. Come on."

He knocked on the door gently.

Dulcie opened the door narrowly at first to see who was there. As soon as she saw Terry she threw the door open wide: "Terry boy, my little grandson. Hello, hello." She kneeled down to give him a big hug.

"Hi mum, can we come in?" Stephen waited until she had greeted Terry and stood up again before kissing her gently on the cheek. "Hi, how are you?"

"Oh fine. I'm fine. Come in and have a cup of tea."

As she put the kettle on Stephen told her he had bought the truck. "I could do with a bit more work for it though. Things are pretty tough. At the moment I have just three businesses I do deliveries for. It's only eleven fifteen now and I've almost finished the run."

"Well you'll just have to go out and look for it son."

Terry drank cordial and watched as they caught up with the news of his aunts: "You know Beatrice is having another baby Stephen?"

"No I didn't. How far gone is she?"

"Two months now. Gosh I don't know how she manages with those two boys anyway."

"They're alright mum; they're just boys."

"Yes but they are getting into trouble at school all the time. Young Joseph didn't come home until eight o'clock the other week. Be' was worried sick."

"Yes but he is fifteen mum."

"You don't know who is walking the streets at night these days. You can't be too careful."

"We used to get trains into the city after school, just for the ride. There was no harm in that then."

"And you had me worried sick too. Wondering where you were. When you hadn't come home by dinner time Stephen, I really was worried about you."

He turned around as there was a knock on the door: "Milko."

Dulcie walked to the mantle clock, which she opened to take a ten-shilling note out to the milkman. When Dulcie returned Stephen was still looking at the clock.

"Yes, I still keep my money in the clock Stephen. Does that bring back memories for you? That time ten shillings went missing from there. You took it, didn't you?"

"No. I told you then that I didn't, and you didn't believe me. You just had me put into that home."

"You were uncontrollable Stephen. I was on my own, in the depression, four children to feed, the mortgage on the house to pay off on my own. You know that cleaning work I did for Mrs Robinson and the Cox's had to sustain us. We were on bread and dripping most of the time."

"But why send me there?"

"You wouldn't go to school, or cooperate in any way, Stephen, I had to do something. At least you went to school there."

"Yes I did, but it was a school of hard knocks. Most of the guys there were in for knocking over houses, stealing cars, fighting, you name it. That's what I learned in there mum."

Stephen had had enough and was on his feet: "Come on Terry, you kiss Nanna good-bye, we're going." He turned to Dulcie. "You could have kept me home, Mum, I wasn't a bad kid then."

"Yes but look at you now Stephen. You have a lovely wife and three beautiful children. All you have to do is to stop drinking. It is a curse Stephen. By all means, do it in moderation, but I've heard that you go overboard sometimes."

"I know what I can bloody-well handle," he suddenly knew he could not get away with any explanation here. "Look, I'll see you later."

He opened the door and swung Terry up into the cabin. The youngster was unaware that this was the first time Stephen had seen his mother for four years. Her last words aggravated him; gnawed away at his psyche until he had to rebel again. He had a taste for alcohol, which would reach the bingeing level very soon.

It started as the occasional Saturday afternoon drink, usually after a morning delivery job until his thirst for the frantic beer swill before 6pm would keep him in the pub until closing time most nights. Shelly was angry when he came home just after six o'clock carrying a carton of beer. There were so many other things they needed before his beer. He was neglecting the payments on the truck and spending the money on booze.

Shelly got into her own habit of sitting the children down to dinner before five o'clock so they would be in bed before he got home. She was frightened, scared stiff, each time he came home pissed and he was doing it more often now.

She dearly wanted him to not bother with the pub; they just didn't have enough money for him to drink, but he'd usually be in such a state when they spoke of it that he would threaten her again.

"I work bloody hard and I'll play bloody hard as I like Shelly," she turned away. "Are you listenin' to me, I'll do as I fucken-well please. You hear that?"

"Yes Stephen, I hear you, but it doesn't help us put better food on the table for the kids."

Stephen would insult her after such an exchange by bringing a drinking buddy home from the hotel, armed with more bottles.

"Get our bloody dinner ready," he ordered. "Me and Roy want our bloody dinner and we want it now!"

She hardly had enough in the budget to feed the family now, let alone some blow-in her husband had dragged home from the pub. Despite this, she fed them with whatever there was.

This night she took Stephen's plate, which had been kept warm in the oven. "Well, what about Roy? What's he gunna eat?"

Shelly was quick and her sarcasm was wasted on them: "Would you care for some bread and dripping Roy?"

"OK, that'll be fine, if it's not too much trouble," she was shocked at the response.

During this binge of Stephen's she resorted to making rabbit stews. These she could 'soup up' or add another rabbit to make the pot last for another night or two. It kept the peace. She heated up the soup and left the room.

This morning Stephen woke to hear his truck engine turning over. On cold mornings it needed full choke, five or six pumps of gas and a few quick turns of the key to get her going.

He heard the grinding sound and raced outside in his underwear.

"What the fuck do you think you're doing?"

The repossession agent went white. He held up a piece of paper in front of Stephen: "This paper says you owe the last four payments on your hire purchase agreement. You haven't honored your agreement; we're taking the truck."

"Who's fucken we, smart arse? I suggest you get your arse out of there and piss off."

The agent complied: "We need a payment immediately or we'll be back to take the truck."

Stephen was fuming when he went inside.

"Well what do you expect if you don't make the payments Stephen?" Shelly protested.

"Look, I'll get them some money today. Maybe that will keep them off my back for a while. I'll try and get that payment from Wilkins Brothers."

He came home that night with the news that he made up two

payments. He also had some "insurance", a German shepherd dog, "Rangie" sitting on the back of the truck.

"Anyone puts their hand near the truck and the dog will rip their bloody arms off."

The next morning he was awoken by a commotion outside. He had to call the dog off before the agent was seriously hurt. He took on the day's events as though nothing had happened, but with only three deliveries, he found he was driving back into the street before eleven this day.

The following morning he awoke to see Rangie in the front yard chewing on a huge bone. The truck was gone. To his credit, Stephen rolled with the news. "It was inevitable," he told Shelly later. "When you can't keep up payments because others haven't paid you the bills they owe you for.

"What can you do Shelly? Go and take it from people who just haven't got it?"

This time Stephen didn't waste any time looking for work and within a couple of days was into his new job, delivering washing machines.

About three months in the job and Stephen was starting to get edgy. The boss kept a close eye on the loading dock and all the while Stephen was getting frustrated at the thought of making an extra dollar from flogging off one of the machines. Trouble was, he thought, a washing machine was not the type of appliance you could pinch that easily. They were too big. On any day he may be delivering up to 20 machines. With that many packed into a load, there sometimes could be just one other there, he thought. He became obsessed with the idea and saw the confusion in the mornings as stock was sorted and placed on the dock ready for loading. He worked out that he would just add one extra onto the dock the evening before. Just try it out.

The wages were fair, but Stephen was more interested in seeing what he could get for nix. He managed to load on the extra machine, which he would off load at Bert's place for freight-on later, after he had teed up a sale. Shelly may have gone for the idea if he had brought a washing machine home for her. Washing in the copper was heavy work with three kids. Her pregnancy made it even harder. Stephen had decided he needed cash for his booty.

Over the next month he took many risks, like wandering into hotels and generally asking if anyone wanted to buy a washing machine, "cheap". The risks paid off for some time and in one week Stephen managed to move four machines and stash some money away. On one occasion he had decided to make up with Shelly and gave her all of the proceeds, but this was a very rare occasion indeed. She held on to the money and within weeks she needed it all to pay regular household bills when Stephen was not forthcoming with his wage packet.

The company he was keeping worried Shelly, especially when an early morning raid from the police awakened the household. In the space of a year there were three such raids, but they never found anything. Stephen would act like the total innocent. Shelly knew he hadn't arrived home until almost three o'clock and here, at 6am, the police were going through the manhole in the ceiling.

"What are you looking for officer?" Stephen would ask in the most angelic of voices, in mock innocence.

"You fucken know exactly what we're looking for Martin, and we'll bloody well find it too," Sgt King did not mince his words.

"But sir, there is no reason for you to believe what you are looking for is here in my home. Don't you need a warrant or something?"

"Look smart arse," Sgt King was down off the ladder in a flash reaching for Stephen's dressing gown. He pulled him close and stared him in the eye: "Listen you little prick; we know what you've been up to for several weeks now, and believe me, it's going to stop and we're gonna get you and fucken-well lock you up. So don't give me any of your shit. If I want to search your place, I'll fucking-well walk right in and do it. You hear?" He pushed Stephen away. "Get me a drink of water, will you."

Stephen backed into the kitchen and brought him back the glass and noticed King grab it by the rim as he drank.

The children were bemused by the antics of the plain-clothed men rummaging through their cupboards. After they had been through the house they would also go outside and look around.

"Are they looking for Easter eggs mum?" Delia inquired.

"No, no darlin', they have lost something and they just think Daddy might be able to help them find it."

"Daddy, do you know what they're looking for? Is it Easter eggs?"

Stephen just pushed her aside: "Come on, Delia, get back into your room and stay away."

This time they left and Stephen did not even notice as Sgt King slipped the glass into his pocket. He considered he had a reasonable set of Stephen's prints from this one. He just wanted his own proof. He didn't give a stuff how he got them.

On the fourth visit that year the larger of policeman, Detective Crilley, stood at the top of the stairs to hoick up a huge lump of phlegm from his throat. He spat sideways over the railing onto a large tarpaulin covering a wood pile. Hours later, after they had left empty handed again, Stephen and Bert could laugh about the incident.

"You could see the fucken steam rising from the spit," Stephen told Bert laughing loudly. Underneath the tarp was the still unopened safe they had stolen from a warehouse the evening before. They waited for darkness before Bert brought his truck over to take the safe to his shed where they used oxy-acetylene to cut it open.

The safe contained about 1200 pounds plus several thousand in cheques, which they burned.

"Listen Bert, I had better lay low for a while. I would not have been home more than two hours when those bulls came through the door this morning. I think we should cool it for a while."

"I think you're right Stephen. How did they know to check you out? You know they also went through Sharkey's place this morning. He rang to tell me. Said they reckoned they knew everyone involved, and had prints to prove it."

"But they don't even have my prints," Stephen thought for a moment. "You don't suppose Sharkey told them to try my place do ya?"

"I don't know Stephen, but I think it would be a good idea if we didn't go showing too much of this money around."

"We should go and have a day at the races and see if we can't turn it into something. Anyway, what's the bloody good of cracking a safe if you can't spend the proceeds," Stephen was feeling the cash. "Just a hundred quid, c'mon Bert."

"Not while they're onto you Stephen. Look, maybe you should leave the rest of that with me for a while, just until things cool down."

Stephen looked into Bert's eyes for a moment and realized he simply did not trust him: "Naaah, I have a place I can put it that's safe enough. Anyway I've been thinking of getting a new car."

"It was as close as you could get without actually being pinched," Stephen lamented to Shelly that evening, "so I told Bert we should lay low for a while."

He told Shelly his share of the haul amounted to almost 400 quid.

"It could very well have been nothing and a jail sentence Stephen. Look, here we are with three children and another just weeks away. You have to stop going out at night, for good."

"Yeah, you're right love. I need to keep away from that King bastard. He's after me I reckon."

Chapter 4

Spring had come around again and the children saw the sunshine as an excuse for hours of pleasure by wetting down a section of lawn in the back yard and running full pelt into it, sliding for several metres on their feet. Once the first fell and slid for any distance, they were running along and diving into the mud to slide on their bellies.

Delia was always instigating such activities, and, even though they knew they might get into trouble, the others would follow. The mud slides had been a regular occurrence last summer until they had dug up the yard to such an extent that Stephen was forced to dig up the section and turn it into a vegetable garden. The remnants of that garden still existed alongside their new slide which four-year-old Terry was enjoying when their father arrived home. He took one look at them and demanded they stop.

"Take a look at you. Your clothes are soaking. You'll catch a cold if you stay in them."

"Oh Dad, we were just having fun," Delia protested.

"Come on, the lot of you, get inside. You can have your bath early tonight."

After finishing off their tea Delia and Terry retreated outside again.

"And don't get dirty again, OK," Stephen insisted.

"Alright Daddy," Terry agreed as he bolted through the back door to see the tennis ball lying on the lawn. Rangie turned to the ball but realized he could not possibly get to it in time but started barking as Terry hurled it to Delia.

Rangie was a good guard dog for the truck before it was repossessed.

He also stopped the police jumping straight over the back fence during that last raid. They could have discovered the safe easily if they hadn't been scared of the dog.

Rangie was pure white but retained the expressive dark eyebrows and movements of the purebred. Shelly was forever warning the children not to play roughly with the dog. She saw him savage one man. So far the animal had been relatively gentle with the children. He may have knocked them over a few times, but for his size, he was gentle.

Delia and Terry would toss the ball to each other, occasionally teasing Rangie by calling for him to fetch the ball when throwing it to one another. They teased him so much he soon learned that if he put the pressure on, one of them may make a mistake in tossing the ball to which he would respond. When he got the ball he wouldn't give it back. To him, that was the game, keep the ball to yourself. As hard as they tried to tug at it, he just hung on tight.

This day Delia found a way of making him let go. Cruel as it was she simply held the ball in his mouth and donged him on the head with something, this time a stick.

She was lucky enough to retrieve the ball at least three times using this method after Terry's quick throws went astray.

On the third occasion Stephen saw what Delia was doing from the back verandah.

"Hey, Delia, don't do that. He'll bite you!"

"No, he won't," the six-year-old responded and tapped him on the head with a small broom she had received as a Christmas gift.

The dog finally worked it out and raced away with the ball next time, spelling an end to their game.

Stephen went down and grabbed the ball in the dog's mouth. He snarled. Stephen demanded lowering his voice: "Drop it Rangie. Drop it." The dog held on prompting Delia to offer Stephen the broom. He tossed it aside and left the ball to the dog.

Shelly was due any day now. The afternoon was wearing on and the last thing she felt like doing was preparing dinner. Terry and Delia were outside and had run out of caps for their pistols. They soon tired of the game without the "crack" made by the caps.

Rangie was running up and down the fence with the ball in his mouth, dropping it here and there near the children, then pouncing just before they could get to it. He was teasing them into a game. On this occasion, Delia was ready and waiting and grabbed the ball from within inches of the dog's snapping mouth and tossed it to Terry.

He caught it, but as the dog came bounding up, he threw it back and the game was on. They managed about twenty rounds of this, expanding their distance apart with each throw, making the dog bound between them just to see the ball whirl back over his head.

On one throw Terry was spooked as the dog bounded towards him and let it go prematurely to see the Rangie snaffle the opportunity and take possession.

"Get it off him," Delia cried, prompting Terry to attempt to grab the ball from between the dog's teeth. Rangie snarled a reply and refused to let it go.

"You get it," he said back to Delia, who chided him for losing the ball to the animal: "You lost it, you get it."

Delia picked up the small broom and took a swipe at the dog who saw it coming and ducked aside. She awkwardly lunged again, and missed before turning to Terry. "You gave it to him, you hit him to get it back."

Terry was not sure about it. The dog had already snarled at him and would not let him near the ball. However he coaxed the animal, ball and all, to where he managed to get a grip on the ball with one hand.

Rangie rolled up his top lip to bare his teeth as Terry raised the broom. He hit home. The dog reacted by lifting to grab the broom in his teeth, but in doing so caught Terry by the ear, bowling him over on the concrete path. Terry screamed as blood gushed from the wound. His ear appeared to have been torn from the side of his head and was pumping blood as Shelly and Stephen rushed to his rescue.

Stephen wrapped a towel around his head and carried him to the car for the ride to hospital. Terry remained conscious most of the way but passed out before they got there.

The doctors rushed him straight into surgery where they stitched the ear delicately back on to the four-year-old over the next six hours.

Terry was totally unaware of what was happening as surgeons worked on him. He was on another journey. He traveled through a tunnel of light, which had a soft, velvet cushion feeling. Something beckoned him through the light and he journeyed on, unafraid of the source. The light dimmed as he came to the end of the tunnel. A blue sky opened up and the path he was on led to a cobblestone bridge. He noticed two people on the bridge, peering over the edge into the water, as he walked toward them. He walked straight up to them before saying "hello", taking a brief look over the side. To his surprise he did not see water under the bridge but, rather, a scene of his own backyard. There were men there, similar to the ones who had visited his father on some mornings. Rangie was there and there was much commotion. He heard a loud bang, and the woman took him away from the edge.

"What are they doing? The people in there, what are they doing? That's our dog," the little boy was concerned.

"It's just what has happened since your accident," the woman's voice was not unlike his mother's, calm and quiet. You are such a nice little boy. Do you like it here?" Before answering Terry looked around and noticed several gatherings of people most of whom were now looking at him, smiling. The garden they were in had what appeared to be over-sized flowers blooming everywhere. He was not afraid. Many of the faces looked familiar to him, but he could not place them. "Yes, I like it here, but I want my Mum," he cried.

A tall man, gentle in voice and manner, approached, prompting the woman to turn and speak: "Look who's come to us."

The man kneeled low and looked at Terry: "Hello little man; I know you would like it here, but I'm afraid you can't stay this time."

The woman protested: "Why can't he?"

"He's not ready yet," the man protested. "He's far too young. There is more work for him to do back there. He must go back."

With this he turned Terry back toward the tunnel pushed him back through. Terry felt himself go although the man's hands were not even touching him. Terry looked back to see all the people in the garden looking. As he entered the tunnel of light they faded from view.

His eyes hurt from the light as he woke from the operation. He heard the familiar voice of his mother, but could not open his eyes until her shadow cast over him blocking out the harsh hospital lighting.

Tears were rolling down her cheeks as she saw his little eyes open up again. He was conscious for the first time in two days. The tubes into his throat suddenly hurt and he ripped at them before his mother stopped him. He was trying to speak, but was restricted by the tubes. His mind raced: "Rangie, they want to hurt Rangie."

"No don't take them away yet. They were for your food," Shelly was trying to be comforting. He was upset at the thought of his dog being taken away. He didn't care for the tubes.

He did not know that the police officers who came to deal with the dog would not even go outside the back door. The child's pet knew something was amiss and barked furiously at the strangers. He knew this was it for him. The officer finally waited until the dog went off the small verandah and down the four steps. He opened the door a few inches and leveled his service revolver and fired. The dog dropped silently. The girls watched in horror from the back bedroom to see the final shakes of their dog. The officer quickly gathered a sack and loaded the animal up to take him away.

Terry knew what had happened, even before Shelly told him. He saw it happen from the bridge in the garden. Another dream followed in the hospital where he saw Rangie in the garden, licking the faces of the people he had seen there. The old man who sent him back approved of his substitute and took to the animal who licked at his nose as he bent down to greet him.

Almost two weeks had passed before Terry was allowed home.

On the journey home he asked Shelly again: "Rangie, what did they do to Rangie?"

"The police came and destroyed him darlin'. I told you that already." Tears welled in Terry's eyes despite what he had seen in his dream: "But why, he was our friend."

"He bit you Terry; could have killed you. The police don't like that, so they had to put him down."

Terry was silent for a while. The depression he felt at the loss of his dog was understandable. He thought for a moment and remembered the dream of Rangie in the garden. He was comforted by the thought the animal was with friends.

"Mum, do you know those people I saw?"

"Where? At the hospital?"

"No. In the garden where the white bridge is."

"Where do you mean darlin'?"

"I saw them and they looked like our family. There were lots of them there. A man was looking at what was happening. I saw the police in the pool. The ones who came to take Rangie."

"Now come on darlin' you sound like you had some bad dreams at the hospital."

"I heard a bang and they wouldn't let me look any more," Terry insisted on finishing. "The people wouldn't let me stay Mum. The man said I had to come back here. So I did."

Shelly hugged him tightly and kissed his forehead below the bandage. He had extensive surgery with 56 stitches all up. The doctor had assured her his hearing would be okay though.

Shelly held him close: "Thank God you are all right, my darlin'."

He did remember the attack. In fact he remembered it so well in his dreams, he woke up several nights running. After a while it faded into a hazy incident somewhere in the back of his mind until Suzanne or Delia mentioned Rangie. Then he felt guilty again. It was his fault that Rangie wasn't there to play with them.

Shelly would tell him not to think that way. "The dog was a bad dog," she'd say.

"But I hit him Mum, I hit him with the broom; I shouldn't have hit him with the broom. Will they come back and shoot me for doing that?"

"No, no darlin', they think that if a dog attacks a child once, he will do it again and again. We love you all too much to risk any such thing."

Terry's bandages stayed on for more than a month but the scars the incident left on them all were to take much longer to heal. The girls were sympathetic and helped where they could. It was the first real trauma they had known as a family. Shelly instilled a caring in Suzanne and Delia which they responded to. Stephen was more helpful too and was keeping regular hours. The family felt closer than ever before after the shock of the attack.

Terry had grown very used to being the baby and being pampered by all except Delia. No longer had his bandages disappeared when his nose was put right out of joint when Shelly arrived home with the new baby. He felt offended when the new arrival gained all of the attention, but he'd soon be over it.

Chapter 5

Delia accepted Terry as her responsibility since the dog attack. She prompted more and more games with him and she had the added advantage having an older sister, Suzanne to talk to when she had run short of things to do with him.

Suzanne assumed the motherly role of looking after Terry when Shelly brought Lisa home. Delia kept him amused in the morning before school and in the afternoons he would wait at the gate for her, knowing he had someone to play with.

Shelly was glad to have the two older ones escort Terry to school the next year. Their schedule usually meant they would arrive at school with just minutes to go before their assembly.

Meanwhile Stephen finally found himself in work more than he was out of it. Even when there wasn't a real job, he now had the contacts across the city and he was always looking for a good bust.

The safe incident was still unsolved. The police knew he hadn't worked enough to afford that MG TC sports car he was now driving. He was a suspect in a number of crimes thereafter, but none of the charges ever brought against him were made to stick.

Barry Adler ran a small fleet of trucks doing deliveries around Melbourne. He often had some work to tide Stephen over and helped with a few duties when Stephen had the truck of his own. He suggested he work the waste paper run which was picking up and he could probably organize a few more clients. At least it was work for Stephen; something to keep him occupied.

Barry always drove one of the trucks himself and would be out of bed at 5:30 every morning to get away before the traffic started to build up. His days were fairly regular starting out at around six, morning smoko around nine, lunch at the Railway Café somewhere between 11:30 and noon. His final pick-up would commence early afternoon ready for his delivery to Smorgons between 1:00 and 2:00pm. He had taken to calling in to see Shelly for a cup of tea on the way home and was often there to greet the kids when they came home from school.

The crisp Melbourne mornings saw Delia and Terry out early, breathing fog, cracking ice on the lawn. They took long bike rides with their friends on Saturday mornings. They'd pretend they were Puffin' Billy in the morning cold.

Terry probably wouldn't have even gone along on some of these impromptu rides if he knew where they would end up.

Delia would get him out of bed at first light. They would have breakfast and set out on their bikes to get someone else to join in. One of these days half the neighbourhood had been looking for them for hours when they rode up the street with about nine other kids, all under eight, in tow.

Terry really liked being with Delia and looked to her for guidance and advice on any topic. She took the blame squarely when they were late home, but sometimes used the excuse she was 'waiting for Terry'. If she peeked at him while delivering the lie he couldn't help but grin.

Delia earned the nickname, "Mouse", after one of their early morning raids on the kitchen. The raisin loaf was just too tempting. After cutting a slice each Terry had shown a love for the fruit while Delia ate the bread. Once they got the taste they simply dug into the bread and feasted until they were discovered.

'Mouse' stuck. Delia was small for her age and had a mousy look about her anyway. The nickname created a further bonding between them, although they were the ones Shelly often had to break up in a fight. They always said they were "just playing" but often the vigor of their play became dangerous. Shelly knew the danger zones of their pitch and was forever stepping in, playing the referee.

Mouse was a regular tomboy and readily played all the boys' games Terry was interested in. She could kick a football as far as the rest of them and bowled down some of the fastest balls when they played cricket in the yard. The problem always arose when she was batting that balls would be lost when she hit them over the fence.

At school Delia had her own friends and they rarely mixed. Terry always enjoyed the afternoons jumping on his bike to find Mouse zooming up beside him: "Last one home's a rotten egg."

In summertime, now they were a little older they could go to the pool unsupervised. Their pocket money for jobs like making beds and doing the dishes, usually gave them enough for entry plus something to chew on later as they lay on the cement, out of the wind, but still shivering. At first their laps would be across the pool, but most of the time they would have fun just jumping in and scrambling to the edge.

On this summer's day, they were at home. Delia spent the morning turning over a small patch of soil down by the chook house. She hounded her mother for seeds and meticulously measured out spaces with a ruler before delicately placing them in and covering them over by hand, with Terry's assistance.

When they were finished Delia got small sticks and elastic bands to hold the labels. They celebrated the garden with a toast of milk and a feast of cookies in the shade of a tree in the backyard.

While they sat and watched the little packets rocking slightly in the breeze they saw the cat appear from the rows behind. Delia jumped to her feet straight away: "That bloody cat."

"What?" Terry was dunking a milk arrowroot biscuit.

"That bloody cat; it's in the garden."

Delia was quick to move, but soon slowed so as not to startle the cat. She didn't yell at it, but rather, moved up to it gently. She was twenty metres away before Terry even got to his feet. The cat simply walked into her arms and relished the scratching motion of her fingers under its neck. Terry was finally in motion but as he approached Delia had turned and was on the move toward the shed. He stuck his hand out to give it a pat as Delia stopped to let him caress the animal.

"Isn't it a nice pussy Mouse?"

"Yeah, but it just scattered and mixed all of our seeds down there when it did a poo."

"Oh, no?"

"Oh yes Terry; so we're going to fix this pussy for that."

"What are you going to do Mouse?"

"You'll see," she started walking towards the small room beside the shed.

"Not the dunny can, Mouse, not the dunny."

"Shush, we've got to do it, so it knows not to shit in our vege patch."

"Well,"

Before he could say any more he found himself following her. As she opened the door she asked Terry to open the lid. He leaned in and complied, repulsed by the smell of the toilet. Delia dropped the cat's back legs through the hole and let go. The cat instinctively grabbed the front of the seat with its forelegs and squealed as she pushed its head down until it let go. Delia snapped the lid closed and sat down for a few seconds as the cat screamed and spattered inside. Terry bolted to the safety of the steps and waited for Delia to emerge. She raced out pulling the door behind her, as the racket from the cat inside grew worse. The noise of the lid flipping open and falling against the downpipe signaled that the cat had got out of the inner sanctum, but he was now trapped in the small wooden room. Terry ran down and opened the door slightly when the cat screamed through the gap making him jump out of the way.

The animal caked in three days' worth of excrement, went straight over the six-foot high wooden fence, clawing its way up the planks with ease.

They sat crouched on the verandah listening as the cat made its way to the Sheldon's back door.

"Hello pussy. Oh what's happened to you - oh yuck!"

Helen Sheldon was storming around her house for several minutes before knocking at their front door. They made themselves scarce by racing down into the woodshed, but they knew they were in trouble by the commotion out front. They hid and talked in whispers as they heard them approaching. Terry and Delia looked at each other as they crouched in the shed alternately looking out their separate peepholes and suddenly laughed. While they were trying to calm down the door opened.

Both were punished with a severe ear bashing and were prepared to take more of it rather than the thought of having to clean the cat that Helen was still holding by the scruff of the neck at arms distance. She waved it in front of them: "How the bloody hell do you clean something like this up?"

Terry suggested they hose it down, but just received a clip under the ear from Helen for the suggestion. Shelly moved in: "Careful, don't you hit him. I'm his mother and I'll handle it."

"You need to give them both the strap," Helen said, her voice peaking in a shrill tone as she stormed out. "If they were mine, I'd be beating them black and blue."

Terry bit on his bottom lip to stop from laughing and dared not look at Delia. They had an early bath and dinner and were sent to bed at 5.30.

Helen was washing the cat daily for over two weeks before it was free of the odor. Her brother, Lance, who was Terry's age, was subsequently barred from playing with them again. The last time that happened was when Delia gave him a Mohawk cut when they were playing cowboys and Indians four months earlier.

This time, Delia was confined to her room for a week by which time the seedlings had started to sprout with the help of Terry's daily watering. He kept her informed of what was going on in the outside world.

"I spoke to Lance through the fence earlier and he reckons Helen still has the shits with you Mouse. She won't let the cat out of the house at all now and Lance reckons it did a poo in the washing basket this morning."

"Serves her right I reckon. Just as long as it doesn't dig up our veges. See I told you that would fix it!"

Terry just nodded and grinned a reply.

Chapter 6

With Stephen now working they were making ends meet a little easier, but Stephen still had his own "cunning kick" for his drink nights. Shelly didn't mind at first. They were still able to cover the bills reasonably well. At least the kids were being clothed and fed although Barry would often lend a hand with a few pounds to Shelly when she really needed something.

On this night out with Sid and Sharkey they busted through a brick wall of the new department store at Frankston with a sledgehammer. Sid had worked on the construction of the building and knew exactly where the cavity would allow someone the squeeze space into the store. Sharkey was first in and grabbed an armful of men's clothing, slacks, jumpers, and two pairs of shoes. He was in the cavity when he heard a car door slam and decided to wait there. Perspiration beaded on his brow and his breathing slowed.

Sidney Godfrey and Stephen were touring through the place when they noticed the light from the night patrolman's car through the front window and were trying to make it to the wall. Stephen knew there was only room for one and saw that Sid was way ahead of him and waited, crouched under a counter, until the light moved away and headed for the menswear display. He froze as the light re-appeared in the window.

The guard thought he saw something move and shone his torch along the aisle right at Stephen. He stood as rigid as a gatepost, arms outstretched, a stupid grin on his face, like a store dummy. The light moved from him to the neighboring store dummy allowing him to take a breath before regaining the stupid look.

"Fair dinkum, I felt my heart was thumping out through me suit. Lucky it was a Buffs night and I was dressed in me top clobber," he told Sid later as they tallied the booty. "Crikey, I got a rush from that."

"Lucky we knew those watchmen have such big areas to cover. If that bastard had walked down the side of the building we were all gone, for sure," Sid was dead serious.

Stephen's drink nights became a little more frequent while Shelly seemed to get the bare necessities. Their problems began to compound. Stephen was home late most evenings, drunk. Sundays, when the pub was closed the regular drinkers at the local would have a barrel in turn in each other's backyards. The rowdy behavior of a bar room brought into a back yard soon narrowed such events to a choice of one or two houses. One of these was a neighbour from across the road and down a few doors. Stephen, like the others, was usually into it until the barrel was empty. During these boozy afternoons many a deal was done and many an opportunity scrutinized. Nev Dorey worked the wharves, along with four of the regulars at his barrels.

"Yer just got to know where everyone is at a particular time," he told Stephen. "Just remember, we're in it for a cut. If we don't get our cut the bloody gate closes."

Stephen decided he might be able to make up a bit on the side. The trouble was he had to find out what goods were being delivered to what wharves and how he could fit them in to the occasional visits he made to the wharves for Barry. This information he managed to glean from one of his brothers-in-law who worked for a shipping company.

Shelly was nagging Stephen about involving family in his nefarious activities while on their way home from her mother's house. As she spoke he reacted by planting the accelerator. The few beers he had consumed made him misjudge one bend and he lost control of the MG. The car careered off the road and overturned down an embankment. Stephen only received a few scratches but Shelly was pinned under the car with a broken arm. Stephen tried to lift the car off her to get her out and in doing so injured his back.

This was the opportunity the Heidelberg detectives had been waiting for.

Sergeant King was ecstatic that Stephen Martin had been drinking that afternoon and crashed his car on his beat.

"Negligent driving causing injury due to driving whilst drunk, that'll do for starters," he said grinning at Stephen. Shelly broke the news to the children with her arm in a sling. They had an accident, and she had been hurt. "Daddy is OK. The policemen just want to talk to him about the cause of the accident," she told a half-truth.

The next day in court Sergeant King sat beside the prosecutor, Les Carlton: "This neg driving, causing injury."

Carlton looked down his sheet: "Yeah, Martin, Stephen, Terrence... yeah."

"He's been in with a group, we believe, have been knocking over every joint from Frankston to the city. Some of his associates are pretty shady characters. Some of those wharf jobs. It's petty stuff, but lots of it. We knew he was in on it 'cause we had a set of prints to fix him with. Trouble is we only legally printed him up last night."

"So what's the brief on this one then?"

"Give him the max if we can. I know the neg driving is fairly minor, but we need to put him away. Teach him a lesson."

Shelly was disappointed, but not really surprised, that Stephen would have to be "away" for six months. They would just have to manage as best they could. She rallied the children to a "family meeting" to tell them their father would not be home for a while. While they were conducive to helping out, she still regimented them. Terry, now in sixth grade, missed his father and tried to fathom how someone could be locked away for crashing a car.

He wasn't to know that the detectives on his case had his prints on a dozen jobs. They had finally found a reason to document him.

The children formed rosters to help as Shelly took on a new job. She was training as a nurse at a nearby mental hospital. She simply needed the money. The job proved to be more than just changing beds and Shelly soon found herself in charge of wards with up to forty deranged patients.

Stephen's closest sister, Dolores and her husband Frank took the children on many evenings. Weekends were taken up with trips to Healesville, 'up the bush', where their grandmother had bought a small block.

Happy Hollow was just an acre surrounded by bush, with a healthy dam at the bottom. Before his incarceration Stephen had helped Frank build the house up to three bedrooms. The wood fire was going all year round and required a constant supply of firewood. Dulcie was nearing 70 and required the weekly assistance of Frank and Dolores to keep on top of everything.

The children loved their weekends up the bush. Dolores' son Phillip led the way in the environment and would lace planks onto old drums to use as rafts on the nearby creek or set the snares around the rabbit burrows in the late afternoons and return in the early morning light.

When Shelly had to work Dolores would be there to see the children to bed and wait until Shelly came home, usually in time to pack their lunches for school.

Barry was regularly there when they came home from school and would ask about their day. He was like a grandpa and they all liked his presence. He continued to help Shelly when she needed money for this or that, although at the moment things were going alright.

Delia and Suzanne lifted Terry when he got a bit moody while Lisa drifted along happily as if nothing had happened. She really enjoyed the social activity of visiting. Weekends up the bush always took their minds off things at home.

The gravity of their situation became all too clear for Terry when a freak accident at school meant he was home one day when Shelly had planned to visit Stephen. He had been leap frogging over posts with other kids in his class when he hooked his shorts, toppling over onto his head. At school, the gash was covered with Savlon cream and he was sent home, much to Shelly's disgust. The wound later received three stitches from the doctor before their visit to Stephen.

The cold grey walls of Pentridge merged into a grey Melbourne sky. Terry followed closely as Shelly went through the routine of gates into a waiting area. It was a huge dungeon of grey rock walls and steel mesh.

Stephen appeared on the other side of the mesh and took one look at Terry who smiled, "Hello Dad". Stephen's gaze turned to Shelly, anger in his looks and tone: "Why'd you bring him here? I told you never to bring him here."

Shelly explained about the incident from school and he calmed down, but he still did not want his son to be there, on the other side of the mesh. Terry didn't get much of a say and the visit was far briefer than any before as Stephen told Shelly: "Get him out of the place".

That was Terry's only contact with his father for five months. Shelly had to explain Stephen's outburst to Terry as they rode home on the cold tram. "He just doesn't want you kids to see him while he's locked away in there," she was diplomatic.

Just four weeks later Stephen's homecoming meant a day off school for all of them. They all received a gift of a 6-inch scale model of a grand piano, modeled from soap. Terry and Lisa were so excited they went up onto the roof of the shed and pretended to play the pianos, which had been painstakingly painted up to look like the real thing.

Some of the toys didn't last the day and when it was discovered they were made with soap they were used in the bath. They were happy that their father was now home, even more than their mother.

Shelly continued her nursing work, which meant nine hour shifts at the hospital while the domestic chores were left to Stephen who became most adept at cooking. In fact he liked the work. He found he could roast a leg of lamb as well as anyone and his oven baking of biscuits and cakes resulted in many delicacies, which could have taken out prizes at any country show. The kids loved his lemon meringue pies.

Shelly was impressed too and after about four months, thought he was spending all day with the duties. However she found he had other visitors. He was drifting again. On several occasions she arrived home to find the children in front of the television waiting for someone to make their dinner. Meanwhile Stephen was helping his mate, Sid, to finish off the dozen bottles of beer they had started on around noon.

"Why haven't the children been fed, Stephen? You know what they're like if they're up too late," Shelly was demanding.

"Oh Shelly. I didn't hear you come in. Sid was just saying that I should get Barry's truck back to him. We had to borrow it today; to do a little job."

"I can guess what sort of job you and Sid would be doing."

"No, no, no, Shelly. This was all legal and above board. Charlie Waldron from the Excelsior over in Prahran wanted us to pick up a piano for him."

Sid almost coughed his beer up into his glass as he tried to talk but laughed out loud.

"What have you got to laugh about Sid?" Shelly protested.

"Well, I was gonna say that we picked it up and dropped it off for him." Stephen interjected starting to laugh himself: "He was offering us a carton of beer to pick up the piano. We picked it up and got it loaded without a hitch. We were just two blocks away from the Excelsior going up that hill on Punt Road and the bloody rope gave way."

Shelly tried to hide her smile as she watched them laughing. Sid continued: "The bloody thing slid right off the back of the truck and smashed into a thousand pieces on the road."

Stephen continued as his mate broke up: "So we decided to go and get the payment anyway."

"Yeah, bloody Stephen went into the bottle shop and just said: 'Hey mate, I've come to pick up the carton of VB for getting the piano for the publican.'"

"But you didn't deliver the piano," Shelly laughed.

"Naaah, it was in a million bloody bits down Punt Road."

"Guess we'll have to find another pub to drink in," Sid laughed.

Shelly moved into the bathroom where she started the gas burner to run a bath for the children. Back in the kitchen she worked around Sid as she prepared dinner.

"Hey, watch out for his beer with those peelings," Stephen joked.

"Just put a bit of body into it. Anyhow, I think I've had enough sustenance for the day. I'd better be going," Sid staggered for the door: "See ya later."

Shelly didn't even look up as Sid left.

"Stephen you can't get on the grog during the day. The kids have to be looked after, you know."

His mood soured quickly with a belly full of grog: "Don't start woman. I did some work today as well you know."

"Yes but what have you got to show for it?"

Stephen grimaced for a moment and suddenly struck out and punched her to the floor.

"Don't you bloody have a go at my mates, you bitch!"

Terry was walking to the kitchen and stood in the doorway as Stephen grabbed a hand-full of Shelly's hair pulling her up.

"Dad, what are you doing? Don't you hit my mum."

Shelly was pleading: "Please Steve, not in front of the kids, please."

He let her go, demanding that his dinner be served up. He turned to Terry still standing in the doorway: "Go on Terry, get in and have your bath, now; your dinner will be ready soon."

As Shelly prepared the dinner he abused her, threatening all the time, banging his fist down so hard on the table that almost everything on it bounced and rattled. The aggression continued as all of the children came in to eat. They went straight to bed after dinner.

All they could do this evening was crouch in their beds and hope he would not hurt their mum any more. On this night Stephen had gone too far.

Shelly was hurting when Barry turned up early to pick up his truck. Barry was annoyed to have to walk a mile and a half through the fog but was furious when he realized Shelly was hurt badly. As her pain became unbearable he took her to the doctors to seek treatment.

Her three broken ribs meant two weeks in hospital in which time Stephen was forced to slow his drinking again and settled back into a routine at home.

When Shelly arrived home from the hospital Terry was relieved. They all were. Stephen had told the children their mother had fallen onto the edge of the table. "That's how she hurt her ribs," he lied.

They knew exactly what had happened.

As a result of her injuries Shelly still required time off work and Stephen was forced to make an extra effort.

Barry refused to put Stephen on again and was disgusted with the little shit. After a few days of searching, Stephen found a job doing deliveries for Woolworths. This meant there were many new food cans coming into the house, which he claimed, had "fallen off the back of a truck". The trouble was, none of the cans had labels on them. Often they would go for a can expecting corn to find it would have sausages and vegetables or sliced peaches.

Stephen could not help himself and hardly a day went by when he didn't off load a carton of something. The final straw for Shelly came when he stole an entire semi with a refrigerated trailer van. He was expecting to see all types of frozen items in the van, but found it contained only one thing, butter. Thousands of pounds of Western Star. The entire suburb had butter in all of their cupboards in what proved to be one of the hottest spells they had seen for years.

Stephen had blamed his brother in law, Sharkey, for his doing time and felt this may be a good pay back and parked the semi beside Sharkey's house.

The vehicle was finally discovered when the freezer unit ran out of petrol and the load started to warm and melt. Sharkey was under suspicion when the police discovered the truck. They watched the place for two weeks before retrieving the vehicle as butter dripped out into the gutter and started to go off. Sharkey was very quiet this summer.

With a few more dollars in his pockets, Stephen was drinking more and coming home late again. There were more arguments, loud enough to wake them all. It was happening with monotonous regularity, however, on this night, there was other trouble in London Avenue.

Kevin Jakes, from two doors up, had joined in the two-hour swill with Stephen before six o'clock closing time. It was around midnight when Jillian Jakes bashed on the front door.

Stephen opened the door for her and she slammed it behind her as she entered: "Stephen, he says he's going to kill me. He had the shotgun. I fell over as he fired, tripped over that stupid fence..." She went silent as she heard a noise outside and cowered behind the lounge suite, away from the doorway.

"Stephen, open the bloody door or I'll blow the fucken thing off its hinges," Kevin was threatening.

"Kevin, calm down, mate. Just calm down. Put the bloody gun down first and I'll open the door."

He was silent and Stephen opened the door to see Kevin standing there with the double-barreled shotgun raised to about waist height.

"Where's that fucken missus of mine? She's gotta make my tea!"

"Look Kevin, she is in here and she's okay, but you had better put that gun away before the coppers show up."

The words seemed to sober Kevin momentarily and Stephen unsnibbed the screen door. "You'd better give that to me, I reckon."

Kevin handed over the shotgun allowing Stephen to console them both over a cup of tea. The children heard all of the commotion, but Shelly kept them in their rooms, assuring them everything was okay.

Jillian cried again the next day as she told Shelly how Kevin had locked their daughter, Glenda, in her room after she came home ten minutes late from a school social.

"I was just asking him to let her out last night when he went off. If I hadn't tripped on that bloody fence out there, I'm sure he would have shot me. He said he thought that he had done it when he saw me go down."

"There, there, Jillian. You shouldn't have to put up with this sort of thing. Is there anywhere you could go?"

"No Shelly. He'd go bloody crazy and hurt the lot of us. I'm sure he would. I'm scared. I'm bloody well scared, but there's nowhere to go."

"You'll get yourself killed if you stay with him. That's for sure."

"No, Shelly, I know there is a nice, kind side to him. It's just when he drinks, he gets all these strange ideas. He's like a different person."

Just two weeks later the children were awoken by screaming at the front door. Glenda Jakes, Jillian's eldest daughter stood there. Her hands were up to her face and blood was dripping everywhere.

At first, Stephen thought she had been shot and raced her into the bathroom where he ran some water in the sink. He pulled her hands from her face and was relieved to find her face was unscathed, there were just a few cuts on her hands.

The sixteen-year-old had thrown herself through a window to escape the room in which she had been imprisoned for two weeks. She fell almost ten feet to the ground after crashing through the window cutting her hands on the glass.

"Dad was threatening Mum and said he was going to kill her. I was calling out and all I could hear was screaming, so I jumped out the window."

Terry saw Glenda and walked into the bathroom about the same time Kevin arrived on the front porch. Shelly had gone down the hallway and saw him outside the snibbed fly-wire door. Delia and Suzanne watched through their front window as Kevin threatened: "Open the bloody door Shelly or I'll fucking well blow it off the hinges."

Shelly was speechless, and moved quietly to the door to unsnib the lock. Kevin pushed past her, through the doorway and down the hall to the bathroom.

Shelly pleaded with him: "Kevin, please, put the gun away. You don't need the gun. Just put it away."

"Be fucked I don't need it; I'm gonna fix her."

Stephen saw Kevin coming with the gun. He instinctively grabbed Terry and lifted him into the bath, away from the threatening barrels.

"It's alright Kevin, she's not badly hurt. Put the gun down," Stephen was saying when Kevin lunged forward, trying to push Stephen out of the way. As he did Glenda started screaming in fear. Stephen kept his cool and managed to lift the barrels toward the ceiling as Kevin tightened on the trigger releasing both barrels simultaneously.

Terry could hear a tinkling sound outside before his ears started to ring from the blasts. Stephen grabbed Kevin in an arm lock, pushing his arm right up his back. He knew what had happened when he heard the snap.

Unarmed and with one arm now broken Kevin was sobered again, crying. This time Stephen took the gun off him and ushered him into the kitchen. Shelly saw to Glenda first before preparing a temporary sling for Kevin. Stephen decided he should now go to the hospital for treatment.

"You just can't keep doing this Kevin. You'll bloody kill someone the way you're goin' and end up spendin' the rest of your life in the can."

"What do you mean, kill someone?"

Stephen looked at him in amazement: "You fucking well threatened to kill your wife a fortnight ago and your eldest daughter tonight mate. That is not fucking on."

Stephen's peace-making efforts with the Jakes family seemed to work and for several weeks he glowed with the aura of a hero to his own family. That is, to all except Shelly.

"I can't stand it any longer Stephen. I think me and the kids should go and live at Mum's for a while. You need to stop drinking altogether."

"You take the bloody kids and I'll kill yer," he responded although he had forgotten this threat in the sobriety of the next morning.

"You always forget that you have done something after you've been on the grog," she told him. "You just go on as if it hasn't happened. Like bloody Kevin."

Terry was in just his second week of high school. Stephen had left for work by the time he got home from his morning paper run when Shelly called the children to her room. Her bags were packed. She had never forgiven Stephen for his violence against her.

"Now you kids listen to me, and listen carefully. I have tried to work things out with your father, but things just are not working out. You kids are old enough to take some responsibility for yourselves now. You are going to have to help your father a lot. I want you to do all of those jobs you have been doing after school. It is very important that you just do them, without any complaints. You know, how you helped me when your father was in jail."

"Can we come with you?" Terry pleaded, tears in his eyes.

"No, it will be better if you don't. I just don't want your father to hurt me anymore. If I take you with me, he's sure to come after us."

"Will you come back Mum?" Suzanne was crying.

"I will see you. I'll see you all. It's just better that I do it this way." She hugged Suzanne and Delia together: "You look after each other, all of you now, you hear me."

They all nodded agreement and Shelly picked up her bags and went out to the car where Barry was waiting. She turned back to look at them: "Come on Suzanne, you have to get everyone ready for school. Get a move on then. I love you darlings." Barry closed the door behind her before moving around the car, climbing in and driving away. Shelly's cheeks were stained with tears as he drove her from London Avenue.

Chapter 7

Terry was in a daze at school. His future had never been so uncertain. All the work he had done with his schooling seemed to be out the door. Shelly was the only one who had helped him with his homework to see he made good grades. Now she was gone.

Harold Sinclair, the science teacher was calling for order in the classroom at Reservoir High. He noticed Terry looking out the window: "Terry Martin, do you have the answer?"

Terry looked around, bemused: "What?"

"Didn't you hear the question?"

"No."

"Well, I suggest you stop looking out the window and pay attention."

Tears were welling in Terry's eyes.

"Now, for homework last time I gave you...."

Terry snapped: "I didn't do my homework. And anyway, it was a heap of shit. You can get stuffed," he stood up.

"Martin, while you're on your feet you can get going straight to the principal's office. Go now. There's six of the best for you there, son, don't you worry about that. I am not going to put up with this behavior in my class."

Terry left the room trying desperately to hold back the tears. His friends did not know what was happening with him. They'd never seen him like this either.

Aubrey Simpson walked down the hallway, stopping for a moment to put his head through a doorway: "Allison Keagan; sit down. No, not there, over there. If I ever see you doing that again, you'll be on detention for a week. You should know better!" He half closed the door again: "Sorry Mr. Whittaker; carry on then."

A sense of dread filled Terry as the principal strode toward him.

"And what are you doing here? What's your name?"

"Terry, sir; Terry Martin. Mr Sinclair sent me here."

"Well you had better come inside."

It was the first time Terry had seen the inside of the principal's office. He went to sit down when Simpson demanded: "No, don't sit down yet. I want to know why you were sent here."

Terry could not think of anything to say: "Err well, Mr Sinclair, sent me here sir. I think I was rude to him, sir." The tears started to well in Terry's eyes again.

"You have been a good student, Terry; why this all of a sudden?"

"I don't know sir. I just feel rotten," the tears were washing down his face.

"What's up lad?"

"My mother has left us sir, just this morning, and I don't know what we're going to do."

The principal was compassionate and listened for a few minutes as Terry told him of the fights and the departure of his mother.

"Listen, Terry. You have a lot of thinking to do, I am sure. These things happen in life. Sometimes people are together who shouldn't be together, and they fight a lot. It is no good for them or for you, the children, when they are like this. Your mother is simply thinking of you all by taking such a huge step. Why don't you go and get your sisters, err, Delia and Suzanne and we'll sort something out for today. Don't worry about Mr. Sinclair, I'll explain everything to him."

"Thank you sir."

Terry arrived back at the office with Suzanne and Delia who confirmed what was happening at home. They were allowed time off their classes and sat under a tree on the banks of the football oval until lunchtime before Terry and Delia headed home.

Terry felt a sense of dread when they walked into their parents' room and realized all of her things had gone. The room, which had always radiated with warmth from Shelly, was now bare and stark. Stephen's soiled clothing lay on the floor in the corner. The pair wandered around the room for several minutes searching for anything Shelly may have left behind. They found nothing.

Suzanne didn't have any answers to their questions when she got home.

She was peeling potatoes for dinner when Stephen arrived two hours later. He took one look in his bedroom and realized something was amiss. He opened the wardrobe to find Shelly's side was empty.

"Where's your mother?" he demanded to Suzanne.

"She left this morning, with Uncle Barry. They didn't tell us where they were going."

"I knew it. I knew it. She's been playing up on me," Stephen was grasping for justification, anything that did not turn the blame on him. "And she's taken off with bloody old Barry. Christ he's twenty years older than her. More!" He ran his hands through his hair. "Well, I'm gonna go and find 'em and drag her back; by the bloody hair if I have to!"

He headed for the door where Delia and Terry appeared: "Can we come with you, Dad?" Delia pleaded.

"No. You'd better stay here," He looked down at them. "Oh okay. Maybe you two can talk some sense into the bloody woman."

They arrived at Barry's house to find his wife Rondel well into a bottle of cooking sherry: "I don't know Stephen. I can't fathom it. I don't know where they've gone, and quite frankly, I don't give a damn. She can have the old bastard. Twenty-five years I've had to put up with that bastard, and now this. Good bloody riddance, I say."

Delia followed Rondel's 15 year old, Angela, into the lounge room. Terry came and sat beside her.

"Where'd they go Ange? Did you know they were on together?"

"No. But mum and dad have been fighting for so long now," she seemed relieved, "I don't think they knew what any argument was about. Mum just gets stuck into the sherry and wants to argue, about anything. She's been at him for weeks now. S'pose I'm gonna cop it all now."

"Yeah, our dad gets pissed sometimes and gets angry for no reason," Delia volunteered.

"Cause his dinner gets cold," Terry contributed, "So he bloody well reckons."

"My mum pulled the bloody bread knife on dad last week," Angela said. "He didn't talk to her at all after that. Cut him on the arm she did."

Stephen suddenly put his head through the doorway: "Come on you kids. We're not going to find her by hanging around here. Let's bloody well go then."

Back home Suzanne had sausages in a pan and potatoes, beans and carrots boiling away on the stove. She automatically served the meal as Stephen came in and sat at the head of the table. Stephen bolted his food down.

"Look I am going to look for your mother elsewhere. Delia, you can wash up and Terry and Lisa can dry. You can watch one hour of television after your bath, but I want you all in bed by eight. I am going to try some other places. I'll find the bastards."

They wished, all together, that evening, he would not find her. They had seen him in similar moods after a night of drinking. Delia heard him through her bedroom wall during one argument when Shelly threatened to leave and told the others as they did the dishes: "He said to her, if you take the kids, I'll bloody-well kill yer." Delia dried her hands on a tea towel: "I think we should all join pinkies and make a wish for Mum."

The four crossed their arms and joined their little fingers together: "I hope Mummy will be all right wiff Uncle Barry," eight year old Lisa said. Delia continued: "Please, we wish, that no harm will come to our Mum."

"Yeah, or our Dad." said Terry.

"And let our Dad find someone else so he can be happy," Suzanne added, "so we can be happy, as a family again." They closed their eyes and squeezed pinkies for a few seconds before breaking the spell.

Four days later Stephen yelled for them to get up and get ready for school as he left the house for work. It was Friday. He usually had drinks after work on Friday. This afternoon he was home early.

Delia heard him come home and looked out her window. She raced into the lounge room where they were watching Hopalong Cassidy: "Dad's home. And he's got a lady with him."

They all straightened up in their seats and looked at the door expectantly. Edna McGrady came through the door, tripping on the step as she went: "Oops, oh shit." She steadied and looked at them: "Cripes, I nearly fell." They looked at one another momentarily before Delia giggled.

Stephen was right behind her: "Kids, I'd like you to meet Edna. She might be coming to live with us. You know, be a mother to you lot."

They stared in silence, dumbstruck, mouths agape. Stephen ushered Edna through the hallway to the kitchen. Lisa followed them.

"But I like our mum," Delia snapped to the others.

"Me too," said Terry, "our mum is coming back. Isn't she?"

Suzanne looked at them both: "The way things are happening, I'm not so sure. Let's go and check her out."

Delia and Terry stayed for a while: "Do you think he means it Mouse?"

"I don't know. You know what these drinking ladies are like. I reckon she's just his tart. Come on let's see if we can scare her off."

Edna was patronizing. She tried her best to impress, but her well-to-do manner and diction repulsed Delia.

"Your father and I have been friends for some time now. He has asked me if I would be prepared to take on four children and believe me, I was not keen on the idea."

"Are you going to sleep in our mother's bed?" Delia asked, stopping Edna in her tracks.

"No, I most definitely am not," she retorted. "There's no way I could live in this dump."

Delia felt she had cut to the bone. The house was not quite as tidy as it may have been just five days before when Shelly left, but it was certainly no dump.

Edna continued: "We are going to look for another house, a little more central than this. If I am going to take on your father and you children, it will be on my own terms, you hear?"

Edna unfolded the packages she had brought. "Dinner tonight is ham and salad. Your father and I have a lot to talk about, so we thought we would make an easy dinner for tonight."

They ate their ham and salad in silence, all the time, waiting for Edna to look back at Stephen so they could look her over. She was a plump woman and appeared to be much older than Shelly. She had short-cropped black curly hair and presented well in her dark skirt and bright red crocheted top.

Terry and Delia finished their meal and went to leave the table: "Excuse me children," Edna retorted. "You should ask permission to leave the table." They looked at one another.

"We don't do that," Delia quipped.

"Well you can bloody well start doing it," Edna was stern, but crude. "A few manners never hurt anybody. So you can bloody well ask permission to leave the table from now on, you hear."

Terry complied immediately: "Edna, can I leave the table please?"

"Yes you may. And Delia?" She waited, but Delia refused, pushing her chair in hard.

"Delia! Mouse, you come back here!" Stephen shouted.

"No, no Stephen, let her go; this time. I think it is going to take some time. Didn't the slut teach them any manners?"

Delia's face was red when she reached the lounge room where Terry was seated: "That bitch isn't gonna be my mum. Never! She called mum something not very nice."

"What? Delia, what did she say?"

"She called her a slut. That's not very nice."

"Yeah and mum doesn't even drink either. She can't be one of them."

"No, no Terry, don't you know anything?"

"What?"

"Don't you know what that means?"

"Yeah, that she drinks and gets drunk a lot. Like Mrs. Pringle down the road. And she gets all those men drunk too."

"No Terry, you've got it wrong. She doesn't just get them drunk with her. She also screws them. They all live around here and everybody knows she is screwing them and that's why they call her a slut."

"Ooh," Terry had never even realized. He remembered waiting outside there one day when Stephen had visited. He smelled the drink on his breath when he came out.

"Terry, that lady's not for us. If it comes down to a vote, go with me will you?"

"Yeah, okay. We know our mum's the best mum ever, don't we?"

Back in the kitchen Lisa had forgotten what she had to say before leaving the table and sat wide-eyed to Edna. Suzanne had made a pot of tea and was starting on the dishes.

"Look, we'll get a paper tomorrow and look for a place. Something near Kew or Camberwell, somewhere like that," Edna had decided she would not spend even one night in this house.

"Look, you can walk me up to the highway and I'll get a cab over to Joss's house. You can meet me there tomorrow."

Stephen was swooning up to her: "How about I just drive you there now and stay with you. The kids'll be all right here. That way we can get an early start."

Suzanne wondered how Edna could sit there without toppling over forward. Her forty two-inch bust line was strapped in tight.

"Okay then Stephen. You talked me into it."

"Suzanne, you make sure they all have their baths and get to bed by eight o'clock. I'm just going to drop Edna to her sister's place. We're going looking for houses in the morning, so I should see you in the early afternoon."

Suzanne allowed them all to stay up to watch the Friday night movie, although Lisa had to be carried to bed soon after it started. During the commercial breaks in the picture they offered their opinions around: "Well there's no bloody way I am going to call that woman, mum," Delia protested.

"Me neither," said Terry.

"You don't know. Maybe she's just a fill-in until mum comes back to us," Suzanne was attempting to be optimistic. "Naah, why the friggin' hell would mum come back to a bloke who hits her."

"But he didn't do it much Suzanne," Terry barked in defense of Stephen.

"Oh yes he bloody well did Terry. What about her broken ribs that time? And that black eye he gave her?"

"Yeah, but she came back after that."

"I think it was only for long enough for her to find something else to do. Anyhow, there is something I have to tell you."

"What?"

"I saw mum today. She met me at the gate after school. She sends her love. She told me she would be okay with Uncle Barry and we'll be able to see her, if Dad lets us."

"Where is she living?" Delia wanted to know.

"Over in Sandringham. But she said they were moving into a new house soon, at Mooroolbark."

"Where's that?"

"It's out there in the suburbs. But look, by the sounds of things Mum won't be coming home again, not for a while at least."

The movie came on again and Delia added: "If we got any choice in it, I would be going with mum and Barry that's for sure. I don't like big tits Edna."

The next morning Suzanne had them regimented into at least making their own beds. She was left doing the dishes from breakfast and lunch when she noticed the truck reversing into the driveway. Stephen alighted from the passenger side and grabbed an arm full of cartons from the back of the vehicle.

"Hi Suzanne, guess what? We're moving house."

"When Dad?"

"Right now. Here's a few cartons for packing your stuff in here. Start packing things into the cartons. Where are the others?"

"Lisa just went next door to play and Terry and Delia went down the road on their bikes."

He spent the next two hours helping his mate Bob Robinson with the furniture. By the time Terry and Delia rode up the street their rooms had been packed into the truck.

"Come on you two. Toss your bikes in the back and go in and check your rooms for things you really want to take with you."

"But where are we going?" Terry asked.

"We're going to Auburn."

"Where Nanna used to live?"

"Just a couple of blocks away from where she lived."

"Can we go and say goodbye to some of our friends?" Delia asked.

"No. There isn't any time. Bob's got to get the truck back for another job tonight."

They all squeezed into the small cabin of the truck. Terry took a last long look at the front of the house and waved to the houses where his friends lived as they passed by.

"Who are you waving to Terry?" Delia inquired.

"To my friends. Someone may be looking out a window or something."

They pointed to houses saying the names of the families and offered a wave as they went by: "Goodbye Sheldons, goodbye Jakeses, goodbye Hillaries, goodbye Walters, Zammits, Dorringtons, Marlows," they ran out of houses and turned out onto the busy Plenty Road.

"Goodbye pub, goodbye fish shop, goodbye milk bar..."

The new house was snookered in the corner of a dead end laneway. Looking from the street it had far more character than where they had come from. There were trees in the street and the park, which Stephen had spent his first twelve years playing in, was just two blocks away.

Terry and Lisa were booked into the same school, which went up to the eighth grade. Auburn Central's facade reminded Terry of a church. He liked the nostalgia of the old desks and looked under many a lid for memorabilia of his father's days there, to no avail. Suzanne and Delia went over to Camberwell High School.

Edna read them the riot act when her furniture arrived the following weekend. "Any breakages or scratches and you will pay for it!" Their eyes rolled in their heads as she said it.

"Look kids, I have never been a mother before. I've had six different husbands and just haven't been able to have children. That's been fine by me, I tell yer. But anyway, now I have four of you; all of a sudden like, so don't expect me to be perfect all of the time."

Stephen interrupted: "Just do as you are told and don't fight amongst yourselves. We have to work in together, all of us, alright?"

They mostly smiled or nodded their approval. "That means you have turns to do the dishes while Edna and I will have turns to cook," Stephen contributed.

"Hey, I thought you promised you'd do all of the cooking Stephen," Edna joked. He smiled back: "We share everything, including the cooking."

Terry missed his friends at first but soon met others in his new, smaller school, and participated in the morning kick to kick sessions.

Just about everything he attempted he could do well. He gained the ethic that if you started something that you really wanted to do, just by starting it would mean you'd be half a chance to complete the task, to succeed.

He excelled in maths and science for the first time through the eyes of a senior teacher in his sixty fifth year. He was in awe of Mr Cain when he said he had seen Haley's comet in the twenties. "It was huge in the sky and lit up half of the night sky with its tail for more than a week as it passed us. You people will see it come around again in the mid eighties; I doubt I'll be around to see that one."

Terry had been quite surprised by Stephen's presence nearly every night. He helped with homework when required and offered fatherly advice. He had finally stopped drinking every night, confining this habit to the weekends. When they did drink Edna was like a cracked record. "I could have been free. And here I am stuck with bloody you and four kids. Cripes, I must have been out of my mind."

"Edna, Edna, it's all going to work out, you'll see."

"What pisses me off is that while we're stuck here on weekends looking after her bloody kids, she is probably trouncing out with that old bastard, tripping the light fan-bloody-tastic."

Edna only unleashed her frustration with a few drinks. She was better performed with an audience and it didn't take long before they were bringing people home from the hotel to pass on their tales of woe.

Terry who was now 13 years old found, all of a sudden, that he was being treated as adult. He did his share of the chores, as they all did, uncomplaining. He dared not push them. Edna tried hard to share little jokes with them when she was sober, but blew it every time she got pissed. Terry was often confused but used his bike to discover a world outside of home.

He rode over to Camberwell one afternoon to ask if there were any paper runs he could do and found himself that very day with a pile of Heralds at the top of the stairs at the station. He was finding independence. A further job arose when a friend from school asked him along to sell football rosettes one Saturday. After that first day with his mate he was allotted a game of his own each week.

The commissions from the sales were not much better than selling newspapers, but enough for Terry. He had two jobs. He got to see a game of footy every weekend and never even had to pay in at the grounds.

He even managed to get onto the pitch during the breaks in play and walk around the centre yelling "footy-colours" holding up his portable display board. Often he would sell out before he was half way around; such was the passion of these fans for their team when it was firing.

Lisa walked beside Terry on the way home from school. They had gone down the full block and turned the corner before Lisa remarked: "Mummy is moving soon. She's gunna let us know where she is!"

"Lisa, what are you saying? Have you seen Mum and Barry?"

"Yes, they were outside the school today. Mummy called me to the car while I was waiting for you."

"How is she? How's she look?"

"Good. She looks really good. She's a bit tired, but she looks really good."

"Lisa, you can't tell dad and Edna, they'll go crook on you."

"It was just Mum," Lisa was indignant.

"I know, but it makes them angry whenever they talk about her and Barry. You've heard them. They tell lies about mum. But remember, it's just their grog talking. It's not the truth."

Lisa's nine-year-old brain was trying to measure up what he had just said. She agreed. "Okay, I won't tell them I saw mum, but can I tell Delia?"

"Of course you can, but just keep it between us, remember!"

After dinner it was Lisa's turn at drying up. Edna was pouring a sherry when Lisa spoke to Delia, who was washing the dishes.

"Mummy's gonna move to a new house soon."

Edna swooped on the line: "Where did you find that out? Have you seen your mother?"

"Err," she couldn't lie, "she was outside school when it finished today."

"What did she say to you? Did she try and pull you into the car?"

"No," Lisa was shrinking under the questioning. "She just said hello and I kissed her."

"That slut," Edna was suddenly in full flight, enraged: "She left you children, kicked you out into the world. Well it's with fucken me now. If you ever see the car there again you are to run inside the school and ask them to ring for the police," her brow was furrowed, menacing Lisa.

Delia could not listen to Edna's tirade any longer: "That's not what she should do. That is our mother you are talking about. She and dad could not live together any more. He hurt her too much. He bashed her."

"No he bloody well didn't. Just a clip across the ears he reckons."

"That's what you think Edna. But can you please offer us some respect by not talking about our mother like that," Delia mustered all her strength not to break into a full-on verbal onslaught with Edna.

"Well she is the one who pissed off. I'm the one who's got to put up with you lot now. So what about a bit of respecting my wishes now too? You know without two wages coming in you'd never be able to afford a place like this?"

They relived the entire incident when Stephen got home from work, by which time Edna had consumed a few more glasses of sherry. Terry couldn't be bothered with it any longer. Nothing he said seemed to matter anyway, so he stayed out of it.

This night he visited Margo from down the road. They had walked together on the way home from school on a number of days. She invited him to call just a week before. Up until now he hadn't been game. This night he needed something to take his mind off things. Margo was just the medicine. She was his age, almost 14, and well developed for her age. Her eyes were wide and compassionate when he told her of the day's events. They kissed. Not just a peck on the cheek type kiss. This kiss started at about seven thirty. Margo was seated on the fence with Terry standing in front of her. Her legs were wide apart to hold him as close as she could. They broke the first huddle shortly before eight o'clock.

"Whew, Margo. That is incredible."

"You don't kiss too badly Terry."

"Yeah," he flashed his eyes skyward then back to her warm brown eyes.

"Let's try that again."

After selling papers each evening Terry would race home, have his dinner and wait for six thirty, when Margo would be clear of her commitments.

The home scene flared up again shortly after when Shelly filed her papers for a divorce. Terry knew it would be one of those evenings as soon as he walked in to hear Edna: "She wants to name me as co-respondent, the bitch!"

"Look, Edna. It's no big deal," Stephen tried consoling her.

"What about custody? Will that affect your rights to custody? Bet you didn't think of that!"

"Look she's not even going for custody," Stephen was trying to be consoling.

"Why not, doesn't she want her bloody kids?" Edna's five sherry start was making her obnoxious.

"I don't think she wants the hassle. And she doesn't want to break them up," Stephen was remarkably understanding now.

"Look Stephen, I can't stand this any longer. I think we should move out of the way. What do you think about moving to Sydney?"

"Well, if there's work there."

"If you don't do that, you can expect your ex to be snoopin' around the streets all the time."

They timed the move to coincide with the end of the school year. As they drove out of the street Terry knew he'd really miss Margo and the footy.

Chapter 8

Stephen found a flat to move into in Leichhardt. It was small, only two bedrooms. The kids were piled into one room with two sets of double bunks.

Terry and Delia hurried to unpack their things and decided to go for a walk around the neighbourhood. Parramatta Road was just a block away and drew them like a magnet. There were lots of coffee shops, milk bars and shoe stores. Their curiosity took them along Nelson Street for several blocks where they discovered their respective schools. It was the first time they had experienced separate boys' and girls' schools, but they would cope.

Stephen started into his new job of driving a delivery truck, as did Edna, the comptometrist, operator of a cumbersome machine in an accounting section in the public service. Terry settled into his new school without a problem. On his first day he met up with Larry, another freshy, from an inner city school. They soon discovered that their birthdays were only four days apart and for most part of their remaining school life they would be inseparable.

Stephen was a new person in this city. He cared about the children, their health, their homework, grades in school. Susan and Delia had few problems settling into their new school while Lisa saw everything as an adventure and developed into a good scholar in the local primary school. At least that was co-ed.

When Terry suggested he would like a surfboard, Stephen responded by buying the first one that came up in the paper. It was huge, a nine footer which Terry could hardly lift. At 14 he was hardly a young Adonis and required help to even carry the thing. After waiting many weekends trying to get Stephen and Edna to take them to the beach he discovered through a school friend that you could carry boards on public transport. The buses were out because the board was so big, but the railway sold a bicycle ticket from Petersham, all the way to Manly. On this day

Suzanne, Delia, Terry and Lisa took the board out. Two of them could carry the thing, as awkward as it was, down to the station. When the train arrived they squeezed into a compartment and felt guilty as boarding and alighting passengers stepped over the cumbersome thing. At Circular Quay they carried the monster down the stairs to the South Steyne and were forced to sit outside with the board.

Their excitement increased with the journey across to Manly where they had to ask advice on how to get to the beach. The walk from the ferry to the breakers exhausted them but they could not wait to launch themselves into the waves. Suzanne was trying to organize the others, as best she could but Terry and Delia were stripped and heading for the surf without delay. They didn't want to get landed with the job of looking after Lisa in the surf.

They soon found that the surfboard did float, but they had a difficult time getting it out far enough to ride it back in. They soon realized that if they backed it out in the white water they could push off the sand and ride in the short distance to the beach or to a depth where the huge fin would dig into the sand, calling a premature halt to their rides.

Delia soon tired of the board and decided to hire one of the surf mats available at the beach. Terry battled on with the board and attempted to paddle it out by himself. This was difficult in that his shoulders were not wide enough to get his arms right across the board. He finally settled for the small ride in the shore break. He would battle out with it and shoot a wave. He was having fun, but he was close to exhaustion after only 20 minutes. When a larger set came through and whipped the board from his arms, it was all he could do to stay on his feet. The force of the wave which stole the board from his grip pulled him under. He surfaced spitting and coughing out water he had taken in through his mouth and nose.

He looked out to sea where real surfers were doing it properly, but wondered how the hell he would ever get this monster all the way out there. He decided it would be suicidal to attempt it just yet and looked to the flagged area, protected by lifesavers where Delia was skimming along ahead of the waves on a hired surf mat.

"Suzanne, will you watch the board while I get one of those mats there."

Suzanne insisted that he get some tanning lotion on first as his fair skin was already starting to redden.

The mat was terrific fun and he and Delia had a ball for hours before returning the floats and moving back to their little patch of beach. Terry looked around to see sun tanned people all around him. His auburn hair and fair freckled skin required only small doses of sun to produce color, and he would never get the deep bronze that these hardened beach goers had.

It was late afternoon by the time they left the beach. The trip home was long and arduous. Lisa was a bit of a handful for Suzanne who, despite her tender years, managed to keep everyone organized and together. Terry did not feel well by the time they had lugged the huge board from Petersham station, back up the hill to the flat in Leichhardt. He was exhausted and went straight into bed when he got home.

Stephen came into the room later to see how he was going and was amazed at the baked body of his son. Out came the vinegar and bi-carbonate of soda, a concoction which fizzed in the bowl and again when applied to Terry's hot skin. He was laid up for three days before he started to peel. And peel he did, from his face to his toes.

The surfboard was stored away at the back of the carport until someone obligingly stole it one evening. Terry was smart enough to wear a T-shirt at the beach on later occasions and was happy to ride on the surf mats, between the flags, just in case he was hit by a dumper and required saving.

It was not long before life in the flat was starting to get on everyone's nerves. The space was cramped and the children took great delight in announcing who had just been to the loo when they heard the flush from one of the floors above.

The house in Ramsay Road, Haberfield, was more expensive, but allowed a bit more room to move. Still the backyard was shared by a couple who occupied a small flat out the back. Terry got along well with its inhabitants, Eric and Gina. Eric had offered Terry some work at a slot car centre he operated and he leapt at the opportunity.

He had started third year in high school and was a well-behaved average scholar. He tried out for the cricket team and found himself as 12th man, getting a start only if someone else didn't turn up. His best innings, when he got a bat, was 16 runs, although he proved himself to be good in the field and was instrumental in many good run outs by hoisting in a quick return.

In the winter months he tried out for the football team but he found playing Rugby a very different kettle of fish to his beloved Aussie Rules. He could not get over the way the guys lined up across the field and threw the ball in the rugby matches. He was again put on the sideline because of his impulse to want to kick the ball ahead each time he got it. The coach eventually realized that he was good replacement when the team required a kick for the line or they urgently needed a field goal. Terry had no problems drop kicking even a rugby ball, but usually had to be within 30 metres to get it over the cross bar.

Needless to say, Terry didn't enjoy the game all that much.

He longed for Aussie Rules again and got his chance with a local Annandale squad, an offshoot of the Balmain Australian Football Club.

He settled into the under16's squad extremely well and enjoyed the competition and social interaction within the team. By this time he was fit again and was starting to muscle up. His prowess as a rover meant he was generally on the ball. On Sundays he would also go to watch the seniors play and before long was pulling on the black and gold of the under 18's.

This Saturday he arrived home to Haberfield to find Suzanne and Delia getting ready to go out for the evening. "Where are you going? Can I come?"

"The Albert Palais. And no, you can't come," Suzanne was terse with her little brother.

"Who are you gonna dance with Suzy. Have you got a boyfriend there, have you?" he teased.

Suzanne responded with a clout across the ears as she pushed him from the room, but Terry peeked back in to watch Delia apply the lipstick. He was intrigued; he had never seen Mouse with make-up on. She had never really been into that girl's stuff before.

"You look silly with all that muck on your face Mouse."

Suzanne turned and threw a pillow at the gap in the door. "Leave her alone; it's her birthday, and we're going out with Colleen and Carla; now piss off Terry." He got the hint and wandered into the lounge room where Stephen and Edna were having their usual Saturday drink.

"What's for tea Dad?"

"What do you think?" Edna retorted. "You're big enough to make your own now. Look in the fridge and see what's there. The spuds are in the cupboard and there are frozen peas in the freezer. Get to it."

Terry opened the fridge and saw the sausages: "There are some snags here."

"Well, poke them with a fork and put them in a pan," Stephen chimed in.

"And peel the spuds," Edna added.

Terry begrudgingly obliged. He could see, by the empties, they had already had a few beers. They were now into the Scotch and he knew that it was not advisable to knock back the suggestion.

Over dinner everyone commented how lovely Delia looked, although Terry thought the make-up was a bit overdone. They joked some more as the girls left with orders to be home by midnight.

The next morning Stephen was pacing the hall yelling back at Edna that he'd have to go looking for them. Terry leapt out of bed to enquire what was going on and was soon told that the girls had not come home that night.

His first port of call would be Colleen and Carla's flat.

Terry was worried about them and relieved to see Suzanne walk up the drive about an hour after Stephen had left to look for them.

She had stayed with Colleen and Carla that night and claimed Delia had done the same after she had fallen down the steps at the dance.

Delia came home with Stephen much later. Two of her top front teeth were missing. She was quiet, subdued and went straight into her room and to bed. She would not elaborate to Terry who was skeptical about her story of a fall. She didn't want to talk about it. Her mood was dark.

Each time Terry tried to enter their room he was quickly dispatched out and eventually barred. He could have understood Suzanne placing such an embargo, but not Delia, not Mouse. He knew something else had happened on that night, but what?

Six weeks later when just he and Delia were at home alone she told him. "This bloke I was dancing with took me from there. All of us were going to his place to party. Suzanne and Colleen and Carla were with blokes too, all mates of his. I went in his car and when we all got to his house he pushed me into a bedroom and overpowered me. Pushed me down and held me there. When I realized what he was doing I started to scream and the bastard punched me. Each time I screamed he punched me. I had to jump out a window to escape the bastard."

"Jesus, Mouse, I'm sorry I acted the way I did. Who is the bastard? I've got mates, we'll fix him."

Delia never did tell Terry who he was and despite his inquiries, neither would Suzanne. As the months passed Delia and Edna began to fight more and more until, after one argument Delia moved out, into a flat with friends.

Terry overheard Edna and Stephen talking in the evenings. They spoke about lesbians and how strange a scene it was, although neither would have known. They read selected scenes from books they had gathered about lesbians. Terry was bemused by it all, but for now he could easily understand why Delia had turned to female company. "At least she got out of here," he thought, "that's a good thing."

Chapter 9

The domestic arguments continued at Ramsay Road especially when Edna started quoting from her lesbian book about Delia's new lifestyle. Suzanne couldn't stand the arguing and after coming home one Saturday found Edna in the kitchen with a carving knife. The table had a number of wounds from where Edna was thumping the knife down.

"What are you doing Edna?"

"I'm gonna kill the bastard this time. The bastard threatened to hit me. I'm not having that; I'll kill the bastard first."

"Edna, don't be so bloody stupid. Put the knife away."

"No stuff it. He wants to play bloody dirty with me; I can do the same with him. I'll wait until he's gone to sleep and stab the bastard."

"Bloody bullshit Edna. You think you have it bad, well you should have seen the way he treated mum."

Edna continued to thump the knife into the table when Terry arrived home to hear the commotion in the kitchen.

"What's going on now?"

Suzanne responded immediately: "She's off her friggin' rocker mate. Now she's threatening to stab dad in his sleep. Well, I've had enough of this shit. I'm moving out." She went to her bedroom where Lisa was playing quietly with her dolls, oblivious to the drama outside the bedroom.

Terry approached Edna and grabbed the knife away from her and threw it back into a drawer.

"Stop this bullshit Edna. You first get rid of Mouse and now you do this to Suzanne. Just stop drinking so much will you. You can't bloody well handle the stuff."

"It's not right what Delia is doing. Living with another woman. It's unnatural, I tell you," she stood up and moved toward the lounge room where she had her small library of books on the subject. She grabbed the first one: "This one says they're suffering from penis envy."

Suzanne heard what was going on and entered the fray again: "Fucken bullshit Edna. The only one suffering penis envy around here is you. All you do is give dad shit all the bloody time and I'm bloody well sick of listening to you."

Suzanne defended Mouse all the way. She was sick of it alright. When Edna realized how enraged Suzanne was she tormented her with more phrases from the book.

"Mouse's situation has nothing to do with your penis envy quotations. That's what you have, you friggin' bitch!"

"What would you know little miss high and bloody mighty, hey?"

Terry stepped in again: "Come off it Edna. Stop talking such nonsense. Whatever Mouse went through has had this effect on her. She's bloody well better off anywhere rather than here. All you and want to do is drink and fight, all of the bloody time."

To his relief she did stop, long enough to pour herself another drink. Suzanne turned, in a huff, off to her bedroom. Terry could see no point in continuing a discussion with Edna and so followed Suzanne. As he opened the door he could see her suitcase on the bed, already half filled with the contents of her drawers.

"I'm outta here Terry. I can't stand that bitch, and now she's threatening to kill dad. She's fucking mad; I can't stand this any longer."

Suzanne was shaking and Terry moved over and gave her a hug. She continued her packing: "I'm going to stay with Carol for a while, until things settle down. I'm sorry, but she's driving me bloody mad and I can't stand the way she talks about Mouse like that all the time."

"Neither can I. Dad hates it too. It's been the subject of their arguing for bloody months now. I don't know why she can't just leave Mouse alone."

Suzanne hugged Terry and Lisa before leaving: "I'll keep in touch, don't you worry. She seems to have calmed down a bit now. Just keep an eye on her Terry."

As she walked up the hall with her suitcases Edna launched another tirade: "Go on then, piss off, you good for nothing bitch. Go on, you'll be whoring in the Cross by next week, you watch."

"Is that what you resort to Edna? The times you disappear for a few days, I mean. You'd be waitin' on street corners for a long time before anyone would want a slob like you Edna." Suzanne slammed the door behind her.

Edna switched on the television talking aloud to herself: "Fucking bitch. What would she know anyway?" She slumped into a chair and fell asleep, spilling her drink into her lap as she did. Terry grabbed the glass and put it on a table before checking the front bedroom. Stephen was snoring away. He had missed all the drama. Terry and Lisa were now stuck with it. They were too young to protest; too young to fully understand, it was thought.

Terry knew though; he knew exactly how much Delia had been humiliated by the attempted rape. It was the final straw. She had seen her mother battered by her father and witnessed the constant arguing and abuse Stephen and Edna had thrown at one another every time they had a drink. He knew the wounds were deeper than anyone else could imagine. She hated the fights at home. Then she had the indignity of some mongrel bashing her. He felt hopeless that he could not do anything for her.

He wanted to kill the bastard who did this. He now had to deal with the stepmother attempting to employ shock tactics on his sister in a bid to get her away from the scene. It would not work; he knew it, but there was no way he could mention it to Edna or even Stephen.

He decided to get the dinner on. He cooked chops and made chips and a side salad. He and Lisa ate theirs alone. "Let sleeping dogs lie," he told Lisa. "Let's not wake them. It'll just be on again."

Stephen and Edna had been able to manage in the months since Delia had gone but they needed the board that Suzanne contributed to maintain the rent at Haberfield. They did their sums over breakfast on Sunday morning. They would have to find somewhere cheaper to live.

Cowpasture Road at Horsley Park was semi-rural with market gardens and grazing stock on five and ten-acre blocks with houses lined up along one side of the gravel road. Stephen chose the house; they would save about $30 a week in rent, a considerable saving in the mid-sixties and they could grow their own vegetables. Well, he had aspirations of turning the soil and putting in a crop or two, but these soon faded when their routine fell into place.

Terry and Lisa had remained at their respective schools in Leichhardt, Stephen was still doing deliveries and Edna was happy in her job. The only difference was now that they all had to travel the 35 minutes to and from Leichhardt every day. The journey would start at 6.00 am with Lisa and Terry in the back of the panel van. They soon learned that it was a good opportunity to do homework. It made the trip seem faster.

The new routine after school each day was to walk several blocks to the home of an old Russian lady who would give them cordial and cookies while they waited for Stephen and Edna to finish work. Mrs Heinsdorf spoke with a deep guttural accent of broken English that entranced Lisa who showed some keenness to the suggestion of learning Russian.

Terry was not that keen at first, but was enthralled when the old lady told stories of her escape from communist Russia through China after the revolution. They heard another installment of Mrs Heinsdorf s' story nearly every day as they settled into a routine.

Lisa was the perfect student. Terry was amazed that she had the ability to turn off to the arguments and actually concentrate, not only on her schoolwork but also on learning Russian.

"Lisa you are only in fifth grade, you don't really need to know Russian," he told her during a drive home one day as she practiced the language on him. But she insisted. She liked it.

Stephen soon had a pen full of chickens out the back which provided a constant source of eggs and meat. Terry had pleaded with his dad to get a dog and one afternoon Ollie arrived. He was a young border collie who loved to fetch sticks. Lisa and Terry spent whatever daylight hours they had left after the journey home, tossing balls and sticks into the paddock for Ollie. Stephen and Edna appeared to be getting along better at home, but often their conversation in the car en-route to work or home would erupt into an argument. They were volatile from the moment they had that first drink. Terry had learned to tune off, especially during the car ride. He simply did not listen to them and concentrated his attention on his little sister who now practiced Russian on him all the time.

The immediate neighbours at Horsley Park lived about 100 metres away. George and Rosina worked a market garden and supplied them with a continuous supply of fresh vegetables. Stephen didn't need to dig up a garden now, but instead offered space down the back for George to extend onto. With the chooks and the veges and the abridged family, the general costs of feeding the family had been reduced measurably, but this simply allowed Edna more money to buy spirits.

Weekends were the hardest for Terry and Lisa. They would lie in bed listening to their arguments, usually about other people. Whenever Stephen called on Delia and later spoke to Edna about it, she would go off again about her relationships with women. The mere mention of her created an excuse for Edna to argue.

They had been on the farm about six months when Stephen noticed some of his chickens were missing.

"That bloody dog is taking the chooks," Stephen ranted. "He'll have to go."

"No," said Terry, "he doesn't take the chooks. Rats are killing them. I heard them the other night when I was going to the loo. It's not the dog."

"How the bloody hell could a rat drag fully grown chooks off a perch and through a fence. It has to be the bloody dog," Stephen was half-tanked and angry after another fight with Edna. She had taken off in the car.

Terry managed to give the dog a reprieve that evening by taking his father out to the pen after they heard the chickens making noises. He flashed the torch on to reveal a rat dragging a chicken by the tail toward the other side of the pen. Stephen raised the rifle broke open the barrel, filled it with rat shot, snapped it closed, aimed and squeezed the trigger. The rat let go and scurried back through the fence, allowing the frightened chicken to scamper back to the coop.

They stayed there for two hours in the dark, waiting for the chattering rats to poke their noses through the fence. When the torch went on they would remain still for a few seconds; time enough for another shot.

Stephen and Terry staked claim to at least twenty hits that evening, but their sport was interrupted as Edna drove back into the driveway. By morning they went around the coop to where they expected to see the carcasses and there was nothing.

They discussed it on the drive in that morning and decided they would use the full calibre .22 rounds this evening. Stephen and Edna had argued, this time about whether or not Terry should be allowed to use the .22 rifle. She stormed off again, taking the car.

It was dark at 7pm. "Bloody women Terry; you can't live with 'em and you can't live without 'em." They were waiting by the chicken coop again. The first rat poked his nose through the fence. Pow! He let out a squeak. "There's another," Terry was holding the torch. Stephen squeezed off another round. Pow! "Got him."

"No you didn't. He didn't squeak," Terry responded.

"He probably didn't have time to squeak before he was dead. Quick the light; here comes another one." Pow!

Their count was about 40 hits on this night, but again in the morning there was no evidence of their carnage, just a chicken. It had been mauled. Its head and guts were missing. Terry was up early and went out to investigate. He didn't have the foresight to get rid of the carcass. Instead he went back inside and put the kettle on.

He noticed the car was not in the driveway. Edna had not returned last night. Suddenly he heard Lisa: "No, I don't want to play."

He looked into their bedroom. Lisa wasn't in her bed. He opened the door to Stephen's bedroom where he saw Lisa astride Stephen. Startled he shut the door. Then opened it again: "What are you doing?"

Stephen was surprised that Terry had walked in: "We were playing horsies."

"Well she's a bit old for that stuff now. Lisa, come out here."

Lisa was relieved that Terry had intervened and quickly got down off the bed and went into the kitchen.

"He didn't try anything with you, did he Lisa?"

"What do you mean?"

"I mean were you on top of the covers. Did you have your pants on?"

"Yes. He just asked if I wanted to play horsies, that's all."

"Well, don't you ever do that again, okay? You are too old to be playing horsies with daddy. If he ever tries anything like that again, you come straight to me alright. Now eat your breakfast." He looked out the window to see the sun shining brightly. "We can take a ride on the bikes this morning."

Stephen waited until they had gone out before emerging from the bedroom and pouring himself a cup of tea. Guilt engulfed him and he was defensive when Terry confronted him near the chicken coop later.

"What were you doing with Lisa in your bedroom this morning dad?"

"Nothing, she just came in to kiss me good morning. She often does that." Stephen changed the subject turning to the chicken carcass behind the coop: "That couldn't have been done by rats. The dog has done that."

"No, Dad, Ollie wouldn't; he's too well fed." Terry could feel the anger welling in Stephen. He could tell he now had it in for the dog.

"Where's bloody Edna? The slut, she stayed out last night."

Terry had no answer for that one and started pleading with Stephen as he headed for the dog. There were some telltale feathers around Ollie's mouth, enough for Stephen to snap.

"He has probably just grabbed one away from the rats," Terry's words were not heard by Stephen as he grabbed a length of fencing wire from under the house and swooped on Ollie, gripping him by the scruff of the neck. Terry soon realized what was going on and pleaded for the dog as his father dragged the animal for 400 metres down the back of the block and into the saplings.

"Come on Dad, he's not a killer, he's our pet."

"A killer dog has got to be stopped. He'll be eating everyone else's chickens next."

Terry was still complaining as Stephen pulled a sapling over and attached the wire around the dog's neck. As he let it go the dog was dragged four feet off the ground and struggled for about twenty seconds as the wire tightened around his throat. Terry turned and raced back to the house. He jumped on his bike and called Lisa to follow him. They rode for miles that day and only returned after dusk.

By the time they got home Edna had returned and they were half way through a bottle of Johnny Walker. Terry made dinner for Lisa and settled in the lounge room away from his father and Edna. He simply didn't want to speak to them at all.

"The dog would have been killing everyone's chickens around here. You just can't have a dog doing that sort of thing," Stephen tried to justify himself.

"Anyway we'll save a bit on dog food now anyway," Edna had to contribute.

"Just more money for you to waste on grog," Terry was speaking under his breath as he walked around them to put the canned spaghetti onto the toast he had made for himself and Lisa.

He remained quiet during the trip into school the next day. Stephen continued with the excuse that the dog would be taking other people's chickens too, "And we couldn't have that. In the bush dogs are for working and if they don't work, they're fuckin' dead."

Terry didn't say a word, only wished for the courage to pull a wire over Stephen's head and choke him, not to death, but enough to frighten the shit out of him. This, of course, was impossible. He feared him.

That evening Stephen and Edna were late to pick them up from Mrs Heinsdorf's. When they did finally arrive, two hours late, the sitter was reticent to let them go, especially when she smelled the pair of them. They had been at the pub for several hours and now expected to drive 30 miles home. Mrs Heinsdorf suggested the children should stay the night, but Stephen wouldn't have a bar of it.

On the way home Terry hugged Lisa low behind the seat, expecting the worst. The journey was erratic. The FB Holden seemed to slide around corners as Stephen took it a bit hard. He was finally jolted into taking more care when he lost control momentarily on a greasy patch of road and only just managed to straighten the vehicle ahead of a deep drain. Edna was spitting obscenities at him and told him to slow down. This just made him angry and he drove even more aggressively. Miraculously, they got home in one piece.

Stephen and Edna continued to drink after they got home. Terry made spaghetti on toast for he and Lisa and locked himself away in the bedroom.

This night they were blaming the long days for their altercation. Terry and Lisa listened to the radio for a while before drifting off to sleep. The journeys in to town for the rest of the week were just as dark, taxing for them all. Anything Stephen said would prompt an abrupt retort from Edna.

Saturday came around ever so slowly and Stephen was gone early. He came home about 10am telling how he'd found a new house, in Elswick Street, Leichhardt. They could move in next week.

Terry was pleased with the new house in that it meant he didn't have to be up at 5.30 every morning to go to school. He also had his own room, as did Lisa and Suzanne was coming back to live there with them.

The move again made a brief change in them. Stephen and Edna were like honeymooners again and with board from Suzanne to help out with the more expensive rent, they had a budget which would restrict their drinking to weekends again.

For Terry the move heralded a new freedom. He was able to visit his mates after school and at weekends. He could play football again, and, most importantly, he found a job selling papers after school. Financial freedom.

The new house in Little Elswick Street, Leichhardt, was only a kilometre away from Delia, and Terry made a visit as soon as he had the opportunity.

He was excited as he opened the gate. Almost a year had passed since she had told Edna to 'get fucked', packed her bags and taken off. Terry approached the door and was surprised as it opened before he even knocked. His broad smile closed as the overweight woman snapped: "Yes, whaddayerwant?"

"Is Delia home, please?"

"Who wants to know?"

Delia was carrying a couple of cups into the lounge room and noticed the commotion.

"Terry, gedday. Come in."

The guardian at the door was not going to budge.

"Get out of the way yer big blacmonge, it's my brother, Terry. Delia leaned close to kiss him on the cheek. "Terry, this is Billy."

"Hi," Terry tried another smile.

Billy didn't respond. She just moved back to allow him inside and retreated with her cup back to the kitchen.

Terry gave Delia a big hug and kissed her affectionately on the cheek. "How have you been Mouse?"

"Not too bad. Although things are a bit funny at the moment, Billy is a really jealous type; she's jealous of anyone, especially men. Gee you've grown since I saw you last. You're looking great. Say, how's Lisa going?"

"Oh she's fine, almost into high school now. She seems to be loving the new house. She has been learning Russian too, of all things."

Terry explained how they stayed with Mrs Heinsdorf after school and filled Delia in on the relationship between Stephen and Edna.

"She shits me that woman. She has no compassion or understanding. After that incident I just wished to have mum close by."

"Yeah, I know what you mean, I miss her too, but I'm afraid to contact her while I'm with them. They talk so badly about her all the time."

"Still?" Delia was truly amazed at the thought.

"Whatever chance they get, and especially after they've had a few. They often talk about you too. But I won't bore you with the details."

"Don't worry Terry, I can imagine. Don't worry about it though; things will work out alright. You'll see. I don't reckon they'll be together for much longer anyway, the way they fight, all the bloody time."

"I miss you too Mouse, are you ever coming back?"

"I couldn't live under the same roof with that woman ever again Terry. She's just too destructive. Are they drinking much?"

"Yes, they drink a lot. Sometimes they're pretty loud and argumentative, but they haven't taken knives to each other yet. He doesn't hit her like he did Mum either. They just argue and argue and argue."

"I don't know what dad sees in her really, but enough about them, what have you been up to?"

"Well, not much really. I have got a good job, selling papers in town after school. It pays pretty well, but she is making me pay board out of my wages."

"The bitch," Delia put an arm over Terry.

"But still, with tips and all I make enough to pay board and have a bit spare for fun times. A mate from school, Larry and I go skating on weekends and I go out a couple of nights a week with the guys from school. How are things with you? With Billy I mean? She acted like I had a disease or something. Doesn't she like me?"

"Well, Billy doesn't like any men. Billy can just be a bitch sometimes too. She's very insecure. That's her problem. It's her headspace. I try to avoid her when she's cranky. Don't worry about her. You're always welcome where I live, any time mate."

"Thanks Mouse, ditto to you too. Please don't be a stranger to us. Lisa would like to see you too. Hey, you know Suzanne is living with us again at Elswick Street?"

"Yes, she told me. She's got a new job in a city pharmacy too. She seems to be doing a heap of courses too."

Billy entered offering Delia another cup of tea. "Would you like one Terry?"

"Yes please," his shy reply prompted a smile.

"You may be the first and last man she has ever made a cup of tea for Terry, I should go and make sure she doesn't lace it with rat poison though," Delia smiled and turned back to Terry. "Really, I think she likes you."

Terry looked around the room. The sideboard was Edwardian, an antique, and the lounge suite, old in style but re-covered in bright, fresh floral material. Extra lengths were draped over the arms to protect the main fabric from dirty hands or spills. Billy came back in, smiling this time: "Here you go, milk-and-two."

"Hold the rat poison," Terry laughed.

Billy smiled: "So, you go to school just down the road here?" She seemed to have lost that initial aggression and was very personable.

"Yes, I'm in third form this year. School's pretty boring though."

As he told her about his likes and dislikes he didn't realize that he was probably the only male person Billy had cared to strike up a conversation with for years.

Terry went away feeling refreshed that his sister was in good hands, but he didn't tell Stephen and Edna where he'd been. When he had her alone he told Lisa who was ecstatic and asked many questions about Delia.

"Can I come with you next time, please?"

"Sure you can Lisa; she's only ten minutes from here. We can go down on Sunday if you like. It's just over the back from your school. So, what have you been up to today?"

"I visited my friends across the road and went down to their church with them. I talked to the priest and asked him if I could become a Catholic and he gave me all of these things to read up on."

"Why on earth do you want to become a Catholic Lisa?"

"My friends are Catholic and I would like to be able to go in with them when they go to church. Father Mayberry said all I had to do was study these things and when I'm ready, he will baptize me. Great hey?"

"If you say so, I really don't see the point though."

"Well I'd just like to; that's all Terry.

Chapter 10

There was safety in numbers when walking the streets of Sydney in the sixties, but Larry Taylor and Terry found that even two out was enough in most circumstances. They had a common bond; they started at the school together. They were born just four days apart and they were both from broken families. Larry lived with his mother and sister in a huge terrace house owned by his grandmother in Wooloomooloo. However their time there was limited as the Railways were buying up properties to make way for a new rail line which would eventually link the city with the eastern suburbs. Larry could visit his father who lived just a few blocks away.

His situation was very different to Terry's in that his mother was the disciplinarian in his household while Terry had his dad and a stepmother to answer to.

"My mum shot through with dad's best mate," he told Larry. "I can't blame her though, 'cause dad used to hit the piss and beat her up."

"Yeah, our household wasn't much different when dad lived with us. They were always fighting and he'd get violent now and then especially when he was on the grog; it was awful for Mum."

"I don't know why my dad is with Edna now; she's not a patch on my real Mum, although I suppose she has been kind to us all. It must be hard for somebody who's never had kids to suddenly be in a family with three teenagers and a primary schooler. It's no wonder they fight all the time," Terry was getting philosophical.

"And look what she has to put up with you, yer red-headed bastard; cripes, mother's worry or what?"

"Maybe that's why they drink so much now," Terry led him on.

"Yeah, you drive them to drink," Larry smiled widely.

"RatFink; at least she didn't get a poon like you," he started.

"A poon? What's a poon," Larry enquired.

Terry got up and started walking away slowly before breaking into a run: "A person who farts in the bath and eats the bubbles.... Like YOU."

"Caw, yuck; you calling me a poon?" He was off, after him.

Larry helped Terry find some independence. He was always keen to make a few dollars and teaming up with Larry saw him take on a paper corner in the city.

Their daily routine from school would see them on the first bus into town, lighting up cigarettes as the school ties were reefed from their necks.

This day was no different except for the old woman on the bus. She was peeved to see two boys in school uniform lighting up cigarettes. "What would your mother think?" she was accosting them before they knew it. Larry and Terry looked at her in apparent disbelief, but without answer. They tried to ignore her, but she went on and on. Her ravings were obviously getting on their nerves and by the time the bus reached busy Parramatta Road they felt guilty. The woman continued her onslaught, leaning towards the passenger next to her. "It's disgusting, isn't it? Seeing young boys smoking, and in their school uniforms yet."

Terry grabbed his bag and stood up, motioning to Larry that they go upstairs. "Bloody old bag. Why can't she mind her own business?"

"So, I'm an old bag am I? What's your name son?"

"Robert Menzies lady, can't you tell by my white hair?" Larry always had a smart arsed answer straight off the cuff.

They disappeared up the stairs and walked right to the front before settling in to a seat. They could still hear her talking, even from there. "Bloody old bag. Some people just need something to argue about.

We'll probably hear Chipsy talking at assembly tomorrow about the boys seen smoking on the bus, hey?"

"Yeah, but who gives a stuff. Lots of guys get the bus from Leichhardt, don't they?" Terry was confident they would not be singled out and propped his legs up on the edge of the window.

"Yeah," Larry was with him on that one.

"Yeah," Terry agreed again.

"Hey Terry, isn't that Amanda Carlson?"

Terry suddenly sat up and peered forward: "where?"

"There," Larry was pointing to the opposite sidewalk, "over there".

"Oh yeah, I see her." He studied the pony-tailed girl with her uniform tucked up in her belt making her tunic as short as possible, slightly exposing her white knickers under the hem. "Geeze she looks a hot little number. Kevin Allison was talking about her the other day. He reckons he scored with her."

"That's bullshit, mate. I reckon Kevin Allison is a wanker. She wouldn't have him anyway, he's too pooncey."

"Yeah, I suppose you're right. I wouldn't mind half an hour behind a shelter shed with her though."

They were craning their necks looking back at her as the bus passed when she looked up at them and smiled. Both smiled back then turned around simultaneously.

"Did you see that. She smiled at me," Larry was ecstatic.

"Nah mate, she was smiling at me, not you."

"You don't even know her."

"Yes I do, I've seen her walking home heaps of times. She only lives a couple of blocks away from my place."

"Bet you haven't said anything to her."

"Have too," Terry lied. "I met her a few months ago and walked all the way home with her."

"You mean you followed her home."

"Well, yeah, about twenty paces behind. I just wanted to see where she lived."

"So you don't know her!"

"Nah, not really, but I know I'd like to. And I think she knows it too."

Larry changed the subject to the recent father and son night at the school: "Your old man was funny last Tuesday night."

"Shit I was embarrassed by that. I knew there'd be trouble; taking him along after he'd had a few," Terry gazed back out the window until Larry slapped him on the arm.

"Yeah but he was fucken funny though. Especially when that guy said 'and how do we know when a young male is attracted to a young female?'"

They both started to laugh as Larry continued: "And your old man stood up and whacked his arm up in the air and said, 'cause his dick stands up in the air like that'," Larry was duplicating Stephen's actions.

"Yeah and when the guy asked him after the meeting if he wanted to buy some of the books, he said: 'I don't need you to tell me how to fuck either'."

Their banter continued all the way into the city. Any bit of skirt they saw sparked an imaginative remark.

"That chic has my name tattooed on her arse Larry," the lies were getting bigger.

"You only wish Terry, that's my sister you mug."

"Oh shit, so it is," they laughed.

As the city engulfed them in lower George Street they were again ready for their couple of hours of watching people from the office blocks pile out into the streets and into subways on their way home. They soon learned who had a Sun and who had a Mirror, and learned the ones who wanted to know the news in the three steps before they reached them. They knew the tippers and the lousy bastards who waited for that one or two copper coins in change.

"Those bastards who wait for the two cents in change shit me Terry," Larry had said on the bus. "I just fumble around with one hand in the bag while I pass papers over their shoulders to the next customers. The really tight bastards will wait for minutes for you to get two cents out for them."

"Probably miss their bloody train too," Terry added.

There were definite rushes of people and if they let them get away they would get around the corner and get a paper from the next kid.

From corner to corner they could gauge one another's progress by the pile of papers and would yell to one another when they needed more Suns or Mirrors. Then the other would have to leave his post for a minute or two and get more papers from the boss they cruelly called "Dragon Lady". Sylvia and her sister would stand at the corner of Pitt and Hunter streets for the best part of twelve hours every day. Terry and Larry worked Australia Square from the western side but got many customers from across the lower end of town who headed for Wynyard Station. They earned about a quarter of a cent per paper, but with tips could pick up eight to twelve dollars a week. After the rush hour they had to wait around for the lingerers. That was the boring time. Often they would throw tennis balls at one another to ease the boredom.

Friday was pay day and a hamburger, hot chips and a coke would usually do as dinner. They loved to "fang" a burger from their favourite burger bars.

This day ordering in a cafe Larry ordered the usual: "Honey roll over and lettuce on top."

"Cheeky thing," the woman replied.

After they laughed together for a moment Larry piped up: "No, sorry, make it two burgers with cheese and bacon," their favorite. When the order was ready Larry grabbed his from the counter. "Thanks very much, it's his shout."

"You fucking liar Larry," Terry had already taken out the correct change for one burger from his pocket.

The young woman was quick: "Young man, please don't speak that way to your friend, it isn't nice to call people an effing liar."

"Sorry lady, forgive me, I know I shouldn't use such language, he's so sensitive too, just look at him." He turned to his mate standing at the doorway ready to do a 'sandshoe', smiling as he took his first bite: "Sorry Larry, you fucken fibber." Larry almost choked on his mouthful of food as he laughed.

"That's better," Larry said paying up his share, "you know it's not nice to fucking swear in front of a bloody lady". She laughed as they left.

They laughed their burgers down sitting upstairs in the double decker bus; they took window seats, one behind the other on the driver's side, from where they could have a perve down into the cars watching for the mini-skirts. They would get great delight in telling one another the colours of the knickers. Just the motion of a bus would leave them with half a roger, embarrassing when they got off the bus on Friday nights heading for Playland, a pin-ball parlour in Pitt Street just off Park Street.

"Why are you walking so funny Larry?" Terry teased as he went to drop a Coke can into a bin, but missed. A man walking behind stopped them; "Hey, do you do that sort of thing at home?"

"No," Terry replied.

"Then what do you do with your empty cans?"

Terry dwelt a moment: "I, I...put them in my pocket."

"And what do you do with them then?" the man was starting to sound like a preacher to Terry.

"I bring them into town and accidentally drop them on the footpath."

The man released his grip as his mouth dropped before he let out a laugh with them before swooping the can up and pushing it hard into the overfilled bin. "Bloody kids," the man was shaking his head.

"Sorry mate, it's just the bin was too full," Terry at least showed a little remorse. "I really meant to put it in there."

Playland was a maze of pinball machines, a fun parlor where they could either exercise their pinball wizardry or lose. Either way one of them would usually get a couple of free games sooner or later and they would go ball for ball on the one machine.

They became pretty good at manipulating the crane machines to pick up goodies such as packets of cigarettes and they became hustlers on the handle manipulated soccer machines and often found an extra dollar or two from some unsuspecting ethnics. Sometimes they took the brunt of a hustle.

They frequented dingy, downstairs city pool rooms and even wagged school to see movies like Felini's Satyricon. They jumped ferries to Manly, and in rough weather would get up front, down below on the mighty South Steyne and get thrown about by huge swells rolling through the Heads. Once they got to Manly, if it was really rough, they'd simply stay on board and go back again just for the thrill of the ride through the Heads.

The fact they hung together for so many events they would simply pool their money so they could have equal fun.

When they went to Luna Park they would search for two girls together and try to chat them up. Terry was always a little on the shy side, but Larry would often make up for this with a quick tongue and a sharp wit. If their money was low they would pool it again and share the rides. What fun is there taking two extra rides on the big dipper by yourself while your mate is standing at the turnstiles?

Just about all of his weekends and nights with Larry were adventures; even working they had a lot of fun. It was such a long way, a million miles away, from the traumas at home.

Chapter 11

Mrs Taylor was cranky that they hadn't done anything around the house. She had left instructions with Larry to do the dishes, but even this simple task had been overlooked this Saturday. It wasn't that they watched TV like many other teenagers might do. They hardly ever watched it because it was in the front room of the little Darlinghurst terrace and Larry and Terry hardly ever spent any time there. They preferred the solitude of the little attic room from which they could gaze down upon half a dozen backyards in its narrow view. Not that they did much gazing out of the window anyway. It was simply their escape route at night.

Larry's new address was just off Oxford Street. It was a lot smaller than his grandmother's house, but just as central. Terry would stay over at Larry's after the paper job on Friday and eventually get home on Saturday or even Sunday.

They never seemed to get bored; they were doing their usual laps of the block checking out the scenery. Sometimes their walk would take them through the city, checking out the shops, especially the pawnbrokers, looking for ice-skates or talking about this or that female they desired; and they desired all of them.

Terry had to admit he did have a latent desire for Larry's sister, Charmaine, but his growing adolescent enthusiasm was squelched by Larry's built-in resentment to her.

With just four days separating Terry and Larry's birthdays the early December celebrations would last at least a week.

They had graduated from the afternoons playing with slot cars at the Rushcutter's Bay Bowling alley and now found their fun at Prince Alfred Park ice skating rink. Their paper runs gave them the money to do just about anything they wanted even after they had paid their board.

They loved the freedom of gliding around the skating rink on thin blades and sliding to a halt at their sou-westerly corner. Pity any poor bastard who dragged himself around the walls in that part of the rink.

Larry and Terry mixed with a tough crew of kids, Sharpies from Surry Hills, Redfern and Darlinghurst. Most were pretty street wise, or becoming that way. Larry had gone to primary school with some of the lads and knew a little of their home scenes.

"We either knock about with them, or become their target," Larry had said when Terry questioned him about the tough guys.

As weeks went by and they got to know them they found the boys were not very organised anyway. Just a bunch of lost kids looking for thrills. It appeared that the ones with the biggest chips on their shoulders were the biggest troublemakers and had to act out the role of being the toughest or bravest in the group. It was their way to sort out their own pecking order. This was all new to Terry.

Despite the anger in some of the young men Terry and Larry managed to keep their noses pretty clean. They wore the uniform, desert boots, Levis and banlon shirts. Being school kids, it was not a problem keeping their hair short; that's the way their parents and teachers wanted it anyway. It showed an apparent conformity to their conservative ideals. In fact, the sixties era was pretty much a short-back-and-side's one, especially in the schools, where lads would be ostracised for having their hair even touching a collar.

The skating was always fun and excellent exercise, but often punctuated by a problem one of the Redfern boys may be having with a learner skater who may have got in his way, or someone who may have upset his rhythm on the ice. Whoever it was, their way of dealing with it was to zoom in, really close, clipping the back of the knees of one of the unfortunates, sending them crashing to the wet ice. The rum they would sneak into the rink in small flasks obtained from any of the local hotels often accentuated the drama of these exchanges. They had a favourite hotel, the Central, where they could go into the lounge and play a juke box and get the oldest looking among the group to do all the ordering. The rest would just talk tough and remain deathly silent when any adult came into the room. They weren't half obvious as underage drinkers and only needed a couple of swigs to loosen up.

When a skating session was due to start they would pile out of the pub and wander through the long tunnel at Central Station to Prince Alfred Park, home of the Bomber's Ice Hockey Club, taking turns at swigging from their flasks.

It was the days of A Clockwork Orange, live in Sydney, and they witnessed many beatings of "hairies" or "whoees" few of which were provoked. Most of the time Larry and Terry would stay well away from any action.

However, like anywhere else, you wear a uniform, or wear your hair a certain way and you become a target for the ones who were targets of abuse the week or the night before. Stephen was concerned for Terry when reading the news reports of the larrikins at the skating rink and some of the bashings which had taken place near the Central Station tunnel: "If you lay down with dogs, you get up with fleas," he'd told him.

"We don't have anything to do with the hooligans," Terry told him.

The ice skating rink had become notorious for loutish behavior and even had its own coppers, in plain clothes, to keep an eye on the hooligan element, but they had their own axes to grind and it didn't appear to be with the younger crew.

Terry copped the brunt of one altercation between a few guys in their crew one Saturday. He had been skating fast around the outside of the ice when he accidentally bumped into one of a group of tough nuts from Leichhardt. After the session Terry was confronted outside only to have another guy from their group step in and "have it out" with him. The boy from Leichhardt ended up with a bloodied nose and disappeared across the park with his friends. The following day Terry was walking with Larry toward the steps of the rink when he was grabbed from behind: "There's one of them," Terry heard one bloke say as he felt a deadening pain across the shoulders from a whack with what appeared to be a newspaper. It was the hardest newspaper he had ever felt. There was an iron bar inside. "You fucking big prick," Terry screamed, flailing the bladed edges of his skates at the three in defence but was struck repeatedly with punches and thumps from the bars. Larry heard his call and came to the rescue and was set upon himself. As Terry recovered at the steps of the building he called to one of the off duty policemen to help.

"Get stuffed yer fucken little hood," came the response.

"You gutless big prick," he screamed as he went back into the fray, this time swinging skates from the long boot laces. He grabbed Larry by the shirt and pulled him free while the thugs dodged the swirling skates, this time at head height. They made the apparent safety of the steps of the entrance way again and started hurling abuse at the undercover cop who had failed to assist.

"Aren't you supposed to be protecting us from pricks like them?"

"Fuck off kid, I got better things to do with me time," came the response.

The irony was that Terry and Larry had been the ones who had broken up the blue the previous afternoon, saving the three who had responded by this attack on them.

They were pissed off and didn't skate that day. They decided to head for the pub instead. A session for these 15 year olds would cost about a dollar fifty each. They exaggerated their alternate feats of heroism with each drink to the compassionate crew and girls who tagged along in sympathy.

Terry was overwhelmed by the attention he got from a young lass from

Redfern, Maxine. He walked her home after the pub session to find she lived in Everly Street. Terry had been falling in lust with Maxine with each drink. He hadn't really bothered with girls before then but she raised a passion in him that rarely got past a pash in the park after skating. A dry root was considered going pretty far in young adolescence, but the resultant wet patch on the jeans often made him wonder why it was termed a 'dry' root. Terry met her mother as they went upstairs, but did not hang around to discuss things on the way out as he was embarrassed by yet another wet patch. He held his skates in front of him as he was leaving. He was learning.

Chapter 12

He was nearing the end of his fourth year in high school when the arguments at home, been fuelled by copious bottles of Scott's whisky, intensified again. After one such crescendo Edna decided to return to Melbourne.

Terry had missed many of these by keeping busy in the evenings, especially around the weekends. Most evenings during the week he would get home about 6.30, just in time to have dinner and by the time the dishes were done he would hear Marty's noisy FJ Holden pull up outside. Marty was a year ahead of him at school and had known his classmates Aiden and George since they were toddlers.

The four of them would chip in 20 cents each for petrol and spend the evening cruising around, visiting other mates or checking out the rev-head haunts. Some evenings they would venture into the city, up to the Cross, to the beach suburbs or their favourite, the Kurnell sand flats.

The sand flats allowed an opportunity for the young drivers to practice their new skills. Most of the passengers would alight as they roared, in turns, up and down the sand, doing huge figure-eight's and generally getting off on the drift of the cars as they cornered. Marty was always fairly cautious and managed to keep his vehicle together, but some tried to corner too hard and ended up rolling their cars on the sand. As a result there were always a number of dented and stripped bodies on the beach.

One night they decided to tie a bonnet from one of the wrecks to a rope behind Marty's FJ and took turns at being dragged around the sand flats. It was very dangerous, but a lot of fun for the one on the bonnet, that is, if the driver didn't give him the whip out across the water. In this case the bonnet would gain speed over the water and often spit the bonnet out in a huge circle back in front of or into the side of the car. They got plenty of thrills out of the game and managed not to get seriously hurt, although Aiden had one close call when he was whipped out over the water and gathered so much speed that he ended up thumping uncontrollably into the side of the car, dislodging Aiden.

Year 10 was finished, exams had been completed and Terry had received his School Certificate results; he had fared well. 'A' level passes in English and Science and B levels in all other subjects except Mathematics which he passed with a C+. He attributed the English pass to assistance he got from the Deputy Principal who he had recently drenched with a water bomb. It had been a hot day and many of the boys had made small paper water bombs and lobbed them at people while they were taking a leak. Terry planned his revenge on the friend he called 'Bugsy' and visited the art room to get the biggest sheet of paper he could find. The result was a water bomb the size of a soccer ball. He was chasing his mate all the while trying to dodge the drips and let fly with the bomb just as Deputy Principal and school disciplinarian, Geoff Peterman, stepped around the corner. Peterman copped it on the chest and was drenched from his shirt down to his trousers. Terry noticed the ink from a pen had also started running from his pocket causing a streak down his shirt.

"Martin, get to my office."

Terry was squirming at the thought of six of the best from Peterman. He had a fierce reputation with a cane and often missed a boy's hand and fingers to connect at the wrist. Sometimes when he was really mad he would collect a boy on the soft flesh of his inside forearm, causing severe welts.

Peterman walked in and, to Terry's surprise, was smiling.

"You've got a choice son; six with the cane or six weeks detention."

Terry was totally aware of his brutality with the cane and was relieved to have a choice in the matter. He took the detention.

This may have been one of the best decisions he made in four years of high school as he found he got excellent one-on-one coaching from Peterman, who was also the English master, for the hour-long detention. The only downer for him was for six weeks, leading up to his exams, he had to make a temporary halt to his city paper run.

Meanwhile, Stephen had been pining for Edna since her departure and was considering a return to Melbourne to be with her. He was now concerned for Terry's future more than anything else. He knew he had made a lot of friends in Sydney and was doing well in his schooling. He could see with his pending entry into fifth form that he was keen to learn. He asked lots of questions, many of which Stephen could not answer, so Terry passed the answers on to him after he had done the necessary research.

In the new-year Stephen mooched around the house. He was bored without his lady, and was torn between his children and his woman, despite the volatility of the relationship. Finally a phone call from Melbourne prompted him to tie up his Sydney association and follow Edna again.

Terry arrived home and was sitting down eating dinner when Stephen came in to break the news that he was returning to Melbourne.

"Do you want to come with me or keep on at school here? You have come to the time in your life that you have to start making decisions about what you are going to do for the rest of your life. You need a career path. Do you have any ideas on what you may want to do?"

Terry was a little overwhelmed with all the questions at once.

"Well Dad, I haven't really thought about it." Terry was now thinking about where the lads may be going when Marty turned up this evening.

Stephen had an idea: "I saw an ad in the paper the other day for a wool-classing school in town. It would be a good job for you. They only shear sheep for six months every year and there would be six months off.

Classers get the best money in the sheds and you would do a lot of travelling around the bush. Would you like me to make some inquiries for you?"

Terry agreed that working for six months and having six months off sounded pretty good.

"It would also give you a chance to see the country too. It's nice out in the country Terry. There are far fewer problems with people in the country. If you work hard there, you'll be fine mate."

Stephen followed up on his promise and two days later came home with a number of forms for Terry's entrance into the College. Terry filled them out and decided that he could continue his newspaper job which would give him the money to pay his board to Suzanne and her new boyfriend, Damian, who would take over the house rental. Lisa had no choice in the matter and had to go with her father. She cried on Terry's shoulder for ten minutes before they drove away.

"I went around to the church yesterday and asked if Father Mayberry could baptize me, and he said I wasn't ready yet," she told him.

"Don't worry about it Lisa, it just doesn't matter. It's what is inside that counts. You don't have to be a practicing Christian or anything to be a nice person. And you're a nice person. Stuff the church love." He regretted his final comment and wished he hadn't said it after she had left.

His routine changed after Stephen had gone. Throughout the holidays Terry lost touch with Larry who had given up the paper run, and as a result he was spending more and more time with his mates from the inner western side of town. When he finally caught up with him months later, Larry was working as a copy boy. He explained he was just doing the job as a fill-in between starting his apprenticeship. He was going to be a mechanic.

Terry, meanwhile, had started the wool-classing course at College and continued straight into the city to sell papers each afternoon.

His time at the College, studying wool-classing and shearing shed management, agreed with Terry. He had learned a lot, but was impatient, especially when he had to sort the same bin of wool into grades for the twentieth time. When the wool was new, it wasn't so bad, he could sort it into all of the necessary categories, but after twenty or thirty sorts it became ratty and required a lot of patience to find the matching crinkles. One staple of wool out of place would mean lower marks.

Through this time Terry's hours had not agreed with Suzanne and Damian. The arrangement was okay for a few months but he was a bit tired of the buses home from the city. When Suzanne and Damian decided they were to marry he felt even more in the way. Things were changing pretty rapidly. When they contacted Stephen about the wedding they were told a week later that he could not attend because Edna had suddenly decided to marry Stephen in Melbourne on the same day.

Terry again met up with Larry this afternoon as he stood at his paper stand. He explained that his wages were just enough to pay his board and bus fares to college.

"Hey, when you finish here tonight, come in to work and I'll introduce you to the copy desk supervisor at the Tele."

Larry knew his apprenticeship was looming and the job would soon become available. He briefed him on the job and added an easy way to bring him a little more money; he knew Terry needed everything he could get: "Tell him you are 18. That way you get six bucks a week more in the pay packet."

Terry went along, and to his surprise, got the job, organizing a 4pm start the following Monday. Perfect, he could continue College and make the Tele in plenty of time to start work each day.

There were set tasks from day to day rostered by the copy desk supervisors, Harvey Levi and ex sergeant-major, Clarence Gray. Old Harvey was their favourite as he would allot bus money for errands around the city which they could pocket by doing the task on foot. The GPO was just three blocks down the road, the TAB a brisk jaunt over the Ultimo bridge. They had taxi vouchers for the rush jobs and they'd use them if the streets were clear. In fact it didn't take long at all to come to the realization of how important every job was in the newspaper.

After the first two hours they got a tea break, which they spent in the canteen. Larry showed Terry the ropes on what to order and they sat looking down on Park Street.

"What happened with your old man then?" Larry asked.

"Love-struck mate. Silly bastard; I don't know why he followed her. He had a good job here, but it looks as though he's found an opportunity there too. Edna's cousin has employed them to look after his chicken farm."

"Chicken farm, what, eggs and stuff?"

"No. Meat chickens; he's got about forty thousand of them in two big sheds."

"How's your sister and her boyfriend, Damian?"

"Oh God mate, he's more strict than dad and he's got all these fucking cats. They breed them; Burmese cats; an exotic sort of breed. They sell them. They're a nice cat though." He looked a girl up and down as he continued. "Damian reckons they were bred as guard cats. Soldiers would have a cat of their own and when they went into battle they'd toss the cat at the enemy and while he was trying to fight it off they'd run them through with a sword."

"Shit ay?"

"Yeah, he's got one that scares the shit out of me sometimes by waiting on top of the door. When you walk through she jumps down on you. She's a cool cat though; Savia."

Larry looked up at the clock: "Come on, let's get back to work."

"What shits me most is that I have to do the Cinderella act, all the time. I have to be home by midnight, even on Friday and Saturday nights."

"Okay Cinders, age before beauty into this lift."

Within a few weeks of his new job, Terry was finding things even tougher at home. Suzanne and Damian were up him about his late hours, which he now couldn't help. He had broken the curfew on a number of occasions in circumstances beyond his control. Marty and the guys liked to stay out late on Saturdays to check out the action at a local burger joint, Beefies. Sometimes they would head out to Homebush where rev-heads from across the district would have impromptu drag races.

He had to work to pay his board and often he'd be on the last bus home from the Tele. Larry came up with the answer: "You can share my room. There's a spare bed there. We spend most of our weekends together anyway."

"But, what about your mum?"

"She's okay Terry. Anyway she likes you. Come on, she's home now, let's go and ask her."

After a discussion with Mrs. Taylor he broke the news to Suzanne, who was quietly relieved at the solution.

The little window from the attic bedroom was their porthole to Sydney in the sixties. On their nights off work they would often wait for his mother to go to bed downstairs and then sneak out of the window and walk around the streets for hours. Larry's father managed a block of flats only two blocks away where they would go and have a cuppa and a yarn and watch the world go by. Two prostitutes did ten and twenty dollar tricks in small rooms downstairs while a couple more worked from nearby houses. From the first-floor window they could see the deals being done with otherwise ordinary men taking their consorts for varying lengths of time. One of Mr. Taylor's girls would come up for breaks and was forever talking about greyhounds she was racing. Terry was surprised to see that she was also an ordinary person and wondered why she was on the game. During one visit he gained enough courage to ask.

"Money," she answered, instilling an eerie silence in them. "I hope to have enough dough to get out of it before I'm twenty-five; it's just my means of getting what I want in my real life," she told them. The insight made them realize that many of the girls on the game were just as normal.

"Some girls," she told them, "are runaways from home who took to the streets to make money for drugs. That's a different scene altogether. I'm not into that stuff and I pity the ones who are. They're heading nowhere fast," she told them.

On work nights they simply did not have the time to take any nocturnal journeys. Their shifts went until 11pm most of the time which gave them little opportunity to do anything else. The copy desk was a place where many friendships were made and from where, many scenes were set for their dislike of individuals in the newspaper game. Some columnists, they considered, to be "up themselves". On the other hand, some of the young lady cadet journalists and secretaries were a constant target for their infatuation and vivid imaginations.

"That Sherene McCauley does something to me guys; I think it's her smell, her perfume, her presence....."

"Careful she doesn't get a whiff of you Terry, I can smell your B.O. from here," Tony Cahill, or T.C. as they had dubbed him, a surfer kid from the North Shore, was being funny.

"That's bloody wool grease mate; I've been sorting wool all day."

"Well I reckon you'd better have a shower before work if you want to impress that one. Anyway, I think she likes me," he joked pointing his thumb to himself.

"What? A seaweed? Fat chance mate."

"That's enough youse blokes," Harvey chimed in, "Now, who's going over to the TAB?" Terry stood up: "I'll go."

Newspapers, in the late sixties, were still done in hot metal and the methods of getting words from a typewriter to the "stone" were laborious to say the least. When assigned to a desk for the night a copy boy's task was to ensure the OUT basket was cleared quick smart. The Chief Of Staff would be assigning journalists and cadets their tasks through the day but at night the place seemed to buzz with excitement as the deadline drew closer and each page was put to bed.

The tele-printer room chugged away with wire copy from other capital cities and overseas, and the copy boys on duty would read many a front page lead before it even got to Mr. Bayers, the revered and feared Cables Sub. Copy boys would be shown such important tasks as loading the machines with paper and how to free the mechanism if there was a paper jam. Terry could soon change a roll of paper while the machine was still printing without missing a take. Once the machines were charged with paper, he would tear off the "takes" of a story and piece them together for presentation to Bayers.

Bayers' rules were simple. Keep the coffee in the cup and copy in the in basket; an old-school workaholic, he became irritable when either was empty. He had a plastic coffee cup that was blackened inside by years of addiction to caffeine and heaven help any boy who failed to keep his cup topped up. Of course, few boys doing the job for the first time were ever warned of his antics. They were chucked in the deep end.

One boy was so riled one evening at being rudely ordered about by Bayers, that he took the mug out to the toilet and pissed in it before making an extra strong coffee and delivering it to Bayers.

He couldn't help himself and had to go to the copy desk to tell the others. For the next half-hour the others on duty had to take a number of strolls to the tele-printer room just to watch him actually drink it.

"Mate, I swear I saw his nose and top lip roll up after he took a big swig," said Larry who didn't like Bayers either.

"Fair dinkum; he doesn't like it but still has to drink it. What a man," Terry added.

They all laughed.

Doing sub-editors' duty meant a late finish, usually about 11pm. Subsequently that roster was exchanged fairly regularly, unless of course, someone mucked up. They would do penance there for a whole week. Subs, to copy boys, were "sub-humans or sub-normals".

The copy boys' job was to ensure the "out" basket was cleared of copy which the subs had marked for size of type and column width and instructions to the typesetters, downstairs, using cumbersome machines that actually set the type in hot metal (lead) supplied from little molten vats beside them. Terry always thought their job looked dangerous. To correct any copy there were people who could read the metal type stacked upside down and back to front.

Copy boys had to roll the copy into little a tight wad and place it into a capsule which was then placed in a tube which would be sucked unceremoniously down to the compositors' room.

Later in the shift the capsules would start flying back up with galley proofs for the subs to check once again.

The subs took great delight in taking the boys away from the crossword with the scream of "boy", as they required the copy to be sent away. This practice of shouts of "boy" annoyed Terry.

In fact, the blokes in this arena would most certainly cotton on to any idiosyncrasy of a copy boy in very quick time and grind him down; little tricks, like waiting until he had just cleared three baskets and chuted the copy. They would wait until the lad had taken his seat and read the first two words of the next crossword clue and: "BOY", there would be another one. They could have a lad on his feet for five hours straight during particularly vindictive times.

This evening Terry was tired. As soon as he arrived to arrange his capsules and paper on the desk he noticed a few of the subs conspiring a night of torture. It didn't take long before it started, "BOY", BOY", "BOY". After about an hour Terry was so pissed off he stood up as bold as brass and approached the table: "Listen you guys, I have introduced myself before; my name is Terry and I am eighteen years old. I consider myself more than just a boy in that I am supporting myself and putting myself through College and I would appreciate it if you could all address me by my name. If you don't, you can shove your bits of paper down the chute yourselves."

That said, he sat down and continued his crossword. One cheeky bastard persisted with the "BOY" routine, so Terry left his copy in the basket and waited until the Chief Sub spoke up: "Excuse me Terry, could you possibly deposit copy from Mr Wimple's full basket, I think he's learned his lesson."

By the time he had done so, the delay he suffered meant that "Mr Wimpshit", as Terry called him to the others later, would have to stick around much later that evening to get his own galley proofs back.

The bold move did influence a number of the subs. In fact, during later shifts on the subs' desk Terry was actually introduced to any new members of the circular table. As a result he showed a greater sense of urgency in the job when treated as part of the team. The senior staff even shared their jokes with him. He nearly always offered one in return and expected a laugh.

Terry enjoyed being rostered in the sports department, especially the racing room. The people there seemed to enjoy their work and as a result appeared to be the friendliest part of the entire newspaper.

Six months into the College year and working at the paper from four until ten or eleven should have been enough, but Terry was about to add another duty into his itinerary, because of his association with the racing men.

Chapter 13

Terry found a new freedom in the form of a motor-bike, a Suzuki T20. The machine was only small, but it was cheap to buy and cheap to run. It allowed him to get around a lot easier than using public transport.

On most mornings he would get up early, just to be able to ride around without the hassle of heavy traffic. This morning he was heading for the beach and, when passing Randwick race-course, decided to call in and watch the horses in their training gallops. He parked the bike away from the track and walked down to a rail near the turn out of the straight. He was wondering how anyone would know which horse was what when he recognized a familiar hat. It was Artie Davis or Clancy as he was known, Clancy the Clocker, one of the guys who visited the racing room at work. Terry admired how he instilled an air of peace and happiness during his visits. He was always jovial and helpful and inspired comic retorts and the latest dirty joke from just about everyone.

"Hey young fella, what are you doing down here?"

"Oh, I just like to watch them; aren't they beautiful."

"Some of them are son, just some of them. Most of them will cost you a packet. They're just sporting animals, equine athletes, being trained to do what they're bred for; to race." Terry was keen to get away, but Artie had other ideas: "Hey, while you're here, you may be able to give me some help, we're a bit short-handed this morning."

"Yeah, sure, I'd love to, but I have to be at Tech by nine."

"Plenty of time mate, plenty of time. Look, if you do all right we can pay you a couple of dollars a day if you like. What's your name again, I forget."

"Terry, Terry Martin."

The mention of money and Terry was suddenly more interested and walked along with Artie when the track was clear. Having just bought the bike he was on the lookout for any paid work.

"Well, what do you say?" Artie motioned to him: "Quickly across here. Horses come down this straight full pelt." They walked hurriedly and Artie asked again: "Well come on, what do yer reckon?"

"Yeah sure, why not? That sounds pretty good to me."

They crossed the tracks into a small stewards' cage in the centre beyond the winning post. Here Terry was equipped with two stop-watches.

"When I say reset, you depress the tops of both watches, like this," he said resetting the watches to zero. "When I say left on, click on the left watch; when I say right on, click the right one. I'll give you a moments warning to switch off and when I do, you read the seconds from the watch, including the tenths, the tenths are very important, you hear."

"Yep," Terry said, looking at the watches.

Artie was businesslike: "Give me the left time first; that one is the full gallop, then the sectional time second, that's usually for the last two or three furlongs. That's going to differ from horse to horse depending on how their gallop is going. Do you think you can handle that?"

"Well, I can only try."

Terry gave it a try out a couple of times as Artie timed as well, to get used to the mechanics of the task and showed Artie the clock to check one of his calls.

"Yeah, that looks okay. Excuse me a minute, here comes boss; I'll get an order and a list going, you just keep practicing there for a few moments." Terry was excited but soon found himself feeling a little pressured as the first line of horses to be timed headed out.

Artie barked orders: "Left on..... right on", at the finishing post he called "stop", and Terry read the times which were logged onto Artie's sheets. He did well. So well in fact that Artie offered $10 if he could help out two mornings a week. Terry jumped at the offer and after a couple of weeks was getting used to the regular early mornings.

This frosty April morning reminded him of Melbourne, in the dark at 4 am trying to start his Suzuki. He was warming up with each kick at the bike, but cursed the two-stroke mixture which seemed to hate cold starts. Eventually he pushed the bloody thing along trying to clutch start it, cursing under his breath as he went. Finally the thing started and he shattered the silence of the neighborhood as he revved away. Randwick was a half-hour's ride in traffic but he could get there in less than 20 minutes at this hour. He arrived to see the track work under way. After parking his bike well away from the horses he walked towards the track. He watched a pair pass on the inside track and looked and listened for hoof beats before crossing hurriedly through the fog. Inside the box he was immediately into work.

"Left on; right on, stop. Time left, time right."

They must have done about 70 horses in the first hour and a half. There certainly wasn't much time for him to pay any attention to the new face in the shed talking to Artie.

"Time left?"

"Fifty-three."

"Time right?"

"Twenty-six," Terry was tired and felt he was on auto pilot.

"Reset."

He double-clicked both hands and waited, looking around at the dozen horses and jockeys wandering around just outside the box.

"Harry's mob have to go first but you can send him up to the six while they're coming." Terry knew they were talking about furlong posts.

"Thanks Clancy, be back in a minute," the new face chimed in.

"Wait till you see this bloke, Terry, he's got a big one coming up this week, but have a look at him."

Terry watched the trainer walk deliberately over to the big brown colt which looked jet black in the early morning light. He passed on instructions to the senior rider holding the horse by the bit while patting his nostrils. The animal glistened in the early morning light; he looked a treat.

"See that shiny coat," Clancy said, "that shows he's healthy; and that high hind quarter, he'd get some spring from that height." They both looked at the horse. He seemed bigger than the average two-year-old.

"He's big too, eh Artie?"

"Yep, bred to perfection, he was on the ground in early August, so his birthday is pretty true to all the others."

"What do you mean?"

"All racehorses have their birthday on the first of August, even if they were born in mid-July of the same year. They're a year older, on paper, on the first of August."

Terry watched the trainer talking to the jockey. He could see the rider leaning forward, nodding as the instructions were received.

His attention was drawn back to the task at hand as Clancy chimed in: "Looks great, doesn't he? Where are those animals?" He peered through his binoculars. "Ah, here they come. OK Terry, reset."

The trainer, who still had not been introduced to Terry, returned to the box accompanied by four others who appeared to have an interest in the gallop. Terry only noticed them after he was knocked aside by one guy trying to find space in the cubicle.

Harry's four worked as planned and he commented to Clancy that the chestnut should give them a good go on Saturday, but all eyes were now on the youngster approaching the six-furlong starting peg.

"Reset, Terry."

"Okay".

"Ready, he's got a good hold of him... not yet; Ready.... Go!"

Terry rarely watched the horses. He couldn't see that far without binoculars and he liked to keep a tab on the sectional times. For this gallop he heard more than his watches clicking as Clancy gave the 'go'.

The horse was striding out nicely but did not appear to be doing anything special until the trainer hit his watch and chimed in: "First in 24. Righto George, get a grip on him, get a grip on him. Gee the little bugger must be fired up. I knew he needed a hit out."

Artie chimed in: "Ready Terry... right, go."

Terry liked to split his own times on the spot too and offered the horse had done 49 for the first two. He looked up now and noticed the horse respond almost on cue to the trainer's quip as he turned into the straight: "Let him go, Georgie; Christ, let him go."

The sheen of the horse could be seen as he appeared to slip down a cog and scoot along despite being held under a fairly tight rein. The post loomed.

"Ready . . . stop,"

Terry's thumbs clicked in unison but he was looking up taking in the graceful stride of this one who seemed to glide along, the jockey not keen to put the brakes on too soon, happy rather, to allow the horse to stride out around the next section of track.

"Time left?"

"1.11," he looked into his right hand and stalled a moment but spoke before Clancy's prompt, "wow, last furlong in 22.2."

"Good gallop Freddy, I got 22.6 that last bit." Clancy was impressed.

"Yeah, he's comin' on good all right. My time was closer to the young fellers though. Hey, can you keep this one out of the paper, we'll be lucky to get any price about him anyway."

"Yeah, sure Fred, but don't go knockin' off the price until I get my fiver on him."

"It's a deal. But you'd better get on before we do; we're going to ignore it completely until they're in the gates. It'll shake a few bucks from the bookies I reckon."

Terry was again pre-occupied with the last few gallops of the day and, although very aware of the conversation going on, he heard enough to know it was a "spesh".

The men were now outside the box. When the last galloper came around he gave the times to Artie, excused himself, and headed for the little cafe in the Cross where he breakfasted on cappuccino and vanilla slice before heading to College and another day of sorting out bins of greasy wool.

Wednesday was a beautiful day. He had slept in until 8am, a luxury. At tech they learned to pull down a set of wool shears to sharpen, a great diversion from sorting one of those bins again.

Later in the day he was thinking about yesterday's gallop as he headed for work. He had told one bloke at the College that the next best run of the morning had been two full seconds outside the flashy colt.

That afternoon he pushed open the glass doors and yelled for the lift. The door opened up again where a smiling surfer Tony stood. He was a chubby kid, with straight blonde, shoulder-length, hair. He was from the North Shore and nearly always boasted of carrying his last two weeks' wages in his pocket.

"G'day Terry."

"T.C., just the man I wanted to see. There's a race meeting at Randwick tomorrow and I've got a spesh." He was talking fast. "Tone, can you lend me 10 bucks mate? I'll pay you back on pay day! Promise!"

"Naaah, not for a bet. I can't loan you money for a bet." Tony was taken aback when Terry cornered him in the lift which had now stopped at the first floor.

"Come on Tony," Terry had not noticed the man enter the lift and Tony held his hands fast in his pockets, gripping his money.

Terry started tickling: "It's a special mate, I saw the gallop, it will win by five lengths. Come on Tony, I know you're ticklish and I'm going to tickle you until you do. Come on mate, it's just 10 bucks until pay day. And you should put whatever you've got on him too."

Tony couldn't stand anymore and lifted his hands from his pockets trying to press his elbows down as hard as possible to stop Terry's protruding fingers.

"Okay, okay, here you are, take it, just stop tickling," he was laughing so much he was embarrassed by the other man in the lift.

"Oh thank you mate; look I'll put some on for you if you'd like; how much you got? Put it all on."

"I got about 50 on me but I don't know, I don't think I want to have a bet, I don't...."

The lift stopped at the third floor and Terry turned around almost bumping into the tall man who shared the lift. His dark pin-striped suit and classy felt hat made him look even taller.

As the door opened the huge frame stopped, turned a little and looked straight at Terry: "Young man, I would like to see you in my office in 10 minutes."

"Yes, sir."

Terry and T.C. looked at one another as the tall man left and turned right towards the executive suites. "Who is that?" Terry whispered.

"Dunno, let's ask Harvey."

The copy desk supervisor was quick to respond: "Him? Oh; he's the boss."

"What?"

"Yeah, he owns the place."

"Oh cripes T.C., I think he's going to sack me for harassing you in the lift. He must have seen it all."

"What's that?" Harvey was interested about what went on.

"Well, I sort of tickled T.C. to get him to loan me some money to put on a horse that will be racing tomorrow. Christ, he saw me tickling T.C. to get him to give me the dough. I'd better go and face the music. Which office is it Harvey?"

"Go down the way he went, turn left and the first door on the right. Say 'hello' to Val for me will you."

"Okay." Terry turned to walk away and stopped turning back at Harvey: "Who's Val?"

"She's the boss's secretary. Say g'day to her for me."

"Righto, I will." Terry's heart raced as he moved down the hallway. The walls seemed to close in because of the bad lighting. He turned left in the dark and headed for the first on the right and quietly tapped on the door.

A woman's voice echoed a pleasant "Come in." He turned the handle and entered.

"Hello, you must be the young man from the copy desk."

"Um, yes, I'm Terry Martin, ma'am."

Val looked at the telephone on her desk: "Mr. Parker is just on a call and shouldn't be very long."

Terry looked around the reception office which reminded him of a 50's American movie. Everything was so orderly.

"Um, Harvey, I mean Mr. Levi, said to say hello too; I almost forgot."

"Oh that's nice, give him my regards in return," she was distracted by a light on the telephone.

"Well, he's off the line now and will be ready to see you shortly. One moment please." Val touched a lever at the base of the intercom: "Mr. Parker, I have a young man, Mr. Terry Martin, here to see you."

A deep, but equally pleasant sounding voice responded: "Oh, very good Val, show him in please."

Val walked to a door and opened it for Terry to enter.

"Take a seat, young man." Parker motioned toward a red leather chair in front of his desk.

"Thank you, sir." Terry felt he had to explain what went on. "Look, I am terribly sorry about that incident in the lift. T.C. is a friend and I wouldn't ......"

"Think nothing of it. I got you in here to, well..." He stalled for a moment, leaning back in his chair. "You know I have an interest in horse racing myself."

Terry nodded, finally starting to relax a little.

"I own a number of horses and one of them is entered in a race tomorrow and I thought I may have something on him. You have been helping Artie out of late I hear!" The big man lurched back in a leather chair and started to light a cigar.

"Yes, at the track. Randwick; two mornings a week."

"He's in race seven that's about the same race as your horse is in isn't it."

"Mmmm, yes sir. Number five, race seven."

"Five aye, I thought so. Well-bred that colt!"

"Sure is."

"What makes you think he'll beat Rover Scotia? He's won three on end; easily."

"Well he's a good horse, he fired the track up yesterday. I don't know if the times made it in," Terry suddenly thought about Artie's deal with the trainer and wondered if he wasn't inadvertently giving Artie up. "Er, because there were a couple of horses who came together at the end of his run."

"What did he do?"

"1.11, and came home two ticks over 22."

"And you obviously think he will win that race?"

   "Well, it was as good a gallop as I have seen there yet sir."

Fred Parker leaned forward on his desk and made a mark on a ticket, before placing it in an envelope which he sealed.

"I would like you to take this envelope down to the TAB for me when you go to put your bet on. Give the lady this envelope and then give her this one in which to seal the ticket and bring it back and leave it with Val, would you?"

"Yes, sir." Terry was still wondering if he had lost his job or not. "Is that all sir?"

"Yes, thank you Mr Martin, er, Terry. You'd better get going then."

Terry took both envelopes and strode out elated that he still had his job. He went straight past the copy desk where he told Harvey: "I just have to run an errand for the boss Harvey. Val sends her love."

"Hoy, Terry. You still with us then, ay?"

Terry was pressing the down button on the lift: "You betcha Harvey, you betcha."

"Hey, Terry, come back here a minute." He pulled a blue note from his pocket. "Put this on for me too will you?"

The colt did not give any of the others a look-in. He jumped in front from barrier 12 and stayed at least a length clear for most of the journey and then cleared away to win by three lengths without being challenged.

On course they bet as good as five to one, but he started at threes after late money arrived. Terry picked up his winnings the following day and noticed someone must have knocked the price off on the TAB as it paid only $25 for his $10 investment.

He was happy to collect despite the disappointment but did not realize that Parker may have backed the colt heavily.

The following Monday he entered the copy desk and Harvey feigned a sad face:

"Terry, I've got bad news for you, you don't work in here any-more."

Terry's face dropped but rose just as soon as he saw the smile beam onto Harvey's face. "There's good news too, you now have a permanent job in sports. Go in and see the Sports Editor, he's waiting to see you."

Gervaise Porter, the Sports Editor, wore a white shirt and grey trousers. His tie always hung on a rack behind his desk, and to this day Terry had never seen it around his neck.

"Terry, I hear you've been helping Artie at the track on a couple of mornings; how would you like a permanent job in the racing room? The pay is a bit better than what you've been getting, and the guys reckon you should fit in pretty well, having an interest and all."

"Why, thank you so much. I'd love to, but I am attending a wool classing course and...."

"Well it's basically a day shift job for most of the week. Have a think about it and let me know tomorrow."

Harvey suggested he take the offer. "You never know where it may lead, son. And it will be doing what you like to do."

Terry decided he would speak to the principal of the College first; just to see if he could delay finishing his studies. After all, he had almost done a year of study which he didn't want to waste.

The principal was a straight shooter and was happy for Terry: "Look mate, I don't know if you have read the news recently, but the arse has fallen out of the wool industry. I reckon your new job offer is a very opportune time for you to get into something really promising. The way the wool industry is going, I don't even know if we will be here for very long. You can always finish your studies at a later date. That is, if the wool industry picks up again. Take your chances with this job Terry and run with it."

Within a week Terry started his new job in the turf room. The form cards provided all of the background information the journalists required to make their selections and to write stories about coming events and create the potted form for the racing guide.

Terry settled in well and enjoyed the days he had to attend the races to keep the cards up to date. Food and drinks were laid on by the race clubs. This was a career he could get used to. He felt privileged to be a part of the team, doing something he really liked and being paid for it.

Chapter 14

Terry reveled in the work and within five months had even made some extra money to take a holiday back to Melbourne to see Stephen.

The chicken farm consisted of three huge sheds each containing 20,000 birds. Stephen put Terry through the routine of changing into special boots which never left the shed. "It helps prevent any diseases which may be in the soil on the outside from getting in here."

There was a sea of birds that spread to each corner of the shed. A ride-on mower, minus the blades, was used as a tractor to pull a small trailer loaded up with feeding pellets. They drove slowly down the rows from one feeder to another, filling them as they went, scattering the birds as they moved slowly along. They had to be careful not to panic them or they may all rush to one end of the shed where a great deal of their number could be smothered.

Terry was amazed that the sheds were all artificially lit; a fine sawdust covered the floor to soak up the droppings and would be sold for fertilizer at the end of the shed. Stephen explained the chickens would be taken away when they reached 12 weeks old. Trucks would load them up and take them away for slaughter, allowing a front-end loader to scoop up the fertilizer before spreading more saw dust in readiness for the next batch.

Stephen was happy with the work which was a little quicker and easier while Terry helped. It took only two hours to load the feeders and check the water drippers which the chickens soon learned to drink from. The feeders hung about an inch from the ground but were gradually raised as the birds grew bigger.

Edna told the story of the foxes that visited the sheds regularly, trying to get in. Since returning to Melbourne she had lived on the farm and saw it as an ideal opportunity for Stephen to get ahead.

'So this was the carrot she had dangled in front of him to entice Stephen from Sydney,' Terry thought.

They were married with a simple ceremony at the Registry Office, enough to satisfy her that they were no longer "living in sin"; she'd had trouble with that for the preceding five years.

"Why did you have to get married on the same day as Suzanne and Damian though? That was a low trick to pull," said Terry directly.

"Well, I looked at it as a way to kill two birds with one stone," Edna replied. "We had just moved here and we couldn't afford to take a trip back to Sydney. Not just for a wedding. We could have our own wedding here."

Terry could accept that his father needed love, but with what had transpired between these two he still questioned his motives to marry Edna, who still had a serious drinking problem. She had always presented overweight and was the first to put Stephen down, especially when they'd been drinking. The evening turned into another debate about Terry's future. Edna had a real bee in her bonnet about what he should be doing with the rest of his life. Terry resented her for it, even though she may have had some good ideas about his vocation.

"I think I can decide what I do with my life, not you," he told her, although he realized that she was patronizing him and anything he might say wouldn't get through anyway. He stormed out as he had done on many previous occasions with Edna, but he could hear them arguing late into the night.

His weekend was cut short as a result. He had only come down to see his father and sister, and was not going to get into any serious debating with Edna, especially when she was on the turps again. There was no point in antagonizing her.

Next morning it was like so many before. She had forgotten the nasty things she had said the night before and acted like she had never said things; as though it may have been someone else passing on her vehemence.

Terry didn't mind as he was returning to Sydney. He couldn't wait to get out of there.

Over the next few months he phoned Stephen at least twice a week. Sometimes he'd be over at the sheds, feeding chickens, when he rang and Edna would take the call. He knew he would have to call back to speak to Stephen when that happened. He just knew she would not pass on any messages. It was her way. He could tell she was drinking through the days now as well as into the evenings. He knew from the sound of her voice and the belligerent attitude she would adopt. He had seen and heard it all before.

On this evening, four months after his visit, he found Stephen at home. He sounded quite sober as he told Terry they would soon be moving again.

"Edna doesn't like the chicken farm any more. She's got a job in town so we'll be moving to Kew next week."

Terry felt for his father. He knew he liked the country lifestyle, even managing a few chicken sheds was better than anything closer to town.

"So what will you do now?" he inquired.

"I'll be driving trucks again; just local deliveries around Melbourne." Stephen seemed happy with the move. "We'll manage somehow, mate."

When he'd hung up Terry felt a lump in his stomach, a hollow feeling, he had felt before as he had attempted to understand why Stephen persisted with Edna.

Ken Raybuck, his immediate boss in the racing room, could see he had been upset from the call, but did not realize until he took him for "dinner" at the hotel downstairs just how much Terry really missed his dad.

Terry, although he was still just 17, maintained the shouts with the crew. By the time they returned to the office he had told Raybuck he should go to Melbourne. "My father needs me... I think."

Raybuck was understanding and made a few calls on Terry's behalf. As Terry arrived back from the races the following afternoon, Raybuck told him he had arranged an interview for him for a cadetship on the Melbourne News.

"It'll give you a chance to get a real career path going, Terry. You are good at what you do and I've passed my thoughts on to the Racing Editor down there. He reckons he needs someone who's keen to help them out down there. It will give you a chance to be with your family again too."

Chapter 15

The Melbourne News occupied an entire block downtown, opposite the Railways. Terry had a brief meeting with the Turf editor, Trevor Kiley, and was set to start on Thursday, the traditional day for acceptances for the following Saturday's races and subsequent form day for the Turf Room.

One of his first duties was to peruse the form cards, which were kept on all horses racing around the state. These were similar to the cards he had filled in at the Sydney paper. It was acceptance day for the Saturday meeting which meant a drive to the Racing Centre where all the metropolitan racing clubs were headquartered.

Terry was enthralled by the process and amazed to see that the acceptances had been made on race book style sheets, all printed up. He was introduced to the people he would be dealing with in coming weeks and years - clerks looking after acceptances and the race club officials, including stewards.

Back at the office the form cards were out, final scratchings were removed and the team separated the races among themselves to do the potted form for the racing guide. The cards were a great idea in that the holder could see every race the horse had ever competed in and very handy information when you are looking for a winner. The cards contained sectional times which had been run, distances from the winner, first three placegetters and the margins from first past the post to last. It contained all of the information the writers required to create their stories. Terry was at the cutting edge of the information, gathering it. It passed through the intellectual factory to enhance the product by informing readers through the Green Guide, a most respected racing form guide. Terry liked it already.

At six o'clock the team adjourned to the local hotel to feast on dim sims and go a round of beer. Terry felt light-headed after the fifth shout despite the fact the beers were just 7oz glasses here. The remainder of the evening went remarkably quick. They knew they had initiated the lad, he'd settle in well.

The tram ride was breezy from the centre of the tram where smokers could indulge. The trip home to Kew this evening, did not seem to take long at all.

As Terry walked up the stairs Stephen opened the door to greet him: "How did it go, mate?"

"Oh, good Dad, I think I'm going to like it." Terry was tired, but excited by the prospect of his new job and related the day's events to Stephen.

"Well I'm proud of you mate. Just give it your best. You never know where it might lead."

"Tomorrow it will take me down to a race meeting at Sale." They laughed.

"Well that's a start."

"Where's Edna? No one was home when I dropped my stuff in this morning."

"She's already in bed. I just waited up to see you." Stephen gave Terry a big hug. "Cripes mate, I haven't been able to help you much, but here you are, doing it by yourself." He poured the tea as Terry now listened to catch up with some of their news.

Lisa was doing well at the local high school, Edna had a well-paid job and Stephen was working the waste-paper run for Barry. He had restricted his drinking to just weekends now.

"How could you broach the subject with Uncle Barry, Dad? All of those things you and Edna said about Mum over the years. I thought you would never want to see them again."

"Well it's not really like that anymore Terry. Barry was always good to you kids."

"What, by taking our mother away?"

"No, not that; I mean he helped us out a lot more than you know. After I got out of the can that time, he got me back into work, helped us out with money and food.

"Look mate, I don't hold any grudges. It was me who broke up your mother and me. When I got pissed there I would have blackouts, time spaces I couldn't account for. I didn't know what I was doing when I was pissed and I was half-pissed most of the time."

"Well you should have been more responsible, Dad."

"What's done is done and can't be undone."

"Okay," he held his hands up. "It is good that you can all speak to one another like real human beings. Is that possible with Edna?"

"She's coming around slowly. She took on a lot you know..." He paused for a moment before finishing. "...bringing up four kids. Anyway it's not like we're all buddy-buddy and visiting there every bloody day. At least it's work and he pays well enough; and I can bring the truck home. It saves a lot in juice and its better than travelling out to Mooroolbark every day."

Terry was pleased there had been communication. He didn't ask any more questions. It was already after midnight and he had an early start the following day.

He was up to get the first tram into town to pick up the car. As he collected the Kingswood the attendant informed him he could have taken the car overnight.

"Thanks mate, I will next time. Say, anything I should know about these cars?"

"Nah, not really, except the radio there can tune to the cops' channel and on channel 15 you can stay in touch with the radio room upstairs."

Terry looked at the radio and turned it on, then turned the volume down. Within minutes of getting clear of the building he turned it off in order to concentrate on his exit route from town.

The drive to Sale took him a little over two and a half hours. He found he could relax a bit once he had cleared the city and was able to look at the countryside. Taking in the scenery he decided he may like to live in the country someday.

At the course he found his way to the secretary's office where he collected his tickets for the Members'-stand and became acquainted with the press box. It contained two small tables and about five chairs. It felt like, and was, as he soon found out, a hiding space under the stairs of the grandstand. He could hear the constant movement on the stairs every time he sat down and decided he'd be better off doing the results back in the office later that evening.

Over lunch Terry chatted with the race callers who spoke of colleagues in Sydney from where he had come. Terry knew some of the people they spoke about and could contribute to the tales that circulated the table. As they spoke a number of trainers came up to say hello to the callers, which prompted Terry's introduction.

This made it easier for him later in the day as he broached at least two of these who led in winners, for comments to make up a story on the day. The race day went rather quickly. The drive home seemed to take forever. He had gone over the story in his head at least a hundred times by the time he got back to the office and it simply flowed onto paper through the typewriter.

He used the self-taught method of typing, like so many others, where two fingers zoomed around the keyboard in the search-and-peck method. Despite this he still managed about 30 words per minute; not bad at this hour.

The results were next and he was careful to maintain the style he had been shown. Price, horse name, weight, jockey, barrier position, placing. The run-on went through to the last horse, the margin from the previous horse, and finally, the time for the event.

The following day he picked up the paper in anticipation of seeing his story across the back page. There was nothing. He found half the story buried further inside the paper. That was something anyway.

Terry was happy to volunteer for the country events. He liked the atmosphere better than the metropolitan meetings. There was a friendlier air about the day and the people, on the whole, were more relaxed.

The stories he wrote were more from anecdotes he'd gained before the races even started as he walked through the holding stalls. He would stop and talk with the strappers and trainers and pick up the unusual yarns, like the horses that needed the company of the trainer's son's shetland pony to travel to the track. He learned of the bush training methods, such as running in the cows with the horse, the inside stories on the horses bred out of an unknown, but favourite, stock horse mare. They were there, all around him. The stories soon found him. Eventually his stories were getting a run more frequently and were far more prominent. He could write to the space allotted by a sub-editor as soon as he got back and many times he would be the last one to file his copy.

He was soon getting pretty good tips on horses to follow simply by listening to the bush talk and watching them run in the country. He followed the progress of many an animal which was headed for the city. At times he was a little overwhelmed with the friendly repartee of the country folk but he learned to enjoy the honesty of these people and the trust they shared with him. In fact, he became part of their day out too; part of their preparations of horses bound for bigger and better things in town. Even with his, so far, limited experience, he could tell a good run when he saw it, but he was still too naive to believe any may be 'pulled'.

Within a few months Terry had been to most of the country race tracks in his home state of Victoria and all of the metropolitan tracks. The talk in the office was always about the up-and-coming horses, events and the matching of one to another.

On Thursdays when compiling the potted form the others were often asking Terry about the runs of horses on the country tracks as they typed out their races. He would give an honest opinion if he remembered the run. This, of course, did not always mean the horse would live up to those expectations, but the questions still seemed to come. He reckoned that if the times were right you could use a good run in the bush, even against moderate horses, as a good indicator for a city run. He mostly referred them to the times the horses had run, rather than to the opposition they had met - a habit he gained from helping Artie at Randwick.

As a result he often tipped a horse which may have put in a good run in the country a few starts back to find it had an early market price of 33/1 or more. More often than not they would get up, or at least run into a place at good odds for him.

The bulk of the work would be done before they went out for tea at 6pm. Most of the talk on this night was about the fancied horses for Saturday. The news-room journos would ask for tips as they related their most interesting story of the day.

Things were read and re-read on their return before tips were finalized and desks were pushed aside for the carpet bowls. Even at a dollar a game, the guys in the sports department were severe hustlers. They couldn't help themselves. They'd bet on anything - the name of a sire or dam, football games, whether Bob Skilton would win the Brownlow, the number of tips they'd get up on Saturday, anything.

After work on pay nights they would go for a drink down town or a game of cards at the home of a colleague. The latter was dangerous territory on pay day for Terry. Stud poker was the game and on a number of occasions was the bane of Terry's week.

The fun of the job seemed to continue well outside it and most of the guys were good enough for a *loner* if anyone had done their arse on cards.

Ironically, Terry only seemed to do his arse on cards when he had found a nice "smoky" for the weekend. He would end up at the races with just his train ticket home and watch a horse he had seen steam home from last on the turn at Ballarat, come out and beat something that all of the so-called experts had favoured and written about. Many times, when he had the money to spare, he gladly took the 20/1 about them and witnessed them saluting the judge.

He felt he may have helped some poor battler out there who had put his hard-earned cash onto a horse through the lines he had written. As weeks went by, he saw the dangers of writing off a horse which recently may have had a number of apparently bad runs. They may have missed its history of good runs at that track and distance last preparation. There was a lot to absorb and he was soaking it up like a sponge.

He rarely saw Stephen and Edna because of the hours he worked, even when he attended the country races he was rarely home before 9pm and on most other days when he started work at 2pm it would be midnight before he arrived home.

This Friday night he arrived home to see more cars than normal parked in the street. He could hear the Irish music from inside and stalled for a moment before placing his key in the door. As he entered he tried to scoot past the entrance to the lounge room to the left, but Edna spotted him and yelled out: "Terry, come in here."

He put his head through the door with the intention of saying a quick 'hello' when he came eye to eye with one of the most beautiful young women he had ever seen in his life. Edna started the introductions throughout the room and Terry was forced to break his gaze away from the girl as the names rolled off Edna's tongue. He shook hands with six people before Sally came around. The gathering was family; Edna's family. Sally, her niece, was very shy and Terry turned his attention to her elder brother Barry so as not to embarrass her.

The party went on for a couple of hours before Terry turned in. He made a date with Barry to go along with him and a few mates to the tavern where a rock and roll band played on Thursday nights. Sally would sometimes go along too. They were hard drinking, hard rocking nights with some of the cream of Melbourne's rock groups playing.

Terry struck out early with Sally and ended up focusing his attention on some of her friends, but again struck out, usually because he had too much to drink before gaining the courage to even ask them for a dance.

On most of these nights the venue was packed to a point where the dance floor would be filled with people dancing with others on their shoulders singing 'Oo-poop-pa-doo'. Lucky for Terry he was allotted a few Fridays off. The Thursday night sessions often ended up at Mordialloc at 5am from where they would hire a boat and go fishing in the bay.

Terry caught a tram into the office throughout the winter months. This Sunday night a bitterly cold wind, direct from the Antarctic, whistled down Spencer Street as he headed for the tram stop. As he wheeled around the corner he saw the tram taking off. Under normal circumstances he would have run after it in the hope of catching up at the first set of lights, however, his attention was distracted by the girl just ahead also disappointed by the sight of the tram clanging its way down Collins Street.

"Were you supposed to get that one too?"

She was a little reluctant to answer at first: "Mmmmm, oh yes, that was my tram. I don't think there are any more either."

"Look we may be able to walk to the other terminus and get the North Balwyn tram. Come on, I'll show you where we can get it."

He discovered Michelle had been in Melbourne for about the same time as he, this time around. She came from a farm in the Riverina where her family grew oranges.

They found the last tram to North Balwyn at the terminus and during the journey, realized they only lived about five blocks from one another. Terry alighted from the tram at her stop and offered to walk her home, but she declined, offering instead her telephone number.

A week later Michelle accepted his invitation to dinner and they kicked on at the local hotel and danced away the evening. She was 18 years old. He lied, telling her he was a year older instead of younger.

It was their fourth outing before she invited him in and they clumsily made love. He inquired about contraception and she told him she used the rhythm method. In his ignorance he thought this meant there was something special in the way she moved during the course of the act.

The relationship was blossoming and after three months of seeing Michelle two or three times per week she dropped the bombshell: "Terry, I think I'm pregnant!"

"How do you know?"

"I'm late, that's how I know!"

"Oh! How late are you?"

"Three weeks."

"Well, what are you going to do?"

"What are you going to do, don't you mean?"

Terry pondered for a moment. "But didn't you say you were on the pill."

"No, it's against my religion," Michelle was getting annoyed.

"Well, what about an abortion?"

There was silence.

"Why don't we just get married?"

Terry was quiet; stony silence filled the room for more than a minute as he stared at the end of the bed.

"I can't, I just can't. I'm too young to marry you anyway, I am only 17."

"Well, what about this abortion?" Michelle suddenly blurted out. "They are illegal you know!"

"I know someone who recently had to arrange one. I'll talk to him and let you know."

He left without even kissing her goodbye. When he rang the next day she was crying. He had inquired through an associate at work who had "got a girl into trouble" only months before. The doctor had a general practice but did the operations after hours. The cost would be $500 up front. No receipts, no questions asked.

"Look Michelle, I have found a doctor, a real doctor who does these operations. Do you still want to do it?"

"No Terry, I want to get married. An abortion is killing a child. I can't do it, I just can't. It's against my religion."

Terry's mind was consumed by the predicament. "Shit, you should have known when it was safe and when it was not."

"What would you care? You wanted to do it every time we were together. Well stuff you, I wouldn't want to marry you anyway, you bastard."

"I can still organize something with the doctor if you wish."

"Fine then, do it!" she hung up.

Terry scoured the form to find one bet in order to get some extra money. He found what he thought to be two "good things" he had seen over the past month and plonked $50 on the first at 5/1. The other horse came up short in the early market; it was odds on. He waited until the last few horses were going into the barrier and saw a bookmaker turn it up to 5/4. He raced in and put his money on. The mare was very lucky to win after leading into the straight. She was headed with a furlong to go but managed to plug on and take the lead again just a few strides from the post.

Michelle didn't say a word when he called to pick her up. He explained that the money had already been paid and she should simply go to the front door at10pm.

Michelle held back the tears as she alighted from the car. He waited for more than an hour before she came out. They were half-way home before she told him that she couldn't go through with it. Her hour in there had been a counselling session. The following day he found the money he had paid was "not refundable".

Michelle's flat mate, Noeline, arrived home with her boyfriend Craig as Terry and Michelle were talking about the situation.

"Why don't you just marry her, Terry? You got her pregnant!" Noeline attacked as soon as she saw Terry.

"Mind your own business, Noeline; piss off and let us work this out together." Terry exploded.

Craig immediately struck out and landed a punch to Terry's face. He was more upset at the situation than hurt by the punch as Craig swung him around and pushed him out through the gate.

"You can just piss off, mate, and I never want to hear you speak to Noeline like that again." Terry backed off as Craig's 6ft 2in frame loomed over him again.

He did not contact Michelle for over a week. He absorbed himself in his work and when Stephen finally asked him what was troubling him, he told the story.

Stephen showed some understanding for both of them, as if he didn't have troubles of his own at present.

"Do you love her, Terry?"

"Yes I do, and no, not really. I'm not sure I know what love is yet. I like her though and I don't want to just leave her. I just don't know what to do. I'm pretty sure I'm too young to be getting married just yet though. Anyway, all we've done since she got pregnant is argue. I don't know if I could handle a relationship like that. I feel it's over already. Maybe it's just starting. I don't know."

Stephen suggested he ask Michelle again about having an abortion. "Maybe she has had other thoughts on it since you last saw her."

Terry was surprised Michelle was conducive to the idea.

Stephen and Edna were fighting more often than not. Now it was about Terry's predicament. The array of boarders they brought into the house just gave them both people to back their side in one of their many arguments. Bronwyn was 23 and worked in an office in the city. She settled in well, but got caught in the middle of an argument between Edna and Stephen. She had a solution for Edna: "Let's just leave, find another place. This is nowhere," she said.

Edna took her advice and this Friday evening when Stephen came home with a carton of bottles under his arm, he opened the door and the house was bare. Stephen took it in his stride and had a drink. He had consumed more than half of the bottles when Terry came home.

"What the bloody hell's happened, Dad?"

"She's left Terry. She left a note to say that she and Bronwyn have found a place together for the time being."

"Where is Lisa?"

"She's gone to stay with your mother for a while. Until..."

"So what's next?"

"I suppose we should go and find something more affordable."

The next day Stephen found another house with some furniture provided and they moved in immediately. With Lisa away and Terry working most nights, Stephen would sit at home by himself and drink. He wasn't very good company at present. He was lucky to keep his job too. Barry had smelled grog on him on a few mornings and frowned.

This Sunday morning he walked up the street to see Stephen out with the buffing pad on the angle grinder, about to do the truck.

"Gee, are you home late or early?" Stephen joked.

"Yeah, I'm just getting home. I had a good day yesterday and we kicked on to the trots and then into the nightclubs last night. I woke up on Kevin's lounge this morning. His bloody dog had slept on me all night and my suit smells like the bludger. I've got to get changed."

"Yeah, I think you better. You are on the bugle a bit; I can smell you from here."

Stephen switched on the grinding disk over which he had secured a soft buffing cloth. As the machine whirred into action he swung his arms sideways to clear the cord. As he did a piece of the buffer grabbed the lead and swished it around the shaft. Stephen was suddenly hopping around the ground at the front of the truck. He was making a "ya ya ya ya ya" noise as he hopped and Terry moved closer to see what was up.

"Are you OK?"

Stephen backed away as he approached and Terry realized his hands were open and the machine appeared to be stuck to him. Stephen wheeled around and bashed the machine on the fence to break the grasp the machine had on his open hands.

"Shhhhhhhhit." Terry went to turn off the machine and was stopped by Stephen. "No, no. It's alive. Elec... elect ...electricity." He was puffing so much he could hardly speak. When he turned his hands up, Terry could see the burns across his palms.

"The bloody thing stuck to me. I couldn't let go of it." Stephen's eyes were bulging.

"Crikey, are you OK? I'll get an ambulance or something."

"No, Terry. I'm alright. My heart's just beating twenty to the dozen that's all. I'll be right in a minute I think."

Terry took him inside, turning the switch off at the power point as he went.

Stephen was sobered by the experience and gladly accepted Terry's offer of a coffee instead of a beer. He was shaking for almost a week, but refused to get medical attention. Terry was worried about him.

A few days later, Terry walked in through the front door. He could smell something burning and headed straight for the kitchen where he thought Stephen may have left something on the stove. A quick check of the kitchen eliminated this possibility. He walked back into the lounge room and noticed smoke rising from the chair. He looked over the back of the chair to see Stephen asleep. His half-empty beer was skewed in one hand and his cigarette in the other. The tip of the cigarette had fallen onto his tie which was smouldering away; holes were forming in his shirt as embers began to fall. Terry grabbed the glass from his hand and threw it over him. Stephen bounced to his feet, hands clenched to fists.

"Whoa, whoa." Terry backed off. "It's just me."

"Oh shit. What'd you do that for?"

"You were on fire."

"Shit, was I?" Stephen looked down and saw his tie had burned right through.

"Have a look at your tie," Terry was still concerned.

Stephen looked down and saw his singlet was still smoking a little. He beat it out with his hand.

"Lucky I came home when I did. Crikey, you could have burnt the bloody house down, and my new suit was in the wardrobe there too."

Terry had to go out again this night. "I need the car Dad. I have to take Michelle to the clinic." He had been saving his money and again, paid up front. This time he went into the surgery with her. Michelle stayed only a few minutes and rushed out the door past Terry before he knew what was going on. The doctor came out and explained that she had not even wanted to get up on the table for an inspection. When Terry asked about a refund the doctor turned and walked away. "You know there is no chance of that."

Outside, Michelle was sitting in the car. "Just take me home Terry, and don't say anything. Don't put me through this again. I am not going to do it. I won't. I am going to have this baby and have it adopted out. That's it!"

A cold wind whistled through Caulfield racecourse on this Saturday. Terry had gained an extra ticket for Stephen but was not prepared for him to go there in such a state.

"Come on, I'm all right to drive," he'd said half an hour before. One smell of him and Terry was trying to get him to hand the keys over. Stephen was obstinate. He refused to be driven.

"I can drive. I can get us there on time. You watch."

The journey was frightening. Stephen was overtaking a dozen cars at a time down the centre of the road, over the tramlines. One driver took offence to Stephen passing him down Glenferrie Road and decided to try to overtake back. Stephen pushed him outside at least two safety zones. The pair raced wildly along until lights halted their progress. The other driver, a new Australian, was irate. He got out of his car and leaned threateningly in at Stephen: "What sort way is that to drive mister?"

"What about you, yer clown," Stephen responded. Terry just rolled his eyes skyward.

"You try to kill me you bastard," the other driver reached for the door handle. Stephen was quick. He flung the door open jabbing the rim of the door striking the man in the head, producing an inch long gash to his forehead. Within seconds he was out of the vehicle, slapped the man two or three times and turned him around to swift kick him back towards his car.

Stephen calmly slid back behind the steering wheel and took off gently running with the traffic: "Who does he think he is, talking to me like that?"

"I reckon you're lucky it wasn't a cop." Terry knew his father could handle himself. "I hope you can calm down for the races Dad. I am just not used to this kind of excitement so early in the day." He looked at his wristwatch. "What, it's only eleven fifty. You're pissed as a fart and you've had your first knuckle for the day. What else could this day bring?"

"He was the one who was attacking me, Terry. I was just defending myself."

"Yeah, but you were driving like a bloody idiot. You were risking our lives, and his, and anyone else who just happened to be driving by."

An icy wind whistled through the bookies' ring at Caulfield. Terry was automatically checking the prices as they walked through to the press box. He hadn't time to do his customary stroll through the stalls this day. The day had taken on its own complexion and it appeared it was not going to get any better. If he backed them for a win, they'd run second. If he took 'em each way, they run bloody fourth. The one winner he did get up he took on the tote when it was showing 4/1 while the bookies were betting 3's. Its tote odds had shortened to 7/4 by the time they jumped.

By the sixth race Stephen had hit the bar several times and was starting to abuse a few jockeys as they returned to the saddling enclosure. He was loud and raucous: "Here's Handbrake Harry. How yer goin' Handbrake? It's working today son. And there's Pullemup Paul. Almost got away on yer there Croakey."

Terry was glad to see the end of the day. He was embarrassed by Stephen and ushered him out of the way. He was a worry to him, and sometimes, like this day, he was a real worry, but he would always bounce back like a pixie from the garden.

Terry decided he should drive home and refused to get in the car until Stephen handed over the keys. Stephen took about two minutes to fall asleep in the passenger seat and Terry didn't even try to move him once they got home.

Next morning he had bacon and eggs prepared for Terry.

Stephen thought Terry was making up a story about yesterday's events.

"I truly don't remember, Terry. I started drinking on Wednesday night and most of everything since then has been a bit of a blur."

"You mean you can't remember *anything?*"

"No. I woke up in the car this mornin' thinkin' 'what the fuck am I doing here?'"

"Dad, I think you drink too much. You've got a problem with it," Terry was ready to let him know what he thought. He was tired of Stephen's chameleon lifestyle. If he was with Irish people, he'd be Irish, with Italians he'd speaka da way they speaka to 'im.

He was lonely now, and there was little Terry could do but let him have the facts. Terry knew Stephen could go straight.

"I think I will really need some help though Terry."

"What about AA?"

"I have to try something Terry. I don't even remember going to the races with you."

Stephen embarked on a life of sobriety interrupted only by another encounter with his Karma. This night he had found out Edna's new address. When they would not let him in, he tried to scale the back fence. They met him with a brick to the head at the top of the fence. He was desolate, lonely. His friend, the drink, would help him through it. And he'd use him as often as needed. These times he was often in need.

Terry could not handle the cold he got from visiting Michelle. Things were over with them. She was frosty towards him. She especially did not want to hear about his father's problem.

"I don't want to hear about it Terry. I have enough of my own problems to think about," she told him in no uncertain terms.

Terry desperately wanted to help her. He knew of a family who wanted a Nanny to look after their children. It was a live-in, well paid, position. Michelle could maintain an income until the baby arrived. He helped her get the job and dropped her at the front door.

Michelle looked across at him before getting out of the car. She had a feeling she would not see him again.

"Do you want me to come in with you?"

"No. I'll be right." She looked at him. "I guess this is it then!"

Terry also knew he may never see her again.

The following day a trip to Healesville trots allowed Terry to make a diversion to see his grandmother at Happy Hollow near Healesville.

She was smaller than he had remembered, but as tough as old boots. Pushing seventy-years-old, she had her own beliefs and was set solidly in her ways.

"We had to go through the Depression, Terry. That was between the wars. It was a hard time for me, it was a hard time for everyone."

Terry seized the opportunity: "He has never come to terms with you putting him in a home Nan, that's part of his problem, the reason he drinks. Why did you put him into that home?"

"He had been naughty; wagging school and running around the neighborhood. I never really knew where he was or what he was doing.

"When the money went missing from the clock, well, that was the final straw. Ten bob Terry. Ten bob was a lot of money in those days. We were on bread and dripping. Ten bob going missing was a lot; especially for us."

"But you had him put in a boy's home. A pretty drastic move for the sake of ten bob Nanna," Terry was accusing.

His grandmother's voice became stern: "I wished I had the money in those days to look after them all, but I just didn't Terry.

"I wanted him to get an education. He had the opportunity there to improve in his studies and he just rebelled against it."

Terry thought about the visit as he drove to the course. The day at the trots proved to be exciting. He was brewing the story through his head on the way back to the office.

A photo finish brought a dead heat decision from the judge therefore halving the results for punters on both winning horses. Terry felt the photo showed how certain one of the horses had won. Its nostrils were totally obscured by the line drawn across the picture. The other horse in the photo had its nose just touching the line. Terry was certain the long shot had won the race. His sub-editor disagreed. Tired at the end of the day he expected the editor would take his word for it. He had a print of the finish. However, the sub was not keen on Terry's angle of punters being *ripped off*.

"You just can't say that. Not in this newspaper. The Tote is a government run organization. The judge will certainly sue the paper, then the race club and anyone else. I am going to straighten this up and I'll show it to you to read over," the sub-editor was doing his best to be polite.

"I thought we were supposed to report the truth," Terry spat.

The sub-editor approached Terry three more times over the evening. He was now losing his patience. Terry wouldn't budge. His mind was reeling with Stephen's problems, Michelle, his grandmother. He could not concentrate for another moment:

"Look, I've written you the story that was there and you want to turn it around into a nice little story about the trots. To me it should not be a nice little story about the trots. It should be the bloody truth. People lost money because of that decision."

The final sheet of paper in his typewriter contained his resignation.

Within a week he left for Sydney. He found a small bed sitting room in the inner suburb of Petersham. He found work with a wire agency for a few months before changing to a better paying job with *The Shipping News*. The shipping industry was being revolutionized with the advent of containerization and Terry soon found himself reporting on the industrial and financial aspects of the changes. It was refreshingly different to just doing races.

The publisher, Max Norton, also had a Sunday paper in Melbourne and jumped at the opportunity to use Terry to do results and reports from Saturday race meetings.

Chapter 16

Roy Pankhurst looked like a character straight off a movie screen. His thick dark hair was slicked back with brilliantine. His suits were tailored from expensive cloth. Humphrey Bogart would have been proud of the look.

Terry, was doing the Arbitration Courts and presenting his copy to Pankhurst, the new sub-editor with *The Shipping News.*

Over a wine tasting luncheon Terry learned Pankhurst had come from up north in the state, a country town where he had worked his way up to sports editor. He also had an interest in racing. By the time the luncheon was out they had arranged for Roy to assist Terry with the Saturday races. The extra money they got for the work would be their punting bank.

Roy had sons around Terry's age and he liked the boy. Terry was enthralled with Pankhurst's stories at the bar about the country. They started doing the races together and it was not long before Pankhurst introduced him to some of the city's illegal gambling clubs.

To their amazement, the news came this day, from their own state premier, that the clubs they had been frequenting "did not exist".

"They don't exist in Goulbourn Street, Forbes Street, Rozelle, Bondi, you bloody name it," Roy joked as he walked up the stairs of the Bombers Ice Hockey Club.

"Hey Roy, I used to play for the Bombers."

"What? There really is a Bombers Ice Hockey Club?"

"Yeah. . . Well, I got to train with the guys a few times anyway."

As they neared the top Roy took over again. "Shhh, keep it down. Just don't talk too loud in here, okay?"

They reached the top of the stairs to be greeted by two very large, suited, men hovering under a dim light.

"Good evening, Roy," one of the men said, opening the door.

"Hi Ross, oh this is a friend of mine, Terry, from the paper. He's okay."

"I am sure he is if he is with you Roy, you may go inside gentlemen. Enjoy your evening."

They entered the room to find a bar down the far side. The atmosphere was quiet, relaxed. People over the roulette table spoke in whispers. A croupier was urging: "Place your bets please."

Roy headed for a blank space at the end of the roulette table and sat down. Terry followed noticing the blackjack tables, six in all, but only two were working. He took a position next to Roy and handed over his $20 which Roy soon had converted into chips.

"I'll show you a system that will keep you going in a place like this. But you've got to stick with it. You can do your dough pretty quickly trying to play the numbers."

The croupier was waiting for the ball she had spun to land, and audibly whispered out the number and color. It was a red.

"Now that was a red we are going to bet one unit on it being black, okay."

"Okay," Terry was taking it all in. They missed on the first spin and doubled the unit on the next and they got a black.

"Okay, now we are up one unit, we change now to a red."

The system was slow and tedious but it gave Terry the time to watch others at the table. There were few playing single chips, like themselves.

The majority were plonking hundreds of dollars around the board with each spin. What appeared to be small fortunes flowed around the table for many hours. Some gamblers played numbers, quadrants of the wheel, which Terry would learn about later.

Their stack of chips fluctuated but soon fell into a rhythm on the upswing. Roy sipped on his scotch and kept control of the chips.

After two hours and just two wins to go before making their projected stake there was a run of black which had the potential of wiping out the bank they had painstakingly built up. Roy stopped after their eight unit bet went down.

"That's three against us. I reckon we should hold for six spins," Roy seemed experienced at such things. Terry just went along with him.

As fate would have it the next six spins were also black. They most certainly would have been wiped out.

Roy chimed in: "Let's put it all on the red now. What do you say Terry?"

"Put it on Roy, put it on."

Lady luck was with them and it came in red.

They enjoyed a cappuccino and sandwich as they split their earnings. Roy placed it down in front of Terry. There you go, one hundred and twenty for you and one hundred and twenty for me.

Terry was keeping track of the colours since they stopped. There had been five blacks, a red, and then six blacks straight, now seven.

"It can go against you Roy, that was seven blacks. That's 64 two dollar chips, to try and make one two dollar unit. We could have blown the lot, easily." Terry had worked it out all right.

"There are variations to a system sometimes. But you've got to look at that last big bet we had."

"Yes. Phew was I glad we got that one up, otherwise we would have done our arse."

"Well, look at it in the right light. We would have done $20 each. Not done our arses. Now we have extra to hit the bookies with on Saturday."

Terry did the rounds of a few clubs with Roy and soon found he could enter most with ease, with or without Roy. He risked his $20 to win $100 at least once a week from then on. The hardest night took about seven hours for him to get home, but he stayed with it. He changed the routine from Roy's continuous doubling to miss a couple of spins after three misses. Most nights it worked for him. Occasionally he would have another bet at higher odds and fluke it. As he played he saw a plethora of characters playing the tables. The display of wealth of many punters was obvious through rings sparkling across two hands with some single stones that would surely cut the blackened plate glass behind the velvet curtains. The men were dripping with gold.

He witnessed the punters arriving at the table with their own chips. The value of these had been determined by the boss, who on these occasions, sat in a tennis umpire's chair hovering above the table. The female croupiers, dressed in evening gowns, often felt the pressure during such a session. The boss would look at the quadrants and see if there were any similarities in the landings. The punters would play these quadrants, plonking extra chips on one or two of the numbers therein. If the croupier kept them there all the time the house was chicken feed.

The boss was quick to respond. A change in croupier would put a completely different spin on the game, literally. The punters would have to adjust, and the house will make money while they do. Terry found his even-money colour changes did not fluctuate all that much. A change of croupier's touch rarely went against him playing the even-money system, but it could have a drastic effect on the bigger punters who religiously marked down every number as the ball fell.

This day, after leaving the casino in the wee hours he awoke lying on the bed in his room. A noise outside on the stairs stirred him. Through the haze of his hang-over he rolled his legs over the side of the bed to sit up. He looked toward the door. The envelope was not sealed. The note inside read:

"Dear Terry, I had been looking forward to seeing you. Our baby girl was born in Melbourne three weeks ago. I had some help through the church and they had me sign some papers so that the baby could be adopted out to a home where people would love her. I wanted to knock at the door but I could not do it. You don't have to worry about anything, I put on the papers, 'father unknown', Michelle."

Tears rolled down Terry's cheeks. Suddenly he thought she may have just been there. Was she the one who made the noise on the stairs outside? He quickly pulled on his shoes and strode down the two flights of stairs. He raced around the corner to the station where he scoured the platform from up at the ticket box. She was not there. He decided not to buy a ticket to get down on the platform and turned away as a train entered the station. Michelle came out of the central waiting room and boarded the train. She looked up and did not recognize Terry walking away. She had her own life to live. She didn't like this place.

"Bloody hell, George," Terry said, "if I hadn't been in a bloody bed sitting room in a boarding house, maybe I would have seen her. I'm going to see the agent about that house down the road a bit."

"Yeah, the boys need a bit of space to play around. That one room and kitchenette business is too small for you."

Terry moved the following weekend. The house had four bedrooms and was roughly furnished. The first night party echoed a warning to the neighbours. He got his first complaint and assured the neighbour over the back that he would get his guests to keep it down. The parties just became more frequent. Pink Floyd, Sunbury Live, The Beatles and the Rolling Stones blared out at peak decibels.

At work Terry had been on the beat with a tip-off through a shipping company. There had always been pilfering on the wharves but with the advent of containerization the handling of goods had been shifted out into the suburbs, away from the wharf areas. Instead of a few items here and there the stakes were now higher. Whole container loads of colour television sets, whisky and tobacco products were going off.

Terry had checked out the first contact at the early opener at Wooloomooloo. Sure, it was happening, but it was not the old guard any more: "They've given them all redundancy packages. There's an organized ring here, and it's bloody big time now. I reckon you should leave well enough alone. Don't tell me those in the know don't know what's going on," said the wharfie, Arnie Poulsen, who didn't really want to divulge too much.

"Who do you mean by *those in the know*?"

"I mean the coppers. Those bastards are getting back at us for the low kickbacks we gave them when we got caught with something'."

Terry pursued the story developing a list from companies who had containers go missing. As the list grew, so did his concern. He was three weeks into his investigation when he got the call from the Metropolitan Harbour Police.

"I think you should come down and talk to me before you go doing any story about the wharves," Sergeant Riley suggested.

Terry agreed to an interview; at 6.30pm that evening.

The sergeant was a big man and hunched himself over the desk as he spoke: "I hear you've been asking questions around the place about things getting knocked off from the waterfront."

Terry shifted in his chair: "I was looking at doing a story about the extent of the pilfering, but I've hit a few dead ends."

"Well, what have you got for me?" Sgt. Riley demanded.

"I thought you may have some information for me, sir." Terry stood firm, although he could feel his stomach turning over.

"About what? Just what do you think I should be fucking-well telling you?"

Terry moved in his chair at the sergeant's tone. "As you probably know from your own informant, I have a list of goods which have disappeared from wharves and warehouses all over the city. How are your investigations going on these cases?"

"Well son," Riley was now patronizing, "the ones that have been reported to us are the ones on my beat. And there haven't been that many."

"What, not many? Six containers in the past month, isn't it? Is that really 'not that many' to you?"

Sgt. Riley's face reddened; his voice grew louder, more threatening in tone: "Listen son, I know how many containers and we have a good idea of who may be in on it too. And we're bloody-well workin' on it. We don't need your paper now scaring the culprits away by knowing where *we* are at with our investigation."

"Can we expect any arrests in the near future?" Terry was pushing it.

"Look son," Terry didn't like the condescending manner of Riley now. "If I were you I would keep your bloody nose out of the whole bloody thing. You know that we know where you live. And if we do, so may, *they*, the people involved in these, er, instances. At the stakes you're looking at there," Riley pointed to Terry's list, "who's to say there may not be a bombing, or something like that, early one morning."

"Are you trying to tell me?" Terry was scared.

"You have just been told, I think. Keep the fuck out of it. Do I need to make it any clearer?" Riley had made his point by sticking a firm forefinger about two inches away from Terry's nose. Terry could feel himself starting to shake. The adrenaline was pumping.

He took the hint: "Well thank you for your cooperation sergeant." He stood up and retreated as quickly as he could. He turned off the tape recorder concealed in his pocket only when he reached the safety of his car.

This incident, he thought, made the whole story and he had it on tape. He decided to run all the details he had so far and hinge it around this final episode. There were gaps and he could hardly quote Sgt. Riley under the circumstances. So he wrote it without him. He used "a spokesman". Editorial manager, Cal Wiley, was not keen on it at all. The story just said it was going on and quoted the number of containers, three or four a week, in Sydney alone.

"We're not bloody crime fighters, we're a bloody newspaper. If you point the finger at someone like this story does, you'll have it bitten off. Go and do some nice stories."

"No way," said Terry, frustrated. He felt he had covered all the bases. "If you're not interested in that story, you can't be much of a news-man."

"It's not the story that would concern me. It's the bloody legal bills." Wiley was serious and knew all about lawsuits in this publishing house. There were threats every other week of legal action, especially when the boss, Max Norton was writing the editorials. "We just can't do it, and that's that!"

Terry went back to his desk and took a few deep breaths. He rolled a clean sheet of paper into the typewriter and typed out his resignation, but decided to put it in the drawer for the time being.

"Give it time Terry," Roy said, turning to the barman in the Menzies. "Scotch and water. Make that two thanks, Ted, and make it Black Label thanks."

Roy settled him down with a few realities. "You know that guy we saw in the club the other night?"

Terry looked at him blankly.

"You know the one, the big punter, the one with his own chips."

"Yeah, I saw him. He had about an hour taking up the whole end of the table."

"Yes, that guy. And the knock on the door at about four o'clock in the morning when they gave us all coffee and asked us to sit around the covered blackjack tables."

"Yeah, I remember that," Terry took a good swig of his whisky.

"They were coppers, Terry. They were all coppers, getting their pay-offs. Don't mess with them and they won't mess with you."

Chapter 17

Terry had had a hard night and Saturday came around too quickly. It was 10 o'clock by the time he surfaced feeling pretty shitty, hung over. The alcohol had left a dry taste in his mouth. It didn't mix well with the saliva he now produced to overcome it. The bathroom was down a short stairwell that he negotiated with two tentative steps and he was soon rattling his toothbrush out of the glass. The smell of the toothpaste overwhelmed him and he stalled for a moment, gasping, before gingerly inserting the brush into his mouth.

He dropped the brush while trying to get it back into the glass perched in the shelves that doubled for a bathroom cabinet. The water was cold, refreshing. Its effect was miraculous and Terry pulled handfuls of it over his hair and face, straightening after he did to see himself in the mirror. He looked closer, peering into the mirror at his own eyes; he was getting focused enough to see they were slightly bloodshot when he realized he was on duty at Warwick Farm today.

It took half an hour to get into his suit and force down a couple of slices of toast and a cup of tea before heading for the station.

He looked through the form on the way to the course and reckoned there were four or five good things in this meeting. He lifted his eyes a few times to study the people on the train. They were the battlers, the pawns in the sport of kings. 'Half of them,' he thought, 'would have a bank of about $10 to play with.' His mind wandered as he looked around the carriage. That guy over there had better win or he'll go home and thump his missus, he thought. Then he focused on the old lady talking of her favourite jockey to the friend she was making next to her.

"Oh, he is lovely. I like the way his hair flows out under his cap. I follow him all the time." Terry pulled his form guide back up and smiled out of the side of his face. If they only knew the guy was a mate with a few underworld figures. Not publicly, but Terry had seen Riley Quayle at a few of the casinos and noticed the preferential treatment he got there. He'd have to do a few favours here and there. He didn't get the nickname, *Maggots* for nothing.

Mug punters, he thought. Few would know anything about what went on behind the scenes. The battery-powered jiggers, the drugs the threats that flew around to trainers and jockeys from some of the big punters.

It had all dawned on Terry that the business was going on all over the city, from the wharves to the police, to the racing industry.

There were set-ups, which the general public just didn't know about, scams to make money for only those in the know. His mind wandered in rhythm with the sound of the train. He wanted to tell them, but stayed quiet as the reality embraced him. He shouldn't have kicked on with the boys last night. He felt terrible, fragile.

The train pulled into the platform at the track and punters hurried off. Most of them in a hurry to get to the betting ring but a few headed for the stalls to get an early look at the horses. Terry always took a stroll around the stables at Warwick Farm and this day noticed just a few shrewd, expensively hatted punters and the old ladies heading for the stalls still jabbering away with excitement.

For Terry it was a ritual. Like a trip to the track in the early morning, he could see the animals which were fired up with excitement, those relaxed, but alert and the ones who looked as if they didn't really want the day out. He noticed shiny coats, the interested, pointed ears and inquisitive heads lifted high. Strappers and trainers were wiping noses with towels or fiddling with bridles while the farrier strained with another hoof, preparing racing plates.

Terry could see the grey horse, ears pricked, head cocked, looking at him from half a dozen stalls away. He stopped in front as the horse nodded and stood still, head slightly askew. Terry thought further about the likelihood of anyone slipping a sugar cube to an animal like this. The soft lips would nuzzle a hand affectionately as any bastard slipped it a mickey. He patted the nose and felt the horse gently lean into his chest: "Hello boy, aren't you beautiful." He rubbed the horse's cheek feeling it lean into him until he realized its hair was getting stuck to his suit. He stepped back, noting the stall number. On the way to the press box he flicked through his race book and found the event the horse was in and added him to his selections for the day. He already had a selection in that race but thought this might be a good saver, in race seven. See how he's going by then.

Terry had been doing the race results and stories for Max Norton since he started at *The Shipping News*. His extra pay for the day usually gave him a good bank to play with, but things were very tight this week. He arrived on course with just a $20 note and a few smaller bills and realized he would have to conserve if he was to make it past race seven.

He did the races as much for the excitement and his love of the animals as he did for the money, but felt it very hard to be on course and not have a bit of a flutter himself. Years of writing up the form and he knew fairly well, how to assess a horse's ability, but he was still learning about the maze of activity going on behind the scenes.

He exchanged greetings with the usual crew as he walked into the small pressroom and found it incredibly crowded for a Warwick Farm meeting. It was carnival time and there were scribes from all other capital cities; a time when racing writers around the country converged on Sydney.

He went through his routine of politely asking his colleagues from the other papers which phones he may use but was told that the phones would be on a premium this day.

When he finally got one, he rang Melbourne reverse charges to advise that he would have to do the results and any stories in two or three small hits this day. The haggling that he went through just to get a phone to do that task set a precedent for the day's events. By the time he got off the line the horses for race one were out of the mounting yard and on the way to the barrier. All the experts in the press box had their stories of how good this or that looked and what a special the other may be. Terry had already made his selection on the train, but usually liked to give them the once-over before investing his hard-earned on the conveyance. For this race he missed out but trusted his form reading judgment to have his little plonk on the nose at 3/1. By the time he had placed his bet he heard they were racing.

By the time he ran up the stairs to the grandstand, they were into the straight. Quayle had his charge three lengths ahead of the field and was riding quietly. Looking good, Terry was thinking.

Lindsay Moir, a colleague from the *Daily Telegram*, yelled to Terry to call the run-on past the post and momentarily distracted him from the race. As Terry looked back at the horses they were about 200 metres from home and his steed was cruising. Then Quayle started jiggling his hands up and down. The process obviously affected the horse's performance and a group started to swamp him. "Leave him alone, Quayle," Terry spoke aloud. The more Quayle threw his hands about the more the horse fought his actions and with two strides to go, he lifted his hands bringing the horse's head up in the air just enough to allow one from the pack to put his head down and greet the judge ahead of him.

The crowd was erupting in the stand with people congratulating and commiserating. The press guys finished the run-on with Terry's help and they were on the move again, back to the room. Lunch was on the table and a few took something to nibble as they headed for the phones. Terry didn't have a chance to get a phone and filled out his race book awaiting his chance.

"Did you see that bloody Quayle murder that thing Lindsay? He should have won by five bloody lengths."

"Yeah, mark him in your book for Randwick. He was dead as a dodo here," Lindsay was deadpan.

"Dunno about being dead, the bastard was three lengths clear into the straight. All the bastard had to do was sit on him and the horse was home. It's got me stuffed how they get away with it."

"Well that was that race, and there are hundreds more going on all around the country today; aren't you lucky you only have to get the results for this one?"

"Yeah, I suppose; what do you fancy in the next?"

Lindsay flicked through his race book; the brown pin-striped double-breasted suit hiding his extra weight. "Not much really, although I think the five has got some show after her run at Canterbury a couple of weeks back."

Terry, interrupted now by the course announcer introducing the horses on the way out of the saddling paddock for race two, shot down to get his bet on. This time he was in the stand as they were moving into the barrier. Lindsay commented that it was bedlam in the press room with all the visitors in town and shared a joke with the guys before they were off in the next race. Terry commented that his horse was another Quayle mount and relaxed as his horse settled third in the pack, right up on the pace. About 600 metres from home, he watched Quayle check the mount severely after it appeared to move up towards the two going head and head in the lead. The check cost the horse a couple of lengths and, despite an impressive finishing burst, Quayle only managed to get the horse home into second place, half a length from the winner.

Terry spewed out the saddlecloth numbers as the rest of the horses passed the post and made a run for the phone booths in the press box. There were none free as the writers who missed this race were filing stories through. Lindsay told him he'd only get a couple of shots this day. He would have to make other arrangements. Terry pencilled in the margins and times for this race and waited around again, taking the opportunity to get into the ring early to see if there was any trend to the betting. His selection again had Quayle up. "Fucking Maggots", he thought aloud in front of Lindsay.

"What's he on this time?" Lindsay flicked to his next page.

Terry held his finger on the selection. "He's just gone down twice, so surely he must be hungry for a win here."

He filled in the riders in his book for the remainder of the races and noticed that Quayle was on four of the five horses he had selected. Two were already down; he had missed lunch and he couldn't get near a phone for love or money. He would give Quayle another try only because he seemed to be on the best horse and at 6/1 he would go each way, the worst he thought he could do would be money and a half back for a place.

He thumped the door to the press box as he burst through to find a phone free. He quickly rang Melbourne to tell them he had Buckley's chance of getting them through and was told to ring the city office where the boss would be working this afternoon.

Four months ago when Max Norton got back from the United States, he promised Terry he would get his own phones on at every course, but to date nothing had been done. Terry felt rushed again as he rang the office and heard over the PA system the horses were heading for the barrier stalls. Norton suggested he try again as the afternoon wore on. "If you have any problems, I'll wait in the office so you can come back and get them on the tele-printer later."

Terry hung up and raced up to the stand as the horses were going into the barrier stalls. 'Maggots' lived up to his name again and managed to stall his mount in the barrier when the gates opened. He came out five lengths behind the rest and despite the efforts of the horse only managed fifth place.

Terry was on him again in a later race and got a second at 4/1.

"Money back, big deal."

Race seven came around too quickly and by this time the pressures of the room were encircling Terry. Quayle was on his first selection again, this one a 12/1 shot. The grey was also in and was showing 25/1. Terry didn't want to risk his money on Quayle again and so had his last four dollars each way on the grey. The horse kicked out well and raced keenly to the home turn where he put on a brilliant burst of speed and kicked two lengths clear and looked home. That is, until Quayle's mount moved up under vigorous riding, with not the slightest jerking to the reins, and cruised past the grey to win by a length running away.

"Fuck me dead," Terry yelled over the din, momentarily forgetting he was in the Members' stand. He was so disgusted that he turned his eyes away from the track and forgot to call the run-on. As a result the others were all calling numbers which were all over the shop and were pissed off at Terry for his error. At last they all agreed on a run-on, but this could well have been a long way from the actual finishing order of the event, except for the first five placings which were emblazoned on the TAB semaphore across the track.

Terry shuffled, defeated, into the press room and saw a free phone and quickly dialed Norton in the office. "Mr. Norton, you can stick the races in your arse." He was immediately interrupted by another scribe, his former boss from Melbourne, who wanted to call Melbourne: "Excuse me Terry I've got to get this through."

At the other end of the line Norton was trying to calm Terry down: "Just come into the office after the last race." Terry hung up in disgust.

The last race seemed to take forever to come around and Terry decided not to have a wager or else he may not have the train fare to get back into the city.

He arrived at Wynyard about 6.30. Norton raised his huge frame from his chair to pour a drink as he arrived. "Had a hard day at the office, mate? Settle down a while, have a drink before you start telexing it through." He was amused by young Terry's description of his day at the races.

"Why do you call Quayle 'Maggots' though?"

"Because he's on so many dead'uns". Norton erupted with laughter and poured another Black Label. This young reporter was a man after his own heart. Norton was impressed that Terry wasn't intimidated by him at all, like so many others. The cheeky little bastard swore freely in his presence and this day went off when the subject of the on-course phones came up.

"If you had just ordered those fuckin' phones before."

"Okay, consider it done, but you'd better get those fuckin' results through that machine over there; they'll be screaming for them soon. Use the one on the left to run the tape and we can feed it through on the right-hand machine later."

Terry looked across the room to the noisy Sagem tele-printer and the old thumpers next to them.

"You know I learned to type on one of those old bastards, but it's against the union rules for me to use them now."

"So fucking what?" Norton boomed.

"So, I am not going to do it. If you got phones on those courses when you said you would, I would probably be seeing my girlfriend by now. You have stuffed my whole day and night," Terry lied.

"You mean me and Maggots have stuffed your day," Norton laughed. "Anyway girls will only get you into trouble."

Terry smiled: "Yeah, well, I suppose you're right, you and Maggots bloody Quayle."

Norton finished his drink and poured another triple shot for himself before extracting another bottle from his bag. He looked at Terry and smiled as he unscrewed the cap.

"I tell you what, I'll put it on tape but you will have to read it out to me in the format it goes in the paper, OK? Is that against your union fuckin' rules, or what?" Norton stood up, laughing loudly, but Terry wasn't fazed.

"All right then, but I think I might be getting a bit light headed drinking this top shelf stuff, so I reckon we should just go steady. Race 1 - "

They were half way through the first race when the machine adjacent erupted into action, clanging and dinging away.

"There they are. I told you they'd be on your case. What's this?" The machine was still ringing, a whole line of bells drew all of the attention of Terry and Norton to it.

As soon as it stopped Norton developed a sickly grin as he read the note asking for the race results. URGENT written top and bottom row of annoying bells.

He touched the keyboard with gusto and Terry roared into laughter when he saw what Norton had typed: "Get fucked".

The pair laughed together as Norton said: "Now that'll set the cat amongst the pigeons."

It took a minute or two for the machine to stutter into life again. The line was direct into the Melbourne office which Terry imagined would be abuzz with life at this deadline hour.

"Who's that?" the message came back.

Norton was straight back: "You find out, dick-head."

The reply came back. "You're fired".

Norton responded: "Fuck off jerk".

Terry naturally took over with the results as Norton handled the task at hand. He knew exactly who was at the other end of the tele-printer machine and how to handle him. He was having fun with him. Pushing his buttons.

"He thinks it's fucking you, Terry. Look at the fat bastard's messages will you? What a bully he is; I should have sacked that mongrel months ago."

Terry was getting a good go on with the results and thought Norton was getting too aggressive now. "Hey Max, he is only doing his job remember; you are the one causing all of his agro."

Norton was not prepared to take all of the blame: "You too, you bastard; come on and get those bloody results finished."

The machine appeared to buzz for several seconds before darting into action again. The message read: "You have one minute to get those results down here or you are fired, and that's final."

Terry laughed with his boss as he typed away. There was just one race to go onto the tape now.

Meanwhile Norton taunted him some more: "Sit on a carrot moron."

"Do you think we should tell him they'll be there in a minute," Terry enquired, but Norton was having too much fun, enjoying the tease. Both he and Terry knew how frustrated the subs in Melbourne would be with an 80-page paper ready to run all but for a few race results, and now this.

Suddenly the tune changed and the tele-printer started again: "Who's that?"

"Not telling," Norton replied.

The phone rang.

"Don't answer it Terry, it's them. They're after you. They're scalp hunting, Ha ha ha ha ha, this'll be driving them fucking crazy. How's the tape going?"

"Almost done," Terry responded, "but there may be a few typo's here and there."

"Fuck'em," he said. "They're paid to sub, let the bastards sub."

They waited for the phone to stop and within 30 seconds the tele-printer roared into action again.

"You're fired. Whoever you are, you're fired. No more mucking around, we need those race results now, or we start the presses without them."

Norton grabbed the end of the long tape that Terry was still working on, ran it through the guides of the adjacent machine and pressed a button which set the tape in motion as the machine simultaneously printed out what was going to Melbourne. Terry had to hurry to finish, but managed to stay with it without stretching the tape.

He watched their machine create the images and noticed the word Maggots thump onto the paper as the first race event went through.

"Oh no, you'll get me shot, you bastard. You wrote Maggots on the results, we can't do that."

Norton was laughing, a deep belly laugh. "Fuck him. He fucked you today, didn't he? Well, FUCK him, and fuck those subs if they don't pick it up."

"Naaah, you can't do that, he's got underworld connections; I'm too young for concrete shoes," Terry was sounding concerned, but soon laughed at his own words as Norton erupted again.

Finally the tape finished.

Norton had poured Terry another three fingers of Black Label and they were laughing when the machine crept into action again.

"OK, Who IS that?"

Norton typed: "Me"

"Who's me?"

"Who do you fucking think, dick-brain?" Norton was laughing and reading the messages out to Terry.

"OK wise guy, WHO is MAGGOTS?" They laughed again before Norton typed back, "R. fucking Quayle, because he's on so many dead'uns." They laughed again until tears were flowing down their cheeks.

"Very funny, but you're still fired, and that's final."

Norton was finding it hard to get a breath as he laughed again: "Doesn't this prick know where to get off?"

He typed again: "To everyone in the Melbourne office; the whole fucking lot of you are fired, so fuck off."

The machine went quiet again and the phone started ringing. This time Norton picked it up. He was still laughing loudly as he said: "Hello, ha ha ha ha ha, tele-fucking printer room, ha ha ha ha ha." Whoever was on the other end of the line would know exactly who they were talking to.

The following Thursday, Norton stopped at Terry's desk to hand him the keys to the phones which he had installed on all of the metropolitan racetracks.

Chapter 18

Preparations were well under way at the Opera House for the official opening to be conducted by Queen Elizabeth II, later in the day.

Terry drove over the bridge and wound his way down to Cammeray where the boat was moored. She appeared even more elegant this morning; the varnish on the handrails atop the decking reflected the early rays of sunlight.

Terry was the first of the crew to arrive and he found Alby Walters, the boat's co-owner and his son Reg on board, still asleep. He woke them up. So much for the 7am start up the harbour.

The others in the crew meandered their way aboard over the next two hours. Sails were prepared for the day's events. Terry helped Reg guide the slides of the mainsail into position, the sail was secured to the boom and the main sheet attached and used to tie the sail up on the boom.

The number one headsail was pushed through the forward hatch but stayed in the bag as boxes and boxes of alcohol were passed on board and taken straight into the icebox.

The skipper, co-owner Bob Gladstone, sauntered down the narrow wharf from the block of flats where he had stayed the night before. The stories of the old boat flowed as freely as the beer from an early hour. The work this crew had done had been split into many man-hours over the past four months. They had virtually rubbed back and re-varnished every piece of timber on the boat. Winches had been pulled apart and completely overhauled, the beautiful teak decking had been rubbed back, relieved of pitch and re-pitched, the topside had all been painted with several coats, and ropes had been carefully measured and cut to length. This was the first time she had been away from the wharf for over a year. They were getting her ready to contest the next Sydney to Hobart Yacht Race.

Terry worked with Patrick pulling the main up to the top of the huge mast. He liked the sail number, 69, it suited the old girl, the skippers and the crew. Today most of them had their women on board too. When the main was hoisted their attention turned to the genoa now hanked onto the forestay. The skipper soon called for it and they started hoisting. Terry did the tailing at the mast with a couple of turns around the winch as Patrick pulled on the halyard from above. As the sail neared the top he got a couple of extra turns on the winch and pulled her up tight before inserting the winch handle to get that extra few inches.

They were no sooner there when the cockpit crew snapped into action and pulled on the sheets to get the flapping sail to set; as they did the boat heeled and they were sailing. The skipper immediately asked them to ease everything off a little: "Spring the sheets a bit, until she gets some speed up, then come back on slowly; watch the wools on the sail there." He pointed, "that's it, there."

He soon asked for the main halyard to be released slightly to allow some shape back into the mainsail which appeared to be on too tight. To do this he momentarily turned the boat up into the wind causing the sails to flap again.

The breeze was only light and they managed admirably despite the flicking of the sails. The skipper dropped the nose again and she was pulling through the water with ease. It was beautiful. Terry had imagined it may be nice, but crouched on the deck in eight knots of breeze aboard this sloop on Sydney Harbour was something else.

Gladstone, who had worked in a number of exotic ports, was right at home at the helm. Terry kept gazing up into the sails, watching the wools, feeling the weight of each puff of wind and how the nose would lift slightly, Gladstone allowing her to take herself to the limit then holding her there for as far as she could go on that one, then easing her in wait for the next, all the while maintaining as much boat speed as he could.

He responded with her so well, she simply wanted to milk the breeze. Another puff and she immediately responded and Gladstone found the slot again.

Patrick passed over a can of beer, which Terry accepted and pulled the tab. They were able to point out through the heads and make just one, tack, "Going about - Leee Hooooo", where they settled, eased all the sails and headed down wind through the centre of Sydney Harbour. There were hundreds of boats; sail and "stink boats" as the yachties termed anything with a motor. Terry went along with them on that. He was in love with the feeling of being swept along and that downhill feeling like there was no wind at all. It was so calm on board at this angle of wind. The boat was beautiful, the day was magnificent, the weather was superb and the harbour was a buzz of excitement.

"Fuck this is great, Patrick, how long has this been going on without me. What a great way to go to the opening of the Opera House."

"Yeah, it's great. Doesn't she fly for such a big boat?"

"You betcha; I feel great. Where are the women?"

They sailed right down the harbour under the Harbour Bridge and headed for the Gladesville Bridge. The return journey was on long tacks almost into the shore in some places before they did a well-drilled 'come about' plus doing a few extra short ones, because the skipper had been so impressed by the last one.

As they'd ease the sheet, Terry would go to that corner of the sail and take it up around the mast as Patrick pulled in the sail from the forestay and ease it into the slot on the other side. They'd both go and settle on the windward side of the deck, the proper sailing position in race mode.

They sailed under the Harbour Bridge again gazing upwards in awe of the structure, watching the trains rattle across to one side. *Revenge* cruised serenely past Circular Quay, Fort Denison and on up to Rushcutter's Bay before they came about and cruised slowly down wind under the main only, into a position directly in front of the Opera House.

"This'll do," Alby yelled as they swept back up into the wind. "Drop the anchor." Patrick and Terry were just about to comply with this request when Terry noticed there may have been a bit of chain with it, but it wasn't tied to anything. He quickly jumped down through the hatch and secured the heavy line to the end of the chain before bringing it back up on deck. They wrestled the anchor over the bow and watched in amazement as all of the chain disappeared and almost half of the rope he had just joined on. While this was going on, the cockpit crew secured the boom with the topping lift and pulled the main down. The spare sheets and braces were then wrapped around the bundled sail to secure it. It was time to settle in to some serious drinking and story-telling.

The party seemed to go for hours before they tuned in a small transistor radio around the time Her Majesty was due to "smash the champagne bottle" over the bow of the city's most expensive building to date.

On board they had a cocktail of drinks and saved the champagne until the evening when the fireworks started going off from the Harbour Bridge and a pontoon a few hundred metres from where they were moored. It was indeed a spectacular event. One of the fireworks even went amiss and landed in a boat nearby. It then discharged its stars, sending the occupants of the boat overboard as the boat caught fire, exploded, burned to the waterline and sank. The added spectacle of the water tugs roaring into position to douse the flames on the already sinking hull was enthralling to all on board and accentuated by fireworks which continued above them: "Wow, this is some show," said Terry, who was leaning against a sail bag.

"Yeah maybe they'll tow a container ship down next with millions of sky rockets going off at once from the top layer," Patrick responded.

"Why not light up the sails of this thing?" he pointed over his shoulder to the Opera House looming out of Bennelong Point. "That'd be different."

There was an obvious finale to the fireworks after which cheers could be heard across the water. When the commotion died down most of the boats began to leave.

"They must have run out of grog," Patrick suggested. Alby agreed and launched into one of his sea stories which had the crowded cockpit in waves of laughter. The party on *Revenge* was still kicking on. The dirty stories were flowing as fast and furious as the champagne and it wasn't until some two hours later that someone suggested they should "weigh anchor".

Terry and Patrick immediately sprang into action but it was not long before they realized this anchor was the heaviest thing they had ever tried lifting. All hands were subsequently called to the anchor rope, but even this was showing slow progress. The ladies on board were laughing as they joined in the heave-ho. They were heaving about six inches with each grasp and it felt like it was pulling them back in.

Alby had the foresight to get the tail of the rope and started winding it around, first one, then two and then another winch. With a concerted effort with every man and woman on board hauling on some part of the line, the anchor chain appeared. After five more minutes of hard winding, the anchor appeared with a huge cable, approximately eight inches in diameter, hooked over it.

The cable, now recognized as one of the major telephone links from the city to the North Shore was stuck fast. They would have to get the anchor, and the cable, right up on deck to release it.

Terry admitted at the peak of the action that he thought the "Warning. Submarine Cables" sign, so visible as they moored there, was a place "where submarines tied up". He copped a jibing from most on board after a comment like that.

Alby, by now was up in the pushpit twisting the anchor with all his might. The bow of the boat was just inches from the waterline. Alby called that the anchor was free and just as quickly the cable slipped over the bow and submerged, causing the bow to rise sharply causing a spill of bodies on the foredeck.

They laughed all the way home about the number of communications they must have upset on the north side and laughed even more when the area from Milson's Point to Cammaray suddenly appeared to darken. By now they were under motor and managed to use all of the buoy light markers to find their way home.

Chapter 19

Delia was glowing when she answered the door to see Terry.

"Hey man, how are you?"

"Great. I spent yesterday on the Harbor waiting for the Queen to open the Opera House."

"Wow, sounds like you had a great day. Hey, I've got something for you." Delia went to the back door and opened it. A small brown dog came racing in with his tail wagging madly.

"His name is Herbie. He's half dachshund and half labrador."

"But how could that happen?"

"I don't know. It just did." She stood back, looking down at the dog, wagging his tail madly as Terry patted him on the back. "He's about six months old and already house trained. He's a beauty, isn't he? He's all yours, Terry." Delia smiled wildly, patting the dog.

Herbie pranced around the kitchen doing a sort of ritual "pleased to meet you", lifting his paw to be shaken.

Terry was beaming and got down to his knees: "Here Herbie."

The dog came straight up and sat in front of him.

"He retrieves things too. Like balls or frisbees, socks."

"Gee thanks Mouse. I can see all of my socks spread across the yard. How are things going?"

"Not bad although Darlene has been giving me the shits."

"Are things not working out with you two."

"Things are fine with me, but she is such a jealous bastard sometimes. The bitch threatened to shoot me the other night."

"Christ Mouse, get the gun and I'll take it to my place. You don't want something like that around while you're bluing."

"Naah, don't worry about it. We've made up now anyway," Delia assured him. "So how did you go with that new job you were going for?"

"I got it. I start in a week or so, when I work out my time with *The Shipping News*."

They shared a pot of tea before Terry decided to go. "Are you sure you don't want me to take the rifle, just to get it out of the way while things are shaky with you and Darlene?"

"Naah, Terry. Don't worry about it. She'll come around, I think. She's really just bluffing. Anyway, we may be going camping next weekend. I'll need it then."

Terry walked home, just around the corner, with his new pet. Herbie claimed a spot on the comfortable lounge as soon as they got home.

Just a week had passed before he decided he had to get out of Petersham. The clanking and rumbling of the trains accentuated his feelings of loss. It was something he had never experienced, been prepared for, in his life to date. She was too young to go, to leave him. Not now, things had just started to happen for him. Sure, he was independent, he had to be, he had no choice. But he had her close by. He tried to think of the happy times and each time he did it made him sad. Not of the memory, but the loss of such continuing into old age, for them both, for them all, the whole family. His thoughts raced back to the morning he arrived back from Melbourne. His first stop was at her place. He wanted to see that she was all right, although he longed for her to have had a change of heart about her relationships.

She had told him once that she would go before her time.

He had not expected the palm reading from Grandma. He was attentive. He had not seen her for seven or eight years and there she was at his mother's house at Mooroolbark, two days before he left Melbourne for Sydney. She enveloped him with her love in a way that only Grandmas know how. She kept referring to him as "my writer grandson". He liked that, and he liked the way she held his hand when he inquired about her knowledge in palmistry. She spoke of lots of things in one's journey of life, stating he would have a very long and full life. He thought he had tested her on questions about finding a mate but was sobered considerably when she mentioned a "great loss" as he was entering his twenties.

"Who? Who would that be?"

"Your best friend."

"Mouse? No. What can I do about that?"

"There is nothing you can do, it is fate," his Grandma looked straight into his eyes: "It may not be Mouse."

"But you said my best friend; Mouse has been and still is, my best friend."

"Is there anything I could do, at all, to stop something bad happening?"

"You will not recollect this conversation until after any event," she had said. "You will be surrounded by beautiful women throughout your life." He succumbed to her changing of the subject.

"Yes, but how will I know when the right one comes along?" Terry asked.

"You will know," she told him.

"Yes, but is there some sort of sign you can give me, so that I'm positive."

His mother's mother, the concert pianist, violinist, mother of 12, tea cup reader and now palmist, thought for a moment: "A sign you say. You want a sign?" She looked to the left and then slowly to the right then back into Terry's palm. Her eyes lifted to meet his: "A sneeze."

"What? I will sneeze."

"I can't say if it is you or her; all I can say is that a sneeze will guide you. But . . .," she said rolling her eyes up at him again, "you will not remember this until after anything has happened. You may then make up your own mind on how to react to a situation."

Terry was fascinated by the information at the time and seemed to remember the entire hour and a half she had been reading his palm, when 600 miles away speaking to Mouse, he could hardly remember a thing of it.

"She said I wouldn't remember anything, Mouse, but I do remember her saying I would have a great loss. She said it would be my best friend, and that's you mate."

Mouse was typical, he thought, in her reaction to that. "Bullshit Terry. I have had my tarot cards read too and there hasn't been anything of the sort come up there Terry; Don't worry about it. Anyhow, when you're dead, you're dead."

"I'd cry Mouse, if you died, I'd cry, a lot. I would put flowers on your grave."

"No you wouldn't, because I wouldn't want to be buried somewhere. I would just want to be burned, cremated. I wouldn't want to be molding away in any grave."

"I would go to your grave and cry."

"I wouldn't want a grave Terry, and I wouldn't want anyone crying about me either. Graves remind me of worms and creepy crawlies."

He remembered during that conversation she sat bare-topped in bed drinking the cup of tea he brought her. They had discussed the family, who was where, doing what, on the morning of his return from Melbourne.

He was back to Sydney, starting into new phase of his life. So little of it was ever planned. He was following his nose, dealing with things as they arose.

Now, a year later, there was the new job, which appeared to be a bit more of a challenge and now, there was a life without Mouse; he just had to get out of this suburb.

The day it happened he felt uneasy, irritable. He had been at a drive-in movie with George and Carla. He was bored with the movie. The night was cold. He couldn't relax. He was in bed within 10 minutes of arriving home. Suzanne and Damian were at the door half an hour later. He opened the door to see them standing there. He knew it was solemn news as soon as Suzanne spoke. She hugged him first. "Terry, come inside and sit down."

"Why? What's happened?"

"Terry," she had difficulty getting it out. "Delia was killed this afternoon."

"No," said Terry, "tell me you're just kidding."

Damian helped out. He wept as he confirmed what Suzanne had just said. "We're very serious Terry. Darlene came out with the gun while she was talking to Suzanne over the fence."

"Not the gun." Terry remembered back to the week before when he spoke to Delia.

"I told her just last week to let me take the gun away while they were arguing. Mouse told me not to worry." Tears streamed down his face.

"She came out with the gun and just shot her, Terry. She didn't suffer, Terry, we knew straight away that she was dead." Suzanne was crying. "She did a sort of flip off the fence and lay on the ground in front of us."

Terry suddenly realized that Suzanne and Damian were right there. They saw it all happen.

"I just grabbed the barrel and took the gun off her," Suzanne said.

They left in silence. Terry was stunned, in shock. Was this a dream? How could it be? He tried to wake Martie who was asleep in the front room.

"Piss off man, I've got to work tomorrow."

"Martie, come on man I need someone to talk to; my sister was killed today."

"I don't care, I have to get some sleep."

"You what?" Terry's rage erupted on Martin who only really wanted to get some sleep. In his half-sleep he was unaware of what he had just said. He knew soon enough as Terry grabbed him by the throat and hauled him up from the bed.

"What do you mean you don't fuckin' care? I'll give you don't care, you bastard."

Martin was suddenly wide awake: "Shit Terry, what are you doing?"

"I told you man, my sister was killed today. You just said you don't fucking care. Well I fucking well care."

Terry saw Martie's startled look and realized that he was just taking his frustration out on him. He released his grip and walked to the door, looking back. "I'm, sorry, Martie. I'm just angry, man; I don't know what to do. I feel like going out."

"Look it's okay man, I am sorry. I didn't hear what you had said, I was asleep. It's okay though, I'll get up; we can talk if you like."

"No, don't worry. I'm sorry for grabbing you like that."

He left the room quickly as he felt tears welling in his eyes. By the time he reached the hallway his cheeks were awash. He walked into the kitchen where he leaned, elbows on the sink and sunk his head between his arms. His vision was blurred by the stream of tears which now pooled on the floor.

Martie emerged and put an arm over his shoulder: "I'll put the kettle on man." Terry straightened up, unable to speak and Martie hugged him. "Come on, sit down."

"How can this happen, Martie? She told me just last week that the bitch was threatening to shoot her. She just wanted to get away from the bloody relationship. I told her to get the rifle and I'd look after it for a couple of weeks; she just told me not to be bloody stupid; not to worry."

The kettle started to whistle as Martie finished preparing a couple of cups he had fished from a dirty pile in the sink.

Terry sat at the end of the table. "I should have just grabbed the bloody thing, I can't believe it Martie, I just can't believe it. She had so much to live for, mate. Who knows what may have happened if she was able to get out of that relationship?"

Terry recounted how Mouse had fallen into the scene. "It was her 16th birthday mate and she had gone dancing with Suzanne and a couple of her girlfriends.

"We lived up at Haberfield at the time and the next morning they weren't home. Dad was very worried about them and went out to search. It was late in the afternoon before they all appeared. Mouse had a black eye and her teeth were missing in the front. They had told Dad that she got drunk and fell down the steps at the Palais. It was months later that we found out a mongrel had tried to rape her that night. The low-life bastard beat her face in when she screamed. That's why she turned to women. Christ, I never blamed her for that, although it was hard for me to understand at the time. Now this. Shit, where's the sense in it all?"

"There is nothing you can do about it now, man," said Martie trying to console him.

"Jesus man, Suzanne saw the whole thing. She was talking to Mouse when it happened. Mouse was sitting on the fence between the two houses talking to her when Darlene came out with the gun and said, 'you can't leave me' and just fired a shot which sent her sprawling. Suzanne grabbed the barrel of the gun off her then and called the police. There was nothing they could do. The bullet hit her in the head. She was dead instantly."

Terry didn't sleep too well that night. His dreams were of the good times he'd had with Mouse; rabbiting up the bush, making rafts for the dam, riding to their rock pool, even their discovery of one of Stephen's stashes in their ceiling. His mind flashed across her friends of recent years and realized there were many nice women amongst them, even if they were "camp". He remembered the way she had defended him in their company when they started on men. "Hey, this is my brother; he's not like that," she'd say. Then there were the women she shared with him after a night of smoking joints. As discreet as they appeared at the time, Delia always gave him a knowing smile in the mornings.

This morning was cold and stark. He felt numb, not from the cold but his state of mind, his state of loss. He went around the corner where it had all happened and hugged Suzanne and stood where Delia had fallen. His heart was heavy; he had never felt so helpless, lost. Damian spent most of the day arranging the funeral. Terry went for a drive around to North Head. He sat at the top of the cliffs and looked out to sea for hours before a shower of rain sent him scurrying back to the car.

The following day, he caught the train into the city to where he was to start the new job. The editor, Mark Hoad, offered him sincere condolences and time off: "Take as long as you need, Terry. It's a terrible thing for anyone to have to cope with. We'll manage here until you're ready to start."

The funeral was the first Terry had ever attended. He didn't know what you were supposed to do. He realized that the faces in the crowd he knew were there for him. The wake was held at Suzanne and Damian's house. Stephen was as solemn as Terry had ever seen him. Shelly was visibly shaken. Terry walked through the sea of well-wishers who attended. He heard the conversations instinctively as he walked by. He thanked people for coming and moved on to the next lot.

He was on the way to the kitchen to get a beer when he overheard the crew of women in the corner. "Delia was a bitch," one overweight girl had said. "We'll get the best bloody barrister money can buy for Darlene."

The tears welled in his eyes as he walked past. He opened the refrigerator to get a beer and looked outside to the spot where his sister was slain. The shaking started in his legs. He put the beer back and walked out to the table where Shelly was pouring a cup of tea. He heard the girls talking over the top of everything else. "We'll get the best bloody barrister. We'll get her off. You watch!"

"They're saying Delia was a bitch, Mum. Can you hear them?"

"Yes I can. I can hear it. It was a terrible accident Terry."

He heard the one woman harping on: "We'll get her off; We'll get her off."

It was too much for him to bear: "Shut the fuck up, you bitch. Murder is bloody murder."

Stephen wheeled through and grabbed Terry by the shoulders,

maneuvering him towards the hallway.

"Dad, they're abusing Delia. That lot are abusing her for Christ's sake. What is this?"

Stephen ushered Terry through the hallway and outside the front of the house. His sailing buddy, the advertising representative from work, Patrick Markham, was there with his housemates, uncomfortable, but there to show their respects. Terry found it hard to talk to them about what had occurred inside. His anger contained, he finally decided to just go home.

He returned later to talk with his family. The conversation under such circumstances was difficult. The subject could not be changed. He had to get out of Petersham.

Chapter 20

Maureen was flamboyant. Her straight, shoulder length blonde hair swung with her every movement. "Hi, you must be Terry," she said opening the door. "Maureen?" he replied.

"Yes; well, come on in and see if you like the place."

She walked to the first door on the right. "That's where you'll be sleeping," she said pointing through the doorway. Terry took a glance and followed her along the hallway on black and white checkerboard tiles which branched into the dining and living area. Stairs led from the living room to a bedroom upstairs. "That's my bedroom up there," she said, pointing over her shoulder as she walked to the kitchen. It was well appointed with a walnut finish on the cupboards enclosing a wall oven. A pine table setting sat in the light of the bay windows accentuated by a colourful tablecloth.

"The house belongs to my boss who is overseas for a year. I told you on the phone what the rent would be, didn't I?"

"Yes, $50 a week?"

"Yep," she strolled back into the dining area past the Colonial dining setting, which would seat 10 people, and on to the bathroom door which she flung open. The whole room was white except for the gold-plated taps and fittings, which reflected all of the light around them.

"It's nothing flash, but it's adequate."

"Looks fine to me; may I look at the front room again, I only got a glimpse as we came in."

"Sure, go ahead. Look would you care for a coffee?"

"Yes please."

"You go ahead; take your time and look around and come out when you're ready."

"Thank you."

He wandered up the hall past the first door. As he touched the handle Maureen quipped again: "That's Trevor's room in there. Whatever you do, don't look in there. No-one goes into Trevor's room except Trevor."

Terry kept going to the next door and entered. There was a long bay window at the front covered with a rich red velvet curtain which could be drawn for privacy. The bed had a leopard skin fabric spread with a flap at the tip to conceal a pillow. There was a fireplace with a small grille set into one wall and a small hearth with a screen to protect the cream-coloured shag pile carpet. The room hadn't seen a fire for some time, Terry thought. A wardrobe and chest of drawers covered the rest of the wall.

He took a quick test of the bed. The mattress was firm, unlike the one he endured at Petersham. As he got up he caught his own reflection in the oval mirror above the mantelpiece which prompted him to pull a comb from his back pocket and run through his curly hair which bounced back to where it was. He spun around again and could see himself in this room. The hat and coat stand in the hallway broke the monotony of the view through the architraves and he found himself attempting to just walk on the black squares as he meandered back along the hallway.

Maureen had the coffee in the cups and was adding milk to her own. "Oh, there you are, I'd thought you may have gone to sleep up there."

"I could have. I gave the bed a try. It is very comfortable."

Maureen offered the milk bottle. "Yes thank you." She poured a little in to whiten the coffee. Terry reached for the sugar bowl and helped himself.

"So what do you think?"

"It's great, I like it, very much."

"I should tell you that upstairs is my domain."

"Sure, that's fine with me," Terry said cheerfully.

"Well, when can you move in?"

"How about tomorrow then?"

"That's fine with me."

Terry told Maureen of his plans to start back at work the following week. His first assignment was to do a tour of New Zealand. He was to leave on Wednesday for two weeks. Over the next few months his itinerary included three more overseas trips away on assignment.

Maureen was vivacious. She was animated in her explanation of doing the accounts for the city restaurant. He was enthralled by the way she held her hands up daintily, waving them about as she spoke. When she walked she took to her tiptoes bouncing along in a happy-go-lucky manner.

He was travelling pretty light, but the move meant a loan of George's car and assistance. Even with this they were forced to do two trips. George volunteered after hearing the "bird", Maureen, was a blonde: "I've got a hard spot in my groin for a well-put-together blonde."

"You always say that, Georgie, give me a break."

"Oh, did you see those fuckin' tits through that T-shirt. I rooted her four times while we were in there," he said as they headed off for their second trip.

"Bullshit, Georgie, you were like a bloody school kid." Terry mocked:

"Would you care for tea George?

"Oh, yes please, if you're making one.

"Would you like milk, George?

"Oh ye-e-es please, ha ha ha ha."

"She had you by the short and curlies, George. I was waiting for you to say you liked to drink it straight from the jugs, I mean jug," he laughed.

"So, smart-arse, I'll bet you don't fuck her."

"Not fair George. I'm living with her, just platonic; rule number one, don't screw your flat-mates. I'm not ready for any one woman just yet. I'm too young."

"Fuckin' piker. Anyhow I bet she doesn't fuck for you, though I know she'd fuck for me. Did you see her checkin' out the crease in my Levi's?" He ran his hand down the front of his jeans and let out a little groan.

"Get out of it George."

They arrived back at Petersham with the bucket, mop, brooms and vacuum cleaner. With all of the furniture moved out of the room they realized just how rotten the boards were in the lounge room. When George walked across it he could feel himself sink. "Whoah. Hey Terry, get a load of this. Don't walk too far in, you'll go right through."

Terry laughed about the times they had there. "What about the time Martie went through it; right up to his fucken chest. Christ that looked funny. The bastard had turned around to pick up his beer, took one step and went straight down."

"Yeah, the most amazin' thing was that he didn't spill a fuckin' drop."

"Yeah, all we did was put a bit of masonite under the carpet and then stapled the carpet back into the corners."

Terry was disgusted at the mess they'd allowed the house to get into. The parties had been so frequent and so full-on that there were ring-pull tops from the beer cans linked into chains that hung like streamers three and four deep from all corners of the room. Others were linked from the picture hooks. The place smelled like the bar.

"The bloody carpet won't last much longer anyway, with the amount of grog that's been spilt on it, George."

"Yeah, I reckon these ring tops were a bad idea; although there's been a lot of fun in putting them up."

"I'll give you that," Terry responded, "I'll give you that."

He cast his mind back to the memories of arriving home from work to a bunch of the guys with a couple of cartons of beer, settled in the lounge room. It was always more interesting than in a pub situation. Most of the time Terry would just rip a can of Tooheys open and join them. George lamented the good times as he snaked ring tops into a garbage bag.

"Come on Terry, you've got to take these with you."

"Naah. chuck 'em. They stink mate, get a whiff of 'em."

When the cleaning was over, he stood back and looked at the house. They went into each room for a last look, missing the bathroom on the way back down the stairs.

"Remember that night when we got the nurses from Lewisham down here?"

"Yeah and Pricey got all heated up with that Rhonda sheila. He fucked her all around the bloody lounge room with that big cock of his."

"Yeah and everybody was lighting his farts as he did it. Christ, that was a funny bloody night."

"Yeah, no-one else was game to have a go that night for fear their dicks would get laughed at."

"Tell you what, I am never going to unleash my salami on anything after that bastard. Shit, he's built like a horse."

"Yeah, it's a wonder the bastard doesn't faint every time he cracks a fat."

"Who's the best sheila you had here?" George lifted his fingers to his mouth. "Hang on. Let me guess. What about Valerie? That little brunette who worked in the job-finding place."

Terry held out one hand and twisted it back and forth: "Yeah, she was good. But I reckon that Tania was one of the hottest I had here. You guys were never around when she was here, except that night you walked in on us."

"Oh yeah, I remember that. She looked terrific leaning up against the fridge like that. There you were, going for your life and I was standing right there as you were trying to piss me off before she sprang us."

"You could have stuffed my chances forever with that woman if she had seen you there that night."

"Why don't you see her anymore?"

"She didn't like me bringing other girls home!"

"Yeah," said George sarcastically, "funny they get cut about things like that, ay? That night Pricey was doin' that girl. He should've had more respect for her feelings."

"Oh she was feelin' him all right. And she didn't seem to mind what she felt."

"Remember that time we put the crabs in his car, and the silly bastard drove off at a hundred miles an hour screaming with the crabs crawling all around his feet."

George placed an arm over his shoulder: "Come on, let's get out of here."

Chapter 21

From the first week he moved in to Clovelly, he was on the go. He decided he should get back to work as soon as possible. It would keep his mind occupied with something other than Delia's death.

His first assignment was a trip to New Zealand. His heart was heavy on the journey over and he elected to stay in Auckland instead of going with the others to the South Island ski fields. He wasn't really into writing fun travel stories at the moment, not yet. He didn't want to have fun. It was too soon after Delia's death for him to expect to have fun. He asked the airline's public relations officer if it would be okay to stay in Auckland. He agreed, and found accommodation for Terry while the rest of the party headed for the south island.

On his first night there, Terry stayed in his room for hours before moping around the city looking for some action at around 10pm. There was none. Most bars were closing down. He was just about to head back to the hotel when he heard a familiar voice. Veronica and Sharon, friends from the Tavern in Melbourne, were out on the town.

"Hi, hi, hi," she said as Terry approached. "Wow, what are you doing here?"

He looked up to see them beaming at him. Veronica was first to speak: "Where do we know this face from?"

"Thorpies!" he smiled.

They were visiting Sharon's aunt and they reckoned the town was dead, compared to their rock and roll heaven in Melbourne.

They hugged hello and exchanged their recent histories. Terry's tale that he had a major crisis in his life sobered them for a moment, but they decided it would be best dealt with if they got him as pissed as they were.

"Let's find where we can get a drink at this hour. I've heard music a couple of times from a place up around the block there. Let's go and see what's happening."

They hooked on to both of Terry's arms and arrived at the door laughing about characters in Melbourne, their trips to the rock concerts at Sunbury and Mulwala; the fun times they had dancing to Daddy Cool at the Civic Centre on a Sunday. The door opened and they were presented with a girl coming towards them on a catwalk. The music was sleazy and the pink lights around the room served only to show the thickness of the cigarette smoke.

"Three beers and three rums," Veronica ordered as she elbowed her way into the bar.

"Take it off, take it off," Sharon was chanting with the 30 males in the cramped conditions. Terry was enchanted by the woman on the catwalk, but thought she may be a bit old for doing such work.

"Come on... take it off," Sharon demanded as the girl got down to a G-string then headed for a pole at centre stage and draped her leg around it for a finale.

The show continued with an array of fairly amateur strip-teasing; really low-key compared to some at Sydney's Kings Cross or Melbourne's St Kilda. After the fourth girl had performed and they had downed as many shouts, Veronica was getting quite vocal about the quality of the acts. "Come on, you girls, you gotta dance to that music. Look sexy for Christ's sake," she yelled, stirring the room into a frenzy of similar calls.

She brought one sensitive lass to tears, prompting the manager to intervene. "Look lady, you got no business telling my girls they can't do it properly. You wanna show 'em how it's done or what?"

Sharon was quick to respond: "I will if you will," she looked at Veronica.

Veronica obliged: "All right then. How much?"

"I'll give you twenny bucks each."

"Fifty," Sharon snapped, smiling.

"Twenny bucks each. That's what you get, take it or leave it. But if you don't do it 'right' then we may not pay yer. You prove 'ow good youse are. And stop givin' my girls a 'ard time."

Both girls put on a sterling performance. They teased and provoked the males in the crowd and smacked the ever-present grabbers clutching out from the darkness below. Sharon was good, but Veronica moved her hips continuously to the music. She picked her favorites in the crowd to play with and ended with prompting Terry to pull down her knickers. He reached up grabbing them by the sides as she swivelled down toward him. She was gorgeous. As she lifted her five-nine, hourglass figure her knickers slid down to her toes. She deftly flicked her foot to swing them up and grabbed them in her hand to swish around as she danced away again.

Terry suddenly felt embarrassed as she collected her things and headed through the door at back of the stage to the cheers of the patrons.

"Wow, you girls were just so much better than any of their 'professionals' and I think we should go back to my motel room and do that again, in private."

Veronica put an arm around Terry.

"Thanks for the offer mate, but it's getting late and Sharon's auntie may be worried about us."

"I can't imagine why she may worry, can you?"

"Thanks for the offer though Terry. Maybe when we are coming back, we can come via Sydney," Sharon suggested.

"You can stay at my place, in Clovelly."

They both kissed him farewell before taking his address and getting into the cab.

Terry sparked up the next day and decided to do a story on the airline's fleet proposals. The yarn wasn't much, but it was something. He flew back to Sydney that night.

Maureen was surprised to see him back so soon, but managed to rustle enough dinner together for them both. Terry discovered Maureen had been married; not once, but twice, already. "My first husband was one of those boring morons who watch television non-stop. I would try to have a conversation with him and he would be forever telling me to get out of the way. He would rather watch what was on TV than converse with me. Now that pissed me off, I can tell you."

"That would be annoying," Terry said as he poured another glass of wine.

"I fixed him in the end. I told him I was leaving and he asked me to move out of the way of the television. He was watching the football. I just picked up the TV and dropped it over the third-floor balcony. Then I said to him: 'John, I am leaving you' and walked out."

"Crikey, what an exit."

"Yeah, he went and looked over the balcony for the TV as I went out the front door."

"So how did you get involved again, after one like that?"

"Sex, good sex. Well it was at first, but Ralph, my second husband, was the jealous type. He tried to lock me away in a house at Bankstown where I could be a good little wifey and do the washing and the ironing and the dishes and wait for him to come home late every night. I found his American Express card one day and decided to do some shopping. He just got the bills and paid them. I think he used the card a fair bit himself. He ended up getting pissed off when I'd ring up the girls and go out."

She slowed deliberately as she spat out: "One night he went too far and while I was out the bastard took all of my clothes from the bedroom out onto the back lawn and burnt them.

"The fucker wasn't home when I discovered it. Lucky for him he wasn't home then. I just left and I haven't seen him since."

"Probably lucky you haven't, I reckon," Terry laughed.

They cleared up after dinner and headed for their respective bedrooms. Next morning Terry was in the shower when she walked in on him. In a reflex action he turned his back to her.

"Oh, don't worry about it Terry. We're going to have to live together so I don't want to have to wait to get into the bathroom." She peeled off the thick white toweling robe and turned to the sink catching her image in the mirror. "Boy, my eyes tell it all after a night on the red wine."

Terry was summoning the strength up to turn around. He washed the soap from his front. Next he felt the flannel on his back. Maureen was in the shower with him.

"Come on, we'll get you finished so I can have my shower."

She rubbed over his shoulders and down his back to his buttocks. He turned around.

"You've already done that part. Go on, out you get."

Terry complained of being forced into the cold and endured watching Maureen soap herself.

"May I help you with that?"

Maureen turned around. "Yes, you can do my back."

He rubbed slowly across and down her back down over the hips. Next time he went up and down over her buttocks, squeezing the sponge at the bottom.

"Thank you Terry, that will be enough."

He retreated up the hallway to dress for the day. Maureen was in her underwear by the time he returned to the bathroom to clean his teeth. He almost spoiled his suit with toothpaste by holding his head up to see her reflection in the mirror.

"What time do you knock off, Terry?"

"About five, five thirty thereabouts."

"I'm usually not free until nearly seven, after all of the bookings are confirmed and they're all seated. I can always get a cab though. Don't ever worry about me, if I'm late I mean."

Terry settled in to the shared bathroom routine very well as the months progressed. The other room-mate was rarely home and he and Maureen found they shared many beliefs about what life and love was supposed to bring.

Maureen, six years his senior, spoke with authority. "We are a liberated bunch of women now, Terry. And don't you forget it."

"Who, me? The guy that agrees with Germaine Greer, that all any bloke ever wants is to get into the pants of the woman he is with, and anyone else, for that matter. Well I reckon she is spot on."

"True," Maureen smiled.

"And I reckon Germaine's real message was for women to explore their own sexuality, rather than have to conform to what other generations may have done and blokes too!"

Maureen had to agree: "She said it was every woman's bloody right."

"Yeah, that's what I reckon too. When I have this conversation at parties and agree with that scenario the girls think I'm a real understanding guy," he laughed, "And then they want to take me home with them; so they can explore their sexuality. I don't mind."

"Too true, get out of here; you're having me on, Terry."

"Well, maybe. But I can guarantee you, it works, sometimes."

"Righto then, my friend Charlotte is having a little party this evening. How about you come along and try it out there. Most of our friends are fans of Germaine." Maureen appeared keen to experience the unusual. This time it would be watching Terry do his stuff.

Charlotte's little flat looked over Rushcutters Bay. The party was an afternoon, early evening do to take advantage of the sunset. They danced to calypso sounds. Kaitlin smiled broadly as Terry shuffled past her dancing and decided to join in. The whole room was dancing. Terry focused on Kaitlin throwing her curvaceous body around in front of him. The slow tune did it. As soon as soon as their bodies contacted, neither felt obliged to move away. They were hot for each other. Terry needed the loving. He needed it badly. In the kitchen, Maureen and her best friend, Charlotte, were paying out on men when Terry danced into the room with Kaitlin.

"Look, anything we say bad about men, doesn't include this guy, okay, he's with me, aren't you darling?" Maureen giggled, rubbing her hand down his face.

"Well this evening I may not be Maureen. You see, Kaitlin wants to show me through her place," he said quietly.

"You horny little bugger," said Maureen. Her comment appeared directed as much to Kaitlin as it was to Terry.

"Maybe so, maybe not," Terry answered and danced out through the front door.

They watched the sun set from the point and walked back to Kaitlin's flat, next to the party. Kaitlin was as white and soft as silk. Terry engulfed himself in the moment. Gentle was the order of the day and that was how they made love. As they caressed Terry thought this may be his true love.

Kaitlin, however, was aloof after this, their first encounter. She left it until Terry had her out to dinner to explain that her boyfriend, a musician, was overseas at the moment. She was just serving her needs while he was away. "I suspect he'll be doing the same in Canada right now."

"Well, why pick me?" said Terry, trying to act nonchalant, but he found it hard to hide his jealousy already.

"We have this understanding of each other's needs, that's all," said Kaitlin who didn't seem to notice Terry's inner turmoil. "Why you? Because I liked you from the moment I saw you at the party, Terry. You are different to most other men." Terry took the comment as a compliment.

He understood she was taken, but for now he was willing to go with the flow when Kaitlin phoned or called around. She was warm after a hard day out on the harbour. She could cook, really well, in a variety of styles and she loved to make love anywhere - the kitchen, lounge room, even in hallway. The bath was a favourite place, but this was always followed by the bedroom. They experimented and enjoyed healthy conversation about a multitude of subjects between their love-making. There was something very special about their relationship.

Maureen had asked Terry if he and Kaitlin would like to dine at the Drummer. The wine bar served delicious crepes and proved to be perfect to launch Terry into a good weekend with Kaitlin. Her boyfriend was due back the following week and he knew this may be their last date, for a while anyway.

Maureen had been entertaining with her boyfriend, Graeme, who laughed loudly at most of her stories. Graeme spent his days looking at hair follicles and his evenings snorting cocaine and laughing. This evening was no different for him. Although Maureen kept his habits to herself, Terry had noticed his crazy behaviour on more than one occasion. This night it was not Graeme they had to be concerned with. Their coffees were on the table when the party of eight walked into the restaurant.

"There's that fucking bastard," Maureen spat the words quietly within the bounds of the table.

"Maureen, keep it down. Shush," Terry was patting her hand across the table.

"But it's him, it's him," she said pulling her hand away.

"Who?"

"Bloody Ralph, my ex-fucking husband. I haven't seen him since that bastard burned all of my clothes." She paused to turn and take a five-second glance at the thick-set man being seated only nine feet away.

"Oooooh," said Terry recalling her story of the clothes burning incident. "Look Maureen, let's just have our coffees and go."

Maureen was on her feet. Terry quickly responded by standing too. She put a hand on his shoulder and pushed him back into his seat. "Look I'm just going to the loo. Don't worry. I'm not going to cause a scene or anything. Back in a minute." She smiled a sickly forced smile at him.

Terry was momentarily relieved, but he had a gut feeling about Maureen. That smile was not her usual vivacious, open-mouthed smile. Her teeth were clenched. He remembered the anger she displayed when she had told him of Ralph burning her clothes.

"Who is it?" Kaitlin enquired. Graeme leaned forward to hear his answer.

"Maureen's ex-husband Ralph." Terry whispered to them: "He burnt all of her clothes."

"What on earth for?" Kaitlan was interested.

"I don't know? Maureen thinks it was because he was a jealous type. He didn't like her going out and having a good time."

"I hope she doesn't get me involved in anything," Graeme was showing his colours now. His coke must have been wearing off. He wasn't laughing.

"Naah. Don't worry Graeme." Terry was reassuring.

Maureen took her time. They watched the table settle in and order their meals as they received mints, coffee and ports at their own table. Maureen waited in the loo until the meals were being served to make her entrance. She was beautiful, graceful, as she stalked past their table. She was so very demure the way she asked the young lady sitting at the end of the table to stand. "May I borrow your chair a moment please?" The young woman was obliging, but was puzzled as Maureen used her chair as a step to the top of the table.

"Hello Ralph." Maureen's voice became loud, slow and precise. "Remember me? Remember that night you burned all of my clothes?" The entire table was agape, in stunned silence. The whole restaurant was now watching. In the silence provoked by Maureen's actions, came the trickling sound as she urinated onto his seafood crepe.

"Is she…" Graeme was dumbfounded, then he burst out laughing. "Yes, she is. She's pissing in his dinner."

"I think we may be leaving," Terry motioned to Kaitlin as he stood up. Maureen had used the same step down from the table and came back smiling at Terry who was now standing. She looked into his eyes: "I feel better now, much better. Let's go."

"No problem." Terry pulled enough money from his pocket to cover the meals and left it on the table and followed the others out the door. Ralph had turned a deep shade of crimson in the lights and was grabbing the tablecloth by the corners trying to stop the flow towards his position.

Outside, Graeme laughed out his question to Maureen who was walking briskly toward the car. "What possessed you to do something like that?"

Maureen didn't answer at first, offering only a wicked smile. Then she had to say it: "He has pissed me off since he burned all of my clothes. I had been wondering if I ever saw him again, what I would do. The idea came to me as soon as I left our table to go to the loo. The only trouble was I had to hold on until his dinner arrived. I nearly pissed myself laughing several times before I got the courage to do it. Now, I'm glad I did."

"There you go Graeme, don't mess with this girl, or she might come back at you one day." Terry's comment was sobering.

As they reached the car Kaitlin decided on an early night. "I have some study to do. I have exams coming up. If you don't mind Terry, I can get a cab." She turned to Maureen: "Thanks for the show, Maureen. That was one of the best I've seen, thank you."

Terry wound the conversation away from Maureen's antics several times on the drive home, but it kept swinging back. Graeme must have said, "and you pissed in his fucking dinner," a dozen times.

Terry admitted he had not seen anything quite like it before and went to bed as soon as they got home.

Chapter 22

The trial put the entire event into clinical legal jargon. Six months had passed before Terry saw Darlene, at her trial. He again attempted to fathom what had occurred. Darlene testified they had been fighting. She was jealous of a relationship Delia had been cultivating with a friend from work. The woman had been having marital problems and Delia was offering solace and advice. Darlene imagined the worst, that Delia may be having an affair. She had meant to simply "teach her a lesson". The forensic report supported this. The doctor who conducted the post-mortem told that the .22 bullet had glanced off the shoulder bone and "entered the victim's skull below the left ear and lodged behind her right eye".

Every news report had to have the tabloid tag, "woman in lesbian relationship" when they reported the inquest and trial.

The money raised by Darlene's friends to mount a defense paid off. The barrister called it a "crime of passion". She was convicted of the lesser charge of manslaughter with diminished responsibility for her temporary insanity at the moment of pulling the trigger and sentenced to serve just six months in prison.

"Christ-all-bloody-mighty, they're handing out worse punishment for people smoking a bloody joint," Terry told George after the verdict had been handed down. "The law is a fucking ass mate. It means if you have the money you can now commit murder and get away with it. Where is the bloody world going?"

"Fucked if I know," George responded, "where can we get a drink around here?"

Terry was numbed by the experience and the whisky he drank did little to ease the feeling. He was sick of drinking after their second shout.

"Suzanne has been able to forgive this woman, George. I don't know. I can't really forgive her yet. There is too much of Delia around me. I see her everywhere. You know those double takes you do sometimes. I keep seeing her, everywhere."

"I don't know how you could forgive her, mate. It's a pretty horrible thing that she did. It's a pretty fucked lot of circumstances for your whole family," George was bravely searching for words that may help. "They say time wounds all heels."

"No, that should be, time heals all wounds," Terry corrected him.

"Yeah, that one too; you can trust me to fuck it up," George was searching for something to say.

"If only I had taken the gun away that day." Terry lowered his head into his cupped hands.

"Hey, you weren't to know, Terry. Nobody knew. Even that bird in the court didn't know she was going to do something crazy, until it was done. You can't blame yourself. There's enough suffering in here to just accept by itself, without any added burdens. It wasn't your fault this happened."

"Yeah, I guess you're right," said Terry, tears welling in his eyes. George stood up and placed a caring hand on his shoulder. "Come on, let's piss off out of here. We'll be waitin' all night for a good sort to walk through here, I reckon."

Terry engrossed himself in his work over following weeks. He phoned Stephen in Melbourne to tell him of the verdict and found he was hitting the grog pretty hard. This time, he thought, he had a good excuse to drink.

Meanwhile, he put all of his own energies into work. He was learning something new every day and taking great joy in passing on the information. He became a vehicle through which stories were told to the industry which had a variety of factional friction. The unions wreaked selective havoc as a new log of claims was under negotiation.

Terry reported on the industry objectively but in his heart he was barracking for the workers, and the unions supporting them. He knew they always asked for percentages far above what they expected to get. He knew that many of the redundancy claims were exaggerated, he knew the terms and conditions were sorted out to get the best deal for the workers at the end of the line, after it had been in the court. He saw in the courts how they had to contend, not only with the employer organization, but also the Commonwealth. Any conditions won under these circumstances were hard fought and each minor point of a log of claims could mean many hours, even weeks, of legal argument. What may have appeared to be a small concession today, could be a very valuable asset to bargaining power in years to come.

After each hearing the court would be booked for the following year. It reminded him of the sheep dog episodes of Bugs Bunny.

After work and at weekends Terry kept busy working on *Revenge*. They were getting down to a deadline for their Hobart race. They had completely re-pitched the decks. Every bulkhead now had a minimum of eight coats of varnish down below and a dozen above deck. The bottom still had to be scraped and anti-fouled. This last week before the event was busy. They scraped for two days to clear the bottom of barnacles. It was back-breaking work which actually made the physical application of the paint a pleasure to do, in comparison.

Alby was usually full of beans, excited about the prospect of getting back onto the ocean. This day he was dark. "They want us to move the boat over to the club to get measured. They reckon it's the only 'official' slip we can use."

Alby had told the race committee they couldn't afford the slipping fees at the club which were almost six times what they were paying on the other side of the harbour. "Fuck it. We're going to Hobart, whether they measure us or not. We can sail unofficially."

Stephen was jolted from his sleep by the phone. "Dad, its Terry."

"How are you mate?"

"Fine, Dad, fine."

"What about you?"

"Oh. Things are OK. Barry has given me the truck to use again. A bit of work from him has helped me try and get out of this boarding house. They're all piss-pots here Terry. I can't get away from it. Lisa has been back with me for the past couple of months."

"Where, at the boarding house?"

"Yeah. She's got her own room. She's all right."

"But Dad, you know it's not a very good environment for her."

"She's fine. She's been still doing her guitar lessons. She's been singing at a coffee shop around the corner from here."

"Well as long as she's safe," Terry showed his concern.

"She's okay," Stephen reassured.

"Good. Well we're going in the Hobart race next week. Wish me luck."

"You be careful, mate. Don't take any risks out in the ocean. It'll swallow you up quick smart." Stephen had sadness in his tone. He didn't want to lose another.

His words came back into Terry's head again on the fourth day of the race. Just the night before Terry and Patrick were on watch when the ocean was black, flat, a mill pond. A mist hung 15 feet above the ocean, lit from above by a moon providing a diffused glow. The sails hung limp, with no breeze at all and it was all they could do to keep the boat on the course. Terry first noticed the luminous trail coming out of the darkness running wide across their bow, about 100 yards away. It came closer, an eerie phosphorescent glistening light at the surface of the water. It was running down their port side but turned straight towards the cockpit where they were sitting. There was no boat speed at all, and so, nothing they could do but instinctively hold on tight.

"What the fuck do you reckon that is, Pat?"

"I don't know but I think it would be a good idea to hold on very tight to something."

They stared as the trail, four metres wide, approached at about eight knots.

"Shit it's going to hit us. Hang on!"

"No it's turning," Patrick stood up and watched the trail disappear under the bow. Suddenly a tail broke the water and splashed Terry, scaring the living daylights out of him: "Fuckin' shit. What *was* that?"

"I don't know but it sure was big." Patrick pointed out off the stern now. "Look, there it goes."

Terry couldn't even turn around to look he was so scared by the encounter. Patrick realized Terry was not feeling the best and suggested they call the watch. It was 2am when Terry crawled into the quarter berth. He was asleep before his head hit the pillow. He dreamed of the good start they had, running the line to perfection then managing to point her nose up to stay up with the leaders on the first tack. Their second "come about" cost them dearly in placings out the heads as Alby tried to skirt the cliffs off Middle Harbour. They had a good start overall and settled into the race running about 30th out of 94 boats. *Revenge* was performing well in the reaching conditions. Alby was heading out wide to run down the rhumb line into Hobart. The tactic had been followed by a number of boats in the fleet. Two had not and slipped along the coast and well into Bass Strait on the nor-easter. *Revenge* was out wide now, becalmed in his dream.

"All hands on deck," came a scream from above.

Terry was jolted back into the bunk when he first tried to get up. He could feel the boat rolling onto her beam. He battled his way toward the hatch, grabbing hold of the nearest purchase point. Plastic plates rattled in their shelves, a few clunking out with a violent pitch that nearly threw Terry backwards again. He gripped the railing to the stairs and pulled himself up one step. The boat slung violently sideways again as Alby barked orders. "Get that bloody head-sail down, quickly." He looked back to the hatch. "No one is to come on deck without a safety harness."

Terry was wearing his belt and clipped to the side railing from the hatchway before pulling himself out on deck. The boat was rising from a trough of the wave where she had been relatively upright. As she rose to the peak of the wave the wind, more than 80 knots, knocked her over. They prayed the railing would hold their collective weight as a huge gush of water ran over them as the boat built speed to push forward down the wave.

"Alby, I'll take her if you like," said Gladstone who had surfaced from below with his wet weather gear on. He was balanced with one foot on the push-pit, one hand on the rail, the other on the backstay. He was feeling the pressures on the boat.

"Sure Bob, just wait until we get back down this face."

"Get a sea anchor out, it may slow her down when we go down the face of the swells," said Gladstone calmly.

"Okay. Cripes, 14, 15, 16 knots. She's off the bloody log again."

"I'll take her now," said Gladstone who immediately threw the helm to port then back to centre.

Up at the bow, they were pulling the number two headsail down. Ralph and Terry were trying to fold the sail down but the wind was pulling it back, almost pulling them overboard. Terry found his way back down the deck and started pushing the sail through the main hatchway.

"Get the storm jib up here. Patrick, pass it up this way," he yelled as the last of the number two disappeared. He held on as they were knocked down again.

The main-sail was still to the top of the mast which was now pushed down by the wind to six feet off the water each time the boat came to the top of the waves. During the knock downs they just hung on tight. The wind was whipping the white water at them so hard it stung any exposed flesh.

Another knock down, they hung on again. As she righted they would build speed again and head down the face of the giant waves and hoped the nose wouldn't dip again.

Terry was near the mast and wrapped his arms around its base as the boat went on her ear. The log whirred in the wind as it lifted from the water. A hole appeared in the water ahead and they were on the way down another face, surfing, in a 60-footer.

"Get that fuckin' main down NOW," he screamed from the cockpit. Two crewmen got on the mainsheet. The cleat holding the main sheet was in danger of lifting from the deck. As soon as they pulled the notch she gave way. Valiant attempts to hold the sheet resulted in rope burns for three of the crew as the force of the gale threw the huge sail into the spreaders. It exploded into bus ticket-sized pieces of canvas which disappeared into the face of the swell. The rope surrounding the sail was all that was left.

Terry looked up to see the mast still whipping from the force of the explosion: "Fuck, did you see that thing blow?"

"Out of the way Terry, I'll go and clip the storm jib on."

"Have you got a harness, Pat?"

"Naaah, don't worry, I'll hang on."

"No way man, you can't go up there without a line. Not in this sea. Here, take mine." Terry unclipped his belt and wrapped it around Patrick. "Now clip it on."

Patrick sorted out the line and clipped it to the rail as Terry went below to pack the sail. Even with the mainsail gone the wind pushed the boat along as fast as she would go. The speed log went off the dial again, and again. Each wave looked like it would tip over on top of them although the top of each wave was now not as violent with the main gone. *Revenge* would lay over on her 89-foot mast and start to sail. Gladstone was throwing the helm around wildly as they went over the top into another high-speed surf down the face of a wave.

"You guys have got to get that storm jib up. I'm not getting any steerage at the bottom," Gladstone was shouting over the din of noise created by the wind and the sea.

Terry surfaced with another safety harness and clipped on. Patrick was forward of the mast and had just moved his clip forward when the surfing boat slammed into the back of the swell ahead. The bow dipped about six feet into the wave and the resulting overflow swept down the deck sending them all sprawling. Terry managed to stay inside the stanchions but Patrick went straight through and was being washed down the outside of the boat. As he reached Terry, he grabbed for one of his legs. Terry instinctively pulled it out of the way and realized Patrick was at the full reach of the harness, grabbing for the railing. He was totally submerged and came out of the water pulling frantically at the railings to get himself up high enough for a gulp of air.

"You OK?" Terry asked.

"I've been better," Patrick responded. "Permission to come back aboard please sir." He always had good manners.

"Yeah sure," Terry said as he grabbed at one of Patrick's legs. "But I'd better ask the skipper first."

"Well can you let go of my leg, so that I can." Patrick's knuckles were white from hanging on.

Terry realized he still had a hold on Patrick and let go, relieved to see him scramble back on board.

"Shit, the sail," Patrick wondered if it went overboard.

"I chucked it back just before it hit. It's stuck in the hatchway."

"Keep a sharp eye on our speed and those waves, you guys." Gladstone was throwing the helm about from one side to another trying to get some feeling of steerage.

Terry held onto the forestay as he clipped the sail on. The halyard had to be freed, prompting Ralph to the position. Terry pulled for a bit of line and decided to hang on to the pulpit as he saw the mountains of sea from the top. The lashings of spray whipped up by the winds slapped his face when he cautioned a look to windward.

The troughs provided protection from this. At the bottoms they could look in any direction and see 40 feet of water looming. The white water in the swells had a sideways jerking movement that had Terry mesmerized. In one silent moment he realized what an insignificant speck he was on the face of the planet. Mother Nature had him in the palm of her hand right now. She could do what she wanted. One mistake and you were dead.

He decided to get out of the way before the sail went up and headed for the halyard winch to help Ralph. They waited until the boat was down in a trough and pulled hard to get it set. The wind catching just the top of the 40 square foot sail was enough to stop them getting it topped. A few turns around the winch and a clip-in winch handle helped get it up, but it was flapping wildly into the breeze again, accentuating the conditions.

As soon as the cockpit crew pulled on the sheet, the first hank holding the sail to the forestay, blew out.

Alby was down the hatchway in an instant.

"A shackle, I'll get a shackle," he said.

By the time he had retrieved one shackle another hank had blown.

"Make it two shackles," Terry said, leaning down into the hatch.

Patrick volunteered for the job of putting the shackles on. It was a dangerous mission in the conditions. Terry was at the mast winch preparing to loosen the sail off so Patrick could reach the clews where the hanks had broken. The sails flapped madly around him but Patrick managed to hook the shackle through the sail and around the fore-stay.

The second one caused a few anxious moments when the flapping sail suddenly wrapped around Patrick, threatening to put him into the drink again. The sail was finally set well enough for them all to experience the prowess of Gladstone at the helm.

Despite all of their problems, they were still racing. A search of the boat failed to find the Tri Sail, a small heavy-weather mainsail, so they were stuck with just the storm jib. They had 130 nautical miles to go and Bass Strait was dishing up some of her worst. The first sight of land also marked their first sight of another competitor cruising past only 500 metres to seaward. The passing boat still had a reefed main up and a storm jib and rocketed past them.

The Organ Pipes seemed to pipe out a warning of their own in the winds of Storm Bay. The route for them into the Derwent was long and varied without a main; they couldn't point very high with just the jib, which meant they had to make around 30 tacks to each one tack of the other boats. Despite the reduction in the size of the swells out in the Strait the winds were still up around 60 knots, pleasantly easing to 45 every now and then.

Terry thought they were within an hour of the finish when they headed into the Bay and a pod of around 200 dolphins joined them. The mammals completely surrounded the boat and gave Gladstone the clues of when to tack for several hours of frustrating sailing.

They watched more than a dozen boats take better courses past them as they did sharp, almost backward tacks on the storm jib, but the dolphins stayed with them, like a security blanket, all the way up the Derwent.

They were four hours into the Bay and they still had not reached the line when Gladstone ordered the whole crew to get their wet weather gear off and get into their "going ashore gear". In turn they all complied and their frustrations were finally eased when they heard the horns of hundreds, maybe thousands of cars tooting. People cheered them all the way into the dock.

As they crossed the line, the dolphins skirted away and disappeared into the Derwent.

Terry watched them swim away thanking them in his mind, for their comfort.

"We made it."

"Yeah, we made it," Patrick said with a touch of irony as they automatically took their positions to lower the storm jib as soon as they heard the engine power on.

Terry unhooked the halyard and headed for the slot on the mast in which he clipped it before Patrick took up the slack. They systematically unhitched the sheet and brace and neatly wound and hung each as they made their way to the wharf outside Constitution Dock.

Terry passed a line to a man waiting at the wharf and was surprised to see a crowd milling around, still applauding. He couldn't understand.

They had run about 30th in the event and they were being treated like they had won the race. He soon realized this was the Hobart welcome for every boat in the fleet.

"Gee, you guys had a bugger of a time up the river, ay? I watched yer come in this morning," one man up on the wharf said to Terry.

"Yeah, no main," Terry replied as he tied her off.

"Land," Terry was keen to touch it. "Dry land, let me get on there."

He pulled himself onto the wharf and felt a couple of pats on his back before he fell over. Everyone laughed. Terry got up again. The people were moving, like the wave shapes out in the Strait. He fell over again.

"Sea legs," Alby yelled out. "He's still got his sea legs. Here, come back aboard, you'll be right soon."

Terry crawled over the edge of the wharf again and landed back on the deck. He sat down but when he attempted it he found he could stand again. His knees were bent as he made it into the cockpit to sit down. Everything on board was wet. The teak decks had leaked like a sieve in the seas because they hadn't been wet down and dried out a few times to allow the surfaces to meld together after the tar re-pitching. The first water the decks had seen was from Bass Strait, and plenty of it.

The party in Hobart became a bit of a blur for Terry. He was amazed at how many young ladies were down at the wharves, apparently picking up the crewmen. He was more amazed that he and Patrick ended up in the hills having a roast dinner with the family of the girls who picked them up.

The party was cut short for Terry on New Year's Day. He had to be back in Sydney for work.

After the race, which Terry logged as a "near-death experience," he took a new look at the arena he was working in. He looked a little deeper into the people he was interviewing. The industries he was writing about were all going through mammoth changes. Shipping companies were getting new container ships, airlines were gearing up to jumbo jets. Freight was being moved in new and modern ways as were people and Terry enjoyed the task writing about it all. The trips on offer were the cream. The luncheons were at the best hotels and restaurants; the company of his peers was jovial.

Saturdays for Terry, when he was in town, now hinged around sailing. He had the bug, and when he was offered a position to crew on a new boat doing the Saturday Harbour races, he jumped at the opportunity. The 36 footer, *Aquababe* proved to be reasonably competitive after a professional coach joined the crew for six months. The sail changes became snappy and every sail was given detailed attention by the whole crew. Tacks were precise with calls from the skipper, "ready about, going about, leah ho". Terry would wait at the forestay until the sheet was completely released and pull the sail together then guide it around the mast and into the slot on the other side between the mast and the hand rail stanchions. He would follow up on the rope, which had gone from a sheet, pulling on the sail to the brace, and ensure there were no snags for it to slip over in readiness for the next turn. He would then find his position back up to windward to await the next orders.

He was now packing turtles; a small bag hung off the bow containing the spinnaker. The rig was designed for setting up beforehand allowing a quick setting of the spinnaker at the mark where the boat was turning down wind.

After five months the boat was very competitive in the harbour races and the crew was prepared to back their combined expertise by risking jugs of beer shouts with guys from other boats on who would get to the line first.

This day Terry came in from a winter sail cold and wet. He was heading for the bathroom when the phone rang. "Terry, it's me, how's it going?" Stephen was sober.

"Gedday Dad, I just got in. You must be psychic. How are you going?"

"I've decided to come up to Sydney, to live. If you hear of any work going, let me know."

"Well, a guy I sail with was saying he needed someone to look after the boat. Maybe I could ask him if he's found anyone. I don't know what it pays."

"It'll be good to see you mate."

"You too Dad, when are you coming? You can stay here until you find something."

"No it's okay, I can stay with Suzanne. I've already made arrangements."

Stephen arrived in Sydney with a bad case of the shakes, he called it, "the Joe Blakes". He knew it was time to stop drinking after he emptied a whole jar of coffee onto a bench, as he tried to spoon coffee into his cup.

The shakes slowed over the next week and Stephen was finally able to go along to an interview. He got the job.

He was supplied with a small van to get to work on the North Shore where Paul Carmody lived. The XJ6 Jaguar was garaged and had to be warmed up for Stephen to drive Carmody into the city office each morning. Stephen would then head to Rushcutter's Bay to hose down the boat and collect anything needed for the next week's race.

Terry was pleased to see his father doing well. He loved the job and kept his promise to stay away from the grog. Things were going really well for him now.

Suzanne and Damian were further relieved when he found his own flat in Glebe and with it, his independence again.

Chapter 23

Singapore's thick tropical air enveloped Terry as he walked down the stairs of the KLM Jumbo. He felt overdressed in the suit, even with a loosened tie and he wanted to get the coat off but could not do so in the hustle to the open-sided bus onto which passengers were pouring for the journey to the terminal. The scenario reminded him of the old wharf buildings in Melbourne. He could smell the avgas and diesel as the whir of the jet engines whistled around them.

In the terminal he noticed the signs on the walls showing acceptable hair length and thanked Christ he had his hair trimmed again before leaving Sydney. "How can a country rule on the length of your hair," he thought. "It is as oppressive as the heat here."

The Holiday Inn was an older-style motel, the foyer well trampled. He likened it to the classic hotel entrances in the movie, *Casablanca*. He noticed the dimly lit bar and dining area beyond the lifts, but was keen to get his bags away. The room had wood-paneling three-quarters of the way up the walls which may have been trendy some time ago but now just helped to create a gloomy feeling. He pulled aside faded drapes to reveal the crowded street six floors below. The smell of diesel fumes had stuck in his nostrils; all the cabs, and most of the other vehicles, it seemed, ran on diesel. The bed felt a bit on the lumpy side, but at least the room had an ensuite and clean linen.

Terry freshened up with a cool shower and jumped into jeans and a sports shirt. It was too late for dinner, and anyway, the plane food was still welling in his stomach.

Patrick Markham had told him of his trips to "Singers" and he was keen to see some of the nightspots he had spoken of, but for now he would start with the bar downstairs.

The dining room was still fairly active for 11pm and the room was buzzing with bodies and conversation in a multitude of languages. Terry sauntered up to the bar and cast his eyes across the shelf of whiskies.

"Chivas Regal, please." He had no sooner ordered when a voice chimed in from behind him: "Ah, and a fine choice, I must say; but have you tried the Glenfiddich, it'll put even more curls in your hair."

"Yes, I think you're right. Could you make that a Glenfiddich, er, two Glenfiddichs, thanks mate," Terry said looking at the man's near-empty glass.

"Another Aussie on holiday. Thank you for the drink."

"Well, a working holiday, you might say. And yourself, what do you do with yourself mate?"

"I work for a Canadian company on the rigs off the coast of Indonesia. The work is boring but the money's bloody good. This is my third tour here. We have to sign up for a year each time." He held out his hand: "Chet Murray's the name."

Terry noticed the firmness of his grip. "Good to meet you Chet, Terry Martin, Sydney."

"Good old Sydney, Australia." Chet pulled up a chair beside Terry. "I've had a few good nights there, I tell you, some of the sweetest little women in the world in Sydney."

"Yeah, I suppose you're right. What about here? Where's all the action?"

"You're sitting in it my friend. You wouldn't believe the women who come in here. Don't worry looking, they'll find you. But keep your wits about you, mind. They can spin the odd yarn every now and then. Just don't fall for anything, man. You sure as hell don't go looking for it here. No siree, no siree."

Terry enjoyed the smooth whisky as Chet spoke of life on the oil rigs and the wonders of Singapore. They were into the second round and Chet was telling about flying to work by chopper doing 12 weeks at a time on the rig before coming to town to spend up. His eyes flicking up and a twist of his head towards the door took Terry's eyes with him. She was about 24, curly blonde hair to her shoulders.

"Take a look at that, you'd think that skirt had been painted on. See what I mean? What did I tell you? She has been in and out of this place six times tonight. Looking to hand-pick her lay. She's looking for something; and I don't think it's me."

"Maybe you're not her type Chet, a bit loud..."

"She's had five goes to get me. If she wants me, she can damned well have me, but I don't think so, man."

As he spoke the girl's eyes met Terry and her body veered towards him. "Hold the phone, I think she's coming our way. This may be my lucky night yet."

"Or mine," said Terry smiling.

"Yep, you may just be right pardner, you may just be right."

She spoke in a deep voice, broken English, from the continent: "May I join with you?"

"Sure can, love. It's a free country," Chet replied, but she was looking at Terry who turned belatedly and pulled another stool up next to him.

"It's too hot in this place, don't you think? It is for me anyway. Hi, my name is Catherine." She said it in three syllables: "Cat- Er-Een".

"G'day, I'm Terry and this is Chet. Would you like a drink?"

"Oh you from Australia. I tell from your accent, it very good, Australia. You here long?" Her eyes fluttered and Terry felt one knee drop a little.

"Just here for a couple of days."

"Oh that is good, a couple of days."

"Where are you travelling to, from here?"

"Back home to Sydney. And you, Catherine, what brings you to this place?"

"About five months ago I came with my sister here from Germany. We have been here since. Well, my sister has gone travelling with a friend. I have been here. It a very nice place when you get to know it. Very; what you call it, cosmer pooli,"

"Cosmopolitan," Terry chimed in.

"Yes, lots of people, from all over the world here."

"Well this is the perfect example right here, don't you say," Chet said, "a Canadian, German and an Aussie drinking in a chink bar." Chet was getting louder again, prompting glances from around the room.

Terry offered again: "What would you like to drink, Catherine?"

"I would like a gin and tonic please."

The barman gave her a familiar look as he placed the drink down and took a couple of notes from Terry's pile.

"Yes, it is an interesting place. I don't go much for the locals though. Not many Won Hung Lohs here," she giggled.

Terry was starting to relax; she was talking dirty, but he didn't have the experience to capitalize on the remark.

Chet boomed in with the skite first. "There's one hung low over here," they all laughed with him.

Catherine slapped him on the knee: "Don't you worry someone will come along for you soon." Chet liked the attention and launched back into the adventure describing the excitement of a helicopter landing on a rig in a gale. Catherine acknowledged him for a while with nods. Terry was getting an instant replay of his first two drinks, but witnessing someone else's reactions to the same story. He prompted Chet into the intriguing lights in the night sky, but didn't get a word in for another 10 minutes until a cute Asian girl walked up and whispered in Chet's ear. He laughed heartily: "Oh Mindy, you wicked, wicked girl; here meet some friends: Terry here from Australia, (Oor-Stray-lyaah), and Catherine (Cat-ar-reen) from Germany. Hey, it must be my shout." Chet was suddenly pre-occupied with Mindy whispering in his ear. He downed his whisky as Mindy consumed her usual champagne cocktail: "Well, Terry, good luck. I've got some playing to do. See you around, Catherine."

Mindy smiled a departure and snuggled in close to Chet as they left.

Terry was about to order another drink when Catherine leant closer to him. "Shall we have the next one in your room?"

"I thought you'd never ask," Terry was off the stool in a flash. He left a couple of bills on the bar, not that he could afford it, but he wanted to impress.

He held her hand when it was offered as they walked from the bar. As they waited for the lift she held his hand in front of her. By the time the door opened she had slipped her tongue into his mouth and flicked it around two or three times before pulling back, looking at him through piercing blue eyes.

They were in a passionate embrace all the way up the hall and somehow he managed to open the door, without breaking the bond. Inside the room Catherine slewed back. "Wow, is it hot or is it me?"

"A bit of both, I think, I'll turn up the air conditioning while you have a shower if you wish."

"That's a good idea." She opened her purse and pulled a small tin from it. "Here, you roll up while I'm in there."

Terry took the small tin and opened it to see a compressed package and cigarette papers. He stared at the tin a moment. He rolled a cigarette. The warnings from friends that drugs meant jail, even death in the East, went out the window with the smoke.

After a few puffs he put the joint in the ashtray, stripped to his underwear and lay on the bed as the sound of the shower stopped.

Catherine emerged naked. Soaking wet, she straddled him. "Did you roll a joint?"

"Mmmm, there." he pointed at the still smouldering smoke. "Come here," he pulled her close and flinched a little as her cool skin touched his.

Catherine took a big suck on the cigarette as she ripped at his bulging underwear.

It was about 3am when he woke with Catherine's hand in his groin. Her sensual touch aroused him immediately to his hour-long episode earlier.

"How come you have stayed here for five months?"

She laid her head across his chest: "When I arrived here with my sister, we met a couple of fellows and got separated. I woke in a hotel room the next morning and my purse was gone, my passport, money, everything.

"Say, can you lend me some money? I can pay you back when I get home."

"Sorry Catherine, but I am on a very small budget already. If I had heaps, it would be my pleasure..."

"You have some money, you must have some money; we make

beautiful love, why can't you pay me for that then? Two thousand, that's all."

"Two thousand. Come off the grass. What the..... Well, I didn't realize you were.... on the game. I didn't expect to have to pay you for this."

"You a bastard," she said gripping his penis hard. "All you think about is this thing." She squeezed so hard it hurt.

"Fuck off Catherine," he said, pulling her hand away. "It was lovely sweetheart, but not worth two grand." He put his arm over her shoulder. "Come here. All I can do is offer you this bed for tonight. You either enjoy that with me, or head off, but I simply don't have the dollars to help you out."

Her whole story sounded like a scam to Terry anyway. The type of thing Chet had warned him about. He wanted to tell her, but felt it better that nothing further was said. Catherine even shed a few tears in his arms but soon reached down under the sheets again.

He awoke four hours later to a noise. Catherine had gone. He jumped out of bed and ran across to check his wallet. He was not sure, but estimated there was about $50 missing from his small roll.

"Worth every cent, I reckon."

He told Maureen about Catherine when he got home on the Monday. "I closed my eyes while I was screwing her and imagined it was you, Maureen."

"Well, it wasn't, was it? Why didn't you bring her home? She'd be a nice little toy for us to play with. I'm getting bored with my vibrator."

He offered his services again but was embarrassed by what he'd said when Maureen simply changed the subject.

Terry mooched around the house for the rest of the week. On Saturday he had a break from the regular sailing and read the papers from cover to cover, making sure not to look at the form guide. He didn't really want to know what was running.

Maureen came down the stairs in her white dressing gown. She didn't look so good this morning. "I need to do something today. What time does the cinema start up at the junction? They're showing *Last Tango in Paris*."

"Gee, I wouldn't mind seeing that myself." Terry had seen shorts of the film. He opened the paper and planned the outing. He joked with Maureen on the way.

During the walk home he stopped her at the corner store. "Hold on a moment, I won't be long."

He emerged with a sheepish grin on his face.

"What did you get? We didn't need anything, did we?"

He held off, but eventually relented as they got home that he had bought a pound of butter.

"Great for your Vegemite toast, Terry, but you're not getting near me with that stuff."

"Oh come on, Maureen. Where's your sense of adventure?" he yelled up the stairs.

"Go away, I am busy," she said, turning on her vibrator.

"What are you doing up there?" Terry enquired. He made one last move. "Just one passionate kiss good night."

The vibrator seemed to double in speed. "Mmmmm, not now, I'm buseeeeeeeeeee."

Terry smiled as he walked down the hallway and went to bed.

Over the following months Terry immersed himself in his work and went to the parties to enjoy the high society trimmings along the way. The parties seemed to be more frequent these days and each had their chance of adventure. Seduction came in many forms and Terry left himself open to as much as possible with no desire to become heavily involved in any one relationship.

A major trip had been offered which would take in Bangkok, Athens, Vienna, Amsterdam and London. The deadline was getting close, his shots had been updated and the ticket was almost in his hand and he had made arrangements to stay with Bruce McEvoy, an acquaintance he met in Sydney a few months before who had moved to a new job in freight forwarding in London.

He had to watch his budget this time. In Bangkok he was offered a buddha stick by an Australian bar manager. Following the few puffs he had had at parties with Maureen in Sydney, he was now open to the suggestion of a puff.

Terry got terribly stoned and eventually bought a packet containing about 70 sticks.

"I have friends in London who may like a smoke," he said as he handed over the $10. He wrapped a couple of magazines around the package and placed it into the lid of his brief case.

Amsterdam was so different to what he had imagined. He enjoyed the art gallery, the window-shopping and the bars. Over three days he prepared stories on the passenger and freight facilities of the airport before heading for Rotterdam on a train.

This day his head was as hazy as the day. The journey was shorter than he'd thought and he caught a cab from the station to the wharf where he was to meet the delegation.

To his amazement, he was given the red carpet treatment. The Harbour Master's launch was packed with officials from the Harbour Organizational Committee. The launch meandered around the biggest port in the world as Terry photographed the well-organized transshipment terminals. They had only gone around a quarter of the port facility when Terry ran out of film. Anyway, he had a flight this afternoon. The smorgasbord lunch sustained him and probably prepared him for the ordeal he was about to go through en route to London.

Customs officers were going through everyone's cases. Terry felt beads of sweat forming on his brow as he offered his brief case for inspection before boarding. He opened the case and flapped down the top section grabbing the parcel in between a magazines he had placed around it.

"Just magazines for reading in here," he said looking down into the case, lifting things with his other hand. "Notebooks, camera..." He managed to push the magazine containing the wad back and re-fastened the press-studs. The Customs officer closed his case, and turned it to Terry prompting him to do up the front clasp.

Terry felt the tension in the air. Military uniforms were everywhere. 'Whew,' he thought as he picked up his case, but it was not over yet. The tarmac had been turned into a gauntlet. There were two lines of armed guards, standing four metres apart for 70 metres all the way to the aircraft. Every second guard had a dog on a leash. Terry wished he was not wearing the suit. He felt hot. He suddenly imagined they were all sniffer dogs and quickened step when one of the animals leaned forward from its sitting position towards him before settling again. The walk to the aircraft seemed to take forever. By the time he reached the plane and got himself seated he was dripping with perspiration. He turned the air nozzle to his face after he had wiped it dry with a handkerchief.

The scene at Heathrow presented a whole new set of problems. He imagined the headlines: *"Journalist held on drug smuggling charges"*. It bothered him. He was agitated and must have shown it. Bruce McEvoy yelled: "Hey Terry, over here."

He picked up his bag from the conveyor belt and gladly walked toward the familiar face from Sydney. Bruce had been working in London for just a few months. They had met at an industry function in Sydney where Bruce told him of his new job. He was larger than life and accompanied by a uniformed officer.

"This is Jack Shrimpton, head of Customs. I told him we should save you the trouble of waiting in those lines. Can't have one of our Sydney journos waiting in lines at Heathrow now, can we?"

Jack extended a hand and Terry bent his knees to release his brief case momentarily to the floor to shake hands with him. "Nice to meet you, Jack. Gee, thanks Bruce, good to see you too, mate."

"How was the flight? Not long at all from Rotterdam, I know, but it can be bumpy in bad weather over the Channel."

They walked through a passageway and out into the main terminal. He would not be having his baggage checked this day. He had contacts, it seemed.

Terry needed the bathroom and asked directions when they were out into the terminal. He seemed to pee for several minutes and took the time to splash his face with water before he came out. Bruce was waiting alone. "Jack had to go back to work, he wished you a nice stay." Bruce was pleasant, but seemed a bit rushed. "Come on, I still have an hour or so to work. You can come with me and wait there, until I finish work. I'll just be an hour or so."

Safely away from the terminal, in Bruce's BMW, Terry pulled out the pack of sticks. "Thank Christ you got me out of there. You wouldn't believe the gauntlet I had to run at Rotterdam with this stuff."

"Wow, what have you got there?"

"I thought you might like some Thai sticks."

"I'd say you will have a deal there, mate. I have a mate coming over later tonight. I reckon he'll take most of that off your hands."

Bruce had an immediate market for the sticks and offered Terry 100 pounds for the lot. Terry was glad to be rid of the packet and used the money to do some shopping in the city the following day. He hitched a lift from Bruce into a station where he could catch the tube into town. He got out at Piccadilly and was pissed off when a photographer snapped him at the top of the stairs and offered to send him a print, for five pounds.

"How did you know?"

"You stick out a bit. It may be the hair do or something," the photographer said.

"Well, give me your card and if I want the picture, I'll write to you."

He took the quick tourist trip around London, stopping only to take in the changing of the guard at Buckingham Palace.

That weekend Bruce and his girlfriend, Anika, drove him around to the places in London they had got to know. They took a run on Saturday and swam in the pool at Eton College. Terry was reluctant at first as it was only about 75 degrees F. He was assured the treat was a rarity.

They lunched at a waterside restaurant on the Thames before he took his flight out on Sunday afternoon.

"Yes, I was booked direct to Sydney, but I have decided to go back to Amsterdam for a short while," he explained to the ticket clerk. He decided he should see a bit more of the city.

On arrival at Schiphol he found himself in a huge tunnel, following the other passengers. Some used the moving footways while others walked along outside. He had stepped from the third footway and was about to board the fourth when the cute, uniformed blonde girl walked up beside him.

"Hello, are you here for long?" she enquired, the top of her head just above the level of his shoulder.

"No, just a few days, maybe a week."

"That is plenty of time to see Holland," she said. Terry was getting used to her guttural speech. She smiled at him. "Do you know where the bags come out?"

"No, not really, I was just following the crowd from the flight."

"I will show you where."

"Oh, you work here, for the airline?"

"For the same company, you might say, for the government. I'm in Customs."

"Oh, that must be interesting for you!"

The officer showed Terry where to collect his bag and waited with him.

"That's it, coming now."

He grabbed the bag and struggled with it momentarily until the uniformed girl volunteered her help.

"I'll help you with that. If you come this way, I'll show you a quick way through Customs." She opened a blue door and motioned him through. To his amazement, the room was enclosed. The girl lifted his bag onto a table: "Could you open the bag for me please? I must do an inspection before you can go."

"What for, why do you want to inspect my bag?" He knew there was nothing for her to find, except the soiled clothes he had carried around in his suitcase. All of the sticks had gone through Bruce. Lucky for him he hadn't brought anything back with him. The way this lady was going through his things she would most definitely find anything she wanted.

She totally emptied his bag, his briefcase and even his toiletry bag before feeling the bottom and sides of the case.

He taunted her a little: "What are you looking for, drugs or something? Do I look like I take drugs?" The officer ignored him most of the time, simply responding with a roll of the eyes as she sniffed at his talcum powder.

"Hey, would you like to strip search me?"

"No, that won't be necessary!" She was terse now.

"Oh come on, be a sport!"

"No, you may pack up your things and you may leave. You go out here and through the red door."

"Typical," he thought. "The red door."

The extra days in Amsterdam were not on his itinerary. He enjoyed the bars, restaurants and the window shopping before finally getting through to his Sydney office by telephone. They wanted him back straight away, and no, they would not send his holiday pay over.

The flight home seemed to take forever. He felt guilty about taking the extra time but at least found he had really experienced a bit of the Amsterdam that drew travelers to it.

The taxi from Mascot pulled up out front of the Clovelly house. Terry noticed the lights were on and knocked at the door. With no answer he pulled out his key to open the door.

Their third house-mate in eight months was emerging from the bathroom as Terry walked in.

"Hey, Charlie, how are you?"

"Oh, Terry. What are you doing here?"

"I just got back from Amsterdam."

"Well, you had better find yourself somewhere to stay. Maureen has done the bolt. Her boss, who owns the house, was around this morning. He has given us until the weekend to get out."

"But I've paid up rent until the end of the month."

"Doesn't matter; we paid our rent to Maureen. She hasn't been paying it to him. He reckons she has cooked the books to her favour at the restaurant too."

The bathroom was lonely next morning as Terry prepared himself for the office.

He walked into the foyer of the publishing house where Carli looked up and stopped him. "Hi Terry. I have instructions to give you this." She handed him an envelope and reached under the table for a plastic bag. "We emptied the contents of your desk into this."

"What about the stories from the trip? I have to write them up."

"That has all been handled by the public relations people. The boss has told me you are not to enter the premises."

"Well thanks a lot, Carli. By the way, how are you?"

Her coldness melted a little. "I'm not bad; Keith and I are going to get married, you know."

"Well Carli, have a nice life. See you then."

His heart was heavy as he walked through Surry Hills. His first port of call solved his housing problem, a friend had to move from his house nearby and had a couple of months left on his lease. Terry also managed to buy some furniture from him which solved them both the problem of moving.

The second call he made was to pay for the printing of the business cards he had done for the trip. Two hours later, he tried to come to terms with how he had gone to pay his printing bill and bought the business instead.

He had his holiday and severance pay, or what was left of it, a new house, a new business and life was rushing along.

Chapter 24

The clank of the small offset printing presses was getting on Terry's nerves. The operator, Shane, was a likeable chap, but lived in a different world, Terry thought. Shane Sutherland lived on painkillers because of the clanking, and swore loudly as paper jammed in the machines. Some days he actually got into the rhythm of the machines and could have three of them humming along at once.

Terry was new to all of this, but he had what he thought were good contacts around the inner city and thought he could make the little business profitable. He inherited Shane, but had to pay Bob Moroney, a former Sydney detective, who had an early leave pass from the force, for the machines.

Moroney called him at 10am and suggested lunch at the local pub. Here he admitted that he had gained a major contract for the Post Office only a few months earlier. It was so big an order he had to farm it out all over town. The biggest printer was cautious and would only do the work if Moroney signed a bill of sale on one of the printing machines as security for the credit they would give him. It was a small unit but had good enough registration to print brochures and the like in full colour. Terry had already purchased some parts for it and was planning a weekend with an engineer to get it rolling.

Bob finally revealed this lunch hour, that he'd delivered the postal job which was about $90,000 worth of printing, but failed to pay most of the sub-contractors. They were after him and he was clearing out. He figured that few of them would go to the trouble of trying to track him down. He reckoned he could lead them a merry enough chase to make it too costly for them to pursue him up north.

"Well, what the bloody hell do I do with the machine?" Terry demanded.

Moroney shuffled a bit on his chair.

"How about you buy it back off me then," Terry continued.

Bob finished half of his schooner in one swig: "My shout," he said, and for a fleeting moment Terry thought he was going to agree to buying the machine back off him. "My shout, for the beer that is, you'll have to sell the machine, I reckon. It's no good to me anymore."

Terry was miffed. "But isn't that illegal?" He was angry, but as soon as he spoke he realized the folly of his comment to this bloke. Moroney was burly and looked like he could hold a bull out to piss, with one hand.

"No, not if you didn't know it was on a bill of sale. Listen," Bob leaned forward on his chair, placing one hand on Terry's shoulder in a consoling manner. "I have been thinking about this and realized I had done the wrong thing by you. You weren't to know, and I want to help you out. Shane has worked with me for five years and he reckons you're all right."

Terry leaned back for a second and looked into Bob's piercing blue eyes as he continued. "I would suggest you move out of the factory, because that's where they will be looking for it."

"Move out? Bloody hell, I have only just moved in. Three bloody weeks Bob. That money I paid you for the machine was all I had."

"I'm sorry, Terry, but you have a machine that is worth maybe three times what you paid me for it. Move it out of there and buy some time. I reckon it'll take them three or four weeks to get rolling on any action."

"Christ Bob, I had some plans for that machine."

"Well, forget them, it was always a dog of a machine even when we had it going well. I don't think you'd even try to get a good colour job off it.

Get rid of it and buy another Multi. There is a heap of work for that type of machine around here, you'll see. You'll probably be able to buy a new one and have change from what you would get for the big one."

Terry knew there was little he could do. Bob was huge; his last four years in the force were with the 21st Division. He was uncompromising. He had been obliging enough; at least, to warn him what to expect now and even suggested how he should deal with it. Terry slowly finished off his beer and passed on a tip he had for the fourth at Randwick the next day. They shook hands and wished each other well and went their ways.

He returned to tell Shane the news that he already knew. Shane had been talking to Bob for a couple of weeks since he left. He had sorted the mail and he knew what the letters meant. They would have to move house. "It's just bloody lucky that I haven't had time to print your cards yet," Shane confessed. He knew all along all right.

Three weeks after kicking off in this new industry, Terry had a steady stream of work for the machines but was now discovering some of the trials and tribulations of the world of business. In journalism he relied on trust when quoting people. The business world had another set of rules he was yet to learn. He'd have to roll with this one, he had no alternative.

It had been one of those Fridays. Apart from Bob's news, all of the things he had attempted to clear out were backlogged at the printer. There was nothing to deliver this afternoon because Shane had the two machines pumping out an urgent order he had to fill. Shane promised to come in at the weekend and clear Terry's work. This, however, meant a list of five people he had to contact and tell them jobs he had promised by the end of the week, would not be ready. A few he handled on the phone, and gave them the courtesy of admitting he was slack, but would make it up to them by delivering early next week. There was a stream of disappointment and surface protestation, but Terry was genuine in his concern. He'd make a greater effort next week. He was learning that Shane had his jobs too and there was only a limited amount of press time. This they would have to sort out, when they moved.

It was 5.30 by the time he arrived home. The two-bedroom terrace house blended into the row of houses which all looked the same except for the number outside. He almost walked into the wrong one again and was looking forward to relaxing once inside.

He opened the door to see the two squatted on the floor. His new house mate, Jennifer, and Angie, the friend he had heard so much about over the past two weeks.

"Heeeey there, Terry," Jennifer giggled. "This is Angie, she's just got back from up the coast and she brought back some mushies and we've already had ours and we left you one up there in that jar of honey." Jennifer was flailing her arm in the general direction of the mantelpiece.

Terry closed the door: "Hi Angie, I've heard all about your shifts at the loony bin with Jenn..."

Angie slung her arm forward: "Oh, I don't want to talk about it; not work, I'm still on holiday." He noticed she was slurring her words a little, a tipsy slur. "Anyway, it's really nice to meet you, but we've already had a few mushies, and it's just coming on to us, so I don't think we can really get into much of a rave right now."

"I've never had this stuff. What does it do? If I have one now will I be...?"

"If you have it right now," Angie said, "I suppose we'll be in similar head space."

Terry understood through the slurs of the girls that they were well on the way. He managed to find out that Angie had arrived about 4pm, so he estimated they had been going for at least an hour, maybe an hour and a half. He looked at the Vegemite jar: "We're happy little Vegemites as bright as bright can be, we all enjoy...." They groaned in unison. "Oh shut up. No singing, please?"

Terry took the jar into the kitchen where he shuffled through a drawer for a teaspoon, before plugging in the kettle.

His throat convulsed as soon as the honeyed button-sized mushroom hit the back of his tongue and he had to forcefully swallow a second and third time to coax it down. Even then he felt he may throw up. Within moments the kettle was boiling and he offered coffee to the others who agreed on the idea. He wondered how long it would take him to join them, but also felt the one tiny mushroom he had consumed would not be enough to do much. "What about the honey? Do you reckon if I had some honey in my coffee it would do something?"

"Yeah, yeah," the girls said.

Four teaspoons of honey went into Terry's mug and he threw one each in for the girls.

"He's really straight," Jennifer had told Angie before he got home. "He only recently started smoking pot, and that was in a bar in Amsterdam, half-way around the world."

Terry sipped on his coffee and realized the girls were somewhere else. He felt light-headed now and quickly made himself another coffee with honey and sat down cross-legged on the floor un-foiling a chunky piece of hash he had secured from a rag trader during his rounds this day.

He had difficulty rolling it, but with perseverance he managed to make the cigarette sprinkled with flakes from a small block of hash.

He lit up and savoured the taste, then took another puff before offering it to Jennifer. She looked at his outstretched arm. After holding his arm outstretched for maybe 30 seconds, he realized she couldn't see it. He moved his hand to the right as Angie's head rose. Her dark eyes glittered as she took a toke, sucking the joint firmly. Terry found himself staring into her eyes. Intuition allowed him to take the cigarette back and as he took a puff he asked again, "What can I expect?"

"I really don't know," said Angie in a song-like voice. "It's different for everyone, like something to do with your metabolism."

"Yeah, but how long will it take? Until I come down, I mean," he sounded like a nervous child.

"Don't worry, Terry, you can't have even started going up yet."

Terry finished the joint and had full intention of rolling another until a realization came over him. He wanted to talk about his day, but felt it not the time or place to reiterate his business hassles. A strange presence surrounded him. Were they speaking to each other by telepathy or something? His mind was wandering as he looked at them staring at the floor. "They sit here, heads bowed side by side looking into their own laps, but they are communicating somehow?" he thought.

He spoke but all he heard was a noise, and as he chased a recognition of the noise in his mind he realized the noise was what he had just said; but it was coming out slowly, as though someone had just taped it and then held a finger on the top of the reel during playback.

He laughed aloud, and listened for the slow motion echo and then realized what he must have sounded like to them when he entered the room. Worse still, what he must seem like to them now. Does it matter that they are not looking up?

"I know now," he said and they looked up at him. "It's okay," he was yelling now, and they laughed. He joined in but stopped soon after to enjoy the slo-mo replay, and then giggled some more.

"Isn't it funny how everything goes into slow motion," he said grinning widely.

Jennifer and Angie were speaking now, but it was confusing to him because he could not see their faces properly, only the tops of their heads again. He had to concentrate hard on what they were saying. After a few minutes he was bored with attempting to track their conversation.

He looked around the room focusing on objects, waiting for them to move or do something. Friends had told him about their experiences with hallucinogenic drugs and he was now attempting to "will" things to happen. He was disappointed that this didn't work for him, but didn't really mind that things still seemed fairly normal. He didn't care if the walls stayed straight, he didn't care that the two lovely women in front of him didn't turn into animals, he liked them as they were. Halter tops, bra-less, flowing summer skirts pulled to their thighs and tucked into their laps. The stories he had heard about tripping were somehow a long way from this. He felt pretty good and thought he may just close his eyes for a moment and feel the thing happening.

It felt pleasant; he was light, weightless. He couldn't feel anything where his hands touched his knees. He opened his eyes and looked straight ahead. The brightness of the light blinded him so he momentarily held his hand out, shielding the light closing his eyes again. As he opened them gently, he was looking down into the room. He could see the three people sitting down there, cross-legged, all heads bowed. He wondered if the girls were seeing the same thing and hazarded a glance to one side, really expecting to see them, up near the top of the room with him. There was nothing, just the strange sensation of seeing the top corners of the room. A moth flew around the light and strayed off into a web in the corner he was looking into. He could see the little moth's wide eyes. The spider wasn't around.

He wasn't afraid, he just took it in for what seemed to him like half an hour. In reality, only minutes passed.

"Hey," he shouted, "look at me." He watched their heads move slightly below. At least they moved. A few more seconds and he realized they were looking at him down there: "No, not there; up here."

Their heads moved from side to side again, but they were not looking up. Then his mind told him that was his body was down there with the other two, sitting on the floor. "Wait a minute, I'll come down. Hang on." To communicate he would have to go back down there.

"Easy does it." He felt as though his elbows were hooked over the top of a giant gold fish bowl. To get back, all he had to do was release them. He felt he was sliding around the inside of the huge bowl and watched the top of his head loom up gently. Closing his eyes he re-entered. "Wow," he said, opening his eyes to see Jennifer and Angie looking straight at him, confused.

"This guy is really crazy, Jennifer." Angie was smiling.

"Well I might be crazy, but I'm not stupid," Terry laughed, and felt excitement welling up in him as he attempted to describe what he had just experienced, not realizing, in the moment, just how crazy he must have sounded to them.

He was insistent: "When I was talking to you before, I was up there," pointing to the top corner of the room behind him. The girls looked at each other, mouths agape.

"That's it," Angie murmured, and the sound came out like a tune Terry knew.

"What?"

"That's it!"

"That's what?" He was starting to get confused a little but lost any sense of paranoia as Angie smiled and said slowly: "It's working on you."

"What's working?"

"The mushies," both chorused.

"Yeah," he said, feeling like he had stretched the word out for about 15 seconds, "it's working on me all right. One little mushie. I like it up there," he pointed over his shoulder up to the corner of the room, "so I think I'll give it another go. See you soon."

He closed his eyes and willed the weightlessness to return. He could feel the lift sensation this time, up until he could see the brightness of the light glowing red through his eyelids and turned his head downward again. Slowly he opened his eyes to take in the circular pattern of the carpet on which they were sitting. He realized by now that it was fruitless to attempt to talk to them from here, although he did give a farewell as he decided to check out the rest of the house. He was in a controlled flight and cruised under the archway and out through the dining room into the kitchen where the dishes were waiting. "Boring," he thought. Terry continued up the narrow stairs but did not feel good about going too far. As long as he could see himself sitting on the floor he was comfortable and moved around the bowl sweeping across the sides, down around the bottom, upside down to right side up.

He was lying across the rim of his goldfish bowl, head supported by one hand, elbow comfortably balanced, when the knocking started. He noticed movement in the others, their heads only. He could hear their voices, but couldn't hear what they were saying. "More, more," he thought. "Yeah, right on," he replied. Suddenly he felt silly, perched on top of the bowl, that they wouldn't even agree was there.

"I can't talk to you from here," he was slipping his legs over the side of the bowl edging his arms down to the rim. He let go and felt the surge as he returned to his body. From down here the girls looked frantic. Angie was shaking him by now. "Well, aren't you going to answer it?" Her eyes were wide and laughing. He felt a permanent smile had been welded to his dial.

"Is the phone ringing? I can't hear it," he said.

"No, the door, some-one's at the door." Terry couldn't work out who was talking back now. Then he caught what they were saying. "The door, the door; some-one's at the door."

Fear suddenly gripped him. "Oh, shit, well why don't you answer it? I was having a great time up there."

Angie smiled: "It's your house; you answer the door."

"Oh, okay," he started to get up, "but what'll I say?"

"Hello might be a good start," Angie's voice was singing again.

As he stood up he felt his head want to continue towards the ceiling again. He held it down with one hand and reached the door latch with the other.

The door flew open and he was relieved to see Suzanne and Damian standing there. "G'day, about bloody time you answered, we've been knocking for two minutes," said Suzanne brushing past him. She smiled a huge smile, so big that her top teeth seemed to hit the tiles in the entranceway shattering at the tips. Terry was shocked at first and responded: "Christ, are you all right? That must have hurt."

"What do you mean?" She was looking right into Terry's eyes. "Christ, you're off your friggin' head. Outta yer tree." She looked at the others and said: "The lot of you."

Terry had to agree and attempted to introduce his flat-mate and her friend.

"Come in, come in, I'll make you a coffee or something."

Damian just had a huge Cheshire-cat smile across his face, taking it all in. "G'day, everyone; what have we been having this evening then?" He had a sarcastic tone to his voice and a knowing pharmacist's intellect.

Terry thought it best to move away from the girls before they said anything silly. He was doing enough silly things for all of them and these were his relatives, not theirs. Suzanne tried to talk to the girls on the way past but soon gave up, laughing at the scene, as they returned blank looks. "She's not to know," Terry thought. "About the strongest thing she's ever had is a bourbon and Coke."

Everything in the house was ballooned to him now he was on his feet; his layout desk which took up space under the stair-well looked enormous, almost twice its normal size. He stopped to look at the M.C. Escher book on its top on the way past. He was entering one of the strange scenes in his mind when Suzanne spoke up again. "Come on then what about that coffee? You look like you need it."

"Have a look at that Suzanne, isn't it great." The Escher print was doing all sorts of things for Terry's mind, but was a bland black and white drawing to Suzanne. "Look at the colours; I've never seen them in it before. Look at those things rolling uphill. How do you suppose he does that? They're moving. Check it out!"

Suzanne leaned across and turned on the table lamp, which blasted light across the whole scene. Her arm looked like rubber to Terry with hands like ET. The diamond from her engagement ring fractured the light into a kaleidoscope of colour. "That's in black and white, you silly bastard. And it's not moving. You, my darling brother, are ripped to the tits."

Terry was still looking at the refracted light and simply agreed: "I'd better make the coffee," he said heading down the two steps into the kitchen. He almost tripped as his feet seemed to float a couple of inches above the tiles. He laughed, but knew he couldn't share the moment with Suzanne who was settling in at the quaint, four-place cedar dining table.

Terry turned on a hot-plate on the stove then spun towards the sink grabbing a saucepan from within. It still contained the remains of potato from last night's dinner. He grabbed the electric kettle from the bench and put it in the saucepan before putting six spoons of instant coffee in with them. He turned on the tap before returning to the table.

"Are you all right?" Suzanne was concerned.

"Yeah, it was just a small mushroom. I've never had them before, but the girls reckon they're okay. It feels bloody weird though. Don't worry if I'm not quite with it. I'll do my best." He had never noticed that Damian's head was so wide. To Terry it was as wide as the table and his eyes were huge and bulging, like a cocker spaniel's. He stared but was afraid to say anything.

Suzanne heard the water still running in the sink and went to investigate. She laughed at the mess. "You silly bastard; I thought you had put the kettle on." She noticed Terry had put coffee into the sugar bowl adjacent the cups on the bench. "Christ, have a go at this Damian."

Damian got to his feet quickly and moved in to survey the mess: "Oh fuck, have a go at it; I think you'd better take over, Suze," he laughed.

Terry just rolled his eyes and smiled: "I think these things leave one just a little uncoordinated, mate."

"Too right, Terry," said Damian to Suzanne laughing. "I think you'd better make his very strong."

Terry got up from the table and walked into the front room. The girls' eyes looked up at him as he leaned down to pick up the piece of foil on the carpet in front of them. They didn't have to say a word. He responded: "It's cool, it's cool."

As he moved slowly back to the table he could feel his body rising. Was it his body, his head, his stomach? He continued into the toilet and leaned over the bowl to throw up. He couldn't look; it must have been the steak sandwich he had with Bob at lunch.

By the time he emerged from the bathroom, Suzanne had the coffee steaming on the table. As she'd waited for the kettle to boil she tidied up after Terry and even washed the dishes. He felt she must have waved a magic wand or something because it all appeared to have happened in the seconds he was in the toilet. He didn't realize he had been in there for 20 minutes and drifted around the ceiling of the cubicle for much of that time.

As he sat he pulled the foil from his pocket containing the nice blocks of hashish. Apart from the blonde cube, there was a small chunk of some Pakistani black.

"Oh, chocolate, yum," said Suzanne swooping on the darker piece and popping it into her mouth before he could react. In fact he watched that she did not even seem to chew it; it just went in and next thing she was swallowing it.

"Hey Suzanne, give that back, you're supposed to roll it in a cigarette and smoke it, not eat it."

"Yuk, that's not very nice chocolate."

He could see she was now chewing at it. "Spit it out, will you."

She spat a small piece back out, but at least half of the chunk had already gone. Suzanne had a real weakness for chocolate.

"What was it?"

"Filthy Paki black, Suzanne; you've just had enough hash to get about 15 people stoned for three days. Give it back."

She hoiked and hoiked for 30 seconds and managed to get another small piece from the back of her throat. Terry grabbed it and started breaking it up to mix with tobacco he had wrung out of a cigarette. Damian watched in amazement as he did it. He knew the effects that this stuff could have. Suzanne took particular notice at the small amount Terry was mixing in the joint.

"Is that all you have?"

"Yeah," said Terry, "this'll do for three or four people for at least an hour or two."

Terry finished rolling the joint and realized that his trip had been curtailed somewhat by his throwing up, but now his sister was entering panic stages.

"What will it do? Will I be doing silly things like you've been doing?"

"No, no, no; just relax and get into it, Suzy. Damian will look after you. Just expect things to be a little different for a while, that's all. Mellow out a bit. Go with it."

Suzanne couldn't mellow out. She couldn't even finish her coffee. She looked concerned, annoyed, that Terry didn't seem to care.

"You ate the bloody stuff love, don't blame me."

"I thought it was chocolate," she yelled.

"You'll be okay. Just don't expect to go out addressing any Cat Club or anything."

"Come on Damian, we're going home." She swept to her feet and was half-way to the door muttering: "Oh Christ, Terry, I feel funny already."

"It's really good shit, Suzanne, just try to enjoy it. Let Damian drive though."

"Crikey, I don't know what's going to happen; how long will it last?"

"I don't know, but you ate a fair bit, I think you have about an hour before it will start to take effect." He was attempting to be more reassuring, but couldn't wipe the mushroom-induced smile from his face. "Look, don't worry Suzanne, just get home and relax and enjoy it. Whatever you do, don't fight it. Anyway, it's only hash."

They left quickly without even acknowledging the two girls still seated on the floor.

As the door slammed, Jennifer looked up and spoke for the first time in ages: "What was that?"

"That was my sister and brother-in-law. Didn't I introduce you on their way in?"

"I don't remember."

"Neither do I."

They all laughed.

Hours seemed to roll by like minutes. Terry changed the record player continuously and they chatted in small bursts, a lot more freely now.

Terry explained that his "journey" must have ebbed when he threw up earlier. "Anyway, I wasn't with you two at all. How come?"

It didn't really matter to him and after he had rolled another joint to help them down he retired to the comfort of his own bed, leaving the girls to their own recovery.

Sleeping was difficult. It wasn't sleep at all. It was all a dream, a pleasant dream. His alter ego had decided the two had fancied him at that moment and had entered his bedroom and covered him in passionate loving kisses.

Saturday's sunlight broke through the curtains and woke him up. The bed was empty. He felt his member, erect, but no sign of any action there.

Chapter 25

Dennis Northey sauntered into the front of the print shop as though he owned the place. "I would like to get some business cards printed please."

Carol was obliging and asked Northey to fill out details for the design of the card on a pre-printed form. Northey was filling in the form when Terry rushed in with an armful of copy and artwork, and almost knocked him over.

"Oh, I am sorry, could you excuse me while I squeeze by there?"

Northey was a good-looking man of medium build with blonde hair, a suave dresser. He straightened up to allow room for Terry to get past and into the back of the cramped shop.

"Shane, we got the Frock Shop; they loved the design and we've scored all of their printing; letter heads, order forms, business cards, posters, swing tags, invoices, the lot."

"You beauty, Terry," Shane said picking up the artwork. "That logo looks great, doesn't it?"

"It sure did the trick."

"It moves, I tell you, even in black and white. Get a look at this one Carol, he's outdone himself here." Shane held it up.

"We get the business, that's what counts."

Carol stopped collating invoices and wandered across to have a look. "Yeah, it really is moving. That's going to look great in their colours."

She noticed Northey look up and moved to the counter with the art board which looked way over-sized for its content. "What do you think?"

Northey peered at the artwork and he, too, appeared to be impressed. "Yes, it does move, doesn't it; each time you blink you see a different angle."

Terry sat behind the counter and noticed Northey's eyes, fluttering at the artwork. "Careful you don't get dizzy."

Northey smiled. "Yes, it does move," he said and added with a rounding sway of his head, "and it really changes colour with the angles. Can you do that on my business cards?"

"What business are you in?"

"I'm just helping a mate out at the moment; a bit of real estate here and there. I have a law degree and handle the conveyancing and we share a few deals."

"Something like that may be a little bit loud for your type of business," said Terry grabbing a folder from the cabinet and unfolding a few plastic leaves. "Have a look at some of these samples; there may be something we can adapt for you. Are you selling business space or domestic?"

"Domestic properties mainly, like houses and units; there are a few moving," he said looking back at the folder. "I think I like that typestyle with this border."

Terry was happy he had come to a quick decision. "Can you call in tomorrow afternoon, about this time, and we should have something for you to look at?"

"Sure, that'll be good."

He completed the order form with Terry's assistance and was out the door.

Carol, who was packing the last few pads together, drew Terry's attention. She was tall and shapely with long dark hair almost to the waist. She had moved in next door to Terry and enquired about work.

Her smile lifted his eyes as she turned. "What about a coffee?"

"You bet, Carol. I'll help you make it."

Shane was busy over the machines again and put in his order as Terry went into the little kitchen and put the kettle on. Carol arrived as the pitch of the water in the jug signalled the winding down of the tap. He plugged it in and turned as Carol went for the cups hanging on hooks.

"It's pretty cramped in here sometimes, don't you think?"

She rubbed deliberately past him, slowly reaching for a cup. "Depends what you call cramped. I'd call it kinda cozy."

"Whew Carol, I'm stuck."

She smiled, picked a cup off its hook and turned back towards him before sliding gently back to a central position. "This is nice, this close," she whispered.

"I'd better get to work on that card for Dennis. Maybe I'll do it at home tonight," he could feel her heat rising from below.

"Do you think you may need a hand to do that? It'll cost you though."

"I reckon I may be able to handle it."

"But why handle it yourself when I'm just next door and we can both do it. I'll jump the back fence; expand the creativity."

The house was a mess when he got home. Jennifer had gone to work at the bar a few blocks away. They would be alone tonight. He spent half an hour hurrying about putting things into places and moving them back again. He operated under an organized mess. Jobs that had been completed covered a pin board. Bits and pieces of jobs on the go covered the desk. He estimated maybe two hours work this evening, depending on where they drew the line.

He had the veal ready and halved his usual quota of garlic before preparing the veges for the steamer. Carol offered two bottles of wine when she arrived. She had showered and changed into jeans and a low-cut blouse revealing a generous cleavage.

Carol was pretty handy at the graphics and enjoyed sitting at the big desk rubbing out Letraset, the type-faces of the day, purchased in sheets with a full alphabet and additional characters of the most used. Terry liked the design side of things but was often bored with the menial tasks. He had already done a rough of the business card with tall buildings surrounding a single house. His idea was to over-set the type on the image – 'Dennis Northey, your property link!'

Carol liked the idea and automatically sat down and started rubbing off the Letraset characters as Terry finished preparing dinner, returning occasionally to check her progress.

The light over the dining table was dimmed enough by the huge circular shade, which left a shaft of light cascading onto the table. It was intimate and made people lean forward a little as they spoke. Her elbows were on the table for most of the evening leaning forward chatting about her home town, Narromine. She left Terry with the impression that nothing much ever happened there. She needed the city. She needed some excitement. She cupped her face in her hands and as she spoke of a disastrous night out with a recent boyfriend. Terry leaned forward. She was still talking slowly and opened her mouth to meet him and they kissed. It was not just a quick peck, but a lingering lip-sucking kiss that neither wanted to break. They rose into an embrace without breaking the kiss for 10 minutes. Neither wanted to break away all the way up the stairs; slowly, at first peeling one another's clothes off. Halfway up and naked to the waist, Terry broke the spell by burying his face into her beautiful bosom as they backed into the bedroom.

They made love and gently caressed one another for an hour before Terry headed down stairs to shower. Carol arrived just as he finished and got into the shower as he dried himself. She was a beautiful woman, he thought, but he had had enough for one night and returned to the bedroom to find some clothes.

He walked home with her and kissed her good night at the door. The sucking full-mouthed kiss almost led him inside again.

Back at home, he had just finished washing the dishes and cleaning up when Jennifer arrived home. He made her coffee before feeding Herbie out the back and retiring to bed. Jennifer insisted he leave the back door open so she could play with Herbie for a while.

The next day Terry was out delivering jobs and picking up assignments; he had photographers to see to get images for the swing tags of one of his rag trader clients and made several calls to down-town customers with order forms and invoice books.

Dennis Northey arrived at the door about 15 minutes after Terry got back from his afternoon rounds. His cards had been printed, but were not quite ready for the guillotine.

He was happy with the job and accepted the offer of taking just 20 cards today. That would be enough as he had a function later that evening where he could use a few of them.

"Crikey, is that the time?" Terry was looking at the clock on the wall which signalled it was almost 3pm. "I have to get a move-on. I have to be at Bondi by 3.15."

Northey responded by asking: "I have to go that way too, do you mind if I grab a lift with you?"

"Sure, but I am meant to see this guy before four. Carol, where's that artwork for John Chambers?"

Carol had it in a folder, ready to go and passed it to him.

"She is so organized, this girl. Thanks," he leaned forward to pick it up and she was only inches away from kissing him. Terry realized and stood straight up: "I should be back around five, okay!"

The printer, Shane, swore again from the back room as another sheet of paper curled the wrong way and jammed the workings of a machine. Terry ignored the commotion as he headed out the door.

The drive allowed Northey to tell Terry about himself, and his law degree. He had not pursued a career in that direction, because he did not like the scene. He claimed real estate was a better market and he could do the conveyancing for clients along the way. The real estate industry had won him the unit.

Terry pulled into the small factory and left Northey with the car as he spent 10 minutes with the client explaining prices for cards, invoices and letterheads. He came out with orders for each and had also talked Chambers into a brochure to canvass his goods around to other stores. The design work had certainly paid off with this customer whom he left extremely happy.

Northey directed him up a few back streets of Bondi to a block of units. "Do you want to come up for a coffee and a joint? Cheryl is home too, it'll give you a chance to meet her."

"Yeah, why not; I'm pretty well done for the day."

The units had a security entrance and he buzzed up to hear Cheryl's voice: "Helloooo."

"It's just me, I've got Terry Martin here, the guy who's done my cards for me, are you decent?"

"Oh," she was silent for a moment; "I will be by the time you get here. Come on up."

As the lift travelled to the fifth floor Terry noticed the classy designer clothes of Northey. His hair was brushed back and his thick moustache appeared to have been combed to the sides. He was into high flying. As the lift door opened Terry noticed the door to a unit open simultaneously.

Cheryl was about 5'4" in bare feet and her attempt to "get decent" was to throw on a T-shirt. The tell-tale projections at the front of the shirt first attracted Terry's attention.

"Terry, this is my wife, Cheryl. Cheryl, Terry; he's done up those business cards I was telling you about. Here, I'll show you," he dug into his top pocket to show her as he walked past, offering a kiss on the cheek. She moved her head back as he did so, causing him to kiss into mid-air.

Northey offered coffee and walked into the kitchen as Terry sat on a stool at the breakfast bar. Cheryl pulled herself onto a stool opposite sitting with a leg astride each side. Terry tried not to look, but now could not help but notice she had only a very thin film of see-through material, the front of a G-string, on down below. She was a natural blonde all right. He kept his eyes up as she spoke, but each time she looked away in her animated speech, he could not help but take it in again.

As Northey walked from the kitchen the show was over, she had moved her legs together again. "What a tease," Terry thought. "What an unexpected pleasure though."

In conversation he found that Cheryl spent most of her time, "stuck in the bloody unit," while Dennis hustled up his real estate deals in conjunction with a number of agents in the area.

He made it back to the office by 5.15pm having accepted an offer for dinner with the Northeys the following Thursday.

Carol had dressed up for the occasion and shared a joint with Terry on the way. He stopped at the junction to buy the wine but when they arrived soon realized it would be wasted on Cheryl. She was chirpy but already slurring her words. She dressed provocatively, in a silk slip. There were no lines to show where her knickers may be.

Carol was absorbed in helping Dennis with the meal as Terry settled in to roll another joint. Cheryl lit up the first one he rolled. She sat in front of him with her legs wide apart and ran her hand up her inside thigh as he paused to pour the wine. She knew he was taking her in. As Dennis emerged from the kitchen she straightened, reaching for her glass.

"Mmm, try some Terry. It's delicious."

"Cheryl has always loved that wine. How did you know it was her favourite Terry?" Dennis was placing a large dish with cheese and crackers on the table.

"Just a fluke, I reckon. I'm glad it's your favourite. It's mine too."

The two couples sat opposite each other over dinner. Cheryl managed to get her foot wedged into Terry's crotch which made him sit in close to the table all night. He discovered on the way home that Dennis had also been warming his toes on Carol as well.

"It was as though they just wanted us to eat and get us horny. I still have a raging fat from her."

Carol leaned over for a feel: "Mmm, feels ready to me."

She undid his fly. "Not here, we're in traffic."

"They can't see me from down here, can they?"

"I don't think so," Terry lied.

Cheryl Northey rang Terry the following day. "Terry, are you over this way any time this afternoon. Dennis has got a couple of jobs in Wollongong he has to attend to. I wanted to see if you had any more of that smoko; if you could bring me some."

"Sure Cheryl, in fact I have to go to Bronte to deliver a job later."

Terry's heart was thumping as he buzzed up. "Hello," Cheryl's voice came through the speaker.

"It's Terry here, Cheryl."

The buzzer sounded: "Open the door to the lift while the buzzer is going."

Cheryl was still wearing the beige silk nightie. She was sober compared to her condition last night. She was also in two minds about seducing Terry. If he wanted anything he would have to seduce her. He was expecting her to do all the work.

"Your foot in my groin was a bit uncomfortable here last night."

"It felt like you were enjoying it," she said. "Coffee, tea or me?"

Terry missed the opportunity and automatically asked for a coffee.

"Does Dennis know you flirt with guests under the tables?"

"Of course he does; we don't keep anything from each other. It's a sort of game we play."

"Like he feels up the girls while you feel up the guys."

"Mmmm. Believe me, last night was pretty tame compared to some of the dinner parties we've had. One night we had a dozen people screwing each other. Bloody Dennis put some Spanish fly into the women's drinks and they all got so horny. I reckon three of the women were sucking face and other parts of each other for a while before they screwed each of the guys. It was a great night."

"So why did you invite me over. Surely it wasn't just to give you a smoke."

"No, I really did want to buy some."

Terry threw a bag of heads onto the table: "Is $20 all right for that?"

"Yeah, that's great. Roll one up for me, I'll get the kettle."

By the time she returned with the coffees, Terry had rolled two joints mixed with tobacco. This stuff is too strong to have straight."

"Not for me, Terry, I like it straight." She lit the smoke he had rolled and took a deep draw. Terry lit up his own. He looked into her eyes and exhaled the smoke: "I thought you wanted to fuck me."

"No, Terry, don't be silly. I have enough trouble keeping up with Dennis. He's such a horny rat."

"But what about last night, at your dinner party? You had your foot in my groin for hours. And what about that other party you told me about. Didn't you join in?"

"Only long enough to get them going a bit. I really don't like sex. I just love the power my sexuality gives me."

To his amazement Terry was actually relieved by the brush-off.

"What the hell am I doing here anyway?" he thought on his way down in the lift.

He had a pound of smoko he had bought at Paddington still in the boot of the car. He would go home and bag up and visit some friends. Terry found the smoke to be his poison, his cheap thrill.

Since Delia's death he would give anything a try, well almost anything. He had drawn the line at powders. That was a heavy scene he wanted nothing to do with.

However. he really enjoyed the little buzz he got from smoking a joint. Good innocent fun, he thought.

He poured the pound out onto a broadsheet newspaper and packed the contents into about 20 full Glad Bags, which he stacked into a carry bag. His run would take him to a dozen friends' houses over about three to four hours. He would take in a guitar lesson, then party from Vaucluse to Bondi, Leichhardt to Coogee.

He was just on the way out the door when Stephen arrived. This evening's travels would be put back at least an hour.

"How's the business going, Terry?"

"Not bad Dad. There is plenty of business out there, but a lot of people take a while to pay. If they get past four months, you have to take them to court."

"Who works the business while you take them to court then?"

"I don't bloody know. It pisses me off. I'm finding out that what you have on your books doesn't necessarily mean what you will get. I told you what happened with that machine I bought, didn't I?"

"Yeah, the bastard."

"Yeah, well I managed to sell the bloody machine a week before the Sheriff came to collect it. I tell you what, it is so good to get out on that harbour every Saturday. It gives me a chance to forget all about all the shit that goes down in this city during the week. How's your job going? The boat has been looking terrific. All those ropes nicely coiled up like that, winches sparkling. It looks great."

"Yeah, I like it. I spend most mornings down at the Bay. I get a lot of peace there, on the water."

"You know, I feel that too, when we sail. You get so absorbed, you think of nothing else but the task at hand. Get to the mark, change the sail, get to the next mark and change the sail. It's really good. I forget about what's happening ashore while I'm there."

"I find I drift off sometimes," Stephen said sugaring his coffee. "The other day I went down below to make a cuppa and sat down to read the paper. I woke up at bloody ten to two."

"Gee. You must have needed it. Bet the boss was annoyed."

"No, he wasn't; I told him what happened and he booked me an appointment with a doctor for tomorrow. I have been feeling a bit tired all the time lately."

"What do you think it is?"

"I dunno, but I have given my body a fair bloody thrashing up to here."

"Mmmm," Terry was thinking aloud at first then added, "You sure have. All of that whisky you and Edna consumed."

He decided to change the subject: "It was nice of Calligan to think about your health like that. Have you been drinking lately?"

"Naah. Just a bottle of wine every now and then. The trouble is I can't just have one."

Terry took a puff on his joint. "Have you ever tried grass? Mouse used to use it. One time when I visited her at that flat over in Bronte she gave me a puff. A friend of hers was there and ended up fucking me silly."

"Well, I've always told you, son, when rape is inevitable you should lay back and enjoy it," he laughed looking at the joint Terry offered: "That stuff, I tried it once or twice. I didn't really know if it was any good though. Just made me dizzy."

"And happy?"

"Yeah, happy too. I laughed a lot; for the silliest of reasons."

"Try a puff, if you like," Terry held the joint out to Stephen.

"No, I better not. I have to see the doctor tomorrow; I better not go there stoned. I think that stuff must be better for you than alcohol though."

They were suddenly interrupted as Jennifer breezed in with an armful of groceries. "Hi, Terry. Oh, Hi Stephen, how's life?"

"Good, good." He watched as she skipped down the two stairs into the kitchen to drop her packages and then went through the bathroom door.

"She's not a bad sort, Terry. Have you given her one yet," he asked bending down to pat Herbie.

"No, although there have been times I've wondered why I hadn't taken an opportunity. She looks great in just her undies, I tell you, but it's better like this, just platonic. That way I can bring anyone I like home. Anyway, she has her own friends. I don't really think she's interested in me."

The following day Stephen was prescribed tablets for his blood pressure and ordered to do just light duties for a while. His only weakness now was the wine and cigarettes. He told Terry over the phone that he'd have to give them both away.

"Just cut back on the fags, Dad." Terry knew the assignment would be tough for Stephen.

Just three weeks later, Terry had spent a rare evening at dinner with Kaitlin. Since her boyfriend returned from overseas he was lucky to see her once a month. They got home to her house heated up. As Kaitlin lay back on the bed slowly unclasping her top Terry suddenly stood up. He held his head, eyes closed. He was getting a message.

"Look Kaitlin, I am sorry, but I have to go. I think something is happening at home." He pulled his boots on quickly, zipping up.

The journey home took about six minutes. As he pulled into his parking position he noticed a man at the door, leaning forward. It wasn't until he got right behind him and said, "Excuse me," that he knew anything was really wrong.

"Terry, Terry," Jennifer screamed from inside the door. "He followed me home from work, I've been trying to get rid of him for half an hour."

Terry stepped back up onto the footpath and walked along the cast-iron fence. One of the lengths of metal was loose and he pulled it out of the fence.

The intruder at the door was defending himself. "She invited me home." He was obviously drunk. "When we got here she changed her mind, or something."

"Well I suggest you piss off then, sport." The drunk turned to see Terry armed with the bar.

"All right then," he said. The drunk was much taller than Terry when he came up onto the footpath. "Fuckin' moll," he said as he staggered sideways. Terry lifted the iron bar.

"Just fuck off out of here, man," he said.

To his surprise the guy staggered off down the street. Terry waited at the footpath to watch as he disappeared around the corner. He could still hear him muttering obscenities.

Jennifer was crying as she pulled the furniture back away from the door to let Terry in. "Oh Terry, he's been trying to get in for half an hour. He said he was going to rape me. He pushed his foot in the door as I came in and I had to pull the couch across to stop him getting in." She threw her arms over his shoulders.

"It's alright now," Terry said hugging her and feeling her melt into his body. She was warm and pressed tightly into him. "Come on, I'll make you a cup of tea."

Terry helped her move the lounge suite back into position and put the kettle on. Jennifer followed him to the top of the steps into the kitchen. He filled the kettle and walked up the first step. She enveloped him again. "Oh thank God you came home, Terry."

"I was at Kaitlin's house. I was just about to get into bed, when I felt something strange. I just knew I had to get home."

"I was sending you messages; you should have heard the things that bastard was saying." Jennifer kissed the nape of his neck before lifting his head to kiss him on the lips. Terry backed away briefly to turn off the kettle. Jennifer was on the stairs to the bedrooms holding out her hand. Terry took her hand in his left and pushed his other hand up her dress. At the top of the stairs Jennifer headed into Terry's bedroom, turned him around and pushed him back onto the bed. She did a slow strip-tease, leaning over to kiss him as each article of clothing came off.

The loving, although clumsy at first, was passionate. They managed to reach orgasm together before collapsing onto either side of the bed. As they shared a cigarette, Jennifer gently rubbed on him.

"Feels weird, Jennifer," he said.

"What feels weird?"

"Us, doing this, after all this time we have lived here without doing this." He rubbed his chin. "What, six months, and now, you're a top little lover, girl."

"It felt really good to me too," she said pulling him towards her as she lifted a leg over him. "And it feels even better now." Terry had to agree and lay back to enjoy it.

The change of circumstances in the household was sudden to Terry. They made love almost every night. In the mornings Jennifer would back herself on to him having aroused him while he slept. Terry enjoyed the attention but found it hard to find the time to do his smoko rounds. He left this for the times Jennifer worked in the wine bar, but would try to be home by midnight, when she got off work.

He would have her knickers off before she took two steps into the lounge room. This night he lay her back on one of the swinging single chairs and licked her. Jennifer lay back in the chair, lifting and sighing with every soft suck and gentle lashing of his tongue.

An hour later, Jennifer was asking Terry to marry her. He took a breath and, in the heat of the moment, agreed it may be a good idea.

Within a week he was wondering what he had done when Jennifer offered him a guest list to "the wedding". He was astounded that the list of 350 people contained just three names he recognized. He was annoyed: "Who are all these people?"

"They're my friends."

"Yeah, but where are my friends?"

"You know Clayton and Eric."

"Yeah, that's two."

"Look, do you have a problem with this?"

"Yes, I think I do. We haven't set any date yet, and I think you're travelling just a bit fast for me. Why don't we just live together for a while. You know, ensure we are compatible in the long term."

"Why should we?"

"So we can get to know each other a bit more." His voice was getting louder.

She screamed back: "We've known each other for seven bloody months, isn't that enough?"

"We've been fucking for four weeks and this is the first time I have seen you screaming like this, in seven bloody months. I reckon I'd like to see you after a couple of years."

"Well there's no bloody way you will. I'm getting out of here, tonight."

Jennifer stormed up the stairs and started packing. She wouldn't accept an apology from Terry: "Aren't you over-reacting a bit?"

The taxi arrived too soon and Jennifer disappeared out the door.

Chapter 26

Terry knocked on the door of the Cleveland Street terrace and turned to shush the others as they waited. He heard footsteps inside, someone coming upstairs. Dianna looked stunning, standing there in her nightie. Her eyes lit up as she smiled. She didn't particularly care about being caught in such attire around midday.

"Dianna, this is Marty, and this is Ando, and Lenny. We were just heading..."

Before he could finish Dianna rolled back to the wall, tilting her head up at Terry who noticed the glazed look. "Open your mouth and close your eyes and I will give you a nice surprise." They all complied as they filed past and down the stairs. Dianna placed a pill on everyone's tongue. Terry waited until he got to the bottom before turning back looking up at Dianna, whose nightie appeared to have shrunk, exposing the bright red of her knickers.

"What was it?"

"Mandies." She seemed to say it long and slow. "I got them on a scrip. I've been to six doctors in the past two days and got scrips from every one of them. We've got plenty, and stop looking up at my crotch." All of the heads suddenly turned upwards except Terry who turned away to notice the shapely form at the end of the couch. He locked eyes with her.

"Hi," was all he could get out as the others watched Dianna's every move on her way downstairs. Dianna introduced Nicole. She was gorgeous, worthy of a glossy magazine spread. He could hardly speak at all, hypnotized by her penetrating gaze. By the time he could say anything he found himself in competition with Ando.

"What do they do to you?" Ando asked.

"Nothin' much. Mandrax. They're a sleeping pill and if you don't sleep on them, you get a high," Nicole was gregarious, smiling every word.

"What, like having a smoke?"

Dianna tuned in to answer: "Naah; oh, yes I suppose so, but different."

Nicole added: "They're really nice to make love on." She was looking straight into Terry's eyes. He felt an immediate rush of activity down below.

"I bet they are," Marty chimed in, eyeing off Nicole's long thin legs.

"Why don't you get dressed and come to the smoke-in at the uni with us?" Marty was still doing the talking.

"Oh, I don't know; we've got other things to do," said Dianna obviously not too keen on the idea.

"What's that?" Marty asked.

"There'll only be a bunch of narcs there anyway." Dianna just wasn't interested.

"Come on, you two; it's history, you know, an event in the history of this city. The first ever marijuana smoke-in ever." Terry finally looked away from Nicole to Dianna: "Come on, Dianna."

"We can't, the kids will be back soon, we have to stay here; who's for coffee?"

Terry had been persuasive with this lady before, but realized soon enough that both girls were in no condition to go out anyway. They sorted out the colours and sweetness of each coffee.

"Oh well, I'd better return the shout then," Terry said as he unzipped his boot, revealing a small foil packet.

"We can have our own smoke-in here, before we go to the smoke-in."

He ceremoniously emptied a cigarette of its tobacco onto the table before putting a flame under the hash and mixing it up. He used three cigarette papers to make the joint and finished off with a small piece of cardboard ripped from the edge of his cigarette papers to make a filter.

"We've already been down to the uni, but we couldn't really see anything going on; that's why we came here to see if you might want to come along."

Terry smiled at Nicole and offered the joint to her. As she lifted it to her mouth he flicked the flint of his lighter. Their eyes met and he stalled. She had to pull away from the lighter to save the end of the joint, which ignited sending a pall of blue smoke into the air.

"How long do these Mandies take to come on?"

"It's really gentle," Nicole answered. "Give it about an hour before you feel anything, but this hash will certainly help it along." She took a deep puff and held it in, and then took another before passing it along.

The guys looked anxious to get on with the day. If these women wouldn't come along, there may be others on the way, or at the event. They took long tokes in turn and drank their coffee quickly. Ando was the most restless: "Come on man, we goin' to a smoke-in or what?" He was already half-way up the stairs with Lenny.

"Okay, let's go then. See you, Dianna." Before following, Terry stopped and turned to Nicole. "Can I see you later today?"

"I'd like that, Terry. Can't wait." She smiled as he followed the others upstairs where Dianna was offering more Mandies, which they pocketed this time.

"To the limo." Terry's recently acquired Humber Super Snipe, was waiting. He pulled her into drive and the boys started speaking all at once about the girls.

"We should have just stayed there and fucked the both of them," Ando was saying.

"Yeah, did you check the tits on that Nicole? Beautiful," said Marty, reminiscing, "I had a babe just like her about four months ago."

"Who knows," Lenny chimed in, "it might have been her and you didn't know it."

"I don't know, I wasn't looking at her face at the time, but those beautiful firm norks..." They all laughed.

Terry kept silent about his planned meeting with Nicole for later that day. It was better they didn't know.

The tape deck was blaring so loud that all of the conversation was yelled by the time they got near the uni.

"Where do we go?" Terry felt confused with all of the drugs in his system.

Marty was in the navigator's chair. "Shit, I don't know. I've never been to this place from this side. Look, we already had one squiz from Parramatta Road side before, maybe we've got the wrong day."

As he spoke Terry saw a break in the median strip and wheeled the car towards a huge set of steel gates.

"Whoah, stop stop stop, man, STOP," Marty was yelling now. "The gates are fucking closed, man."

Terry slowly reacted and managed to pull the car to a halt just six inches from the closed gates. He whipped the car into reverse and completed the three-point turn. He was simply listening to the commands and trying to comply. "Down this way. Yes; there's an open gate there."

Terry made another right turn, this time negotiating his way through an open set of gates. The road they were on was narrow and headed down through the university.

"Turn left, left; LEFT HERE MAN! Oh, Jesus Christ, where did you get your licence?" Marty was laughing.

"Bought it off a wog in Leichhardt," Terry replied.

"Is this a road or a footpath?" Ando let out from the rear seat.

"Shit I don't know, but both wheels seem to fit, so let's keep going."

From the back seat Ando and Lenny were having their three pence worth. "First sign of any narcs and we're out of here, okay," Lenny sounded serious. There was general agreement before Terry noticed a bitumen track leading up to the left.

"Let's try up here," he said, wheeling the car up a ramp of about 45 degrees. They went up for about 10 metres before the car seemed to go airborne and thump down onto brick paving.

"Watch out, Terry, there's a guy in a wheelchair there. Christ, where are we? This ain't the smoke-in, man. Slow down, man."

"Where the bloody hell are we?" Terry was now starting to panic.

Marty gripped the dashboard peering out through the windscreen: "Shit, I think, I know where we are; I think we're in the hospital. It's the courtyard of the hospital, how the hell can we get outta here?"

Terry wasn't game to stop. He couldn't see any other exit. Patients and visitors were flying in all directions trying to get out of their way. Terry finally stopped. "I'm going to have to turn around and go back the way we came."

Nurses and people in white coats yelled at them from either side of the path. The down ramp was hard to see and the car made a horrible scraping noise as he ran up the gutter and back down.

Wheeling the beast left at the bottom, a relieved Terry laughed.

"Whew, glad to be out of there. Did you see that guy in the wheelchair move?" They were all laughing now.

"Yeah, but what if someone calls the cops?" asked Marty who was now getting paranoid.

"I think that Mandy must be starting to work on you a bit," said Terry who had a firm grip on the wheel.

"Never mind me, what about you, driver?"

"Not a problem, I'm perfectly helpable of caping myself." They all laughed again.

Finally they bounced over another gutter onto a much wider section of bitumen and the passengers cheered at the feat of finding the real roadway which wound its way through the sandstone buildings to a central garden area.

"Hey, watch that bump, man," said Marty, hanging on. "Slow down a bit, will you?" Terry looked at the speedo: "We're only doin' 12 miles per hour."

"Look at the road, look at the road." Marty's voice was shrill, "Around there," he demanded.

"Where's this smoke-in supposed to be?" Ando sounded bored and a little reluctant now.

"Over there," Marty was pointing across Terry. "To the right; that guy looks like he's lighting a joint."

"There's a few over there too, maybe that's it," Len said.

"How about you get out and ask someone?" said Terry.

"Not on your fucking life, mate, he may be a narc."

"Look guys, how are we supposed to know we're at a smoke-in, if we don't ask someone. I'll pull in here and we'll all go, okay?"

"Okay," they all chimed together. Group decisions were easier.

Terry walked up to the first guy with long hair and inquired: "Is this it, man?"

"Is this what?"

"The smoke-in."

"Dunno mate. All I know is there were about 50 people here a while ago all smoking joints, but now this is about it."

Terry looked around to see maybe 30 people standing around in small groups, each looking one another over trying to spot the narc.

One hippie-looking dude approached them: "Hey man, have you got a light?" He had the biggest joint Terry had ever seen. It was like a Havana cigar, straight out of Cheech and Chong. He lit it for him and accepted a toke and quickly passed it on, coughing. The whole scene was animated. Everyone wanted to smoke in public as a protest to the marijuana laws, but they were all shit-scared, paranoid, that the guy next to them may be a cop.

"Is this it?" Terry said again, nervously.

"Yeah, man, I guess it is. There were a few more here a little while ago; some fine drugs too, but as soon as a guy came along with a camera, people started ducking for cover everywhere. I think there are still a few of them around here on the campus. Dunno though, it might have started earlier and we missed it. Here get your laughing gear around this."

Terry grabbed the cigar again. "No, we were here earlier and there wasn't," he coughed again as the smoke burned his throat, "anyone around."

Ando accepted the joint and took a couple of hefty puffs. "Well if this is it, I vote we bolt."

They chorused in unison: "Let's do the Harold…"

"Thanks for the toke, man, but we gotta go."

"No problem, buddy, keep cool, you guys."

Within a minute they were back in the car. The euphoria of their consumption for the day was catching up. The adrenaline buzz from the hospital wasn't bad either. Terry drove out slowly as the others looked around the gathering, searching for eyes looking at them. One group appeared to have about four joints circulating in unison, but apart from that, there didn't appear to be anything happening at all. All they knew was that they didn't seem to trust anyone who was there.

"Some fuckin' smoke-in, man," said Marty, in a slow drawl. "I thought there'd be thousands there. Double J has been pushing the event for a week."

"Maybe these are the only smokers in Sydney," Terry contributed.

"Bullshit man," said Ando who was feeling a bit woozy. "Every bastard smokes now-a-days; I reckon they were just paranoid, that's all."

"But we did it," Lenny smirked. "One day we can tell our grandkids that we were four of the 30 stupid bastards who risked getting fuckin' busted by attending this stupid fuckin' smoke-in."

"And I reckon they wouldn't have even legalized it by then," Marty added.

They decided they would go back to Terry's and have a smoke in comfort and took turns at checking their rear with each turn. Terry took a winding track back home, just in case. When they arrived, they all piled out of the car and flew through his door as though they were being chased.

"Shit man, why are we all so paranoid?" Terry was excited, his heart was pounding.

"I think we should just take that other Mandy and relax a bit." Marty was full of good ideas.

"There is too much money in it for them to legalize it, I reckon. Black money," Ando said as they lined up for a sip of water to wash down their Mandies.

Marty was in the lead and reached for the refrigerator: "Oooh, Heaven. Tim Tams, Coke, cheese, spring onions, pickled onions, dry biscuits. Yay, Tooheys!"

"I reckon they think people will stop drinking piss if they legalize dope. Now where would that leave us?"

"It would be a much cooler world, I reckon," Ando was reaching for a Tim Tam.

They recounted the day's events as they listened to the latest Steely Dan album over a coffee, but the conversation of the hospital adventure and the smoke-in soon reverted to the shape of Dianna and Nicole's tits.

"I saw right up that nightie from the bottom of those stairs," Ando said. "Fair dinkum, I saw right inside the girl."

"Ring them up, man, and get them over here and we can all fuck 'em," Lenny was sounding anxious, excited at the prospect.

They impulsively rolled a few more joints and each realized they were pretty out of it by now, especially Marty who instinctively curled up on the lounge just a wink away from sleep. Ando and Lenny were talking incredibly fast. It was a wonder they could understand one another. Terry was having a hard time taking in what one had said before the other replied and then found himself a couple of sentences behind the conversation.

He finally broke the spell: "Shit, you know it's dark outside already?"

"Well, I'm off," Ando said. "Want a lift, Len?"

"Naah, I'm gonna ring them sheilas and get a fuck."

"Bullshit man, come on, let's get outta here. We'll go by the Cross on the way home if you like."

"You got me, I'm as horny as a rhino. See yer, Terry. We've got some business to do."

"See you guys, go carefully now." Terry was heading for the bathroom as they shut the door and came out feeling a little woozy. He opened the fridge and saw the makings of a meal.

He pulled a pan from the cupboard and put four lamb chops on to sizzle away. He returned to the fridge and found eggs and tomatoes to round off the meal. When it was nearly ready, he stepped up into the lounge room to wake Marty.

He was disoriented as he woke: "Shit man' what's the time?"

"About 7.30; I've got some dinner on, the guys have bolted, so whadda yer say we have some tucker and ring the girls."

"Yeah man, now that sounds like a good idea."

They laughed about the events of the day as they ate dinner. As soon as he was finished Terry picked up the phone. Dianna was busy trying to get the kids to bed. "Here I'll put Nicole on, you talk to her."

Terry sat on the second step near the phone leaning against the banister: "G'day Nicole, are you ready to show me how good these Mandies are to make love on?" he said winking at Marty as he spoke and then nodded her agreement to him.

Nicole's voice sounded slow and sexy. "I don't have the money for a cab, though."

"No problem, I'll come and get you. See you soon."

In his haste he forgot to even ask about arranging anything for Marty with Dianna.

They debated for a few moments about whether Terry was sober enough to drive.

"No problem, man. It's just a few blocks from here. I'll be back in 20 minutes."

"I might have a kip while you're gone. Can I use the spare room? Your couch gives me a pain in the neck."

"Yeah sure; the bed's made up. I'll see ya soon."

Terry's heart was racing in expectation. He slid behind the wheel of "the limo" and cruised down towards the main drag where his plan was to turn right, go up a block and left to drive straight through to Dianna's place.

After five minutes waiting for a break in the traffic to get across four lanes he decided to go around the block to the left so that he could get across the busy road at the traffic lights a block back. He flowed with the traffic wheeling left, then left again and then again. It was familiar territory driving down between the factories on one side and the high-faced terraces. "Aaah, through the lights down here and we're away," he thought. The green lights reflected off the wet windshield, giving the impression there were about six sets in the air; then there were orange ones, six sets again. He was getting off on the designs they made on the windshield. When the lights turned red the whole viewing image shone. It appeared like there were about 40 sets of lights. Terry's mind was trying to work it all out when he was jolted to a halt. BANG! There were four cars stopped at the lights ahead of him. He had just rammed the last one. He could see the stoved-in boot lid, the crumpled bumper bar and the tow bar, bent up almost to a right angle.

He felt like slapping himself, but saw the driver ahead alighting from his vehicle. "Think quick, Terry, think quick." He told himself. He opened his door and put one foot out onto the ground pulling himself up with his right arm over the door, propping himself up.

"Ah, sorry, mate; just got your tow bar." The words just came out of his mouth as though someone else was saying them.

The driver ahead acknowledged the comment by waving his hand and settling back into the driver's seat. He had heard the cars ahead of him start to move off with the green light. To Terry's surprise, he just drove off across the intersection.

Terry was trying to work out how to get back into the car without stumbling. Luckily, there were no other cars behind him. It took him a couple of minutes to work out how to release the hand brake and he rolled slowly down to the lights which had turned red again. He waited there for several changes of the lights until another car came up behind and gave him a toot to get him moving.

He blessed the automatic transmission on the limo and gained enough composure to make it to Dianna's without further incident. He alighted and walked towards her gate and realized he was parked about a metre out from the curb. "Holy Christ," he said, looking at the crumpled metal above one of his double headlights but wasn't game to make any closer inspection. "The things one does for love."

He tapped on the door gently and soon forgot his ordeal as Nicole wrapped her arms around his neck, their tongues embracing for what seemed like a minute. He finally broke clear. "I had a prang on the way over here. Shit, it was close. Somehow I managed to convince the guy that there wasn't any damage. He just drove off."

Nicole showed some concern as she saw the car but Terry dismissed it just as quickly. "Just dented above the headlight and a scratch on the bumper, I think."

Nicole closed the door behind her and headed for the car. Terry stopped and held her hand, pulling her back. "What about Dianna? Can she come too? Marty's still at my place."

"No, she's busy, with a friend. Ken brought the kids home at about four o'clock and she raced him off into the bedroom. She only surfaced to get the kids to bed. All I've heard from in there have been her love groans, for hours. I'm so glad you rang. I'm so glad you're here." She pressed her body firmly against Terry, lifting up to her toes as she kissed him again.

Terry held her just as firmly, relishing the fact that he was going to get into this little lady's pants in a matter of minutes, if, that is, he could drive.

He opened the passenger-side door for her and closed the door as she melted into the leather seat. He looked closely at the damage again as he moved around the front of the car, annoyed that he could have done such a silly thing.

Behind the wheel he poked around for the keyhole and pulled the set of keys up into the light to find the right one to kick her over. "Can you do me a favour Nicole?"

"Sure Terry, what?" she leaned over and touched his upper thigh.

"Can you just keep talking to me and make sure I respond. Keep talking all the way home. Can you do that?"

She started talking about her and Dianna, how they'd met when she had to do a shoot for Dianna's boyfriend Ken - lingerie and underwear for a catalogue, how she and Dianna shared a guy one time, a Mandie session which lasted for hours. Terry listened and drove.

He was amazed at how quickly this day had appeared to go in this condition. He found it hard to recall many details of the smoke-in. When she asked, he just said it was a non-event. "We may have just got there before it had started and then, again, after it was finished. I dunno if it was even on." He forgot to tell her about the hospital. He was trying to work that out in his head when his familiar street-parking place loomed up. His street was narrow and the locals pulled their cars onto the wrong side of the road so as to park right in front of their gates. This time was no different, although Terry had to have a couple of goes at reversing into the space.

Inside he offered coffee and a joint, but Nicole's mind was on other things. She loosened his belt and pushed his Levi's over his backside and dropped to her knees as she pulled them down to his ankles, causing him to lose balance and flop back onto the couch. Nicole unlaced his shoes and took them off to allow the jeans to slip away. From the floor she ran her hand up the inside if Terry's leg, rubbing gently as she went until she reached his jocks which, by now, were bursting at the seams.

"I want to make you come and come and come."

"Me too," he replied, "but not here though. I forgot Marty is still here. Let's go up to the bedroom, in case he wakes up." Nicole slowly kissed her way up to his mouth but did not let go of his dick. With her free hand she loosened a string on her dress and it dropped to the floor. Terry cupped a hand under her soft white breast and awkwardly leant down to run his lips gently over the nipple. He felt her shudder slightly and pulled his arms under her to carry her to the bedroom.

He had taken about eight steps to the bottom of the steep stair-well and realized his knees were like jelly.

"There is no bloody way I can carry you up those steps," he laughed, putting her feet on the second step, hugging her from behind and kissing the nape of her neck.

They moved one step at a time, Terry running his hands down over the front of her silken knickers, gently rubbing the mound. Each of the 12 steps to the bedroom seemed to take an eternity as they enveloped each other in the pleasures and heat of the moment.

At the top of the stairs Terry glanced into the spare bedroom to see Marty sleeping and gently pulled the door closed as Nicole pulled him into the master bedroom. His senses were heightened by this time and he tried, for a second, to recall just how long his senses had been worked on. Since he first set eyes on Nicole early in the day he had been dreaming of this moment.

Holding her hands he lowered Nicole gently back onto the bed and pulled his T-shirt up over his shoulders. She arched her back pushing her stomach high off the bed as Terry was kissing his way down from her neck. His tongue roamed freely around her midriff and she giggled as his head wedged in between her legs. His tongue searched in circular motion and she lifted again holding herself where she wanted. She couldn't stand it and whispered for him to take them off, but he kept his bottom jaw moving, occasionally slewing his tongue to the side and up the edge of her panties. At this she grabbed one side and held it across allowing his wet, soft mouth more access.

The knickers finally began to grate on his tongue and Terry slipped a finger into the elastic from behind Nicole and pulled them down. She assisted by kicking them off from her knees and gently pushed his head back home.

Her grip increased on the back of his head as she started rocking faster and faster against his face bringing her to a noisy climax.

He felt her juices on his chin and kissed his way up over her perfectly formed breasts, nibbling the nipple extremities gently, sending her even wilder. "More Terry, I want more; hurry, roll over on your back."

She straddled him and they were enveloped in the sex. After half an hour of lovemaking he was yet to come. "Shit, under normal circumstances I could have come three of four times by now," he thought as she kept grinding away.

Just the thought of it started a rumbling down below, urged on by Nicole. He had expected her to pull off as he was about to come and warned her what was on the way. She simply pushed her pussy hard down over him. It was a huge explosion. The initial release was followed by a rapid fire which seemed to last almost a minute.

"Now that is a feeling I don't think I will ever tire of, Nicole. You are magic."

Nicole slipped her mouth away from his and holding her hips high she directed him home again. There was no rush. Terry was about one-third of the way in when he jiggled slightly. Nicole moaned with delight as she pushed a little harder, beckoning him to plunge all the way, but he held her weight on his inner thighs. "Give me all of it; come on, I want all of it."

Terry allowed another centimetre with each plunge before pushing her high into the air with an arch of his own back, but retracting again just as quickly. This excited Nicole even more. She was moaning as though it hurt, but she wanted more. They entwined, kissing, probing each other with their tongues; quickening with excitement and climaxing together in a rapture which seemed to hold for longer each time.

"This is truly a night to remember," Terry thought, and pushed Nicole back over, onto her stomach, before sliding into her again. She closed her legs when he was in providing a snug fit. The position provided yet another sensation for both of them and they rolled slowly over and over, finding interesting ways to delight one another.

"Christ, that was beautiful, Nicole. I don't know if I've ever felt it quite so magic. Bloody hell, look at the time." It was almost 2am. They had been at each other for hours. Despite all of its hard work, Terry's penis stayed erect and Nicole wanted more: "Fuck the time," she said. "I want that thing again."

It was 10 o'clock in the morning when he woke from his dream. It was the most wonderful feeling. At first he thought she was still attached to him but as he opened his eyes, she was not there.

"Must have gone home," he thought.

He was in a dream-like state, contented as could be, but the urge to relieve himself soon had him out of bed and stumbling downstairs to the bathroom.

"Aaaaah," he was so pleased with himself and shook the drips away before running the water in the shower. The hot water felt so good, but not as good as Nicole. He suddenly longed for her again as the warm water rushed over him and felt the rising with the very thought of her.

He grabbed a towel from the rack and realized it was wet and registered that Nicole must have showered before leaving. He grabbed another from the cabinet to dry himself off. "Wow, what a woman," he thought.

He wrapped the towel around his waist and headed upstairs, his head still spinning from the thought of Nicole. He could hear the wonderful moaning sound she made as they climaxed together, for what seemed like an eternity.

He was near the top of the stairs now, wondering how he could remember those beautiful tones so well. He walked into the bedroom and lay on the bed. He rolled over and sniffed at the sheet. Her smell was still there. He closed his eyes and could hear her moans again. What an effect this girl had on him. "How wonderful is this?" he thought.

Suddenly he opened his eyes. Sure, he could still hear her. "But this isn't a dream," he thought. He stood and walked to the door which met the door of the spare room. He held the handle and turned it, quietly opening the door a couple of inches. His heart dropped to his stomach. There she was, with Marty, having a great time.

He closed the door quietly, so as not to disturb them.

He shook his head and rolled away: "Fucking women," he thought. He smiled as he lay back on the bed, listening. Marty was having a great time. His smile widened as he closed his eyes falling back into dream-enchanted sleep. The Mandies were still working.

Chapter 27

The day's sailing was great. The crew worked hard and managed 16 slick sail changes around the busy course to finish in third place. Terry helped clean up the boat and pack sails before heading to the bar for the mandatory jugs, but this evening he didn't stay long.

He dropped his bag as soon as he got inside to be greeted by Herbie, tail wagging madly. He bent down and gave him a pat.

"G'day boy. How are you then?"

The dog sat in front of him with a tennis ball in his mouth, urging Terry to throw it. He waited until Herbie dropped the ball and kicked it across the dining room and it rolled down through the kitchen, the dog hot on its trail. Herbie had the ball back at his feet within seconds.

"No more, boy; I'm too tired tonight."

Terry dragged himself to his feet and checked the refrigerator on his way past, pulling a few sausages out for dinner. He showered to wash the salt from his skin and threw the sausages into a pan as he headed upstairs to find a change of clothes.

He was in deep thought about the day's sailing. He thanked Heaven he at least had that to take his mind off things. A check of the books at the office the day before meant he had to let Carol go. He knew she'd find work elsewhere, but still he felt guilty at having to put her off. It wasn't that they weren't doing the business. There were plenty of jobs. In fact, the machines were continually in motion at the factory. It was the bigger jobs he'd done, the ones he had to sub-contract out to other printers. He was meeting deadlines all the time, but having to hustle for the money more and more. The 10 per cent he allowed for handling the work, simply wasn't enough for him to hold the debts for any length of time.

He looked at the pictures on his desk. They were the last ones ever taken of Delia, on the beach and one taken at one of the clubs she liked to frequent.

"What will I do, Mouse?"

He expected an answer to hit him immediately, but nothing came.

"I've got to do something to get back on track. When the money is not there you lose the incentive. What would you do?"

He sat and absorbed the silence as he ate the sausages he'd prepared with a zucchini, onion and tomato. He gave the leftovers to Herbie and glanced at the books sitting on the top of the desk. Half the money that was owed to him was owed by so-called friends.

"Why can't they pay up?" He slammed the books closed and decided he would make these things his priority next week and moved into the lounge where he settled in the large swivel chair before flicking through the channels looking for a movie. He started watching, but succumbed to sleep as the hard day's sailing caught up with him.

The banging at the door would not stop and jolted Terry from his sleep. Stephen stood in the doorway with a sheepish grin on his face. "G'day."

"Christ Dad, you're as pissed as a fart, you old bastard. Aren't you supposed to stay sober these days?"

Stephen grabbed his girlfriend by the hand and pulled her into the room, allowing Stephen to close the door behind them: "This is Marlene. Marlene, this is my son, Terry."

Marlene was as drunk as Stephen and acted shy.

Stephen was slurring badly as he told Terry he had been to three hotels that afternoon. "All 'round bloody Redfern," Marlene chimed in, slurring too.

Terry did not want to get involved in a conversation with them. It was 1am, he realized when he went out to put the kettle on. Stephen was telling Marlene it was all right for them to stay as Terry poured the coffees.

"Look Dad, I've made you both coffee; the spare room is made up, if you want to stay; I'm going to bed."

In the morning Stephen was still asleep in the spare room. Marlene had gone.

"Dad, what are you doing with yourself? Can't you do any better than bringing home some drunken old gin? Christ, what about your medication? You're not supposed to be drinking any more. Aren't you concerned about looking after yourself?"

"Terry, Terry, Terry, please don't lecture me, boy! I just needed to get out and do something. I've been bored shitless sitting in that flat every night. Yesterday I just decided I needed a drink."

Terry tried to change the subject: "Have you seen Suzanne and Damian?"

"Yeah, I saw them during the week. Suzanne is still going out all the time. Things aren't so good with them at home, I don't think."

"Why? I thought they were closer than ever, since Delia's death."

"We all have our own ways of dealing with things, Terry. I don't know about you, but all I have wanted to do is avenge her death."

"Hey Dad, you can't think like that. It wouldn't solve anything. It's the violence in her life that caused her death. All the violence she had to witness."

"What do you mean?"

Terry was venting his anger now. "As a child, she saw her father beat up her mother and then you and Edna on the piss, constantly bickering."

"But I was always kind to you kids!"

"Yeah by scaring the shit out of us driving home drunk; by killing my bloody dog...."

"I had to do that, he was killing the chooks."

"Shit Dad, that's all you know how to do, isn't it? Meet violence with violence. You have got to stop thinking that way. I know it hurts. We've all been deeply hurt by it."

"I have just felt like it would be the right thing for me to do. All I dream about is the good times we had together," Stephen said, verging on tears.

"Me too Dad. I can't remember anything bad about her at all." Tears welled in his eyes. "I miss her Dad. I fuckin' miss her a lot."

Stephen placed an arm over Terry's shoulder, then hugged him tightly: "There's nothing we can do about it now. She's gone mate, but she will be with us forever."

"I feel her around me all the time. I talk to her, ask questions about what I should be doing about this or that. Sometimes I even feel she answers, although I don't hear her. I just decide on something and find it was right, or wrong sometimes. It's like an inner strength she gives to me."

"Well, hang on to that feeling, Terry. You hang on to it," Stephen said, sitting back in the chair opposite. "You know I blamed myself when it happened. I thought about the upbringing that I had given her. I reckon that night of her 16th birthday was just the last straw. That's why she wanted something different. After the funeral, when I went back to Melbourne I just hit the piss, really heavy. I think I was drunk for about four months solid."

"Drinking doesn't help, Dad. It has the opposite effect, I reckon. It provokes violence. It always did with you. Look at the times you used to come home from the pub and beat Mum up. And those never-ending arguments you and Edna used to have. What was that all about, anyway?"

"I know, Terry." Stephen looked up from the chair, tears welling in his eyes.

"You know how I have contended with her death Dad? By fucking anything that moves and getting shit-faced stoned. The same as you, I s'pose."

"You just be careful though, mate, you know some drugs can lead to heavier things. I remember when I drove cabs for a while in Melbourne there. I had to use those yippy beans to keep going through the night. When bloody lampposts started hailing the cab, I had to give it away. I just felt tired all the time."

"Dad, there's a lot of bullshit goes on out there about one drug leading to another. I have virtually decided now that if I can't smoke it, I won't touch it."

He didn't tell Stephen about the mushrooms or the Mandies he had consumed but knew that Suzanne would have related the experience to him when he brought up the subject.

"What about that stuff Suzanne had here that time? She was off her tree for three bloody days, she reckoned."

"Dad, I promise you I will never get into the heavy stuff, like heroin. I am just not into that scene. Bloody Warwick who has been staying here is bad enough, I tell you. Six bloody months and I haven't seen any rent from the bastard."

"Kick the prick out, mate. You don't want people like that around you," Stephen was stern.

"He's working in a band on a cruise ship at the moment; not due back for another month or so. When he gets back if I don't get all the back rent, then he's out, that's for sure."

"Well just be careful, mate. Bastards like him will drag you down with them if you let them."

"One good thing about having him here is that I get free guitar lessons."

"But just don't get involved in any of his heavy drugs. That shit kills people."

"No way, Dad."

"Just be careful, that's all I can say. You don't want to end up in jail."

Terry took the advice. "Say, do you want some smoko? I'd rather you had a puff than a drink any day."

"Naah, I'll be right. I'll go easy on the booze too. I just find that I can't just have one drink. I've got to have more and more once I've started."

Terry pulled a Glad Bag from the cupboard and put some heads in it and offered it to Stephen: "There you go; next time you feel you want a drink, just sprinkle some of this into a fag and smoke it."

Stephen pocketed the bag.

"Say, we had a great sail yesterday; got third. The boat would go faster though if you got rid of all those trimmings like plates and stoves and seats and stuff down below."

"He likes it like that, mate. He wants customers to see a boat all decked out for cruising."

"Oh well, I suppose we can handle that in the future then. By the way, next time you arrive on my doorstep with a woman in tow, make sure she's got a bit more class about her."

"I've told you before, Terry; a standing prick has no conscience."

"Yeah, sure, but will it still love you in the morning? You're incorrigible, Dad. What hope have I got with you as an old man?"

"Well what are you up to today? Can you give me a lift home? I came out without the car yesterday."

"Sure, I was goin' to call over to Marty's place. I'll wait until you've had a shower though. You're a bit on the bugle."

Chapter 28

Terry's heart was pounding as he crouched low in the front seat of the car. The lights from the foreign vehicle sliced across the mini-van, marooned in the car park. The vehicle looked official and pulled up to the door of the Customs Hall.

He stayed low until he heard the car door slam and took a peek as the driver headed through the huge glass door, shouldering it open as he went. The guard on duty met him in the hallway where they struck up a conversation, unheard by Terry but momentarily animated by the waving of arms and gesturing. He couldn't look and slumped low on the seat willing Warwick not to come down that gangplank. Not now!

He took another peek and noticed the gesturing arm movements had subsided. One man had pocketed his hands and strolled slowly along with the driver as he reached for the door.

"Shit," he whispered to himself. He could now hear them from his crouching position. He lay flat so he would not be seen. What if they came over and discovered him? What would he say? Even worse, what if Warwick comes around that corner now? Terry knew he'd be dressed in a duffel coat; this was a hot summer night; the coat pockets, he imagined, stuffed to bulging.

He lay still, feeling a cramp in one leg wishing he had a larger vehicle, like "the limo" as Warwick called it. The Humber Super Snipe was a limo compared to the bland little mini. He had to sell the bloody limo before Warwick took his little trip on the cruise ship.

He lay there, deep in thought. He had known this guy just over a year, maybe 18 months and so much had happened. Time raced along. He should have realized that something like this would happen. He could see it now, eyes closed, body flattened across two tiny front seats. The guards were talking; just a few words recognizable from this distance, but they were loud enough to cause perspiration to mill on his brow.

He tried to remember his first meeting with Warwick Lomond. Memories were vague on that point because the time had gone so fast. He had consumed so many drugs. They had done so much together, but Lomond was still not what Terry could call a "mate", not like George or Marty. They were acquaintances; yeah, acquaintances was more like it. His mind was racing. How did he get so involved?

One thing had certainly led to another. The music, the smoko, the women and the gigs. It was a fantasyland; no, an indulgence.

Terry liked the way Warwick took the piss out of everything he saw on television. His comments were absurd; they would sit and watch movies with the sound turned down on the telly and music on the stereo up loud. They had the characters saying the craziest things and laughed loud at their creativity in the dialogue. That was fun to do when you were stoned, and they were stoned all the time.

He knew Warwick had lied to him; at the same time he knew there was a lot of truth in many of the things he said. The trouble was he couldn't figure out what was real and what was bullshit about this guy. He insisted Warwick refrain from using heroin while he lived there. He moved in soon after Jennifer left.

Since then, Terry had watched him nod off, fall asleep, in mid-sentence and wake two hours later to finish the sentence he was delivering, all the time denying that he was on heroin. Terry would simply act as though seconds had passed too, instead of the hours. He was amazed that Warwick could convince himself that he had not nodded off. Terry had never seen a smack freak from such close quarters. He had laid down the law when Warwick moved in: "No needles, no smack".

"Of course, man, I'm cleaning up the act, I tell you."

"Bullshit; you're a bad lad. I know it and you know it, so cut the crap. Just don't use it here."

Warwick played bass guitar and impressed Terry with his prowess of ripping off the licks of some of the finest studio musicians with apparent ease. He had been playing for about15 years so it wasn't hard for him to impress Terry who was taking his first guitar lessons.

Warwick was 17 stone when he played around the city circuits of Sydney, Melbourne and Adelaide with some of the big-name bands from the sixties and early seventies before he took the holiday to Thailand. He disappeared for almost two years; settled in to the lifestyle and the dollar value. In that time he developed a raging dependency in Chang Mai. Heroin and opium transformed him into to a trim 11 stone that could claim a "straight" look. Well, at the right moment anyway. His bulging eyes usually gave him away.

He shocked many of his buddies from just a few years before. "How long has this guy been gone anyway?" his drummer mate, Alby Freeman, asked on his return. It was hard for him to remember. He looked so different. The weight difference was the most amazing factor, from fat slob to dapper and suave. Alby had to wait for him to speak before really recognizing him. As a slob, his hair was long, bedraggled, and he mostly went unshaven. Now he was style-cut and dressed to impress. The gold glittered from his neck, wrists and fingers, for the time being anyway.

On his return the band work did come, albeit irregular, a bit here and a bit there, but the bands now had to make allowances for Lomond. At any one time he could be using anything - heroin, speed, pills, and smoko, opium, hash, oil, sticks and heads. He boasted of his indulgences and was known as slightly crazy. If he wasn't holding, he knew of and was always visiting someone who was.

He had lady friends who fed him Mandies when there was nothing else around. Four and five tabs at a time were his go but he couldn't be held responsible for what he may have done or said in such condition. He learned from Dianna and would do circuits of five or six doctors a week complaining of restlessness, irritability and insomnia. The cure? Downers.

Grass and hashish were a warm-up to him and from the first day Terry and he met there appeared to be a continuous stream of sweet-smelling smoke coming from his general direction.

Terry was 21 when he met Warwick through a couple of photographers he knew. His guitar tutor, Jack Barker, also knew him well from former bands. He respected his playing, "but the man is a worry," he'd say. He was at the Annandale studio on that first meeting which ended up turning into a party, especially when the girls arrived.

Warwick, fresh from the journey, was relating excerpts of life in the Triangle. He certainly was a good talker, a Gemini, describing one of his disappearances from the scene. He had the floor for hours while the others watched, wide-eyed, at his adventures, none of them really absorbing the gravity of the experiences, under the circumstances.

In comparison, Terry appeared naïve. He came across Warwick a couple of times a week after that. He was often at Jack's house, working out tunes to do with a new band they were working up when Terry turned up for guitar lessons. Warwick would get a lift with him nearly every time he was heading home. It didn't take long before Warwick included Terry's house on his list of calls where he elaborated his stories of the mansions in the hills of Thailand, guarded by armies and snarling Dobermans.

On one meeting about eight months later, sampling some delicious Lebanese blonde hash, he claimed to be "sort of married to a Thai lady". He did not elaborate at the time. The mystery he created in his stories enthralled Terry, but his tales always got to that point where he didn't really know if Lomond was telling the truth. He always had to cross that line. Add a bit of shock value. They were absorbing yarns nonetheless and Terry was a good listener.

Lomond spoke tough of his knowledge of the drug trade as though he was talking about a grazier he knew who sold wool. The runners, Bernie and Lance, were Warwick's smoko contacts. Terry knew them, but he did his deals elsewhere. He was small fry compared to them. The sweat-shirted Bernie and Lance pulled on designer running shoes to jog, every day, around the eastern suburbs. Each carried a gear bag, packed with little bags of green, for clients at drop points spanning a six-kilometre radius of their respective homes. They made a packet from breaking "The Greek", as the Griffith grass was known, into $25 bags. They worked hard at it. It was no longer a supply to just the mates for them; it was business, big business. They worked hard and they got fit and they were getting wealthy. Semi-trailers brought loads up the highway. These guys had pooled resources with dealers from other suburbs to buy in bulk. Warwick was one of their calls on this night.

He was practising new bass lines when Bernie arrived. The Paddington house Warwick shared with fellow band member Paul and his girlfriend Jayne was warmly lit. They exchanged gratuities before Bernie produced some of "The Greek" for a smoke and, after rolling a joint, offered the bag to Warwick: "Here, have it," he said. "We want a word with you about Chang Mai."

"Oh yeah, what do you want, a geography lesson, or what?"

"I'll be straight with you; we want to do a run, but we'll need some help. We've got $150,000 to invest and we want to turn it into something."

Warwick was definitely interested, although a little surprised to see his skills of such matters required so soon. The cash register started ticking over behind his eyes; he knew there would be a few dollars for him in this one if he could point them in the right direction. Warwick had more front than a rat with a gold tooth; he could role play and carry out many charades.

Bernie and Lance had a master plan, but they needed his information of places and people who could organize things at the other end. He would give them enough to get started, but not enough to go through with it.

He planted the seed; gave them the hotels, the bars, the people to contact and how it should be done, but he was wary when the boys wanted him to go with them. They'd pay the fare and all expenses; all he had to do was introduce them to the right contacts. He was too smart for that. "Look I'm hot over there, I can't go back."

Better still, he would tell them where to go to secure the load, knowing all along they would need him. "They didn't even use the stuff," he thought. "How are they even gonna *taste*?"

He went through the routine with them and told them the etiquette, the protocol of getting what they wanted. He even went through the procedures of checking a sample.

To them every second person in Bangkok was Lomond's mate. They didn't know, however, how close he had come to going to jail over there.

He didn't tell them the story he later told Terry, about shooting the cop whom he discovered raping his Thai wife. Warwick did not tell them how he grabbed the revolver as the cop was about to give his girl a fatal last hit. She had been tied to the bed and raped several times before he produced the syringe filled with a lethal, almost 100% pure hit.

The cop demanded, and got, whatever he wanted in this illicit trading arena. He was ramming himself home to her as she was dying when Warwick held the gun about an inch away from the back of his head and blew him away. Terry had always wondered since Warwick told him the story, how long he may have been watching the macabre event.

"I was lucky to get out after that. I had to make sure I was on that plane before the deaths were discovered," he said. When Terry inquired, he told him he put the gun into her hand before leaving.

Paul and Jayne knew where Bernie and Lance had gone. They were pissed off about Warwick getting reverse-charge calls from Bangkok and Chiang Mai for a week, and told Terry so when he called in this Monday night.

A barbecue on the front lawn of the house the day before saw them all smile for a photographer up the road. Their barbecue provide a perfect opportunity for the Drug Squad camped a 100 metres down the road.

"They could have been taking pictures of the house across the way; after all, it is for sale," Paul was justifiably concerned. He had a gut feeling. Something was going on and it was getting awfully close to his environment.

The house across the way was empty and provided what Lomond thought to be the perfect address to mail the package, a statue of Buddha.

"Jesus, you'd think the guy had just read *Snow Blind*," Paul said to Terry. How were they to know that the package had been sent two days earlier? That's why Bernie and Lance were on the blower so often. They were anxious about the prize, whether it had arrived.

On the Tuesday Warwick waited for the postie and quickly moved in to collect when a package arrived across the way. Little did he know the postie was Drug Squad. The van salesman just a few doors up was Drug Squad and the Ford Transit van with darkened windows parked outside for the past week contained another four members of the Drug Squad, complete with phone-tapping and other listening devices. Everything that had gone on in the house was on tape.

Five o'clock on Wednesday morning they moved in, with their weapons drawn. Paul, Jayne, and Warwick were rudely awakened as the door was smashed open. The squad knew Warwick had been scratching in the dirt outside the night before and soon found his own stash, about two ounces of powder. However, they knew there had been four kilos in the parcel. They were to spend the rest of that day and evening interrogating him.

Terry called in about noon, seven hours after the raid. Paul and Jayne were still furious. They were in shock, shaking, as they recounted the bust and wanted Warwick out of the house. "When and if they let him out." He was still detained.

The next day Warwick was at Terry's door, suitcases in hand. "Can I stay for a couple of days, just until I find somewhere?"

Terry was silly enough to agree, but only after feeling pity for Warwick who cried over coffee describing how the "Narcs" had held phone books against his head and bashed truncheons against them: "So as not to bruise," he said. "Then they put me inside a coat locker and threw it down the stairs." He claimed he was forced to take that journey 13 times and described the feeling of each in graphic detail to Terry.

Six more months had gone by and Terry had not seen any rent from Warwick. There was plenty to smoke with a deal of hustling, but Warwick was back into his old habits. Terry wondered where he got the money for it. He was surprised to see from his court appearance, complete with embarrassing press for some of the more popular artists he had played with in the past, that Warwick received a six-month suspended sentence and $5000 fine. The fine was Warwick's excuse for not having any money. He told Terry he was paying it off... on the dole. Terry wondered if there had been a misprint in the paper when they reported he was attempting to import just two ounces of the drug. He had been told there was four kilos of the stuff.

He waited for him to arrive home flush with cash and pleasant stories of life aboard the cruise liner. "For Heaven's sake, working in a band, seven nights a week, for an eight week cruise, surely, he had the dough to pay his rent now?"

Warwick strung him the line that he drank a lot on board ship and he only had a couple of hundred dollars left. However he knew how he could get the rent paid up and more, "for one night's work".

He claimed to have "picked" a guy on board as being a potential smuggler: "It was written all over the guy's face. I knew he had something. As it turned out it was 4000 Thai sticks; had them bulk in a suitcase. I helped him hide them by wrapping them in paper and pressing them down in the ship's printing press," he told Terry.

"When all that was done, I discovered the best place to hide them was in the showers. We undid all the screws around the bulk head and stashed all of the packets in behind them."

"Yeah, but what's this got to do with you paying your rent? I told you before you left that if you weren't paid up, you're out."

"I can pay up; all you have to do is drive me there, Darling Harbour, where the cruise ships come in. You can have the grand that I owe you and a grand for your trouble. Whadda yer say?"

Terry was caught between the devil and the deep blue sea. "A Catch 22, mad if you do and broke if you don't," he thought.

Here he was, crouched over in the front of the mini waiting for the bastard to come wandering off the cruise ship in a bloody duffel coat, in the middle of summer, right into the waiting arms of two Customs officers having a little chat at the front of the building.

"Shit," Terry was thinking aloud then risked a glance as he heard the car door slam and sounds of closing conversation reverberated from 50 metres away. The car started up and cruised slowly out of the car park. Terry stayed low but chanced a peek to see the officer on duty sauntering back up the hallway towards his office that looked straight out on to the gangplank. Warwick was descending the gangplank; he hit the bottom and turned left and out of sight of the window as the guard opened his door and disappeared into the office.

The bulky figure approaching looked completely out of place and most certainly would have been pulled up by the Customs officers if they had another minute's worth of conversation left. He opened the door and crouched down into the car. Terry had it started and drove deliberately, slowly, out of the car park.

"What took you so long? Doesn't matter; you're lucky it did take so long. Those guards were right at the entrance there five minutes after you went in until the minute you came off. Shit I'm shakin' like a dog shittin' razor blades." Terry really was shaking.

"Hey, it's cool man. I had to undo about 60 screws in the shower to get at it, and then put them all back, the way I found them."

"How much you get?"

"About 35 or 40 packs, I think."

"What about the Kiwi guy; was he there? Did he help...?"

"Yeah, he wants three bucks each, so whatever we can get over that is profit."

"Jesus Warwick, I don't need rushes like this."

"Hey, wait till we get home and steam open one of these, it'll all be worth it. Shut up and drive, driver."

Terry took as many back streets as he knew on the way home and kept checking the rear vision mirror to the irritation of Warwick.

He had been kind to this bloke and forced to play "getaway car" on a very tricky little assignment, which he had absolutely no control over.

"Luck of the Irish; I must be Irish," he thought.

The hot plate started to glow as Warwick unpacked his coat. Terry put a saucepan under a tap for a few seconds splashing water over the narrow kitchen and forcing him to rise to tip-toes to turn it off quickly. Enough dribbled over the edges of the saucepan to create a steamy fizz as it hit the hotplate. Warwick was still counting, an excitement in his voice, no longer controlled. "Thirty-seven, thirty-eight," he stalled to undo his belt and reach into his crotch, "thirty-nine... there was another one somewhere." He lifted the duffel coat from the floor again and reached into a pocket normally designed to stow away the hood.... "Forty."

The first of the packets, each not much bigger than a 250-page paperback, were neatly stacked, but the rest were strewn across a couple of metres of floor space. Looking at them now, it was hard to imagine how the hell he had managed to carry so many in one hit. It sure was risky.

Terry looked at Warwick. "Well, get one open, we'll have to try it out."

"Don't you worry, this is good shit; quality assured."

A heavy packing tape sealed the ends of what appeared to be newsprint, about four layers, insulated inside by a thin layer of plastic wrapping. The package was so tight that Warwick was hard pressed to pull even a small sample out through the top and had to completely unfold the parcel in the order it had been folded and sealed.

Unwrapped, the compressed clump looked appealing to connoisseurs of fine smoko like these two. "Rip some off, and roll her up," Terry was now anxious, the adrenaline must have been wearing off.

"No, we've got to steam it first," Warwick swooped on the block and headed for the steamer in the now bubbling water in the saucepan on the stove.

They watched in amazement as the bulk of the block grew, within 30 seconds, to more than twice its size. Soon Warwick was grabbing at the steamed block with kitchen tongs, shaking it gently as the smell of the resin wafted through. "Christ, take a whiff of this steam."

"Oh wow, man, who needs to smoke the stuff, quick grab me that one." Terry was back at the table expelling tobacco from a Winston cigarette into a small pile on the table, ripping a piece of the Buddha from the stick, admiring it. "Sure looks like the primo goods, Warwick." He lifted it to his nose. "Smells good too. Smells, well, foreign."

"Yeah, now all I've got to do is move it; I hope you know someone who might be interested."

Terry looked up: "What can we get for them?"

"Look, the Kiwi wants $2.80 a block, sticks go for $10 on the street, there must be someone interested in them wholesale at, say, seven, or six...."

"Wait a minute," Terry kept his cool, "you have people you know all over this city."

Warwick jumped in. "I can't, not since the bust; I can't go near any of my guys. I'm hot, they know I'm hot."

Terry knew someone likely to want it, but stalled for almost a minute, rubbing his chin and scratching his ear in between the ritual of joint rolling.

"I suppose I may be able to interest Paddo Mick." He carefully ripped off a strip of board of the papers and read the "50 Gummed Cig.." as he rolled it neatly onto a match end and placed it into the slot at the end of the two-paper joint.

"Get it into yer," Warwick said, fingering the makings for himself, complaining a little about the fine bamboo thread holding part of the head to the narrow stick.

A couple of puffs and Terry handed it over, coughing. "Shit," he spluttered, "damned filthy weed."

Warwick took a toke and held the smoke in. Before exhaling, he sucked again on the end of the smoke, watching the fine red tip emerge from the ash at the other end. Finally, he coughed it up too, which put his head into an immediate spin. He wheezed: "I like that cough rush."

They sat and smoked the next one, turning up the latest Steely Dan on the record player... "Green ear-ring.... I remember...." Warwick sang it with a Peter Lorre accent. They agreed with one another about how good the smoke was for another 20 minutes over coffee before Terry hit the phone. "Chris, can you tell Paddo Mick I may have something for him; it has a lot of strings in the song." There was a pause at the end of the line.

"What are you on about, Terry? Do you know what fucking time it is?"

"You know what I mean, Chris, there are about 70 bars in each tune and I reckon they may make 40 or thereabouts. Ideal for 40-year-olds, in fact," said Terry, laughing at his own cryptic messages. "Look, Chris, you mind if I come over and we can talk?"

"Okay, I'll see you at the factory in 20 minutes. Bring a sample." Terry put the phone down, "Get that lot into that sail bag and let's go."

They drove in the back lane entrance to the Annandale factory and were greeted by Chris who prepared coffee after a look in the bag. He was soon on the phone to Paddo Mick who was on the way. Chris sat back in his office chair and sampled the smoke and they all agreed to agree again that it was pretty good stuff. Chris had cut himself in to be able to buy back from Mick at cost. That would be enough for him, for the sake of a phone call.

Mick arrived and was immediately impressed, without even sampling the sample, and readily paid the $420 per packet. He took the thirty-eight packets offered and, as he was leaving, inquired: "If there is any more, I'll take all you've got at $380." Terry was just about to speak when Warwick chimed in: "About the same again is all I can manage."

"Alright, when?" Mick was cool.

"Give us an hour and a half to get back here."

"OK, done." He left with the sail bag.

Warwick was divvying up the money, for the mysterious Kiwi. "$11,200 to him and we'll get a couple apiece."

Terry thought it was pushing the luck driving back into the Darling Harbour car park. He picked the very same spot and watched as Warwick disappeared up the gangplank. Within minutes of his disappearing, a car came in. He stayed low. This time the guards chatted about what they'd rather be doing this night and finally said their farewells. Terry kept down for 20 more minutes until he sensed movement. Warwick opened the door and crouched into the passenger seat as Terry started the car and hammered the accelerator.

Warwick acted pissed off. "He made me pay most up front for the rest," he lied, "plus I gotta go back and pay him the balance."

Terry just wanted to get rid of the stuff now. Despite his condition he was tired and really didn't want to hear about Warwick's "problem". Mick was waiting and the exchange occurred. Within two minutes of arriving at the factory, they were on their way home.

Terry smiled as Warwick counted out two grand for him. Warwick kept the rest. Terry roughly calculated that Warwick, after paying off most of his debts, must have made close to $5000 for the evening. If the Kiwi guy really existed, that is. If not he was about $25,000 better off.

Morning light had almost caught up with them and Terry made Warwick stash the remaining packets before they crashed out. As his head hit the pillow Terry realized the trouble he could have been caught up in on this night. Lomond would have to go.

Chapter 29

Terry approached the bar in the Kings Cross club. Almost midnight, he was full of smoke and exchanged smiles with three different ladies as he ordered a scotch. Warwick told him he would meet him there after midnight. He had an idea for him. Terry was glad Warwick had moved out and Warwick obviously didn't want Terry to see that he scammed him. Terry knew it, but he felt Warwick was scamming himself more than anyone else.

"I just front up to the girls at the bar and say, 'S'pose a fuck's out of the question,' said Warwick, tongue in cheek when talking about this bar. This night Terry decided to try it out. A band cruised away on stage. He leaned against a wall from where he could see both the band and the babes. One young lady, wearing a tight red dress, appeared to be blinking at him. He walked up and laid the line. To his surprise she responded: "Wouldn't you like to dance with me first?"

"Not particularly." He was committed now, although a little embarrassed.

"All right then," she took his hand and knocked down the drink in front of her. Terry knocked his down just as quickly.

The girl was intense. She wanted to hurt him during their lovemaking. She bit him, scratched him, thumped herself unmercifully into his groin so hard it hurt. As soon as she was finished she called a cab and left.

Within 10 minutes he heard a knock at the door. Dennis Northey came in brandishing a small medicine bottle. "Boy have I got some nice smoko for you. Hash oil, some of the best I have ever had."

He sat at the table and unscrewed the cap from the medicine bottle, turning it upside down. "Look how thick this stuff is, I'll have to dig some out with a match."

"Did you go down the club tonight?" Terry asked but he was only vaguely interested.

"No, I've been at Gino's place smoking this stuff. He's got six pounds of it. Have a taste, you'll want one."

Terry took the joint and lit up, taking in a lungful, trying to hold it in. He coughed several times, trying to gain his breath. "It's not bad, Dennis. Not bad at all."

"If you want some I can take you over to meet Gino tomorrow."

"I reckon you've got a date there," he said taking another toke.

"Good. So what have you been doing?"

"Generally keeping busy doing bloody nothing, I think," Terry said looking up at him. "I still have a few jobs for the business, but it is pissing me off chasing money all the time. At least when you hand out a bag of green, you get the cash straight away."

Northey sipped on coffee between puffing on the hash joint as Terry launched into a replay of his Friday. It had been hectic from the start as his printer, Shane, had let a dozen poster jobs go out without payment.

"Not to Brian Pilchard, I hope. Shit, now I'm going to have to chase him," Terry recalled.

Terry chased him that day. He told Northey that Pilchard sat behind his huge desk giving Terry a lecture on business. "See these files," he told him, casting his hand around behind him where the whole wall was taken up with 40 filing cabinets, each with four drawers. "In every drawer there are 100 people I am paying off." He opened one drawer and pulled up a card. "This guy supplied us toys worth $1200 for a factory party in 1968, he gets 48 cents a week.

"This guy," he grabbed another card, "supplied $700 worth last year. We pay him thirty cents a week."

"Look Brian, I couldn't give a shit how you rip people off. You owe me a grand and I want it."

Pilchard was condescending. "I'm just showing you how you have to play the game here, in the big city that's all."

"Just sign me a cheque and I'll get out of your way. Our deal is for cash and that's that."

Pilchard signed a cash cheque and offered it to Terry. He headed straight for the bank just two blocks away and stood in line. Ten minutes later he reached a teller and offered the cheque. He was not amused when the teller started to giggle as she shared the joke with her friend next door.

"Have a look at this," she held the cheque up to the window adjoining the teller's cubicles. "A cash cheque from Brian Pilchard; what a scream." The second teller laughed. "I wonder who has earned the cash he wants us to give; certainly not him."

By the time he snatched the cheque back from her hand there were four tellers laughing about Pilchard's cash cheque. They all knew Pilchard only too well.

On the way back up the road, Terry was seething. He noticed a couple of loose bricks near the house next door to Pilchard's office. He picked one up and lobbed it through the rear window of Pilchard's prized 1956 Mercedes Sports parked at the front of the building. He was leaning in the smashed window to retrieve the brick when Pilchard came on to his balcony shouting down at Terry. "What the bloody hell are you doing?"

"I'm getting my brick back. By the way, your cheque was worthless at the bank."

Pilchard was now concerned. "What are you getting the brick back for?"

"I'm going to throw it through your fucking windscreen."

"Hey, hang on a minute, don't do any more damage. Everyone's looking. Hang on, I'll give you the money. Do you know what that car's worth?"

Terry was still holding the brick as he met Pilchard half-way up the stairs. Pilchard pulled a huge wad of notes from his inside coat pocket and peeled off $1000 for Terry: "Here, take that and fuck off."

"Thanks Brian. I can't say it was nice doin' business with you. You had better find someone else to do your art-work and printing in future."

Northey laughed at the thought of Terry's antics but knew the payment he received meant Terry may be flush enough to do some business with Gino.

The Lebanese restaurant at Glebe had just six small cubicles along one side, each big enough for two people to sit face to face. They got the rear cubicle and drank Turkish coffee from small mugs. Gino came out with a tea towel over the plastic take away food container. It was thick all right. Gino flipped the container and held it upside down for almost 20 seconds before the contents started to move slowly and prompting him to turn it over again.

Terry had to heat the oil to get it to flow into the medicine bottles Northey had offered. They went off like hot cakes. One client, an acquaintance of Northey, looked at the consistency of the oil and asked Terry if there was any more. "Any bulk of this stuff?".

He said he would see and contact him.

The following day Gino told him there was just one left and he would meet him that evening a few blocks away from his Surry Hills house, "at my girl-friend's house". Terry had the money; he was making about 15 per cent on the deal. "Okay," he thought, "for making the arrangement and then a 10 minute round trip."

He got the container back to his house and walked in where the client waited. The buyer looked nervously at the movement in the container as Terry put it on the table and furrowed his brow.

The lid came off so quickly some of the liquid slurped out. "Shit, that's not the same stuff, it's been cut. Cut fuckin' heaps. I don't fuckin' want that."

Terry stared at the waves in the top of the container. He grabbed the lid and pushed it gently back on: "I'll take it back. I've got to hurry, he said he was going out."

The client put his hand into his jacket pulling a large silver-coloured handgun out to rest on the table: "There better not be any fuckin' problems," he said, eyes glazed with anger.

"Five minutes, I'll be straight back. Five minutes, okay."

Gino was in his car and just about to pull away when Terry screeched to a halt in front of him. "Gino, Gino, what are you trying to do to me? The fucking stuff is cut. It's all runny, like bloody cooking oil."

He reached inside and grabbed Gino's keys from the ignition. "Here's your stuff; he doesn't want it. The fucker's got a gun. Give me the money back, quick, or he'll be coming after you."

"Hey, that stuff is all right. Did he smoke it?"

"He didn't have to smoke the shit, man. It's runny. It's not stiff like the last lot."

"Yeah, it's hot. Summer-time, it goes like that," Gino was trying to con Terry into taking it back.

"Gino, I'm not giving your keys back until you give me the fucking money back. I'm fair dinkum, man."

Gino begrudgingly offered the money back and almost dropped the container Terry thrust back at him. As he counted the money, Terry realized his journey into the drug world, so far, had been relatively harmless. He had luck on his side when helping Warwick with the sticks. This experience reminded him of just how easy it would be to go down in a bad deal. This one he may survive. "But what if Gino had not been there when he got back?" he thought and decided this was the last time he would do any bulk. The gun was put away when he handed over the cash at home. The visitor left threatening Terry all the way to the door. He was glad to close the door, close him out of his life.

He had just settled down when the phone rang. Suzanne was calm. "Dad was found passed out down Parramatta Road earlier tonight. He's in Lewisham Hospital, in the cardiac unit."

Terry was anxious but Suzanne settled him down: "He's okay, but they think he may have had a heart attack. A taxi driver pulled up and revived him before getting an ambulance. He'll be all right, they reckon. We're going to visit tomorrow evening. Can you make it?"

"Of course, Suzanne, I'll see you there."

Terry looked at the clock. It was after 10 already. He felt drained. The phone rang again. "Terry, Chris here. Can I drop over?"

"Sure Chris, but don't make it too late."

"I'll be right there."

Terry recounted his near-miss to Chris, knowing he would understand. "Shit, that guy you were buying for, I think he's one of the really heavy guys I met over at Willoughby one night. He's fuckin' shot people before. You're lucky you didn't get kneecapped, just for fucking him around."

"Thanks a lot, Chris. Cheer me up why don't you. That bloody Northey put him on to me. I wonder what deals he does with him?"

"Smack, I'd say. Hey, the reason I came over Terry was to see if you could to a photographic job for me. We need an ad for the local cinema.

They need slides. Can you shoot it for us?"

"Sure can. When?"

"The ad has to be ready next Friday. I think we're gonna have to shoot it on Saturday morning. Can you be at the factory about 10 o'clock. We should have some samples and things ready by then."

"Yeah, I think I can get up early enough for that. I was going to have an early night anyway. I need it."

Stephen was in intensive care. A saline drip was in his arm and other probes were attached to his chest, monitoring his heart rate. Terry looked at the machinery in awe as he kissed Stephen.

"G'day mate."

"G'day Dad, what happened?"

"I don't know really. I had been drinking at the Prince and walked outside to hail a cab and next thing I remember I woke up in here with fucking tubes everywhere."

Suzanne arrived with Lisa and both gave Stephen a hug hello.

"Well you nearly bought it this time, you silly old bugger. The doctor told you not to drink any more. What possessed you?"

"I didn't have that much to drink. In fact I had only had a couple of beers and I felt too crook to have any more." The meters on the machine near Stephen's bed started to increase in tempo.

"Come on, Suzanne. Go easy. We all got a bit of a shock from this. Don't give him another heart attack by arguing," Terry said defensively.

"But he should be off the grog; I mean completely. Now the doctor reckons he should give up cigarettes too." Suzanne was upset, but she meant well. They all knew Stephen would do what he liked to do regardless of advice from doctors, or his family.

"Dad, I brought you a book to read," said Lisa handing him the novel. "It'll give you something to do while you're in here. I hope you just get well soon."

Terry decided to leave the girls to it and kissed Stephen goodbye: "Don't you go trying to chase the nurses around in your condition. That little brunette out there may be the finish of you."

Stephen smiled. "You should see the one who's on in the mornings. I woke up this morning with her tucking me in and I thought I was in Heaven."

Terry kissed them all good-bye and left, thankful his Dad had survived this one.

Saturday came around quickly and Terry was sizing up the shot through the lens of his Nikon when Chris disappeared from view.

"Gerry, Colleen, it's great to see you?"

Three people had entered - Chris's friends, Gerry and Colleen and another girl. She was about 20, her thick curly blonde hair was slightly teased out. She noticed Terry looking at her as the others were greeting each other. She sneezed. Then again, and again.

"Bless you," Terry smiled.

Gerry finally turned around to introduce the girl. "This is Karen, a mate of ours from New Zealand."

Karen sneezed again between "hellos", apologizing for her sneezing.

"It must be the inks out the back," Terry said, offering another "bless you".

Terry was beaming. He could not wipe the smile from his face as he looked at her.

"Say, why don't you be our model for this shot. You're going to look better than these two scruffy-looking buggers any day."

Karen was shy at first but after a little prompting from Terry, decided to get in front of the lens.

"She is perfect," Terry thought. The roll of film was finished and he was sure he had the shot they needed for the ad but loaded up again and used up another roll. Karen was so photogenic he just wanted to maintain the momentum.

With the shoot complete, the visitors disappeared as quickly as they arrived. They were heading for Bondi and invited the room to a party that evening, to welcome the new lot from New Zealand. Terry could not keep his eyes off Karen at the party. Her generous smile lit her face up each time she spoke. He noticed that as she answered the door she sneezed again.

"It must be the spring flowers or something. I don't know what has been making me sneeze. It seems like I only do it when you're around. I must be allergic to you!"

"Want to risk it and come out with me tomorrow. I'll show you around the city."

"Sure, why not?"

Terry was on his best behaviour. He didn't swear once. He had taken George's advice and taken Karen into the glass pyramid in the Botanic Gardens. They stopped for their first kiss at the centre of the structure. They broke as she went to sneeze and Terry's mind rolled back several years to his grandmother's palm reading.

"You're her, aren't you?" he said. Karen was rather amused: "Who?" she said.

"My grandmother read my palm several years ago. When she spoke of the woman in my life I asked her how I would know, if I would get a 'sign'. A teacher, she said, and you keep sneezing."

"Yeah, but that might mean that I am allergic to you or something."

"Maybe, but I reckon you are the loveliest, most beautiful young woman I have ever met. I know we don't know one another very well yet, but I think we could make a go of something, if you don't have any other plans, that is."

"You're pretty direct, aren't you? I don't really know, I just got here yesterday. Let's just play it by ear for a while, hey?"

Terry had already made a decision about the printing business. Disillusioned by the atmosphere of business in the inner city, he decided he would sell the machines to his printer and just concentrate on doing artwork for clients and contract the printing work out. For the first time in two years he was motivated, working every day and getting a lot of jobs through. He continued into the evenings, dropping off bags, a habit he knew he would have to kick if he wanted to impress Karen. There was something special about this one.

They were on their third date when Terry suggested they go home for a coffee and an after-dinner joint. The music was a little loud for her so Terry suggested they go upstairs. "It'll be just right from up there." He was happy to just hug and kiss her for more than an hour. She eventually peeled her top off, signaling a clearance for him. He wanted everything to be perfect. It almost was.

He never felt like pleasing a woman as much as this one. She felt like she had been individually moulded for him. This time, he thought, it was love.

Weeks later, they were sitting down to Chinese food Terry had prepared. He was pouring Karen's wine when Warwick walked in the open front door. "Mmm, something smells good."

Terry had told Karen a little about Warwick, including the times he was most likely to turn up. Here he was and he would appear at around six o'clock for weeks to come. He'd usually eat and get going, occasionally stopping to have a joint and watch some television. Terry no longer knew where Warwick was living. He was happy not to know. All he knew was that the guy was trouble, positively dangerous. He had decided not to get involved with any more of his scams.

He was not surprised three months later to see Warwick turn up with Dennis Northey. The pair had big plans for Terry and Karen which had been seeded by Gino.

"Yeah, just like that pound of oil Gino passed off on me to sell to that mate of yours Dennis. He pulled a fuckin' gun on me. I don't want any part of that shit."

"Terry, Terry, I'm just telling you what Gino said. All you have to do is carry a suitcase through Customs. You get ten grand plus the holiday to Kabul. You have nothing to worry about. You're straight, Terry. No one would ever suspect you or Karen."

"Yeah, well I am not going to give them the chance. I'm not interested in doing it. If it's so fuckin' foolproof, why don't the pair of you go?"

Warwick chimed in: "I'm too fuckin' hot to do anything like that."

"Yeah, and I got busted for some grass once. They'd be on to me too," Northey offered. "You're a clean-skin Terry. Maybe you and Karen could go for a holiday. You'd only be bringing in hash oil. Nothing else, honest." he sounded so insincere.

As Karen prepared the dinner, Terry watched as Dennis and Warwick closed their eyes almost simultaneously, nodding off to sleep on the couch. He went to the kitchen. "Don't worry about dinner for them; they're out to it."

"What?"

"Asleep; they're both asleep. They just nodded off in unison, the fuckin' smackies. They were just offering you and me a holiday in Kabul. Reckon it was to carry some suitcases for them. How do you like their cheek?"

"They just want to use people as heroin couriers. Get rid of them, Terry."

"Well, I can't right now, they've both nodded off. Shit, they couldn't give a stuff about anyone, could they? Look at the bastards smacked out of their heads." he mocked their earlier comments: "There's no smack involved, honest."

Karen looked across at them while she and Terry had dinner. "Who do they think we are, Terry? Blind Freddy could see they were using. This is the first time we've ever seen them together. Did you know they were acquainted?"

"No I didn't. Not this deep. Not before today. At one stage I thought Dennis was a narc. His wife Cheryl was into it pretty heavy. She always appeared out of it, but this is the first time I've seen him out of it like this."

They completed dinner and decided on a movie and snuggled into one chair as Warwick and Dennis slept on. The movie was almost over when Northey woke. He immediately gave Warwick a shake.

"So, what do you think Terry?"

Terry and Karen looked at him in amazement: "What?"

"So what do you reckon about the holiday?"

Terry estimated three full hours had passed since they started the conversation. Northey acted as though he had just blinked heavily rather than slept for three hours.

"Is the stuff you want us to carry the same as what you've been using today?"

The question caught Northey by surprise. "Yes. Yes, it is; good hash oil." He rubbed his eyes a little. Gee, did I doze off for a minute there or what?"

"Or bloody what," Karen laughed.

The pair rose to their feet as though they had not heard Terry's refusal. "Well, I can let you know some details about the trip. You'd be away about a fortnight. Is that okay?"

Terry placed his hand on Northey's shoulder, slowly guiding him and Warwick towards the door. "Find some other sucker, Dennis. Do it yourself. You nodded off on the couch about three hours ago. I have never known hash oil to do that to someone. If you guys want to get involved in this shit, go right ahead, but leave me and Karen out of it."

He opened the door. "We may see you when you get back; if you get back. Then again we may not. Just don't come around here with any of your offers again. I don't need it. The pair of you are full of shit."

Terry blamed Northey for the episode but Karen wasn't sure Warwick was altogether blameless.

"Jesus love, he was probably just with him because he was holding. I don't know. Warwick has just been through a big heap of trouble trying to import stuff. He wouldn't be organizing that stuff anymore."

"Bullshit Terry; he's been off his face nearly every time he comes around for dinner. He would sell his own grandmother for a quick fix. I am sick of it. It's me or your friends, like Warwick and Dennis. I think you better choose, now. You can't go on just dealing dope around town. The law or a bloody bullet is bound to catch up with you one day. And I don't want to be around when that happens."

Karen was serious and decided to visit a friend in Tasmania, leaving Terry to sort out his own life. He was not to know about her own dark side, the reason her friend lived in Tasmania, it was close to the poppies.

Warwick told Terry that Northey was pushing shit uphill. "I told him before we even got here that night."

Warwick continued his habit of arriving at dinner-time at least five nights a week. Warwick actually felt safe around Terry. He helped him with his guitar lessons by showing him patterns on the fret board that were used in the records he listened to. It helped him get by when he was hanging out; gave him something to do, an interest to take his mind away from his craving for the drug, so Terry thought.

"Well, I'm packing it in, Warwick. Fuck the drugs and fuck you guys into your weird scenes. I have to try to get my woman back now, but you guys have got to stay away. Whatever you do, don't come here with any offers like that again."

Warwick did the right thing and steered clear of Terry for two months.

Terry wrote to Karen twice a week. He pined for her while she was away. He wasn't even interested when old girl-friends rang up inviting him to parties. All he could think of was Karen.

She finally replied and said she was prepared to come back, if he was prepared to get out of the rut he was in. Terry jumped at the opportunity and offered to meet her at his mother's house in Melbourne. They could drive back to Sydney together.

Shelly and Barry knew they were in love and Terry had to endure Barry's teasing during their stay. They spent three days driving back to Sydney via the coast road.

They had been home less than a week when there was a loud banging at the door. Terry stumbled down the stairs in the dark, grasping for the door handle.

"Warwick, what the bloody hell are you doing at this hour?"

"I've got a little present for you. Can I come in?" Terry was reluctant. "It's five am. Warwick. Fuck, you're off your head, aren't you?"

"Yeah, opium. I brought you a taste."

"But I don't use it. I only like smoko. That's enough for me."

"You smoke this stuff, it'll get you shit-faced. I'll roll one up for you. Put the kettle on."

Terry complied before going upstairs to get dressed.

"Who's that?" Karen inquired sleepily.

"It's bloody Warwick. He's got some bloody opium this time."

"Shit. Get rid of him."

"I'll try," said Terry as he pulled on his jeans heading for the stairs.

Warwick's eyes looked puffy and dark. His thin physique was taking on skeletal proportions. This morning he looked as grey in the face as the opium he was smoking.

"Look, Warwick, I really don't need to smoke your stuff. I have some of my own."

"Oh why don't you try some, Terry? It won't hurt you. You're not going to get hooked or anything."

Terry hesitated as Warwick offered the rolled joint "Just have a puff or two. Can't hurt!" Terry took the smoke and carefully took a puff, then another before handing it back to Warwick. He headed for the kitchen to catch the kettle before it started whistling. As he spooned coffee into the cups, Warwick offered the joint again.

"Christ, this stuff just makes your guts turn. I feel really queasy," he said handing the joint back to him. As he did, Terry raced for the bathroom. He felt like he had to vomit, but nothing came. He was dry-retching for two minutes before he regained enough composure to go back.

"Fair dinkum, Warwick. That is rubbish. All it does is make me want to puke. No more for me."

Warwick took a sip from his coffee as he finished the first joint and then lit another he had prepared. Karen came down the stairs rubbing her eyes and automatically took the joint Warwick offered. She took a puff and coughed the smoke out immediately. "That tastes weird, what is it?"

"Opium; grey rocks," said Warwick whose eyes had disappeared into two fine slits. Karen dropped the joint in fright. "Yuck, that stuff is horrible." She headed for the bathroom. Terry gave her a moment and then went in to offer assistance.

"It made me feel crook too. Just a couple of puffs had me wanting to puke."

"Terry, I don't know if I can handle this lifestyle any more, having people blow you out at dawn."

"I know what you mean. I think I should get rid of Warwick, if he hasn't passed out on us, that is."

Warwick was surprisingly cheerful. He knew his indulgences irked Terry. But he knew he could laugh his way around it. To Terry he was a tragedy waiting to happen.

"Listen Warwick, I just don't want to be around to hear someone tell me you have overdosed on something. Fucking hell man, every house in the street got knocked over while you lived here. You're bad news pal."

"Have I ever tried to get you into anything you didn't want? I always went outside to have a taste. I never tried to push you into it."

"Well I can't do it any more Warwick. I have a good woman now. I'm going to get us a life. You and your drug fiend friends aren't going to be part of that. I am sick of it, ma, sick of trying to help you, but you won't help yourself."

"I've never done anything to hurt you, Terry."

"Yes you have, man. You've abused yourself and then lied to me that you weren't using heroin while you nodded off for hours on end. Then fuckin' Dennis's mate pulls a gun on me during a deal and next you and he come here offering us some big-deal fucking run. Now you wake us at five o'clock, make us both sick with this shit."

"Well why don't you jump in the car with me and we'll go and get Alby shit-faced too."

"Warwick, you're fucking hopeless. Leave everyone else alone. Just because you must have this shit. Don't fuckin' try to suck others into it."

"Well, if you don't appreciate me around here, I'll piss off then."

"Good-bloody-bye then, Warwick."

Terry and Karen went back to bed for a few hours and immersed themselves into the dreams induced by the opium.

When Saturday came around, Terry bought all of the major papers. He needed to get back into a regular earning situation. Five jobs stood out from the others in the columns. Terry applied for each. Within a week he was ready to start work in the Sydney office of the news-agency when another letter arrived.

"Karen, how would you like to go to the North Coast to live?" The Murwillumbah paper was after a general reporter. His application inspired an immediate offer.

"If we stay here, this city is going to consume us, Karen, I just know it. Every day we wonder if Warwick or Dennis or any of the other guys knock at that door. Let's not wait around just to watch them go down."

Chapter 30

The drive north of Sydney started to get more interesting around Byron Bay where Terry decided to take a detour and breakfast on the beach. The water was so clear after the cloudy foreshores around Sydney.

After feasting on rockmelon and pears he threw himself into the water and surfaced to look out onto the border ranges, dominated by the mountain which would be his alarm clock in the years to come.

Murwillumbah was less than an hour's drive north and as he got closer his heart grew bigger with the acceptance of the forest-clad mountains. The town first reminded him of a western town, the only difference was the cars parked at a 45-degree angle up the main street. One of his first stops was the music store. He checked if they stocked his brand of guitar strings and as he looked around, saw the small sign on the office in the rear of the shop; the proprietor was also a real estate agent.

After introducing himself the agent allowed Terry to elaborate. "I have a job with the local paper; I'm starting in about two weeks...."

The agent heard him out for at least 10 minutes, in between answering the phone and tending the shop, as he waited for his offsider to return. Then he appeared to have an idea. "If you don't mind doing some gardening and general upkeep, I do know of a nice place out in the hills. The owner is going overseas for six months."

Terry willingly jumped in his car for the five-kilometre journey from town. The valleys opened up, one into another, some areas with banana plantations covering the hills up to the winding road along Nobby's Creek. As they swept around onto a ridge, the car pulled into the left and down a long concrete driveway. The first house down the driveway was currently used by the owner and they traveled another 100 metres into the large carport.

Terry was impressed, but felt he may be in a league outside his budget. The size of the house impressed him as soon as the owner took him through the front door. There was a bedroom to the immediate left and another straight ahead which joined another dressing/sitting room.

Another bedroom was down the hall on the left opposite the bathrooms, one completely fitted out, the other containing a spare shower and toilet. The bedrooms looked straight out at the mountain which caught the first rays of sunlight each morning.

"But this is such a beautiful place, why aren't you living here?"

"It's just too big for me to keep up with. I'd much prefer the flats down the way," the owner Mrs. Smith responded with an incredibly British accent.

Terry was already impressed but again had flushes about how he could afford such a place. They arrived in the kitchen, a huge, well planned room, with cupboard space all around and an island in the centre along one end of which the gas stove and oven were contained. The rest of the island was a food preparation area with a further bench along one side containing the sink. Terry was still admiring this as he opened doors through the servery into the dining room.

The dining setting could accommodate 12 people and the room extended even further into the plush lounge-room. The whole side of the house was filled with hopper windows to take in the view of the mountain. Outdoor settings provided several cosy spots to sit and have tea or breakfast in comfort at different times of the year.

Terry was still trying to fathom how much rent they would be asking. He was thinking about the $110 a week he was currently paying for a two-bedroom terrace house in Sydney when the agent chimed in. "I know I could get around $80 a week but there is a fair bit of mowing to do. Do you think you could handle $50 a week."

Terry's mouth dropped open enough for him to start the answer with: "Aaaagh, yes, that would be fine."

His head was full of the good things he had managed to help fall into place this day as he walked into the newspaper office to introduce himself to his future colleagues before starting on the long journey back to Sydney.

Stephen was in two minds about him leaving the city. He was happy for him getting back into newspapers, but was saddened he would not have him around.

"Look Dad, Terry said over coffee, this city just doesn't do for me what it used to. This city killed Mouse. I don't want to be next."

"But I am here, mate; I will miss you so much if you go."

"Dad, the job pays well and we'll be living in this mansion out in the hills. You can come up and stay for holidays, any time you like. You'll love it there. I've just got to get away from all the shit that has been closing in on me here."

"What about the sailing? You'll miss that too, I bet."

"Well, yes I will, but not as much as I'll miss you Dad. You just have to make sure you don't get on the booze again."

Stephen dismissed the suggestion: "Not since that last time mate. I know I will be risking death if I do that again."

He put up enough of a smoke screen to take Terry off the scent, but Suzanne knew she was going to have to keep an eye on him.

Karen seemed excited at the prospects for them both as Terry told them all about the new house they were going to.

Over dinner with the family Terry told Stephen, Damian, Suzanne, Lisa and Karen. "I seem to have had this feeling here that my whole life depended on the pulse of this city." He stopped. "You hear that?" They all craned their necks slightly as Terry opened the back door. All they could hear was traffic from busy Cleveland Street.

"Hear that noise?"

"What, the bloody traffic?" Damian was quick to respond. "Yeah, that's not too bad is it?"

"Well how long has it been since you've heard the sounds of silence?"

"I go out in the bush for that," Damian responded.

"Well that's what we'll be waking up to, up there. We will hear just the sound of the birds and the crickets and the frogs. For too long I have really believed that I was tied to the pulse of that traffic noise we can hear out there right now. I reckon I have found something better and we're out of here. I've got a chance again, half a chance, at least to make something of this. We've got to take that chance."

Terry had a small going-away party the following weekend although his close friends like George and Martie and Larry had found their way to his place for days before. They were emotional about his leaving, but most wanted the best for Terry anyway and were relieved to see him making such a positive decision.

"If I hang about here mate, I'm going to get old too fast. I have got everything I want from this city plus a lot of heart-ache, anxiety and torment to boot. There are better things waiting. Anyway, I need to get out and see this great country of ours. Shit, here I am, 22years old and all I have seen is Melbourne and bloody Sydney, plus a jaunt to Ayers Rock once. I want to see it all and I reckon this is the best way for me to get out of here."

Terry's first drive from the back hills of the Tweed into Coolangatta to work again reminded him of how lucky he had been. Even the rain did not affect his demeanor on this, his first day at the *Daily Blues*. The instinct he had developed over the years for a good story was still with him. Once the readers saw what he produced, the stories came his way thick and fast.

His interest in racing also gave him the opportunity to cover the local race meetings which also gained a boost in interest as Terry sifted through the many stables for stories to do as previews to the meetings.

He approached each day with an optimistic air.

He realized now, he was one of the survivors. Most importantly he knew he had made the right move with the love of his life, Karen. And here, in paradise, they had half a chance of a good life for them both. Only time would tell.

ABOUT THE AUTHOR

Danny Mortison worked as a journalist for newspapers and magazines for almost 40 years. He freelanced for many of these to write adventure stories from the wilds of Australia's North Queensland resulting in his work being published in magazines and newspapers all over the world. He also published his own newspaper, North Coast Issues, for seven years in the coastal northern New South Wales town of Ballina which will provide grist for the mill for planned future works.

He currently lives in similar country from where he continues to write, play rhythm and blues music and play golf.

www.ingramcontent.com/pod-product-compliance
Lightning Source LLC
Chambersburg PA
CBHW050030030726
47506CB00001B/200